W
PR

The Smug... ...ore Sur

"Alyssa Alexander captivates with a potently drawn Regency suspense that will keep you turning pages far into the night. With perfectly paired protagonists . . . Alexander delivers a lively, twisting romance with an undercurrent of gritty realism. With wicked dialogue and well-researched historical facts, Alexander is clearly an author we ought to watch *and* read." —Jennifer McQuiston, author of *Moonlight on My Mind*

"A thrilling, wild ride of a spy thriller that sizzles with passion . . . A maze of plot twists and turns. Like an intricate puzzle, Alexander has all the pieces of the ideal romance and arranges them in the perfect picture. She is a rising star you won't want to miss." —*RT Book Reviews*

"Hot, suspenseful, and wildly romantic. A lushly told romance that takes you back to the fascinating Regency world of small village drama and international politics—all converging on the white-hot attraction between a sexy spy and a daredevil smuggler destined to trump fate." —Kieran Kramer, author of *Sweet Talk Me*

"Romantic suspense at its very best. Alyssa Alexander weaves a tantalizing tale of moral dilemma, political intrigue, and enough heart-thumping romance to keep you turning the pages." —Tracy Brogan, author of *The Best Medicine*

"Well-drawn characters, superb dialogue, and a decent plot will keep pages turning." —*Publishers Weekly*

Berkley Sensation titles by Alyssa Alexander

THE SMUGGLER WORE SILK
IN BED WITH A SPY

In Bed
with a Spy

ALYSSA ALEXANDER

BERKLEY SENSATION, NEW YORK

THE BERKLEY PUBLISHING GROUP
Published by the Penguin Group
Penguin Group (USA) LLC
375 Hudson Street, New York, New York 10014

USA • Canada • UK • Ireland • Australia • New Zealand • India • South Africa • China

penguin.com

A Penguin Random House Company

IN BED WITH A SPY

A Berkley Sensation Book / published by arrangement with the author

For information, address: The Berkley Publishing Group,
a division of Penguin Group (USA) LLC,
375 Hudson Street, New York, New York 10014.

ISBN: 978-0-425-26953-4

PUBLISHING HISTORY
Berkley Sensation mass-market edition / December 2014

PRINTED IN THE UNITED STATES OF AMERICA

10 9 8 7 6 5 4 3 2 1

Cover art by Aleta Rafton.
Cover design by Diana Kolsky.
Interior text design by Tiffany Estreicher.

To Joe
Because this one day,
you met a crazy person,
and she wanted to write romance novels.
Then you married her.
All my love.
Always.

ACKNOWLEDGMENTS

An author lives in fear of leaving someone out of a dedication. This is one of those hazards of writing. I hope if I inadvertently forget anyone, they won't hold it against me.

The first people I must thank are readers. Thank you so much for loving Julian and Grace in *The Smuggler Wore Silk* and asking for Angel's story! Without your support and enjoyment, this whole endeavor wouldn't have meaning!

To my agent at Holloway Literary Agency for her constant support and answering my silly questions. To my editor, Julie Mianecki, the copyeditor, art department and everyone at Berkley. Thank you for all you have done, and for believing in me and this book!

To Kelsey, my sister, for reading this book in the early editing stages. The last hundred pages are different. Enjoy!

To Jennifer McQuiston, Tracy Brogan and Kimberly Kincaid, my Three Cheekas who are Honey Badgers to the end and who teach me so much about life and writing every single day. Plus, we laugh every single day. Without you, well, this book would (1) have a bad ending, (2) have a bad beginning and (3) have a sagging middle. What would I do without you?

Also, to J, The Closer. Thanks. Those last hundred pages are the best pages of the book. Plus, you gave me sunshine, and I heart you for it.

To Kieran Kramer, for simply being there and saying the right thing when I needed you.

And a special thank-you to Leslie L., for her advice on fencing; to the Beau Monde for historical advice (you ladies rock!); to Mid-Michigan RWA for their unending support; and to the baristas at Biggby Coffee. I wrote almost the entire first draft of this book at your coffee shop. I made new friends, saw some friends leave and always, always enjoyed my tall skim chai latte, extra hot.

And then there's the friends who aren't writers and who find me baffling because of it, I'm sure. You have always supported me, and I cannot thank you enough! But there are two people I must thank particularly, Kimmie and Molly, who are my comrades in arms when it comes to the joys (also trials, tribulations and scary moments) of mothering. To Molly, for so many things that cannot be listed, not the least of which is a good margarita and some awesome skinny jeans. To Kimmie, just because. There is no one else in the world who gets that side of me better than you. And you know the side I'm talking about.

To Brooke, Marty, Robin and Nancy, because I miss you. And to Bruce, the Best. Boss. Ever.

And of course, to Mom, Dad, Kara and Kelsey. I don't think there's much to say here, except I love you!!! A special thank-you to Sharon, for all of your support!

Finally, to Josh and Joe. Joshua, you are the brightest light of my life. Sometimes I wonder how I was so blessed to have a child whose every day is a miracle of discovery. I hope you never lose that thrill!

And Joe . . . well. For every day. Whether I'm living in my head or in real life, on crazy-busy days and normal ones, crabby days where I didn't get coffee and lovely days when I got sunshine. Nights where I sat at the computer and nights where we had a "date" on the couch in our jammies. Hysterical phone calls when I lost my wedding diamond and thrilling phone calls when I sold a book. Without you, my life would be boring.

Prologue

June 18, 1815
On a bloody field near Waterloo

THE WOMAN SHOULDN'T have been in the thick of battle. But
she rose out of the acrid smoke, perched high atop a chest-
nut horse and wearing the blue coat of a light cavalry officer.

The Marquess of Angelstone staggered through rows of
trampled corn, shock rippling through him as the woman's sabre
flashed. A shrill whistle sounded overhead. Instinctively, Angel
ducked as cannon artillery pounded into the ranks, blasting into
the earth and showering him with dirt and black powder.

The woman on horseback didn't flinch.

He staggered forward, coughing, ears ringing, as soldiers
around him fell or scattered. Pressing a hand to his jacket
pocket, Angel fingered the square shape of the letter he carried
there. He hadn't known he'd have to fight his way to Wellington to deliver it.

The horse turned a tight circle, one of the woman's hands
gripping the reins while the other brandished a cavalry sabre.
Her grip on the blade was untrained, her movements awkward. But fury and hate blazed from her eyes and fueled her
sabre as it sliced across the chest of a French soldier. The man
collapsed, shrieking and clutching at welling blood.

The woman turned away, already arcing her sabre toward another enemy soldier, and Angel lost sight of her.

Reflex sent Angel's bayonet plunging as a Frenchman reared up in front of him, face contorted by fear. When the man screamed, regret shot through Angel before he forced it away. It was kill or be killed. There was no time for regret.

He surged forward with the ranks of foot soldiers, compelled to look for the woman. The muddied ground sucked at his feet, threatening to pull him beneath thundering hooves and panicked soldiers. Broken cornstalks slashed at his face. The sulfur smell of black powder burned his nose, mixing with the scent of men's fear.

He fought past a charging enemy soldier, spun away from another and saw her again.

Soot streaked her grim face. She grinned at the enemy standing before her—and the smile was terrible. The man paled, but aimed his rifle at her. He was not fast enough to beat her sword.

When that soldier, too, fell under her sabre, she looked up. Over the dead soldier and through the swirling gray smoke, Angel met her eyes. They were a chilling, pale blue and held only one thing.

Vengeance.

She pulled on the reins and her horse reared up, hooves pawing at the air. Angel planted his feet and braced for impact. But the hooves never struck. The woman kept her seat, her jaw clenched, and continued to hold his gaze.

The battle faded away, booming cannons falling on his deaf ears. The gray, writhing smoke veiled every dying soldier, every hand-to-hand battle being waged around him.

He only saw her merciless eyes. Blood roared in his ears and the beat of his pulse became as loud as the cannons. A high, powerful note sang through him.

The woman's horse whinnied as its hooves struck the earth again. Standing in the stirrups, she thrust her sword aloft and howled. The battle cry echoed over the field and carried with it the sting of rage and unfathomable grief. She wheeled the horse, spurred his sides and charged through battling soldiers, her blond hair streaming behind her.

And she was gone, obscured by clouds of dark smoke and the chaos of battle.

Chapter 1

July 1817

ALASTAIR WHITMORE, MARQUESS of Angelstone—code name Angel—coughed into his gloved hand in the hope of discreetly hiding his laugh. A man shouldn't laugh when a fellow spy was being hunted by a woman.

"Oh, my lord," the brunette tittered. "Truly, you are a remarkable figure of a man."

The Earl of Langford—poor hunted bastard—lifted his annoyed gaze over the short matron and met Angel's eyes. The woman leaned forward, her powdered cleavage pressing against Langford's arm.

Angel quirked his lips. The brunette's fawning was highly amusing—since it wasn't directed at himself.

"If you will excuse me," Langford said, "I must speak with Lord Angelstone about an urgent matter."

"Indeed?" Angel didn't bother to conceal his merriment. "I wasn't aware we needed to discuss an urgent matter."

"It has just come to my attention," Langford ground out. He extricated his sleeve from the woman's grasping fingers and eased away from her.

"Must you go?" The brunette pouted rouged lips. Feathers trembled on her turbaned head as she sent a coy look toward

Langford. "I truly feel we should further our acquaintance, my lord. You have been in the country for *months*."

"With my *wife*."

The brunette's mouth fell open. "But, you are in London. She is not here this evening. I thought—"

"My dear lady," Angel said smoothly, sliding between the pair. He might as well stage a rescue mission. "As I'm sure you are aware, his lordship has many demands on his time. Not the least being his wife and new daughters."

"I see." Without even a single remorseful glance, she turned her back on Langford. Sharp eyes flicked over Angel. Subtle as a stalking elephant. "Well. You are unmarried, Lord Angelstone."

"Indeed. But alas, I am otherwise engaged for the evening." Angel raised the woman's chubby fingers until they were just a breath away from his lips. "A pity, for you would have been a most enchanting diversion." He wondered if his tongue would turn black after such lies.

"Perhaps another day, Lord Angelstone." She preened, patting her bosom as though to calm her racing heart. The cloying scent of eau de cologne drifted up, and Angel fought the urge to sneeze.

"Perhaps." Angel let her fingers slide out of his. He bowed. "Good evening, ma'am."

As the brunette waddled away, Langford sighed gustily beside him. "A female predator, that one." He brushed at his coat sleeve. "She was getting powder everywhere."

Angel smothered a grin. "You've been married and ensconced in the country too long, my friend, if you've forgotten how our society ladies once adored you."

"Not as much as they currently adore you."

"True. A title does that. Now, did you truly have something to discuss?"

"No." Langford palmed his pocket watch and flipped the lid. He frowned at the small glass face. "But I do intend to make my escape. I've had enough weak punch, innuendos and pleasantries for one evening. And Grace is waiting at home."

"How is your countess?" With a wife such as Langford's, he could understand the desire to hide in the countryside.

The frown cleared and Langford grinned at Angel. "She is still tired from the birthing, but she shooed me out for an evening when she learned of my assignment." The watch disappeared into a waistcoat pocket.

"Ah. I wondered if you were here for business or pleasure."

"A little of each." Langford's shoulder jerked up in a half-hearted shrug. His eyes roved the room. "You?"

"The same." In truth, it was always business. A spy never did anything simply for pleasure.

Angel studied the ballroom. It was an impossible crush. Guests bumped up against one another as they laughed and flirted. Diamonds winked and painted fans fluttered as women entertained suitors and friends. Footmen threaded through the crowd carrying trays of gold champagne and rose-colored punch. Surrounding it all were the subtle notes of a string quartet and the scent of candle wax.

Such was the glittering and dazzling world of the ton. But underneath the gleaming polish of society were passions and intrigue and secrets. It was his mission to seek them out. And beyond his government assignments, beyond the political intrigues, was the enemy who had assassinated a woman four years ago.

His woman.

Gemma.

Cold anger turned him from the scene. "I believe I may follow your lead and make my escape as well." He wanted his own hearth, a brandy and his violin. The constant din of voices grated, the endlessly changing pattern of dancers was visually dizzying. He scanned the room once more. A wave of people ebbed and flowed, came together and parted.

And he saw her. No cavalry coat. No sabre. Only a gown of silver netting over white muslin and a painted fan fluttering languidly near her face. No howling battle cry now, only the sensual curving of her lips as she bent her head toward a military officer.

Something clutched inside him as the battleground superimposed itself over the ballroom. Twirling women became French soldiers, stringed instruments became the whistle of a blade. The scent of gunpowder stung his nostrils and the pounding of artillery rang in the air. The scene swirled around the woman, though she was no longer on horseback.

Two years since Waterloo. Two years since he'd seen a bright halo of hair and pitiless eyes full of retribution. He shook his head to will away those memories.

But the woman remained. A bevy of men were gathered around her, jostling for position. Striped waistcoats of the dandies clashed with the brilliant red and dark blue of soldiers' uniforms. Then, like an echo of his memories, the Duke of Wellington himself approached the woman. She smiled warmly as he bowed over her hand.

The bevy of suitors stepped back in deference to Wellington, leaving him as alone with the woman as two people could be in a crowded ballroom.

"Who is that lady?" Angel spoke softly, nodding toward the woman. "The one talking to Wellington?"

"Lilias Fairchild. Major Jeremy Fairchild's widow. He was killed at Waterloo." Langford raised a brow. "Did you know the major?"

"No." Angel watched Mrs. Fairchild's fan tap lightly against Wellington's arm. A sign of affection rather than flirtation. "What do you know of her?"

"Both Grace and I found her pleasant enough, though one can sense a spine of steel beneath the attractive exterior. She's known for being private, which has only increased the gossips' chatter." Langford lowered his voice. "She followed her husband on the march. They say when the major's body was brought off the field, she was wild with grief. She took her husband's horse and sabre and joined the battle."

The gossips were correct. There had been a wildness in her that day. Across the room, her hair caught the light of the candles and turned a bright yellow-gold. "I'm surprised she's allowed into this ballroom." A woman on the march with soldiers, one so unladylike as to fight and kill, should be ostracized by society.

"There are some doors closed to her. But with Wellington himself championing her, society as a whole has accepted her."

"She should have died." He'd assumed she had. Her face was the clearest recollection he had of that day, and he could not think of the battle without thinking of her. He had never considered she would live, and was vaguely sad to think such a vibrant creature had been struck down. Seeing her alive and whole seemed to defy fate.

"If you ask the troop she marched with, death was her intention," Langford said softly. "The French called her *L'Ange de Vengeance.*"

Vengeance. It seemed he and the Widow Fairchild were two of a kind.

"I know her just well enough to introduce you." Langford's glance turned sly.

She wouldn't remember him from Waterloo. One soldier meeting another on the field of battle was nothing. Not that it mattered. It had been only a moment. A fleeting breath of time that would barely be remembered. Never mind he'd seen her wild, vengeful eyes in his dreams as often as he'd seen Gemma's dying eyes.

As Wellington bent to speak to Mrs. Fairchild, the woman angled her head and let her gaze wander the room. She should not have seen him. Guests danced and flirted and laughed between them, blocking her view. But like an arrow piercing fog, she trained blue eyes unerringly on Angel.

There was no vengeance there this time, but still they seemed to blaze. The color of them, the shape of them, ignited a visceral beat low in his belly. As did the lush curves even the most flowing gown couldn't conceal.

Recognition flared in the widow's eyes. Her lips lifted on one side before she flicked her gaze back to Wellington. The duke bowed his farewell and retreated into the crush.

"Introduce me."

"You're asking for trouble with that one, my friend." Langford laughed. "Which means it would be my pleasure to introduce you."

Langford pushed through the crowd. Angel followed, brushing past silks and satins and elaborate cravats. Mrs. Fairchild's eyes tracked his movements across the floor. Odd to be studied with such interest, even as he studied her. Flanked by soldiers and gentlemen festooned in evening wear and vying for the position closest to her, she seemed to be an island of calm.

He narrowed his eyes. No, not calm. Confidence. There were no affectations, no feminine vapors. A woman who killed a French soldier in the thick of battle had no time for vapors.

"Lord Langford," she said as they approached. Her eyes flashed briefly in Angel's direction, then back to Langford. "It is good to see you again. How are your wife and daughters?"

"Quite well, thank you. The twins are a handful already." Langford grinned. It wasn't clear whether the grin was for his daughters or Angel, as he slid an amused glance in Angel's direction. "Mrs. Fairchild, may I present the Marquess of Angelstone?"

"Lord Angelstone." Her voice moved over him like velvet, smooth and rich. "But we've met before."

"We have indeed, Mrs. Fairchild." He bowed over her hand. "Though the circumstances were quite different."

Langford's brow rose. The message was clear enough.

"We met in battle." Mrs. Fairchild tilted her head. Candlelight shadowed dramatic cheekbones and full, ripe lips. "I'm afraid names were not exchanged."

"My condolences on the loss of your husband," Angel said.

"Thank you." Her face softened. "He was a good man."

"And a good soldier, I've heard," Langford added. "Will you be in London long, Mrs. Fairchild?"

"Through the Season, I think." She smiled, a subtle, feline turning up of her lips. "Will you dance with me one night, Lord Langford? So I can pretend I'm not too old for all this nonsense?"

"For you, Mrs. Fairchild, I'll brave the dance floor—but not tonight. I must return to my wife."

"A flattering escape."

"Indeed. Now, I see your punch glass is empty. I'd offer to get you another"—Langford looked toward the table holding the punch bowl—"but I have no desire to fight this insufferable crowd."

Mrs. Fairchild laughed, low and throaty. The sound sent desire spiraling through Angel.

"Go then," she said, shooing Langford with her closed fan. "I can obtain my own punch."

"Allow me." Angel stepped in, offering his arm. Langford, the cur, grinned. Angel ignored him. "I would be honored, Mrs. Fairchild."

Behind them, the bevy of gentlemen suitors bristled, almost

as one. A pack of wolves defending their queen. Or a gaggle of geese flapping uselessly at a predator.

"Thank you, my lord." She cocked her head to look up at him. A smile flirted with the corners of her lips. "I would be most grateful."

The gaggle hissed in disappointment.

She set her white-gloved hand on his arm. The touch of her fingers was delicate on his sleeve. As they crossed the room, she splayed open her painted fan and waved it languorously. A lazy ripple of painted wildflowers in the wind. The scent of her skin rose into the air. Clean. Bright. And when she smiled at him once more, his body tripped straight into attraction.

Chapter 2

S HE HOPED HE wasn't an idiot.
     So many men were. It was one of the facts she'd learned since returning from the Continent and entering society. Though perhaps it was simply the bored, titled gentlemen. The seasoned soldiers she knew were infinitely smarter.

Lilias angled her head and looked up at Lord Angelstone. He didn't appear to be an idiot. He looked like a golden angel—a fallen one judging by the roguish gleam in his eyes. Luckily, his face was saved the burden of perfection. He had a crooked nose. She wondered how he'd broken it.

His hair was also longer than was fashionable and tied in a queue at the base of his neck. How unusual. And how interesting. Something about that queue gave the impression Lord Angelstone was barely tamed—and just on the edge of dangerous.

She hadn't particularly remembered him from Waterloo until she'd seen him. She'd met hundreds of men on the field. Most she would never remember. But this one—oh yes. He could not be forgotten. He'd fought with brutal elegance, his body dancing over the battlefield, his sword efficient and decisive.

"This evening's venue is rather different than the fields of Waterloo," she said as they wove through the crowd.

"Not as different as you might think." He nodded toward a corner of the ballroom. "Do you see the debutantes?"

"The two girls giggling behind the potted palm?"

He lowered his voice. "The enemy still lies in wait." The baritone timbre shivered through her. "They're ready to ambush the unsuspecting soldier."

"And their spies—" she countered in a whisper, "are everywhere."

"Is that so?"

"A pair of match-making mamas are watching you even now," she said, waving her hand at two beady-eyed matrons. "It's quite frightening."

"Rescue me from their clutches, Mrs. Fairchild. Walk with me on the terrace." He leaned down, leaned in, and she saw that his eyes were tawny gold. They gleamed as his lips curved. The movement brought something alive in her—something she'd forgotten how to feel.

The keen edge of desire.

"A wise retreat from the battle of the marriage mart," she murmured.

"I learned strategy at Wellington's knee."

"Then I shall take advantage of your strategic experience and retreat as well." The group of her hopeful suitors had grown tedious, poor souls.

Within moments they'd escaped to the flagstone terrace. Another couple stood at one end, talking in low voices. Angelstone led her to the opposite side.

She leaned against the balustrade and contemplated the night sky. It was nearing midnight. Stars twinkled merrily against the blanket of darkness. It had grown cold outside. She tugged her shawl around her shoulders.

"Have you ever noticed that the stars are the same, no matter what part of the world you are in?" she asked, studying the play of light from the windows over Angelstone's handsome face. "Whether you're standing outside a London ballroom, on the march in the bitter days of winter or watching death take your husband on the field, Orion is still Orion."

His attentive silence made her feel foolish.

"Listen to me!" Laughing lightly, she looked again into the night. "I'm becoming maudlin on this lovely summer evening."

"The loss of your husband is still painful." Angelstone's

words were quiet. Over them she heard the click of his boots on flagstone as he stepped closer.

"Yes. And no." She sighed, letting the clean night air fill her lungs. It was difficult to explain the horrible grip of grief, the slow acceptance and the ultimate need to survive. "It's been two years. Two interminable, never-ending years. Yet it seems to have gone in the blink of an eye."

"Grieving takes time." Knowledge resonated in the low tones of his voice.

"Have you lost someone close to you?" Curious, she turned to lean on the balustrade so that she faced him.

He paused. "My brothers."

There was more. She'd heard it in the empty silence before he answered, but didn't pursue it. "I'm sorry."

"I had two older brothers, both with wives and one with a daughter. In fact, I wasn't supposed to inherit the title. It was assumed that between my brothers and their future progeny, the title would be secure."

"So you were free to go off to war."

"Precisely." Self-deprecating amusement sent his lips twitching. "I thought to make a name for myself in India, fighting in the jungle and bringing back trunks of gold."

"Ah." She understood the hard shock of reality. "Youth."

"Youth, indeed." He laughed, and the sound rumbled through her.

"War is not the adventure it seems, is it?"

"No." The word was quiet and full of meaning. His eyes met hers. "But you know that, don't you, Mrs. Fairchild? You followed the drum. You marched with Wellington."

"Yes." No more needed to be said.

She searched Lord Angelstone's shadowed face. Something there held her breathless. Her skin prickled, a small current of energy running from her head to her toes.

"Life must still be lived," she said softly. "Despite the memories."

"Are you ready to live again?" His voice threaded through darkness and surrounded her, warmed her.

"Yes." It was a truthful answer, and one she doubted she could have given in the light of day. But the dark felt oddly safe. "Are you?"

For a moment, no words were spoken. Candlelight from the windows played over the dangerously sharp edge of his jaw, over expressive lips. The murmur of voices and beat of music seemed to quicken, rising and swelling as pleasure grew.

Or perhaps the quickening was her pulse beating a touch faster.

"A valid question, Mrs. Fairchild." He leaned over the balustrade, resting his forearms on the stone. They stood side by side now, and when he turned his head his gaze fell to her lips.

She couldn't quite seem to draw a breath.

She straightened, trying to breathe in the night air. Her reticule slid from weak fingers, hitting the flagstone terrace with a dull thunk to break the spell. For a moment, she could only stare at the shadows at her feet. The frivolous little accoutrement had fallen open, its contents partially exposed. She looked up. If that twitch of his lips wasn't amusement, she was Boney's spy.

"Allow me," he said, bending to retrieve the reticule.

"Thank you, but—" With a huff she took it from him and crouched on the terrace. Her gown pooled around her, a froth of cream and silver that matched the beaded reticule. She pushed the skirts aside and her fingers brushed against an embroidered handkerchief, a small comb. Both returned to the pretty bag. Pulling the drawstring tight, Lilias stood again.

She felt ridiculously silly. She was no better than one of the debutantes.

The notes of a waltz filled the air. Another set was beginning. She couldn't see inside the ballroom, yet she could imagine the couples swirling around the dance floor—gowns brilliant in the candlelight, jewels sparkling, surrounded by the long notes of the violins.

At the other end of the terrace, the other couple laughed aloud and moved inside, leaving Lilias and Angelstone alone with moonlight and violins.

Notes floated through the night, smooth and long. The rich tones mingled with the sweet, clear sound of a flute. The music wrapped around and between them, a warm and velvety embrace.

"A lovely sound, isn't it?" The tone of it, the bright joy of it, seeped into her. Lilias closed her eyes and drew in a breath, wishing she could bring the music into her. "I've always thought the violin to be a beautifully full and powerful instrument."

"Do you play?" His deep voice melded and mixed with the song.

She fluttered open her lashes to find him watching her intently. "No. To my everlasting regret, I have no talent."

"But you clearly love music," Angelstone murmured, leaning once more on the balustrade. He was so close she could feel his breath, the heat of his body. His scent rose, sending her already heightened senses jittering. "Would you care to dance?"

"I haven't danced since my husband died."

"Two years?" His smile was a challenge. "That's a long time to go without dancing."

"Is that so very long?"

"You are well out of the traditional full mourning period, Mrs. Fairchild. Society wouldn't bat an eye if you danced again." He turned slightly, leaning on one arm. "I promise, you won't have forgotten the steps." His voice lowered so that it slid through the night as smoothly as the violins. "Or the rhythm."

She arched a brow. "And if I *have* forgotten?"

"You would have your choice of partners to remind you of the movements."

"No doubt." Oh, he was wicked. She knew well he wasn't speaking of dancing. "Would you be one of that number, my lord?"

He grinned, teeth flashing white in the darkness. "That remains to be seen, doesn't it?"

She turned her face away and looked out into the July night. Once, it would have seemed impossible to make love with a man who was not Jeremy. There had only ever been her husband. His arms around her. His body against hers. But Jeremy was gone. She missed him, and would always feel the loss of that bright, shining love they'd shared.

"Two years *is* a long time," she whispered into the dark.

"I wonder, then, when will you dance again?"

Angelstone was close beside her. Only a step away. How amazing it was to feel him next to her in the dark. She knew where his arm was, where his shoulder was. She didn't *hear* his breath. She felt it. Her body reacted with a ripple of awareness.

"I don't know when I will dance again." It was the truth,

though she wasn't sure whether she meant on the dance floor, or with a man. Straightening, she backed away from the balustrade. Angelstone did the same. Light from the windows slashed across his face.

He didn't quite look as he had on the battlefield—nothing could compare with the look of a man fighting for his life. But the tawny eyes held the same purpose, the same focus. The same heat.

Something in her answered that heat. It had been a very long time since she'd felt such a stirring. She missed that slow burning and the awareness that accompanied it. For the first time since Jeremy's death, someone interested her.

For the first time, she was tempted.

Angelstone reached for her hand. Glove met glove, silk slid against leather. Her reticule bumped softly against his wrist. Stepping forward, he brought her gloved hand to his lips.

"Save your first dance for me," he whispered against her fingers.

Lilias angled her head. She knew what he was intimating and should be offended. But she wasn't scandalized.

She was tantalized.

Heat rushed through her, filling her belly with a thousand butterflies. She stepped forward so that their faces were only inches apart, their lips a breath away from a kiss.

"I'll consider your request, my lord."

Challenge leapt into his eyes. She felt the tension coil in him, saw his lips part. The need to feel alive, to be loved—however superficially—nearly drove her straight into his arms.

But logic stayed her. Not here, not now. Not without careful thought.

She turned toward the ballroom and the light and music spilling from the terrace door. Sending him a come-hither look over her shoulder, she smiled.

"I'll consider your request," she repeated. "But I make no promises."

Chapter 3

FASCINATING. ABSOLUTELY FASCINATING. Angel studied Mrs. Fairchild's retreating back, covered by an elegant silver shawl. The avenging goddess of the battlefield was well hidden, even as that wildly curling hair was subdued in a tidy coiffure.

But he had seen her eyes flash. He'd heard her battle cry.

What had Langford said? Steel. Yes, he could see it. Steel wrapped in lush curves and sensuality. He had the most intense desire to unwrap those curves and explore the center of her.

He stepped toward the French doors leading into the townhouse, thinking to find the card room and cool his ardor. The toe of his boot kicked something and sent it skidding across the terrace. A circular metal object, only an inch in diameter, lay on the patterned stone floor. Mrs. Fairchild must have dropped a coin.

He bent, reached for it—and his blood ran cold.

Candlelight glinted on a small medallion, coloring the silver a burnished gold. In the center, an inlaid onyx symbol shone dull black. His breath wanted to hitch, so he clenched his teeth and drew air between them. It wasn't rage that gripped him, but an icy calm.

He folded the medallion into his palm, squeezed. The

round shape bit into his hand. Flesh held memory. He'd held a similar medallion once before—only that time, he'd stood over a woman as her life was just beginning to seep from her body.

The medallion was the sign of the Death Adder. An assassin that struck quickly and silently, before slithering away into the dark and leaving only the medallion behind as evidence of his kill.

Flipping the disc over, he studied the reverse side. There it was, glinting in gold light from the windows. The twisting "A" stamped into smooth silver. He turned it again to view the onyx symbol and ran a thumb over it. No two assassins used the same symbol on the front of their medallions. He'd always thought it a mark of pride as much as a calling card. This one he recognized easily enough. He had spent months meticulously researching that single French gypsy symbol.

Here we have to take revenge.

It had been revenge against him that caused Gemma's death. Now, here in his hand, was the same sign, which indicated it was from the same assassin.

His fist clenched around the silver circle. Mrs. Fairchild carried the same assassin's sign as Gemma's killer. If he hadn't seen a man running away that day, he would suspect it was Lilias Fairchild who had stolen that vibrant life.

He looked through the terrace door. The Widow Fairchild laughed with some poor sod who was dancing attendance on her. Damn if that smile didn't look genuine. But he had seen her wield a sabre, had heard her war cry rise above the battle.

Ah yes. She could be an assassin.

And she had the medallion.

IT WAS RIDICULOUS.

She was thinking of having an affair with Angelstone. Her cheeks warmed at the thought and she lifted one hand to her face. The exhilaration that had whipped through her at Lord Angelstone's words still hummed along her skin two hours later. She very much wanted to see him again.

The Fairchild carriage rocked on its springs as it turned a corner. Lilias shifted in her seat and pulled her shawl closer.

"Are you chilled, my dear?"

"No, Grant. I'm comfortable." She smiled at the man ranged on the seat across from her. Her husband's cousin. She'd known him for as long as she'd known Jeremy and his face was nearly as dear to her. "I'm quite warm, in fact."

"Good. It's cold this evening." The carriage lamps gilded Lord Grant Fairchild's burnished hair and threw his broad shoulders into relief. "I don't want you to catch a chill."

"Oh, she's fine, Grant." Catherine Fairchild nodded her head knowingly, sending the black feathers anchored in her hair quaking. "You insist on coddling her, but all of society knows she's quite resilient."

Lilias shared a laughing look with Grant before responding to the third occupant of the carriage. "Thank you, Catherine." Her mother-in-law knew her well, even if Grant thought her a delicate English flower.

A feather drooped over Catherine's ear. She shoved uselessly at it. "You wouldn't have followed my Jeremy all the way to hell and back if you weren't resilient, dear."

"Catherine!" Lilias coughed into her glove, trying to hold back the laugh threatening to spill out.

"Nonsense." Catherine waved her hand dismissively as the carriage rumbled to a halt. "As I always say, men do tend to forget the good Lord created women for childbirth. Thus, we can do anything. Now, Grant, help me down. I'm old."

"You are anything but old, Aunt Catherine," Grant said, stepping down to the walkway. He turned and offered his hand, then grinned at Catherine as she set her hand in his. "You're slim as a fairy and delicate as a rose."

"I may be slim and delicate, but I'm still twice your age," Catherine snorted as they ascended the steps of the townhouse.

Lilias followed the pair up the steps toward the bright light spilling out of Fairchild House. As she stepped through the front door and into the soaring foyer, she thought for the hundredth time how blessed she was that Jeremy's family had accepted her without a qualm after his death. She'd had nowhere else to go and little money. And she'd desperately needed a place to heal.

"Good night, my darlings," Catherine called out as she

tottered up the carved staircase toward the next floor and her bedroom. With decorative feathers bouncing in her white hair, she looked like an ancient sparrow flitting around the townhouse.

Lilias laughed quietly at her own fancy and let her shawl slip from her shoulders. Gathering the embroidered Kashmir in one hand, she pulled up her skirts with the other to follow Catherine upstairs.

Looking over her shoulder to say good night, she found Grant watching her steadily from the door of his study, an arrested expression on his face. He filled the opening, his wide shoulders elegant in black evening clothes.

Foot poised on the lowest step, she paused and raised her brows. "Grant?"

"May I have a word?" he asked.

Skirts rustling, she changed course and followed Grant into the study. He stood before the fireplace, his back to her.

Curiosity drew her forward. He seemed to be contemplating the three sets of binoculars displayed on the mantelpiece with great seriousness. When she stepped beside him and looked up into his handsome face, he met her expression with sober eyes.

"I don't think I've said it yet, but I'm glad to see you're out of mourning, my dear." His eyes flicked over her cream and silver gown, down to her cream gloves, then up again to her face. A smile tugged at one corner of his mouth. "Though black did suit your fair coloring."

"Thank you." Though it was an awkward compliment. She draped her shawl over the arm of a nearby chaise. Peeling off her gloves, she laid them over the shawl.

"What finally persuaded you to leave mourning behind?"

"It's time." Lilias breathed deep, so deep the thin fabric of her bodice strained at the seams. The comforting scents of wood smoke, beeswax and lemon mingled on the air. "I finally feel whole, Grant. I'm ready to live life again."

The words were an echo of her conversation with Lord Angelstone. She felt a tingle in her veins as she pictured that strong face, the tawny eyes. Her stomach did a long, slow roll that left her breathless.

"I'm happy to hear it, Lilias." Grant's quiet words drew her attention again. "As is Catherine, I'm sure. You were so lost after Waterloo."

"Only my heart had been lost." It had seeped into the ground of the Netherlands, along with Jeremy's blood. "But that was two years ago."

"Jeremy would not want you to mourn for so long."

"No." But she would never forget. The long, hard marches they'd endured together and the interminable wait when she was left behind. The deaths from disease and exhaustion and hunger. And the laughter and camaraderie that still prevailed in the end. Life always triumphed over death. "Truly, I'm ready to live again."

She skimmed a fingertip over the bird feather lying on his desk. It was both soft and prickly against her skin. She had not the slightest idea what bird it came from, though it was a bright yellow color. Grant would know. He knew birds and feathers and bone structure and species. But for all his knowledge, there was a space between them. He would never understand the horror of bathing blood from one's arms and hands.

"Where did you go, Lilias?" Grant asked softly.

Fingers jerked against the feather. "Forgive me."

Grant's quiet words drew her attention again, as did the gloved hand that skimmed down her arm to her fingers. He raised her hand, set it against his lips. A faint alarm rang in her head and she considered tugging her hand free. But his touch was soft, and when his gray eyes met hers she saw genuine affection there.

"Lilias. You are free to marry again. A suitable amount of time has passed—more than suitable, in fact." His eyes darkened. "*We* are free to marry."

"Grant—"

"Please, listen." He looked so serious, so determined, that she understood why he was an effective politician. And as he had so kindly invited her and Catherine to live with him after Jeremy's death, she owed him much more than a few minutes of her time.

He dropped her hand in favor of curling his fingers around her shoulders. Gloved thumbs brushing lightly across her skin.

"I need a wife, Lilias. One who can act as a hostess and

understands politics. One who will withstand the rigors of foreign travel and comprehend the nuances of foreign ballrooms. I need a partner by day—" He cupped her cheeks, his fingers warm even through his gloves, and brought his lips within a breath of hers. "And a companion at night."

His lips touched hers. Gently, although she could feel the tension in his fingers and sensed the controlled passion beneath the gentleness. She dug deep inside herself and tried to find some tingle inside her. But she felt nothing. No tingle in her blood, no frantic beating of her pulse. No passion. No love.

Grant's lips left hers, but his hands still cupped her cheeks. Firelight flickered over his face—a face most women would think devastatingly handsome. To her, he was simply Grant. Her husband's cousin. Kind eyes, broad shoulders she could depend on and a smile that charmed other women senseless.

"No." Reaching up, she placed her hands lightly over his and drew them away from her cheeks. "No, Grant. I cannot."

Understanding flickered and his face blanked. "Don't refuse yet. Think about my offer. Give yourself a few more weeks, even months, to decide." He stepped back, and her hands fell helplessly to her sides.

"I don't need time to—"

"Just wait a little longer." He strode to the door. His hand gripped the doorframe when he stopped at the threshold. He didn't turn, but he spoke. "I would make you a good husband, Lilias." Then he was gone, and all she could hear was his slow, heavy footfalls as he made his way to the upper floors.

"I know," she whispered, her heart aching for him.

Picking up her shawl and gloves, Lilias followed more slowly, her steps light in the quiet house. When she reached her room, she lit a single candle and set it on the nightstand. Her shawl, gloves and reticule dropped to the floor. She lowered herself to the bed and gripped the edge of the mattress. Leaning forward, she stared into the dancing candle flame and tried to envision marriage to Grant.

Debutantes considered him a catch. Wealthy, titled, handsome. Young enough to be thought in his prime. She would be the perfect hostess for him and was accustomed to the travel. She understood war and politics in a way some women did not. Marrying Grant would be the most sensible course of action. She could not be a poor widow forever and depend on his generosity.

But having felt desire again—even briefly—she knew she couldn't marry Grant. Not ever. Her first marriage had been for love, and with that came a passion that had never waned. Not even in a tent worn thin by the elements after marching for miles in the bitter winter cold.

A discreet knock sounded on the door and a young maid stepped in.

"D'you need help, missus?"

"Just the buttons and stays, please," Lilias answered vaguely, standing and turning her back toward the maid. The girl made quick work of the buttons and laces before slipping from the room, leaving Lilias alone to change into her nightclothes. Lilias let the gown fall to the floor, a whisper of sound in the silent room. Her stays followed before she slipped out of her chemise and let that slide to the floor as well.

Reaching up, she pulled the pins from her elaborate coiffure and laid them on her dressing table, one by one. Ropes of hair fell down her back, thick and heavy and full. She fingered a strand, pulling the length between her fingers. She hadn't cut it in six years, not since shortly after her marriage.

She looked into the mirror, studying the curling blond locks and the way they tumbled over her bared breasts and swirled around her naked hips. The long strands shifted over her body, shimmering and glowing in the candlelight.

The Marquess of Angelstone flashed into her mind. He was rough and virile and—masculine. She thought of him now. Of those eyes gleaming when he looked at her. How would her hair look spread across his pillow? Across his body? Would it look the same against his skin as it did against hers?

It had been a very long time since she'd thought of her body as anything but a shell that needed food and sleep. Now, she saw those round breasts as something to offer to a man.

Sucking in a breath, Lilias pulled her hair back in quick, rapid strokes. She braided it in a familiar rhythm, *right, left, right, left*, until every lock was tucked away, then slid her nightgown over her head.

Pulling a small wooden box forward on the dressing table, she lifted the lid. A miniature lay inside. It was a simple painting of Jeremy's plain, familiar face. His boyish grin flashed and his smiling eyes beamed up at her. She ran a finger down the painted face. They'd been so young when they'd married. Nothing seemed to matter but being together. And yet they had learned that life was hard. Tough. Loved ones died. The world turned on its axis.

And then life went on.

She turned her gaze away from the miniature. Beside the portrait lay an empty bed of black velvet, waiting for Jeremy's last gift to her to be nestled in the soft fabric.

Lilias looked up and stared blindly into the mirror, seeing not herself, but Jeremy as he had been in those last moments of life. Gray skin, blue lips, bloodied chest. She had never told another soul that Jeremy was alive when they brought him off the field. She'd never told anyone—not even Catherine—that she'd held him in her arms as he breathed his final breath. Or about the small medallion he'd given her as his final gift and that she carried everywhere with her.

She searched the room for her reticule, found it on her dresser where the maid had set it. Lilias opened the pretty beaded bag and dug inside for the silver and onyx medallion. When her fingers didn't find the item she was searching for, she pulled the drawstring open wide and turned the bag inside out. A comb dropped onto the dresser, as did coins, a handkerchief and a vial of smelling salts she never used but always carried.

Nausea rose in her, filling her throat with bile.

The medallion wasn't there.

Chapter 4

H E HEARD THEM before he saw them. Voices. Laughing. Female. The bright sound spilled from the yellow salon, like cheerful butterflies fluttering and tumbling into the hall.

Pausing in the door, Angel studied the women inside. Four of them. Two young widows, an orphan and a mother who had lost her husband and two of her sons. Yet there they were, laughing as though they hadn't a care in the world.

Once, he had imagined Gemma among them.

The youngest of the females sat on the floor, tongue trapped between her teeth as she carefully arranged tin soldiers in formation. Her fingers were precise in their movements. A six-year-old general commanding her troops.

"Watch out, Boney! Uncle Angel's going to get you!" She swiped a hand across the field of battle, scattering the troops. Leaping to her feet, she hooted and danced around the fallen soldiers. Braids flew in all directions. "I told you, I told you! Uncle Angel will get you all!"

Laughter again from the women. He smiled and joined the conversation.

"Well, Maggie, aren't you a blood-thirsty chit?" he said.

Four pairs of female eyes turned in his direction. He grinned when Maggie raced toward him, her rounded cheeks pink with pleasure.

"Uncle, you won the war again." Spindly arms wrapped around his waist, hugging tight.

"So I see," he said. A small face tipped up, lips pursed. He obliged and presented his cheek for a kiss. She smelled of childhood and sweets. "Mmm. Peppermint drops."

Maggie giggled, squeezed once more and then danced off in favor of the soldiers. "Mama said I could have only one peppermint drop because we'll be having luncheon soon. But I told her I need two. I'm *starving*!"

"You're always starving." Maggie's mother, Lisbeth, smiled fondly. "You're growing. We've had to order all new dresses— again!" Though most of the light in Lisbeth's eyes had died with her husband, it returned when she looked upon her daughter.

"Just like your father. He outgrew everything as soon as he put it on." The Dowager Marchioness of Angelstone laughed as she pulled a needle through stiff white fabric. Her thin countenance and spare body lent her an air of severity that showed nothing of the generosity and joy beneath.

Maggie beamed delightedly. "I love being like Papa."

Ah, the simplicity of childhood. Maggie wanted to look like Hugh, talk like Hugh, play with his boyhood toys. Hence the battered tin soldiers.

"Can I play, Maggie?" Elise, the widow of Angel's oldest brother, tossed aside her needlepoint.

"A wise decision, Elise," he said. "I think your needlepoint is on fire." Even from across the room, the garish combination of orange and pink embroidered flowers struck Angel blind.

Elise laughed and waved the unsightly design away. "I know. It's perfectly ugly. I love it." Then she was down on the floor, bringing the dead soldiers back to life and grouping them into formation. Maggie settled beside her.

Angel studied Elise's bent head as he worked off his constricting leather gloves. She should have had children. She and John should have had a dozen children and spent their lives as the Marquess and Marchioness of Angelstone. Now she, too, was a widow, her husband carried off by putrid fever and with no child to comfort her.

He stuffed his gloves into his pocket and flexed his fingers. Better. He turned toward the ladies still sitting by the window.

Sunlight spilled over them. The sight of them sent a pang through his heart.

"How was the ball last night, Angel?" Lisbeth asked. The sun turned her ordinary brown hair to shining mahogany.

"Did you meet anyone interesting?" The dowager marchioness looked down her long nose at her son.

"What you are asking, Mother, is did I offer marriage to anyone last night."

"I hope you would tell me if you were planning to offer marriage to someone." She sniffed, then sent him a sly look. "But, yes. That's what I'm asking."

"No. I did not offer marriage to anyone last night." Instead, he'd found an assassin.

"It's time, Angel, dear. As you well know." The needlepoint fell unheeded into her lap. "You're the last of the Whitmores. If you don't produce an heir, some distant relation in America"— her bony shoulders shuddered—"will inherit the title."

"Mother." He kissed the dowager's soft cheek, marveling at how few lines there were on her face considering the difficulties of the last few years. "I am aware that the demise of my freedom is at hand."

"Demise." From the floor, Elise snorted. Her striped ice blue gown looked decidedly unpleasant with its Pomona green trim. How an earl's daughter could have such an abysmal sense of style had baffled all the Whitmores. "Marriage isn't *all* bad, Angel. There are occasional benefits to marriage, you know."

"Like what?"

"Regular relations, for one thing."

"Elise!" Lisbeth sputtered, followed by shocked laughter. "Maggie is present."

"Oh, for heaven's sake—"

"It's fine, Mama," Maggie said matter-of-factly. "I know what relations are. Lord Pemby in Number 4 next door has relations with Mrs. Bider in Number 9. Grandmamma says they are quite indiscreet."

"Heavens, I said no such thing!" The dowager tried to look innocent. It didn't work.

"Oh dear." Lisbeth buried her face in her hands, even as laughter shook her shoulders.

"Relations aside," Angel said, trying to keep a straight face, "what other benefits are there to marriage?"

"Ah. Well—" the dowager began. "Um." She fingered her needlepoint contemplatively.

"There's always . . . hm." Lisbeth stared out the window.

"A wife can warm your bed," Maggie piped up. "Your bed must be very cold, because Grandmamma says that half of the women in London have tried to warm your bed."

"Grandmamma!" Lisbeth slid down in her chair while Elise snickered from the floor.

"I suppose a warm bed would be nice." Amused, Angel watched his mother's face flush with embarrassment as she busied herself with the needle and thread.

"And then of course, there's love, isn't there?" Maggie finished. Every eye in the room fastened on her. "Grandmamma says she married for love, and she was happy her sons did as well. She says no one should ever marry for anything but love."

"Your Grandmamma is a very wise woman," Angel said softly, eyes on that solemn pixie face. "I hope you listen carefully to her."

"Angel." The dowager's needlepoint lay forgotten. "Isn't there anyone . . . ?" But she stopped. She always did. She had never met Gemma, but she'd known there was someone. He supposed mothers usually did. Then it had all ended, and there had been no one important since.

"Excuse me, Mother. Ladies." He bowed to the collective female company. The only woman not watching him with some pity was Maggie, who was busy with her soldiers. "I was informed I had a missive waiting for me when I arrived. I must attend to it."

———

THEIR VOICES ECHOED down the hall and into his study long after he had left them. He kept the study door open. He wanted to hear that bright, feminine sound.

He broke the seal on the message, smoothed out the folds in the paper. He sifted through multiple sheets, thumbs skimming across the smooth surface. What had the lovely Widow Fairchild been doing in the last few years? And where had she come from?

If the reports were to be believed—and they should, as he'd asked his best informants—she was the daughter of a country squire. She'd married the only son of a neighboring family, who went to war against his father's wishes, but with the support of his mother. And her own family? What of them? The report did not say.

The quill on the edge of his desk was light in his fingers as he made a note to pursue information on her family. Then he turned to the next portion of the report. Lilias Fairchild had followed Major Fairchild on nearly every campaign, usually traveling with the troops, though she did occasionally travel separately with other families.

He had a good idea of her experiences on the march. She might sleep anywhere from a local inn with clean sheets to a tent in an open field. Perhaps even a makeshift hut, if necessary. Disease, low rations. Cold. God, he remembered the cold himself. It didn't just seep into the bones. It pierced with such bitterness a man could barely sleep or eat. Worse was the danger of retreating armies after a battle and the plundering that occurred.

Not a pretty tale. But she had lived it, according to the official military records. The question was, what part of her life was not in the official records?

He could find nothing untoward in her history, so he turned to Major Fairchild's military record. It was exemplary. He had earned his promotions, was well respected by his men. Angel studied a list of campaigns the regiment had been on. He ran a finger down the rows of letters. They had not been in Pamplona when Gemma had been killed, but the regiment had been at the siege of San Sebastián. Only fifty miles. Less, perhaps. It had been a two-month siege. Plenty of time to travel to Pamplona.

It could be done. But it was not Mrs. Fairchild's hand that had held the knife. Gemma's killer had been a man. Still, there was more than one Death Adder, and they did work in pairs on occasion.

And she had the medallion. He could not find an explanation for that.

The silver disc lay on his desk, beside Gemma's file. Beside all the files.

Forty-two dead. That was the number of political and

military figures killed at the hands of the Death Adders. Their files were permanently on his desk, though he usually kept them at the bachelor's quarters he maintained to escape his family when needed. He rarely looked at the files. The names and identities were permanently burned into his memory, but he occasionally scanned them for any information he may have missed.

But there was one name that never left him. Not even in sleep.

No one should ever marry for anything but love.

Gemma hadn't been pretty. But, oh, she'd had a joy inside her. She lit any room she walked into, even when she was undercover for the Service. They had not married, though he'd asked. Repeatedly. But Gemma had always gone her own unconventional way. It would have been a disastrous marriage—tumultuous, fraught with worry and complicated by duty. But it would have been full of passion.

Pulling open his top desk drawer, he retrieved the miniature he kept there. Laughing brown eyes met his. A wide, upturned mouth that should have been too big for her face smiled at him. Such delight. Such love. She'd been amused by life, by the vagaries of people, even by the game of espionage.

He'd wanted her fiercely. He'd loved her fiercely.

And now she was dead. Four years dead. He should have forgotten her by now. Moved forward. But he couldn't. It was his assignment to hunt the Death Adders. In those four years, he'd only brought in two men alive, and neither one lived long enough to tell him anything. The rest defied discovery. He only found what they left behind.

The dead—and a medallion.

He reached into the drawer again, hands closing around a second silver medallion. He'd found it beside Gemma. In her blood. He swallowed and tucked that memory away. It was a hellish moment to remember. He must make a better effort to bury it.

He lay Gemma's medallion beside Lilias Fairchild's. He turned one, so the symbols were aligned. Side by side. Sunlight caught the edge of the disc that had been left with Gemma. The black onyx inlay seemed to writhe. He flicked his gaze to Lilias Fairchild's medallion. They appeared identical.

It was an easy matter to bring out his glass and test the similarity. He bent over them, eye to glass, and studied the magnified marks in the silver. The long line of onyx on each front ended in the outline of a diamond. The center of the diamond shape shone silver. Precise cuts, onyx and silver perfectly aligned. No gaps between the materials. He rubbed a thumb over the surface of Mrs. Fairchild's medallion. No raised or loose areas where craftsmanship had failed. Though he knew each mark in Gemma's medallion, he studied it again. Front, back, edge. The stamped "A."

They were identical, barring the minor marks time left on metal. The same workmanship. The same symbol. The same assassin.

Savage anger swelled in his chest. It clawed, howled, trying to fight free from that deep place in his heart where he'd buried Gemma. Her body might be lost somewhere in Pamplona, but that did not expel her from his memories.

With one swipe, he sent the medallions and the miniature into the desk drawer.

The agony of failure never lessened.

He closed the study door. He didn't need the caring women of his family disturbed. He'd learned to lock the door when he played his violin, and they'd learned to pretend they didn't hear him.

It suited them all.

The violin case was worn and battered. When he'd first purchased it, the leather had been soft and supple, the wood beneath strong. He ran his fingers over the scars. There was a hole from a rifle in Austria. That had been a near miss on the instrument itself. A scratch ran the length of the case. A knife fight in India that had ended well for Angel and badly for the case.

With patient fingers, he opened one latch, then the second, then the third. The hinges barely sighed as the lid slowly opened. The instrument called him. He heard it, as clearly as he heard his own heartbeat. He trailed his fingers across the strings. They were hard, small ridges that dug into his skin.

Lifting the violin from the case, he nestled it beneath his chin. It was like coming home. It fit perfectly. Flawlessly. The curve of his shoulder against the curve of the wood. He breathed in the scent of leather and wood and rosin.

Lifting the bow, he set it against the strings.

The world lifted away. The fist gripping his heart eased, the burning anger gave way. He'd carried that violin from London to Paris to Lisbon to Brussels and back again. He'd carried it to the wilds of India, where he'd met Gemma in a pasha's palace. He'd played for her while she'd danced for him, wearing nothing but bells on her ankles.

With that image in his head, he played for Gemma. Playful, seductive, fast. He caught the joy of her, his fingers flying, the bow a blur as it stroked the strings. Notes licked the air, bright and lively.

The song ended. Sound faded.

When he closed the lid on the violin, he locked away another memory.

Chapter 5

"YET ANOTHER LOVESICK swain falls at your feet, my dear Lilias." Grant delivered the words with a sardonic grin, leaning down to murmur the words near her ear.

"Lord Spencer is not a lovesick swain," Lilias corrected, tapping a censorious fan against Grant's arm. The black ribs of the fan faded into the sleeve of his elegant evening coat.

"No?" One corner of his lips quirked up, an expression she knew well. He was trying not to laugh. "Are you certain?"

Unfortunately, Lord Spencer chose that moment to raise his hand in farewell and beam a besotted smile in Lilias's direction. But he was standing at the edge of the line of dancers in a crowded ballroom. A young lady bumped into him on her pass around another couple, tripped over Lord Spencer's feet and nearly went headfirst onto the floor.

"Perhaps he is a bit lovesick," she amended, flicking open her fan and hiding an unbidden smile. Lord Spencer was sweet, but dim, poor dear.

"I have no doubt he'll be calling on you soon." Grant's eyes met hers. "So many offers of marriage to choose from," he murmured.

"Hush," she reproved, glancing at her mother-in-law. But Catherine was chatting with another elderly matron, their elaborate curls bouncing as they bent their heads together. "If

you tell Catherine, half the city will know about—about—"
Lilias struggled to find the right word.

"My lovesick offer?" Grant suggested.

Lilias slanted him an amused look.

"Oh, don't worry." Grant waved an elegant hand. "I'm not
about to publicize my proposal. Do I look to be as much of a
fool as Lord Spencer?"

"Do you truly want me to answer that?" she asked pertly.

"Hmm. Perhaps not." He smiled, then gestured vaguely
over the crowd. "I see a few members of the House of Lords
going into the card room. Please excuse me."

Grant nodded his good-bye and disappeared into the
crowd. Lilias sighed as she watched his back disappear. He
refused to accept she wouldn't marry him, instead pretending
she hadn't answered at all. Which left her in a muddle. She
and Catherine were dependent on Grant. At some point, his good-
will would run out.

Sliding her fingers along the edge of her open fan, she lis-
tened half-heartedly to Catherine's chatter.

"Those poor ladies. Every one of them still at the Angelstone townhouse, too," Catherine tsked. "Well, his lordship
has kept them on, as he should, of course. So I suppose there's
something to redeem that rake."

Lilias angled her head and eyed her mother-in-law. "Are
you discussing Lord Angelstone?"

"Of course, dear." Catherine's dark eyes sparkled gaily.
"Who else? He's been watching you for nearly ten minutes."

Lilias froze, the fan clutched in her fingers momentarily
useless. She narrowed her eyes at Catherine. "Are you quite
certain?"

"I'm old, Lilias, but I'm not blind yet. That *gorgeous* man
has been watching you most intensely."

"I wish Lord Angelstone would look at *me* like that,"
Catherine's elderly companion tittered.

"Oh, don't be silly, Leticia. You came out the same year I
did, which makes you over twice his age, the same as I." Catherine gave her acquaintance a chiding tap on the shoulder.
Then she offered up a naughty grin, at odds with her white hair
and papery skin. "But I wouldn't mind him undressing me with
his eyes as he's doing to you, Lilias, dear."

The sound that tumbled from Lilias's lips was part snicker, part gasp. She tried to hide her amusement behind her gloved hand, but it triumphed over her shock and she laughed aloud. "Catherine, you truly are a darling."

"Oh, oh! Look! He's coming over," Letitia whispered sotto voce. With obvious preening, the plump old matron waited beside Catherine, her face expectant.

Lilias's heartbeat quickened, but she kept her gaze on Catherine's dark, elated eyes. Catherine, of course, pretended she didn't see Angelstone coming.

"Mrs. Fairchild," a low baritone drawled behind her. "How delightful to see you again."

His voice rumbled through her body, concentrating itself low in her belly. She fought against the shiver that rushed up her spine.

"Lord Angelstone." Turning toward him, Lilias let her amusement linger on her lips. "Are you enjoying your evening?"

"I wasn't particularly." His eyes gleamed. "But I am now." The warm candlelight glowed on that barely restrained queue of hair. He bent his head slightly and smiled down at her. And oh, it was a wicked smile. A knowing smile.

Behind her, Catherine sighed.

Angelstone's eyes flicked toward Catherine. "I don't believe we've met, madam."

"Catherine Fairchild, my lord." She extended her hand. Her tiny fingers folded into his. Angelstone raised them to his lips, lingering as he would with any young, available lady of the ton. Catherine's cheeks pinked with pleasure. "I'm pleased to make your acquaintance, my lord."

"And Lady Letitia, we've met, of course." Angelstone bowed over the other lady's hand.

Then his eyes arrowed back to Lilias. "Mrs. Fairchild, would you do me the honor of taking a turn about the room?"

Lilias tipped her head to the side, considering. Angelstone had already singled her out once at a ball. If he did so a second time the whispers linking them would begin within minutes.

Angelstone's eyes were bright. His shoulders squared in the elegant coat, his snow-white cravat a shining beacon in the gold candlelight. He watched her intently, his body still. The quiet before the storm. Or perhaps the predator waiting to pounce.

Twin thrills of danger and desire sang through her body. In that moment, she yearned to be touched. To have even the most fleeting sense of passion and love. It had been so long since she had simply been held. So long since her lips had touched a man's.

Would Angelstone taste as delicious and male as he looked?

She smiled, slow and inviting, as her very skin shivered in anticipation. "I would be delighted, my lord."

His lips curved as he offered his hand.

Lilias wondered if it was an invitation to heaven, or hell.

———

A SPY COULDN'T abduct a woman in the middle of a crowded ballroom. Nor could he interrogate said woman when she stood next to a pair of ton gossips. Angel kept his smile in place and calculated how best to get Mrs. Fairchild alone.

Petticoats rustled as she stepped forward and set her fingers in his. A light touch, an elegant brush of glove on glove. The smile Mrs. Fairchild sent him was full of mischief. It seemed remarkably genuine. For the briefest of moments, he thought that hint of mischief was purely feminine. A woman flirting with a man, and nothing more.

But she had carried the medallion. Why, if she were not playing an assassin's game?

He needed to get her alone. He needed her at his townhouse. Interrogation, questioning, simple conversation. Whatever direction the investigation took, he could not continue it here.

She fell into step beside him, tucking her hand in the crook of his elbow. He curled his fingers possessively around hers to hold them in place. She slid him a glance, amusement hovering around her lips. A slight elevation of her chin acknowledged his grip, but she did not protest. Which could mean nothing. Or everything.

"Don't be long, dear," Catherine Fairchild called as they began to stroll away.

They threaded their way through the glittering crowd. His shoulder brushed against hers. The froth of blue ribbon on her capped sleeve trembled against the black of his evening coat, as a tiny bird would tremble against its captor.

"Must I conquer the dragon at the gate?" He looked over, studying the lovely picture she made. He'd never dealt with an assassin wearing a fashionable gown the color of bright blue delphiniums. The Adders were all men, as far as he knew. But then, the element of surprise was a brilliant strategy. More so when a woman used desire to put her opponent at a disadvantage.

"A dragon? Catherine?" Mrs. Fairchild laughed lightly and shook her head. "No. She is only reminding me we are leaving shortly to attend Lady Smythe's soiree this evening. Will you be attending?"

"I hadn't planned on it." His thumb rubbed the back of the delicate hand that rested on his forearm. "But perhaps I will."

"You are quite intent on your quest, are you not?" Mrs. Fairchild slowly opened her fan, fluttering it lazily. She did not look at him.

Did she know he had the medallion, or was it simply an interesting choice of words? The medallion's circular outline pressed against his chest—just to the right of his heart, and to the left of the knife hidden beneath his coat. Both were a stark reminder. "When a man wants something, he works to achieve it."

He guided her to a corner of the room, stationing them behind a mass of green fronds issuing from potted palms. Her eyes were bright, her lips tipped up on one side. A woman with a secret. "But you have not yet succeeded, Lord Angelstone. I have not decided if I should accept your invitation."

Ah yes, his invitation to *dance*. The idea of *dancing* with an assassin would be a noteworthy occasion in his life. If he lived, of course, which would be an uncertain prospect if she were a Death Adder.

"It seems a gentleman's plight is to forever wait for a lady to decide," he said. But he didn't want to wait much longer to interrogate her. He had wanted to storm the Fairchild townhouse when he'd found the medallion. Every delay chafed. So he pressed his suit. "Perhaps you require persuasion, Mrs. Fairchild. Perhaps I cannot succeed in my mission without a demonstration of our various abilities."

"Perhaps," she said, angling her head to study his face. She touched the end of her fan to her lips, tapping the painted silk over her amused smile. A flush tinged her cheekbones. Not embarrassment. Excitement, if he could judge by her swift inhalation. Some spies were like that. Excited by the job. He imagined some assassins were the same. She said, "We all have a mission, don't we? A need to fulfill."

She did know he had the medallion. She *must* know.

He drew breath to speak. To press her further. But the arrested expression in her eyes held him. She was thinking. Discarding ideas. Making plans. That amused corner of her lips tipped up, then down.

Hell. A smart woman was a damn attractive thing.

She sent him a sultry look. Her fan continued its unhurried wave, but he saw the shift in her expression. Whatever game she played, she had made a decision.

"A test, then, Angelstone. A sampling. Let us see if the rake can live up to his reputation." Her body shifted toward his, a bare half inch. But it was enough to send her fresh scent into the air. Enough to feel the slightest brush of her breasts against his coat. Enough that his body reacted with a line of fire from head to toe. She said, "Come to the blue salon. Fifteen minutes."

Then she slid out from behind the palm fronds and leisurely strolled into the crowd.

Chapter 6

DECEPTION. SHE WAS well trained in it. If the Death Adder medallion wasn't weighing heavily in his pocket, he might have believed Lilias Fairchild. In fact, he might have believed his own performance.

Then again, any good performance had its base in truth. They were attracted to each other, and there was no denying that. He had an awareness in the skin, in the bone, of where her body was. Each shift of her limbs, the angle of her head, the sweep of her lashes. He'd seen it all. Felt it all, as though each movement rippled the air and then touched his skin.

But that did not change the facts. Lust did not affect the truth. He dipped his hand into his inner coat pocket. The contours of the medallion were smooth against the fabric of his glove. Doubt niggled at him, but he pressed it back. Angel, himself, had collected all the Adder medallions left on the victims. There were none unaccounted for.

Fifteen minutes. The next stage of his deception would begin then. He wondered which lie would be revealed first. His? Or hers? But the game had to be played. He had plans for her this evening—as did his commander—but it was best to let her show her hand first.

The blue salon was nearly dark when Angel arrived. The single candle on the mantelpiece cast a golden glow over the nearby settee and side table, but the remainder of the room lay in shadows. He couldn't see Mrs. Fairchild and wondered if she'd lost her nerve. Then he saw the candlelight flicker and dance over her curves as she stepped out of the shadows.

"You're late." With a siren's smile, she slowly closed her fan and let it dangle from her wrist. It bumped against her beaded reticule. "I could take offense." She cocked her head.

"But you won't."

"Are you so sure of yourself, Angelstone?" She pursed her lips in the most seductive moue he'd ever had the pleasure of seeing.

He prowled forward, assessing his prey. She seemed light-hearted. Flirtatious, even.

"Why did you ask me to meet you, Mrs. Fairchild?" It would be interesting to see how she answered his straightforward question. A spy could be caught by lies. Presumably an assassin could as well.

"I'm thinking." She watched him, her eyes unreadable in the semi-darkness.

"What are you thinking about?" He was thinking of the curve of her cheek. It was smooth and delicate. He wanted to run his finger across the skin, then the slight ridge of her cheekbone. Perhaps even the sharper line of her jaw.

"You. Me." Her breath caught. "Us."

"A combination brimming with possibilities." The game had to be played carefully. She would be every bit as well trained as he. He sent her an inviting smile.

"I confess, I hadn't thought of another man since Jeremy died. And now"—she touched the tip of her tongue to her upper lip—"I am."

"Is that so?" She was good. Very good. He would swear desire flushed her cheeks. "Don't you think you should gather sufficient intelligence to make an informed decision?"

She laughed, low and sultry. "Perhaps I should."

It was she who stepped forward. She who set her hands on his shoulders. And it was she who pressed against him, tipping her face up toward his. His heart pounded as heat flowed through him, a torrent of need that shocked him.

"One kiss, Angelstone. To appease my curiosity." She whispered it, just before her lips brushed against his.

Her lips felt like they looked. Lush and soft. Her mouth opened and her tongue danced lightly over his lips. It was like being caught in the glow of a hundred candles. A bright, burning radiance that warmed the skin and heated the blood.

His hands skimmed down to her waist, pulling her closer. Beneath her gown, he could feel the indent of her waist, the stiff shape of her stays. His fingers itched with the need to touch skin. He hated wearing gloves, and now he chafed at not only the barrier of his gloves, but the thin silk of her gown and the stays beneath.

Her hands slid up his shoulders. Fingers curled against the back of his neck, the silk of her gloves smooth and cool against his skin. He was flirting with death and didn't care. Not when he knew where her hands were.

She made a small sound, a low, throaty hum that shot straight through his body. He cupped her cheeks, plundered her mouth. Fingers dug into his shoulders. Her body trembled, just the lightest quiver of her muscles. Her desire for him was real.

But she wasn't.

Assassin. The word battled through the voracious hunger that swamped him. He drew back slightly, looked into pale blue eyes framed by long, gold lashes. Her warm breath fluttered across his lips. Her lips were rosy pink in the candlelight, and turned up in a seductive smile.

"Is your curiosity appeased, Mrs. Fairchild?" The taste of her lingered on his tongue. "Or do you need more?"

"I certainly have something to think about." Her fingertips glided along his shoulder, then rested there.

The kiss clouded his mind. She was more than accomplished. She was lethal.

He set his lips against the column of her neck, grazed his teeth along the sweep of skin that ran to her shoulder. Her breath shuddered out. Her scent rose from her skin and surrounded him. Fine tendrils of hair curled against his jaw. He raised his head and slid his hands down her soft arms to circle her wrists.

He leaned toward her lips, slowly. When he was a breath away, when the heat of her skin warmed his lips without touching them, he stilled. Fierce hunger raged in him.

But it could not be satisfied.

"Mrs. Fairchild," he breathed. He felt a shiver run through her. "I suggest you accompany me to my townhouse."

She pulled back from him, but he set his hands around her waist. A man always held his enemy close.

"You go too far, Angelstone." Her eyes were bright and sharp. Gone was any sensual invitation. "One kiss doesn't mean I'll accompany you to your townhouse."

Ah. So she did not give her body lightly, even for her profession. Gemma had not, either. Then he would not lure Mrs. Fairchild to his townhouse with lies and subterfuge. The direct truth would serve.

"You're very good, my dear. I almost believed you. But it's not a kiss that will bring you to my townhouse." He bared his teeth in a semblance of a grin. "It's murder."

Her eyes went wide. Her lips fell open on a puff of air. "I don't know what you mean."

"I think you do." He captured her wrists. With one swift jerk he turned her around and twisted her arms behind her.

"Stop it. Let me free." She bucked, but he held her wrists tight.

He pressed forward, crowding her, so that his chest touched her back. The vulnerable nape of her neck was in front of him, and though the need to taste her skin was an intense craving, he denied himself the pleasure. In seconds he'd pulled a fine, tightly woven cord from beneath his coat—an easy item to conceal if one knew how. In another few seconds, she was satisfactorily bound.

He spun her around. With her arms bound behind her, a pair of ripe breasts were pushed forward. That gorgeous flesh swelled high and proud above her gown. Damn if he didn't want her. Still.

"We have some business to attend to this evening." He reached into his pocket, then lifted his cupped palm. The medallion lay in the center.

Her eyes flickered. Lashes swept up toward his face, then down to his palm again.

He knew he had her.

"Where did you find it?" She surged forward, stumbled, righted herself. "Let me go."

"No. I was quite taken in by your charms the other night,

my dear. But then I found the medallion and suddenly your charms were not quite as appealing." He dropped the medallion back into his pocket. Her eyes followed the movement. "I've already arranged for a message to be delivered to your family that you've been taken ill and returned to Fairchild House—"

He didn't expect her foot to hit his bollocks full force.

He fell to his knees, then propped himself on one shaking arm. "Son of a—" He coughed. Swallowed. Incapacitated by the crushing ache, he struggled against the urge to retch. His arm gave way and he hit the floor shoulder first. A groan erupted from his throat.

Then she was on the floor beside him, twisting, wriggling that erotic body over him. Her bound hands fluttered around his sides, found his pockets. Fingers groped for the medallion, limited in their movements by the cord, but no less crafty.

He should have seen that tactic coming. Instead, he was lying on the carpet and trying desperately not to vomit. Fighting nausea, he rolled away and onto his hands and knees. He was still faster than a bound assassin, thank the fates.

"Bloody hell, woman." He was lucky she hadn't found his knife.

"Give me the medallion." She scrabbled away from him, hampered by her skirts and bound hands. With a clumsy lurch she rose to her knees. Pinned beneath her, the cream gown pulled taut against her body.

She isn't running, his mind whispered. *She's fighting.* He expected nothing less of an assassin.

"We're not going to settle this here." He coughed again, then reached for the cord binding her hands. Hauled her to her feet.

"I won't—"

"It doesn't matter." He pulled her around to face him, pain still fueling his temper. Her eyes shone bright and angry in the candlelight. "We've business to discuss."

Chapter 7

I T DIDN'T SEEM possible a person could be abducted from a London townhouse in the middle of a crowded ball. But it had happened.

Now here she was, sitting in Angelstone's carriage, with the faint glow of the lamps highlighting his inflexible jaw and cutting cheekbones. All lean legs and broad shoulders, he filled the vehicle's interior. In the partial light, with his unreadable gaze and his unruly queue of hair, he looked much more dangerous than a fallen angel.

"Angelstone."

"Mrs. Fairchild." The words were clipped. No seductive purr, no sensual smile from those lips. Lips that had kissed her senseless and reminded her she was a woman with needs and desires. Even now, she could still taste him. Rich brandy and wild heat.

Embarrassment washed through her. She'd been forward and shameless, and look where she had found herself. Hands bound and trapped in a man's carriage, destined for parts unknown and heaven knew what treatment.

"I demand to be released."

"No."

"Why am I here?" she fired back.

"I think you are quite aware." He watched her steadily as

he pulled off first one glove, then the other and stuffed them in his pocket. It was an unpardonably rude gesture for a gentleman. Obviously, he was not a gentleman.

He was close enough she could kick him. But she wouldn't be able to open the carriage door quickly with her hands bound. And he had the medallion. The final gift from her husband, one he gave her with his last breath.

She refused to leave without it.

"The medallion is mine," she said.

"Is it? Interesting." The conversational tone of his words was oddly frightening. "Well, now the medallion is mine." Propping his elbows on his knees, he leaned forward. He filled the space between them until his face was only a foot from hers.

The instinct to shrink into the seat was overwhelming.

So she leaned forward to meet him. And smiled. Slowly. "Give me"—she angled her head insolently—"the medallion."

"Oh, but your smile is a formidable weapon, Mrs. Fairchild." He reached out, tracing a bare thumb over her bottom lip. His skin was calloused and sensitizing. "Wicked, wanton and willful."

Heat pooled low in her belly as desire warred with temper.

"Why, thank you." She flicked the tip of her tongue over his thumb, tasted salt and man. Lilias hid a smug smile at Angelstone's quick inhalation. "So is your voice. It's by turns chilling and erotic."

"Erotic?" he said. "A strong word for a woman."

"I'm a strong woman."

The carriage shuddered to a stop and they stared at each other through the darkness. The clip of the horses' hooves rang on the cobblestones as the animals paced a step or two. Above them, the coachman called out to calm the horses.

Large hands tugged the hood of her cloak forward to shade her face.

"I'm surprised you care for my reputation enough to cover my face while you abduct me," she said.

"Only mildly."

The hood concealed everything from her view but his face. Just there in front of her. Lean and male—and frightening given the circumstances.

But she wasn't beaten yet.

He stepped out of the carriage and onto the London street. For a moment, she couldn't see him through the door and she wondered if he'd disappeared into the night. Then a strong hand reached into the carriage and gripped her arm to guide her out.

She had little choice but to accept his help. She couldn't leave the carriage with her hands bound behind her back. Getting out the door, maneuvering the steps—all were a feat she knew would best her.

Lilias studied the street. They were still in Mayfair, but away from the fashionable West End. It was a perfectly respectable area, if not the wealthiest. She could scream and someone would look out. She could run to any door on the street and find assistance.

"Don't." He gripped her upper arm, hard.

Apparently he could read her thoughts.

The front door to Number 12 opened as they approached. The man standing in the lit opening flicked expressionless eyes over Lilias before stepping aside to let them pass into the hall. No, not expressionless. Concealing eyes. Secretive eyes.

"He'll be here shortly," the man said.

He shut the noiseless front door with careful, deliberate movements, then turned to face them. Her gaze fell on the pistol held easily in the man's hand. She swallowed hard and studied his face again, the barest hint of nighttime stubble on his jaw, the unsmiling mouth. His jacket was tailored to broad shoulders, but it was not livery. He was no common butler.

"Good. Thank you, Jones." Angelstone's grip loosened, but his fingers remained curled around her upper arm. "We'll be in my study."

The man nodded once in acknowledgment, face serious, brows low, before disappearing into the nearest doorway.

She let Angelstone propel her down the hall and into a room full of heavy masculine furniture. A fire roared in the hearth. "Your study? Is this your home?"

"In a way."

"Cryptic answer."

"Sit down." He didn't give her much choice in the matter. He pushed her into a seat facing the desk.

Anger bubbled up in her, shot through with fear. But she knew how to bury fear. "I want the medallion."

"Here it is." He tossed something silver and circular on the desktop. The disc struck with the dull ping of metal hitting wood before rolling across the surface.

"I thought it had been lost." She couldn't reach for it. Her hands were still uselessly bound behind her. She gritted her teeth and scooted forward in the seat, her eyes on the medallion. "I don't understand why you abducted me for this."

"I did not know the Death Adders counted a woman among their assassins."

Her eyes jerked up. Shock pinged around in her chest. "I don't—What do you mean?"

"That is quite a virtuous look, Mrs. Fairchild. If I didn't know better, I would think you were innocent." His voice had changed. It was hard. Cold. His eyes, too, had changed. The deep amber was as sharp as the edge of the gem. He stalked forward, a predator in elegant evening attire.

"I *am* innocent of—" *What was he insinuating? Assassinations?* "I am."

"Indeed?" He tipped his head toward the medallion. "Your little token? It's the sign of the Death Adders. Only an assassin carries it."

Chapter 8

ANGEL WATCHED HER carefully, searching for signs of guilt or innocence.

Her features blanked for an instant, as though there was simply no thought in her mind. Then her eyes darkened as the pupils dilated. Color drained from her face. She swallowed once, hard.

He would swear she was innocent. A person can control movement, words. Tone of voice. But not pupils. Not the color of their skin. She was either shocked he had discovered her secret, or shocked the medallion was the sign of an assassin.

"I don't know what you mean, Angelstone." Her tone was brisk, the words clipped. "But I suggest we discuss it."

She recovered well. Admirably well. "A wise choice," he said.

She sat daintily in the chair, her spine straight, her chin high. Bound hands were hidden beneath her cloak. He saw her throat work as she swallowed hard. "Explain to me why you believe the medallion belongs to an assassin."

"Explain to me why you have it."

She held his gaze but did not speak. Her chin tipped up, showing him the slight hollow beneath her jawbone where candlelight danced.

He stayed silent, waiting. Watching. She did not struggle against the bonds, and he found that strangely admirable.

Giving her a moment to think, he rounded the desk and sat. Still, she did not answer.

"We are at a stalemate, Mrs. Fairchild. One of us is going to have to break the silence or we'll never have a discussion."

"Irritating, but true. Very well, my lord." She shrugged delicately, rounded shoulders curving up, then down. The cloak rippled around her. "The medallion was a gift from my husband. The last one he gave me."

"An odd gift for a wife when a man is going off to battle." He couldn't think of a more horrific gift.

She shook her head. "I don't understand." Blond curls bounced along her jawline. She tossed her head to flick away the loose tendrils.

"One would think a man would buy a trinket to remember him by. A book of poetry. A pretty bauble. Diamonds or some other gem. But a medallion? One that is not even pretty?"

Mrs. Fairchild's nostrils flared. In agreement or denial? She did not speak, so he did.

"A fascinating story, but highly doubtful." Angel leaned back in his chair, eyeing her over the desktop. She was selling him a story, and he could not decide if he should buy it. She appeared calm, her voice even, but the lovely flush that usually covered her face was still noticeably absent. "Try again."

"It's true. I don't know when he purchased it or how long he carried it, but he gave it to me when—" Her breath hitched. "When he lay dying."

His instinct stirred. The doubt flickered again, for entirely different reasons. *When he lay dying.* Angel forced his muscles to relax. "The major died at Waterloo."

"Yes." She looked up, met his gaze. There were no tears there. No grief. The bright blue was clouded with memory. He wondered how similar the memories she carried were to his own. "But you know that already."

"How did he die?"

"A sabre cut to his chest," she said flatly.

Such a cut could wound a man or kill him. It was all in the angle of the sabre, the placement of the cut, the depth of the wound. An assassin would know precisely the right method.

It occurred to him Lilias Fairchild knew how to handle a sabre. She'd wielded the weapon with rudimentary skill at

Waterloo. Perhaps, if she were an assassin, the sabre was not her weapon of choice, but she could certainly kill with it.

"Now it's your turn to answer my question." Her lips tilted up in a mocking smile. "What is the medallion?"

He studied her face again, searching for an assassin beneath the beautiful exterior. Was she an Adder? The Adders were skilled at deception. But then, he was skilled at unearthing lies.

He'd seen her grief-stricken eyes two years before. *L'Ange de Vengeance.* Yes, she had been full of vengeance, but also honesty. War revealed truth. Brave men became cowards and the humblest soldier became a hero. Mrs. Fairchild had fought, but not with any glee. Not with the skill of an assassin. In battle, soldiers did not conceal their skill or they would die. She could use the sabre, but not with enough skill to show she'd been trained. An Adder would be skilled at every weapon, or at least more skilled than Mrs. Fairchild had been.

He knew the truth in his gut, even if his brain questioned her possession of the medallion. When espionage was a man's business, he learned to trust instinct. The brain could overthink things.

But that did not mean she was not the key to finding the Adders—or Gemma's murderer. She still carried a medallion.

He stood and walked toward her. In a moment, the cool hilt of his dagger was in his hand. He saw the slight stiffening of her spine, the quick intake of breath. Fear. Temper. It wasn't clear which emotion had stolen her breath. But she tipped up her chin and met his gaze squarely. Much like a brave martyr meeting the guillotine, eyes full of defiant determination.

"A deadly skill," she said, "to hide a knife so easily in one's coat."

"One learns what one must." He moved behind her chair, looked down at the nape of her neck. A vulnerable place, that exposed nape. Her shoulders tensed and he knew she felt that vulnerability. His gaze traveled the length of her spine, to the hands tied uselessly behind her.

A swift slice and the cord binding her wrists fell to the chair.

He replaced the weapon before moving around to face her again.

"And then the knife returns to the same nowhere from which it came." She chafed her wrists. Narrowed eyes scanned his body once, likely imagining just where he'd hidden the knife. Then her eyes flicked to the medallion on the desktop. She snatched the disc, ran her hand over the onyx as though wishing to feel the surface through her gloves.

"The medallion is the sign of a group of assassins called the Death Adders." He leaned a hip on his desk. Her head was bent over her cupped hands. The curls and coils of hair piled on her head shone like wheat under a late summer sun. "They leave it at the scene of every assassination to identify their work."

Her body jerked. The medallion tumbled out of her hand and landed on the thick rug. The onyx emblem lay faceup. They both stared at it. The emblem resembled a many-legged spider at this distance.

"Death Adders." Her whisper barely reached him.

"Assassins for hire." He had some sympathy for her, but he did not change his tone. "They kill for politics, succession to a throne, inheritance of a title. As long as they receive compensation, they'll take a life. The medallion is left on the victim or delivered to the individual that hired the assassin upon completion of the assignment."

"Why would Jeremy have a medallion?" This statement seemed to revive her. Her hand darted out and she picked up the medallion again, fisted it. "Why would my husband have one?"

"A very good question, Mrs. Fairchild." One he would find the answer to.

"Jeremy was not an assassin. I would know." Her tone was low and fierce, her eyes bright. "I was married to him for six years. I lived with him. I marched with him through foreign countries. I slept beside him nearly every night."

She spun away, the medallion still clutched in her hand. Pacing to the window she stared out. "How could I not know? If he were—if he—It's not possible. It's simply not." She opened her fingers and stared down at the medallion. Anguish contorted her features, turning beauty into despair. "And if he were not an assassin, then his death—" Her lips pressed together. She did not complete the thought aloud. She did not need to.

Her shoulders hunched forward, creating a rounded valley between them. Protection of the heart. His bare fingers reached out, almost touched the creamy skin and delicate lace covering her shoulder.

But he did not. The subtle arch of her back also protected her from him.

"Do you know what you have done?" She turned to face him. Her agony had been replaced with rage. She was magnificent with it, brilliant and powerful and bright. "Even if your vile accusations aren't true, I will always wonder if I truly knew my husband. I will always wonder if my marriage was a lie. Jeremy isn't here to ask—" Her voice broke. She turned the medallion over in her fingers. Firelight flashed on the medallion's smooth metal back. "He isn't here to ask, so I will never know."

Well, damn. Somehow he'd shrunk until he was two inches tall.

"My apologies, Mrs. Fairchild. But—"

A throat cleared. Angel spun toward the doorway and found his commander standing there.

"We may not be able to ask your husband about the truth, Mrs. Fairchild, but the circumstantial evidence carries great weight." Sir Charles Flint wasted no time or space striding into the room. Decisive footfalls rang on the wood floor, then muffled on the rug. He was not particularly tall, but he filled the room with broad shoulders and a barrel chest.

"Sir." Angel felt off balance, being only two inches tall. It was decidedly uncomfortable.

Sir Charles paused as he passed Angel. The spymaster's brows rose—the question was asked. Angel shook his head, the movement barely a tremor—the answer was given.

Lilias Fairchild is not an Adder.

"I apologize we must meet under such circumstances, Mrs. Fairchild." Sir Charles took a chair near the fire and folded his hands in his lap. "I'm Sir Charles. I can't give information on my position or the office I work with. I'm sure you understand."

"No. Frankly, I don't understand. I choose not to play your games." She shot Angel a dark look. "I demand to be released. Again."

"You cannot be released until we have received more information," Angel interjected, stepping forward. Sir Charles would say the same, but Angel would see to it.

"If I do not return to Fairchild House soon, the other members of my household—including my cousin-in-law, Lord Grant Fairchild—will wonder where I have gone. They will start a search for me." Her chin tipped up and she gazed steadily at Sir Charles. The damsel staring down the dragon, though there was no fear in the damsel.

Angel stationed himself beside Sir Charles's chair. His commander would remain seated to portray a nonthreatening demeanor. It was one of his strategies.

It was not Angel's. He smiled. All charm. All polish.

Chapter 9

I F THE MARQUESS of Angelstone believed his smile was charming, he was quite wrong. The smile did not reduce the underlying wild and dangerous power of him. In fact, it only increased it. A wolf in sheep's clothing is still a wolf.

"Mrs. Fairchild." Angelstone's tawny eyes trained on her. "I've approached this harshly, and I apologize. I believed the medallion to be yours, and that is my mistake."

"'Approach' is a tame substitute for 'abduction.'" She tapped the disc in her left hand, the rounded metal making a light *thwack* as it hit her kid glove. "The medallion is mine. It was gift from my husband, as I've already said. He was no assassin."

"You maintain he never killed anyone."

"Do you think I'm an idiot? Of course he killed. He was a cavalry officer during the war. It was inevitable. But he did not kill in cold blood." She swallowed hard as bile rose in her throat at the thought. Jeremy could not have been an assassin. It simply did not make sense.

Not her husband.

"Mrs. Fairchild." Sir Charles gestured to an armchair, an easy expression on his face. "Please take a seat. You will be more comfortable if you are seated."

"I prefer to stand, sir." She did not believe for a second he was worried about her comfort. She sent her gaze to

Angelstone's face. "I mentioned a moment ago that I am not an idiot. You wish to subtly interrogate me about my husband and my marriage in the hopes of discovering whether he was an assassin or whether he was killed by one."

The words were out now, those horrible words she could not say before. Perhaps because she was speaking to a man she had not kissed just an hour ago. Had it been only an hour? Her world had shifted on its axis in the space of sixty minutes. Only three thousand, six hundred seconds.

Sir Charles smiled benignly. The smile did not reach his eyes. "You are correct, Mrs. Fairchild."

"I shall tell you what I know then, sir, so there will be no need for subtle interrogation. My husband was a good man. He loved me. He cared for the men that marched under him, seeing to their welfare before his own. He would go without food if one of his men was starving. You cannot reconcile that man—that officer—with an assassin."

"Were you with him every moment of every day during your marriage?" Angelstone prowled around the side of the desk toward her, the smile gone from his face.

She flicked her eyes toward Sir Charles, whose expression was still mildly pleasant. Perhaps just a bit curious. A benevolent uncle asking how she was feeling.

It was like facing one good spy and one bad spy. And Angelstone was not the good one.

"No, Angelstone. I was not with him every second. Sometimes we were separated. A few weeks, even a month or two. But I knew him, and I knew what he was capable of."

Angelstone stepped closer, his gold eyes deepening. "Everyone is capable of taking a life, Mrs. Fairchild." His voice was low and knowing. "It is only the motive that changes. I believe *you*, of all people, would understand that."

Something dark reared up inside her. Remorse for those lives she had cut short. For the families, the wives. The children they would not have. It often tried to weigh her down. She refused to let it. She'd been wild with grief that day. Seized by uncontrolled madness. Jeremy had fought for his country, for a cause he believed in. That cause had killed him. She'd wanted nothing more than to finish what he started, to avenge him, even if it meant her own death.

Angelstone was right. Everyone was capable of taking a life. Even her.

"Perhaps I do understand that darkness in the soul," she said softly. "But I also understood my husband, and I refuse to believe he was capable of what you accuse him."

"Then, if he was not an assassin, he must have been assassinated." Sir Charles said it so calmly, Lilias's legs nearly buckled.

She locked her knees. "Then I suggest you start looking for the man who assassinated him, sir," she said. "Because I want a few minutes with him."

———

SIR CHARLES PULLED the door, leaving only the slightest crack between Mrs. Fairchild in the study and himself and Angel in the hall. The set of the commander's mouth was grim.

"A high-priced Prussian courtesan has been assassinated." Sir Charles didn't waste time or mince words. "A few weeks ago."

"I've heard." And Angel regretted it. One more death by the Adders he hadn't been able to stop. "She sold political secrets as well as her body."

"You knew her?" Sir Charles's eyebrows rose.

"Not in that way, sir," he qualified. "I met her a few times on assignment."

Sir Charles glanced at the study door, then down the hall to where Jones stood patiently in the front entryway. He would be waiting dutifully for his own assignments. "We need to shut them down, Angel. The Adders are spiraling out of control. There have been six deaths in the last six months."

He knew every one of their names. The method of death. Even the secrets of their lives. But it was never enough. "I have no guess as to whether Major Fairchild was an assassin or simply a target, but either way, Mrs. Fairchild will have key information." Angel grimaced. "She only has to remember it."

"Make her remember."

A shadow fell across the open sliver of light between the study door and doorjamb. She was listening. Or at least close enough to hear. Angel tipped his head down the hall. They shifted away from the study and walked toward the front door.

"Give her a few days. Set an agent to watch her." Sir Charles lowered his voice. "Let her come to you, Angel. She's hurt and angered by the betrayal now, but she'll want answers. By asking questions, she'll give us the answers we want."

He wasn't so sure. "I don't intend to give her more than a few days. We need to move forward. Quickly."

"Indeed." Sir Charles's eyes turned sharp. "My foreign counterparts are beginning to believe the Adders are under my control."

"You can't be serious." Shock rippled through him.

"Unfortunately, I am. We know there is a man in London directing the Adders' assignments. At least three of my foreign counterparts have hinted they suspect the leader is myself. I have been advised that if we do not locate the leader of the Death Adders in London, they will send as many agents as necessary to do it for us."

Sir Charles turned sharply and strode down the hall. Jones handed him a cane and hat before opening the front door. Sir Charles turned to face Angel, his sturdy frame blocking out the light from the foyer candles.

"You must find the leader, Angel, before England is overrun with foreign agents."

Chapter 10

IT WAS A miracle Angelstone's unmarked carriage brought her home before Catherine and Grant returned from their social engagements. She just had time to sneak in through the rear door, slip out of her gown and plait her hair before she heard the wheels of the Fairchild carriage rumble on the cobblestones.

Her room faced the street, and she quickly blew out the single candle she'd disrobed by. Flicking back a pretty yellow curtain, Lilias peered at the street below. A footman lowered the carriage steps, and a moment later the open carriage door framed Grant's shoulders. He stepped down, greatcoat swirling around him, before turning to assist Catherine. The carriage lamps outlined his square jaw as he smiled at her.

After a sharp call from the coachman, the carriage rolled off toward the mews. Grant and Catherine disappeared below her as they moved into the townhouse.

Not once did either of them glance at her window.

She was not certain if she was pleased they trusted her enough to believe Angelstone's lie, or if she wanted them to worry about her.

Lilias let the curtain fall closed, blocking out the street below. Moving easily through the dark room, she stepped toward the dresser. The case holding Jeremy's miniature sat on top. Taking the painting from its velvet bed she ran a finger around the gilt frame. She didn't light a candle to look at it, afraid of what she might see in his face. It would not have changed, would it? The paint would not somehow shift over the ivory to reveal a man she did not recognize.

When the light knock came at her door, she jumped nearly a foot.

"Lilias, dear?" It was Catherine's thin, reedy voice. Barely more than a whisper through the door. "Are you well?"

"Yes. I'm better. It was a headache," Lilias called softly, in compliance with the lie Angelstone had already told. The frame of the miniature bit into her fingers as she clutched it. She must not let Catherine into the room. She could not face Jeremy's mother with this question haunting her. "I'm just tired now."

A pause, then, "Good night. I shall see you in the morning." Quiet footfalls faded away in the hall beyond her door.

Lilias sighed, pathetically grateful for the reprieve. Rubbing a thumb softly over the painting, she felt the brushstrokes. Doubt and fear and betrayal swarmed through her, though she tried to bury them and think logically. Jeremy was not an assassin. She would have known. A man couldn't hide that kind of darkness from his wife. He must have obtained the medallion some other way—perhaps even during the battle— but it could not have belonged to him.

And if it did?

She refused to believe him capable of it. The man she'd known laughed and loved easily. He'd earned respect from his men and cared about each one of them. He slept in mud, bled from multiple wounds, starved when necessity demanded. He'd believed in his country enough to fight and die for it. And he had loved her.

Such a man could not be an assassin.

She would prove it.

With careful fingers, she set the miniature back into the case and closed the lid. Then she dropped onto the edge of the bed and waited while the house settled into sleep around her. A few doors opened and closed as the last remaining servants made their way to bed. Floors creaked, walls sighed.

When she was certain no one remained awake, she lit a single candle and shrugged into her wrapper. She opened the door to the hall and, shielding the candle from drafts, made the first step forward. Shadows flickered in the corners as she crept down the hall and up the stairs to the attics. They were quiet beyond the snuffling and snoring of sleeping servants. Soundlessly, bare feet chilled from the wooden floor, Lilias passed closed doors until she reached the storage area.

The trunk had not moved since her return from Waterloo. It had not been opened since she'd closed and latched it in the Netherlands. She could not have borne going through it then. She had simply taken it up and brought it home, side by side with her own trunk.

Setting down the candle, she kneeled in front of it and smoothed a hand over the scarred leather surface. It had traveled across the Peninsula and the Continent with Jeremy, following him on the baggage trains from one bivouac to another.

She supposed it was time to open it. Two years was a long time.

Heart drumming in her ears, she set her fingers to the latches and flicked her thumbs up. Rusty with disuse, the metal latches moved slowly, but they snicked up and open. She breathed deep and lifted the lid with damp palms.

Musty air assaulted her nostrils, bringing with it dust that had her sniffling to keep from sneezing. Clothing was piled within. On the top were Jeremy's dress uniform, his medals. Evidence of his exceptional career. Evidence of his honest beliefs and ways. Swallowing hard, she set them aside. The pain near her heart was a dull ache, but one she'd grown accustomed to.

Beneath those items lay the sabre. She wrapped her palm around the hilt and drew it from the valise. Her mind flew back to the battle, to the cries of the wounded, the pounding of the artillery guns and thick black smoke. She did not regret fighting for her country.

But by God, she had better not regret fighting for her husband.

She set the sabre beside the uniform. Clothing followed, then a comb, a shaving kit. A pair of boots. Each item was familiar and foreign. A reminder of other days a lifetime ago.

Tears wet her cheeks, but they were soft. There was no evidence here against him. Angelstone was wrong. Jeremy had been exactly what she'd thought: the good man she'd married. Relief flooded through her, sweet and comforting and reassuring.

Until she saw the hole in the bottom of the valise.

Stomach churning, twisting, she bent closer. There was space where there should be none. She stuck a finger into it— and touched metal.

"Oh, God." The word sobbed out as her breath clogged her lungs. Frantic fingers tore at the hole, clutching linen and ripping it away from the bottom.

She nearly wretched when she saw the matched pistols nestled side by side with a set of knives. Her fingers shook as she lifted one of the pistols. It was not military issue. That inexpensive pistol had been reclaimed by the government for another officer to use. This one was exquisite, with its engraved silver flintlock and pearl inlayed handle.

She had never seen it before. Not in six years of war and marriage.

Gulping in air, she examined the knives still nestled in the valise. Coiled beside them was a thin, tightly woven black rope. What did a man need a short rope for? Why would he hide pistols and knives when he was a soldier?

She could think of only one reason.

But how could she not have seen it? She would have known. There would have been signs. A woman didn't live with and love an assassin without suspecting something wasn't right.

Had there been signs, and she had been too in love to see them?

Pieces of her life began to break apart, then shift and re-form, like small sections of broken glass soldered together to form a stained glass window. Only it wasn't nearly so pretty. An alleged message delivery to Prague, which Jeremy's commander could not recall ordering. A stranger loitering outside their rooms in Brussels and a jittery Jeremy watching from inside. A week he should have been home from leave, but he never came.

Something tore inside her heart. The sharp, jagged edges of it sliced into her. She let the pain fuel her anger. *Lies. All lies.* And there were more. More half-truths, more confusion.

She had overlooked and excused all of it.

She drew her knees up to her chin and set her forehead against them. But she did not weep. She seethed and thought of betrayal. She thought of battles and worry and grief and loneliness. And she remembered a dozen other things. Small questions, a bit of confusion.

She had been blind. Each time, she had simply believed his explanation. Sometimes she had not even asked the questions.

Worse, she remembered nights spent in the arms of a man who deceived. Making lazy love on a summer afternoon and letting a veritable stranger plunge into her body. Had there been any honesty in her marriage? In the arms that had held her close, in the secrets she shared with him?

She had been in love with an assassin—one who barely bothered to hide his weapons from her. What did that make her? Too stupid to notice what was in front of her face, or an accomplice?

Rage was a living thing inside her chest, beating a rhythm against her ribs as it fought its way free. She stood so quickly the candle almost flickered out. Jeremy's dress uniform was in her hands before she realized what she was doing. She heaved it across the room, her breath catching in her throat. Then the medals, one by one, were hurled against the wall. The boots followed, each thudding against the plaster.

It wasn't enough. Nothing would ever be enough. Breath shuddering, she looked down at the pistols, now lying at her feet.

These she would take, along with the knives and the sabre. They were hers now. Payment for betrayal.

And a reminder of lies.

HE FELT STUPID, chasing after Mrs. Fairchild. Perhaps he should have waited for her to find him, as Sir Charles indicated. But the delay of even twenty-four hours was grating on his temper. The need to act grew steadily, straining against the need to be patient.

And, if he were honest with himself, he wanted to see how she'd fared after the blow he'd dealt her.

Now he was slinking along the edge of the ballroom, looking for that bright crown of curls surrounded by the cropped hair of gentlemen that would signify Mrs. Fairchild and her ever-present suitors. When he saw her, he stopped short, unable to take another step forward.

She glowed like fire among the pale, watered-down

pastels. Her dress was a deep ruby red trimmed in creamy lace. Slashed sleeves revealed crescents of shimmering ivory. Pearls glowed against her skin and dripped from her ears.

She had been beautiful before. In deep red, with a sparkle of energy swirling around her, she was stunning. Sultry and sensual and full of life. Lust reared up and gripped him by the throat. So visceral, so consuming, he sucked in a breath.

A crowd had gathered around her, both men and women. Drawn to her like moths to flame, each vying for her attention.

He cocked his head. Looked again. Her smile was too bright, too sharp. The energy surrounding her was frenetic, even brittle. He strode forward, pushing through the moths to reach the flame.

She saw him coming. Her eyes narrowed slightly, though her smile widened in false welcome.

"Lord Angelstone," she said smoothly. "How delightful to see you again."

He ignored the moths around her. "Mrs. Fairchild, would you care for a stroll around the room?" Angel took her hand and set it on his arm, giving her no choice.

"No, thank you." She pulled her arm away, temper sharp in her eyes.

"It would be an honor if you would walk with me." Angel reached for her again.

A tall man stepped between them, angling his body in a protective stance. "Your rank doesn't entitle you to order people about, Angelstone." Cool brown eyes snapped over a square jaw and lips pressed into a thin line. "The lady said no."

Angel looked down his nose at the other man. If he were impressed by an ostentatious cavalry uniform, he might be intimidated. "I don't recall being introduced to you."

"Major Jason Hawthorne. A very old, very good friend of Mrs. Fairchild's." That could mean any number of relationships. Major Hawthorne wasn't a peacock, or one of the gaggle that followed Mrs. Fairchild like blind geese. Which meant he was important to her. "It is my duty to protect her from unwanted advances."

"Hawthorne—" Mrs. Fairchild interjected softly. She set an ivory-gloved hand lightly on the man's arm, though her eyes were riveted on Angel's. "I'll be fine."

Hawthorne sent Mrs. Fairchild a long look. Something

passed between them that clearly required no words. Another man might have felt a twinge of unexpected jealousy. Angel, however, reminded himself he had no reason for jealousy. She was not his woman.

"I don't want to stroll, Angelstone." She tossed her head, the curls around her face flirting with him. Her eyes met his straight on. Bright. Steady. Full of challenge. "I want to *dance*."

The force of her eyes, her words, hit him full in the chest. She wasn't talking about dancing. At least, not in a ballroom.

His mind filled with nothing but the vision of her naked beneath him, her limbs entwined with his. He went hard instantly. Lust was a living thing inside him, roaring its approval.

Her knowing smile only fueled the hunger.

"Excuse us, Hawthorne." Angel flicked his gaze at the tensed soldier. Tried not to exude victory.

Then he met Lilias's gaze again and dismissed all thought of the other man. He heard the rich tones of violins on the air now. A waltz. He offered his hand, palm up. She set fingers in his, her movements slow and elegant. The scent of her skin rose and stirred the beast inside him.

He drew her to the floor, hands still joined, eyes still locked. He lifted their linked hands to the proper position. His opposite hand slid onto her waist.

Her lips tipped up. "It seems I've saved my first dance for you, Angelstone." Fingertips trailed across his shoulder as she set her hand there. "Let's see if I remember the steps."

"If you don't, I'll remind you."

He swung her onto the floor in a breathless spin. It was still a scandalous dance in some circles, and one not performed everywhere. There were standards to ensure it was proper. He couldn't remember any of them.

He pulled her close. Not so close they touched, but still the space between them heated. Her cheeks flushed rosy.

"You look particularly fetching." He didn't even try for charm. Just fact.

"I've heard that frequently this evening."

"I can't imagine why." He swept his gaze over the body revealed so daringly by the gown. If she shrugged her shoulders in just the right way, her breasts would be bared to the entire ballroom. "You seem to remember the steps."

In fact, she more than remembered them. Their bodies moved in tandem. Spinning, whirling. The room beyond was a swirl of color and music, a soft, unfocused mix that insulated them.

"I need to speak with you about my husband," she said.

"Ah, so it is business that brings you to me." But the quickening of her breath betrayed her. She was as aroused as he. "Why?"

"Because I believe you." She said it fiercely. Her fingers dug into his shoulder as they spun across the floor. "Jeremy was an assassin."

"Indeed?" Angel's brows rose. "What changed your mind?"

"I've thought back over the entire six years of my marriage." Her velvet skirts moved around and between them, a swish of fabric brushing against his legs.

"And?" If his pulse hadn't already been pounding from lust, it might have spiked with the thrill of the hunt.

"Jeremy was everything you say he was—and nothing I thought he was."

"If you want to speak of espionage, why are we waltzing?"

"Because I've chosen to dance again." Her eyes met his. "But only with you."

The music's tempo increased. So he swung her around and around, faster and faster, bodies almost touching. The lace rimming her bodice brushed against his coat. Her lips parted in shock and her breath shuddered out.

"Only with me." He repeated it as the beast within him roared.

She had come to him, as Sir Charles had said she would. But it was not the way he expected.

The set ended and they stood there a moment, joined hands trembling in each other's grip. His other hand still rested on her waist. He could feel the measure of her breath, in and out.

She relaxed her fingers and stepped away. The fan that had been dangling from her wrist snapped open. She fanned herself in long, slow movements. "Send your carriage for me. Midnight. Do *not* let the coachman sit in front of Fairchild House. I'll meet him at the northwest corner." She spun on her heel and disappeared through the crowd.

His fingers twitched reflexively.

She wanted to dance.

Chapter 11

"WOULD YOU CARE for a drink? Wine, perhaps?" Angelstone gestured to the sideboard in his private study as they entered.

A decanter rose from the mahogany surface. Its crystal shape was one long, sinuous line accented by the ruby liquid within. Such an elegant picture. But Lilias didn't feel elegant. That was too nice of a word for what she felt. "I would like something stronger, please."

He raised his brows. "I promise the questioning won't be that difficult to endure."

But he poured brandy into two glasses just the same. The squat, cylindrical glass suited her better. Not a snifter, but something much more practical, and filled with a good, fortifying liquor.

"Difficult is relative, Angelstone." Her heart jittered around her rib cage, a hard rock tumbled by a brutal flood of emotion. The river that had been dammed was now rushing uncontrollably.

She took the glass he offered. Gloved fingers brushed. His lingered there, just a moment, while he watched her. It was a heady thing to be so intensely watched by a man such as Angelstone. It was not open desire in those eyes. That had been banked for now. But the quiet focus of those eyes, only on her, could make a woman aware of her body in the most fascinating way. A tingle along the skin, the air between him and her, the position of her legs, just so, as he walked past her.

Lifting the glass to her lips, she sipped the smooth brandy and let the fire rest on her tongue. Clearly, her choice in men was suspect. Her husband had been an assassin. The man she now wanted as a lover was a spy.

She had very poor judgment.

At least Angelstone didn't lie to her. At least there was honesty between them. Or there would be, once she told him everything.

She cast her gaze around the room. She had been in his study when he'd abducted her, but hadn't noticed the décor then. It suited him. Elegant, spare, masculine. Not dark, but not the light, pretty colors associated with women. And it was practical. A locked cabinet in the corner containing untold secrets, an unobtrusive pair of pistols, side by side on a table. A wall mount that held knives. Three spaces were empty, tiny arms waiting for their respective weapons. Was he wearing those knives under all his evening clothes? Her eyes flicked over his body. What a stimulating idea.

"What is this place, Angelstone?" she asked. "It is not your family townhouse."

"My bachelor's rooms before I inherited the title."

"Ah." She leveled her gaze at him over the rim of her glass. "Now you use it for spying?"

"And other things." His grin was tempting. The rogue. "Please, have a seat."

She settled into the chair he gestured to. It was the same one she'd sat in when she'd met Sir Charles. Soft, comfortable and without even a hint of femininity. She envied men their comfortable retreats.

Angelstone remained standing, the dangerous spy hidden by fashionable clothing. She could almost imagine he was a titled gentleman enjoying a drink at the conclusion of his evening.

Almost.

"Mrs. Fairchild—"

"Don't call me that." The words whipped from her before she could stop them.

"I beg your pardon?"

"Don't call me Mrs. Fairchild." The name tasted acidic in her mouth. She hadn't been aware of her revulsion for it until he'd said it aloud. "I don't wish to be called by my last name at the moment. Particularly by you."

"Why not by me?" His eyes narrowed with curiosity.

"Because you, of all the people in the world, know the truth. You're the *only* person who knows the truth." She set the glass on the table at her elbow. It was disconcerting to have no sense of identity. She wasn't the beloved wife of Major Fairchild any longer. She was the wife of some other man. The name would have to stay, but she didn't have to use it—at least not with the one man who was as close to a confidant as she would have. "Call me Lilias."

"Lilias." The name sounded like a caress on his gilded tongue. "Tell me what you know."

"He lied to me. That's what I know." The brandy was no defense against the fury gnashing its teeth inside her chest. "In a dozen large ways and a hundred small ones."

"Run me through the lies, then. I need to understand the man. I can talk to other soldiers, other officers. But no matter how much information I obtain from them, I can only learn the man from you." He sat on the edge of the desk just in front of her. Arms crossed, legs extended so his boot tips brushed against the edge of her skirt. "I've investigated his rank, his military record. It's exemplary. Not a blemish."

"That would be just another lie, wouldn't it?" Sitting still was impossible. She pushed to her feet. She couldn't know if Jeremy was an admirable soldier that cared for his men or whether it was a performance. Where did reality end and deception begin? "There were so many small things I never would have questioned Jeremy about. I simply accepted what he said."

"Why would you question him?" Angelstone's gloved hands flexed, like two caged animals trying to break free of their restraints.

"Because odd things happened." She took the brandy with her when she prowled the room. The glass in her hand was solid. The liquid a known flavor. Brandy didn't change. It was always warm in the throat, stinging the nose. At least some things stayed the same.

"Give me an example," he said.

"We were in Spain a few years ago after Salamanca. I had taken rooms in Madrid with other officers' wives during the occupation. We went to the opera with a group of English diplomats and ambassadors. Jeremy was supposed to be in the barracks—illness was spreading through the troops and provisions were low. He said he needed to be with his men." The glass stayed round and smooth when she rolled it between her palms. Amber liquid rippled and shifted, a small storm inside the crystal ocean.

"We met Jeremy in the street as we left the opera. I bumped into him as he was passing. I thought he was a stranger at first. When I recognized him, he said he'd returned to town early and hoped to join us at the opera."

She stopped. If she said the words aloud, they would be true. Truth could not be unsaid. She took a large swallow of liquor. The brandy burned less than the emotion bubbling inside her. But she would finish the memory.

"And?" he asked. "What made the incident odd?" He was pulling his gloves off, one finger at a time. Why the sight of Angel's bare hands—long-fingered, tanned, natural—should comfort her, she could not say.

"He wasn't dressed for the opera." The words had their own will. She could not hold them back. "He wore riding clothes. When I asked him why he hadn't changed into evening wear, he said he'd been too eager to see me. And I *believed* him, as I was eager to see him."

"Perhaps it was true." Angelstone shifted onto the table and began to swing a leg. He set his gloves beside him on the desk.

"You are playing devil's advocate." He was irritatingly rational about it.

"It is the only way to obtain the truth. One must confront all other possibilities and rule them out."

"That sounds like a maxim you learned at a school for spies. Jeremy's words outside the opera could have been true," she agreed. "But they weren't. He was shocked to see me. I didn't think anything of it then, as he recovered quickly. But I remember the shock on his face, then the briefest look of panic. I dismissed it. I was so glad to see him alive and not succumbing to the fever spreading through the barracks."

He rounded the desk to sit behind it. He looked comfortable there. Comfortable and competent. He smoothed a bare hand over a piece of blank paper. "What was the date?"

"I don't remember."

"Try."

"Why does it matter?"

"Because I need to compare the date with known assassinations during that time—in the event your husband was the assassin." His eyes turned dark, boring into her. Was he determining whether she would hold up to the accusation? Perhaps he expected her to have the vapors or something equally ridiculous.

Dipping his quill in ink, he waited expectantly. A droplet of ink formed at the tip of the quill. The black sphere shimmered in the firelight. He was writing down the information. Keeping a record. Words written on paper were final. They could not be unwritten any more than spoken words could be unsaid. Even if the paper were burned, the record had been made. Ink on paper. Black on white.

But neither could death be undone. Lies could not be unsaid. Betrayal could not become truth. Whether Jeremy was an assassin or simply involved in something disreputable that resulted in his murder, he was not the man she'd believed him to be.

Closing her eyes, Lilias searched her memories. Battle merged with battle, city blended with village, acquaintances with friends. She sifted through details, through time.

"The middle of August 1812. I'm quite certain. The opera was *La Viage in Grecia*." She opened her eyes and hoped no hate showed there. The problem was, she didn't know who she hated more: Jeremy for deceiving her, or herself for being hopelessly in love with an illusion.

Angelstone scratched a notation. She couldn't read the bold scrawl from across the room, so she simply looked away. She didn't need to know what he was writing, but she could guess. So she continued.

"Once, I saw a man standing in the street across from the rooms Jeremy and I had taken in Brussels. Three hours he was there. I mentioned it to Jeremy as we readied ourselves for bed, wondering what the man could possibly be waiting so long for." It was as though she couldn't stop the words and memories from tumbling out of her. The floodgates had opened. "Jeremy was jittery after I told him. He went out, ostensibly to speak with his commanding officer. But when I looked out the window again, the strange man had left as well." She drew a deep breath. "It was nothing. It seemed like nothing. I barely thought of it at the time, dismissing it as the man in Brussels had left the street."

She did not dismiss it now. Neither did Angelstone. The quill continued to scratch its inky path across the paper.

"What else?" he asked.

"I don't know," she snapped. "It's all muddled in my brain. I can't tell what is reality and what's not." She set the empty glass down with a sharp snick. The heat of the brandy was beginning to tangle her thoughts.

"There must be more than these two incidents, or you wouldn't believe he was an assassin."

"Fine. There are more. There are dozens." Anger poured through her in hot waves. Taking a deep breath, she struggled to force it back. She pressed cold fingers against closed lids and ignored the scrape of chair legs and rustle of clothing as he stood up.

"Tell me, Lilias."

When his hands touched her shoulders, she nearly shuddered. The touch was soft. His fingers were calloused. The rough patch on each thumb grazed the skin of her upper arms.

Oh, she wanted to put her head on his broad shoulders. To lean against that solid chest and feel his arms come around her. His heart might pound beneath her cheek. His skin might smell of citrus, or spice. Certainly it would smell of man. Taste of man.

She breathed deep. Perhaps speaking of Jeremy would exorcise that demon. Or perhaps Angelstone would make his notations and perform his research and tell her it was all a lie.

But it wasn't a lie, so she told Angelstone everything she could remember. The occasional stranger Jeremy seemed to know so well. Midnight meetings she assumed had been related to his military position. The occasions when he'd been at one location when he'd told her he was at another. Messages that were delivered and quickly burned.

She had never questioned him. Because she'd loved him.

Desperate to fill the void, to smooth out the edges, she poured a second glass of brandy. She sipped it and watched Angelstone scribble his notes as she spoke.

A lock of hair had fallen from his queue so that it skimmed his sharp cheekbone. His full lips were pursed slightly as he wrote. When he looked up, his gold eyes were dark and focused. She wasn't certain if it was concentration or something else that put that look in his eye.

He set the quill beside the paper and leaned casually back in his chair. "It seems you know more than you first thought."

"So it seems." Lilias stared into her brandy. She did feel better. Having said it aloud, sharing that burden, had dissipated the hard rock jittering around in her chest. "It was all just there, staring at me. Fool that I am, I never guessed."

He cocked his head. "How could you guess? Women don't suspect their husbands of being assassins. Perhaps an affair—but not murder."

She raised a brow. "Is that supposed to make me feel better?"

"My apologies."

"Oh. You have nothing to apologize for. Not really." She glanced at the low fire burning in the grate. "Is it warm in here?"

"I'm comfortable, but you've had two glasses of brandy."

"Mm."

The brandy was mellowing her. Warmth infused her muscles, light-headedness swamped her mind. But her heart didn't lay easy in her chest. Her husband's betrayal had scraped a raw, fresh wound there. A hollow that chipped away at the core of her.

They sat quiet a moment, the crackle of flames the only sound in the room. When she looked at him, his gaze was lingering on the neckline of her red gown. There was no fichu to hide the swell of her breasts. The fabric hugged her curves, moved with her when she walked so that it slid over her body like a lover's hands.

She'd known it when she dressed for the ball that evening. She hadn't intended to entice anyone specific, but only to feel desirable. To feel like a woman after being a widow for so long. To fill that aching hollow Jeremy's betrayal had left behind.

"Angelstone." She said it softly, so that he was compelled to look at her face. Calmly, to hide the churning inside her. Desire twined with loss. Lust merged with the need to belong. The smile she sent him was full of invitation, the finger flicking at her bodice a deliberate temptation. "Are you ready to dance?"

His eyes went dark. Jaw clenched. A quick indrawn breath rippled the air.

And then she *was* desirable.

"Indeed?" she mused aloud. He had seemed difficult to read, his thoughts hidden behind a wall of charm and the impassive mask of a spy. Apparently he had lost his ability to hide his thoughts. Desire was something she recognized plainly enough, and it sent a wicked thrill singing through her. It was good to feel that way again, however fleeting.

It wasn't the brandy that caused the reciprocating desire coursing through her. She'd found him attractive before. The brandy only stripped away her better judgment. Falling in lust with Angelstone—a spy—would be the height of folly.

At the moment, it seemed the most reasonable thing in the world.

"Do you know the worst part of this entire situation?" After setting down her glass she moved slowly forward, watching him watch her.

"I can't imagine." Tawny eyes gleamed, stalking her every move.

"I spent six years of my life making love to a man, and I barely knew him. I don't know if his love for me—his *desire* for me—was real or an act." She couldn't move backward in time to find out. But she could move forward. She *needed* to move forward. She needed to erase six years of uncertainty. Angelstone was just the man to do it.

"It would be a mistake." He pushed his chair back from the desk, but didn't stand. His eyes held no shock, only intense focus. His gaze skimmed over her breasts, down her hips, then back up to her face.

Heat swirled in her, rising up and sending her blood pumping. "Yes. It would be a mistake." She didn't care just now.

She came around the desk to stand in front of him, settling herself just beyond his reach. Her eyes followed the long line of his body, appreciating the glory of lean muscle and strength. He was relaxed in the chair, a little slouched, legs outstretched, his fingers playing idly with the chair arms. His cravat had gone the way of the gloves at some point and his collar lay open, exposing the hollow of his throat. She imagined pressing her lips there, where his pulse beat.

The brandy swirled in her head, in her heart, in her loins. She was hungry for love. Hungry for something she could pretend was love, even for a short time. And she was no longer married. There was nothing holding her back but loyalty to the dead husband who had lied to her.

So she sent him a long, slow smile and stepped between his knees. Her skirts brushed against his breeches, then her leg bumped against his. Even that small contact sent a jolt through her.

"Are you seducing me, Lilias?" His deep baritone slid along her senses. He looked up at her through his lashes.

"I am. What say you, Angelstone?"

Chapter 12

HIS JAW WORKED once before his eyes fell to her lips. Held there. He did not speak, but she could see he was weighing his decision. *It is only sex*, she wanted to say. *Nothing more.* She would not let it be anything more. But she did not say the words. She could only will him to give her the elusive something she craved.

Then his legs opened wide, making room for her between his muscled thighs. The breath she'd been holding sighed out of her in a delighted exhale.

"I would say that's answer enough." She laughed, light and low, as a thrill stole through her veins. "We'll both regret this tomorrow, Angelstone, won't we?" His thigh was hard under her finger as she skimmed its length. The muscle beneath flexed. She reveled in that little relinquishment of power.

"Lilias." He reached for her hand, lifted it. His lips brushed her knuckles. Gold eyes fastened on hers. "You are beautiful."

"Angelstone—"

"You *are* beautiful. And desirable."

Her legs trembled beneath her skirt. Her breath quickened. How could he know what she felt? How could he know she needed reassurance to anchor her?

"What happens between us here, now," he said, "will be separate from the rest." He stared at her, eyes glinting. She could not read those depths, and was not certain she wanted to. "There is no espionage here. No memories. There's only a man and a woman."

"Do you think that will stop the regret?"

"No." He set his hand against the curve of her waist. Fingers slipped over her velvet-clad hip. His touch was gentle, even wondering, as though his fingers touched a woman for the first time.

Pleasure radiated through her body, starting at those light spots of pressure. Four fingers curved just around her side, a thumb pressed against her abdomen. She drew a deep, jagged breath as his touch moved up, thumb feathering over her belly. She let her head tip back, losing herself in the sensation of having a man's hands on her. It had been so long. *So long.*

"I don't care, just now," she whispered. "I don't care if I have regrets tomorrow."

Approval growled low in his throat. "I don't care, either." He gripped her hips with both hands. Harder now. He looked up at her and she thought again that he looked like a wicked angel. His sensuous lips curved in a grin. "Seduce me, then, Lilias."

Exhilaration coursed through her, centering between her legs. She would match the wickedness in that grin. Would bring it inside her. She needed something to fill that empty space within her. "As you wish, my lord."

Bracing herself on the arms of the chair, she bent and took his lips with hers. Softly at first, running her tongue against his lower lip. They did not touch anywhere else, simply their breath mingling, lips meeting. His mouth opened, so she danced her tongue against his. He tasted of brandy and of man. Of the forbidden.

He drew her in, sliding his arms around her back and bringing her close so she sat on his thighs. Heated fingers played with the bare skin at the nape of her neck. She could feel each place where they touched as though a brand lay between them. Buttocks to thighs, fingers to back, lips to lips. Her hand cupped his cheek as she angled the kiss. Stubble roughened her hands, the rasp of it tingling her skin.

How could the need for a man be so primal? But it wasn't just a man. If it was not Angelstone, it would not be anyone. Not just now.

"I need—" She didn't know how to name this *thing* that gripped her. It left her vulnerable and yearning. "Make love to me."

She felt his control snap. It whipped through his body like a blade through the air, whistling quick and sharp. His hands suddenly molded her breasts, his teeth nipped at her lips. She fisted her hands on the lapels of his coat and matched his fervor with her own. Insistent mouth, demanding tongue. She plundered, taking his mouth with all the hunger washing over her.

It was not enough. She wanted to feel his skin, to feel the weight of him above her. To be filled by him. Deft fingers released the buttons of his jacket and splayed it open. The buttons of his waistcoat followed before she yanked his shirt from his waistband. Running her fingers across the hard planes of his stomach, she reveled in the feel of hot skin stretched tight over muscle. She had not touched a man this way in two years. That was a long time to be alone.

Angelstone's head tipped back and he groaned as she moved her hands beneath the shirt. A quiver of muscle, the jagged edge of his breath. Ah, that was desire. That was need. Her hands moved up his chest, slid beneath linen to feel the hard contours of his shoulders. Her fingers skimmed the ridge of a scar, a thin, hard line that ran from shoulder blade to bicep.

It reminded her of what he was. Of what she was. But the pulse beating in his throat called her. She nipped with her teeth, then feathered hot kisses against the hollow between his collarbones. The beat of his blood pulsed hard and fast against her lips.

More.

Pulling herself away, she looked at him. He sprawled in the chair, legs outstretched, lapels crushed from her hands. He watched her with hooded eyes, a half smile hovering on his lips. He was gorgeous. Golden and lean and so, so male.

The intensity of his gaze drew her in. She couldn't look away. God, she wanted him. Wanted with a breathlessness that sent her head spinning. So she gathered her skirts with a rustle of velvet. She set her knees on either side of his hips so that the core of her pressed against his arousal. He was hard and hot beneath his clothing, and she could feel the weight of him against that most intimate place. She ached there, ready and wanting to simply be touched.

When he opened the flap of his fall front trousers, she raised herself so that she was poised just above him. She sank down slowly, her body accommodating his heat and strength. She had forgotten what it meant to be joined with a man, to have him fill her. It was a simple matter to accept him, a thrill as he thrust into her.

Then they were joined. He did not withdraw, but simply filled her as deeply as possible. His muscles strained as he paused—but no. That was control, not strain. He held himself still. Hands gripped her hips. Then, *yes*. A long stroke as his hands guided her hips up, then down. Petticoats swished and pooled around them as they moved once more.

He pushed them out of the way and his eyes flashed down to the stockings riding high on her thighs. His gaze went dark and she heard that quick intake of breath she was beginning to recognize. Rough hands slid up her thigh to linger on the place where silk stockings met skin. Fingers dipped beneath silk, a quick stroke that matched the rhythm of her movements on him.

Her eyes drifted closed. His fingers held magic as they drifted higher, skimming thigh, hip, then that juncture where everything met. All sensation, all heat, all desire spiraled to a single place. Suddenly her thighs did not work. She could not raise or lower herself. Only her inner muscles clutched around him.

"Angelstone." The word became a sigh as his hand pressed against that small center of her being. She had not been touched there since—but she could not think. Her mind fuzzed as her body bowed back. She rose high on those clever fingers and let their devastating skill overwhelm her.

Her fingers searched for purchase, found solid shoulders to anchor her. She opened her eyes to find him watching her with heavy-lidded eyes. She did not wonder if he desired her. She did not need to. The deliberate focus of his gaze, the movement of his chest, his thrust inside her. They were truth.

Her body tightened unbearably as he continued to pleasure her until she pushed over the edge of reason. A thousand thoughts crystallized, then broke apart. Regret and release spiraled together and she let her head fall back.

Then his hands were sliding up her body to cup her cheeks. He drew her down and ravaged her mouth. His finesse turned to hunger. Satisfaction was a dark edge on his moan. But her mind was a step behind, lost in morality and fidelity and widowhood.

Her bodice seemed to simply slip beneath her breasts under his swift hands. A quick tongue flicked at her nipples, one, then the other. Any thought of morality and fidelity dissipated. *Please, just let me forget.* Her head fell back again as she fisted her hands in all that thick, gorgeous, golden hair. His tongue slid between her breasts, up, drawing a line to her lips.

"Lilias." The ridged calluses of his thumbs brushed her cheekbones. "It is only me here. Me."

She gasped, her breath coming in sobs. "Angel."

"I know there is a void in you. I know you need to fill it." His lips pressed against hers, wreaking havoc on her control. He drew back and rested his forehead against hers. "But there is only me and you here. No one else."

She knew what he was asking, even if it was not a question.

"No one else, Angel."

And then there was no one else. Only Angel. Hot skin beneath her hands. Firm mouth. Strong hands, with those calloused fingers building sensation upon sensation, touch upon touch. Thrust upon thrust. The scent of his skin, the taste of him. A hand against her cheek, another playing with her thigh just above the stockings.

Body to body, she rode him. Lost herself in heady sensations until he drove her to the peak and over a second time.

When she felt him withdraw from her and heard his sigh of satisfaction, then felt the wetness of his seed on her leg, she dropped her head to his shoulder and wondered why she wanted to both laugh and cry.

Chapter 13

SHE DREW A deep breath and turned her head so it rested on his shoulder. She ignored the trembling of her hands and gripped the back of the chair.

Fool. Utter fool. Closing her eyes, she studied the play of candlelight against her lids. Her body felt loose and limber, quite satisfactorily used, in fact. But her heart was still heavy. It was silly of her to think sex would ease all that anger and need and grief in her.

"Regrets already, Lilias?" he whispered near her ear.

Her eyes flew open. She leaned back to look at him, half reclined in the chair. His cravat was still lying about somewhere, and his shirt was open to reveal his throat and the fine hairs sprinkled across his chest. He looked exactly like what he was—a man who had recently been seduced.

He cocked his head. "Do you feel better?"

"Not particularly." She lifted herself up, started to move away from him, but he was using his handkerchief to clean up his seed. Quite matter-of-factly. The gesture made her heart stutter. It was embarrassing, and yet . . . and yet.

"I didn't think you would." An amused, self-deprecating smile spread across his face. The handkerchief dropped to the floor beneath the desk. "Are you sure? Not even a little? It would be a blow to my pride otherwise."

"A little better, perhaps." Strange. His teasing lightened her heart more than the sex itself. "You're an exhausting lover."

"I had a need for you. Such fierce eyes." He leaned over and brushed his lips against hers, just the lightest touch. A residual flutter of desire bounced around in her belly. Then again, perhaps it was new desire. She tipped her face up and met his kiss. He was an expert, nibbling and tasting as though he hadn't just had his fill of her.

She sighed when he finally drew back. "A mighty weapon, that mouth of yours."

He grinned and gripped her hips to guide her to standing. She settled her skirts down, and when she looked at him, the front of his trousers was already buttoned. He stood and picked up his gloves from the desktop, then retrieved the cravat from the floor where it had fallen.

He straightened, and his face turned serious. "*Do* you have regrets, Lilias?"

She couldn't answer. She didn't know.

He watched her, eyes full of secrets. Then he turned away to pick up her cloak from its heap on the floor. Wrinkles clung to the wool. He spread it out for her, an unspoken offer of assistance. All she had to do was step into it. With a sigh, she stood and turned her back to him. He slid the cloak over her shoulders, hands lingering.

"I have no regrets." He spoke softly in her ear. He feathered a kiss at the nape of her neck. "No regrets."

———

HE LIED. QUITE convincingly, in fact. He had all sorts of regrets.

There is only me and you here. He had almost deceived himself into believing it was only the two of them. It wasn't true. She'd used him to exorcise the ghost of her husband. They both knew it.

If he hadn't looked into those blue eyes and seen pain and uncertainty, he would have said no. He didn't like sharing a woman, even with a ghost. But he *had* looked into those eyes. He'd seen a lost warrior. A woman who'd fought her demons years ago and won, and now had to fight them again.

It was her eyes that had pulled him in. If she had maintained that sensual awareness, the knowing, confident woman, he could have resisted. But the pain deep inside had simply shattered his resolve. Gemma had always said he was an easy mark for troubled women. She'd been right.

The thought didn't cause him the pain it usually did.

The uncomfortable idea flitted into his mind that perhaps he was exorcising his demons just as Lilias was exorcising her own.

He looked over at her. She stared out the carriage window. Lamplight slipped across her face, gilding the curve of her cheek. Full lips parted as she breathed slow and steady. He could see the outline of her cloak rise and fall with her breasts, leaving just a hint of pale skin moving between the shadowed depths.

She was lovely. Beautiful and sensual and full of passion. Whether that passion was on the battlefield, the dance floor or in bed. Well, a chair, at any rate. Just watching her now, his body stirred to life.

God help him. She was a lead to the Death Adders. The closest he'd come to finding Gemma's killer in four long years. He'd prepared himself to use her for information. But damn if he didn't like her, even with all that stood between them.

"If you think of anything else about your husband—" he began.

"I'll come to you." The words echoed in the carriage, a stark reminder of his mission. She turned to look at him. A lock of hair had fallen from its pin and brushed her cheek.

"The information you've provided is a start. But I need more," Angel said. There was no getting around the Death Adders, even if he wanted to forget about them in favor of a beautiful woman. "I need to know routines. The company he kept. Weapons he carried."

"I'll give you everything I know." Her breathing sharpened. Small exhales of anger to hang in the air between them. "I already told you I would."

Why was it that women—any woman—could make a man feel like some slinking animal that bellied across the ground? But perhaps it was not her. Perhaps it was himself.

"If you think of something, come to my bachelor townhouse. If I'm not there, Jones will send for me."

The carriage rolled to a stop and the echo of the horses' hooves faded away. They were at the corner of the square, as she had requested. Fairchild House was tucked in the middle of the row of townhouses. Windows were dark, the street was empty. Even those members of the ton who had stayed through to the last ball had now sought their beds.

"I have a key to the rear door," she said. "I don't wish to be seen."

"I'll accompany you." He pushed open the carriage door, letting in the cool evening air.

"You don't need to."

"But I will just the same. I'm still a gentleman." He shot her a conciliatory grin. "Mostly."

Her slow, knowing smile heated his blood. "At least you admit it."

And just like that, they were on even ground again. She set her hand in his without hesitation when he offered to help her from the carriage. Tucking her arm beneath his elbow, he led her through the mews. She moved quietly beside him, her footfalls as soft as his own. When they arrived at the rear door of Fairchild House she tugged her arm free. Reaching into her reticule, she pulled out a slim key. Her breath puffed in, then out.

"I don't regret anything, Angel." The hood of her cloak shadowed her eyes. The moon sprinkled silvered light on her mouth. "But it was still a mistake."

That lower lip called to him. Plump and smooth and shining in the moonlight. He ran his thumb across it. "One we'll likely make again."

"Are you so sure?" That full lip curved up beneath his thumb.

He captured her mouth, sinking into the softness. The taste of her was beyond tempting. He caught her lip between his teeth. Nipped. Her breath tumbled out, a quick gasp as she opened her mouth, tongue tangling with his.

He cupped her cheeks, skimming his fingers over her skin. Soft as flower petals. "We should have nothing to do with each other, beyond the investigation," he whispered.

"We're fools, Angel." Still, her mouth sought his. "This is madness." She pulled back, stared at him. Her eyes were colorless in the dark, but no less compelling.

"A happy madness." He jerked his head toward the door. "Go to bed."

She gave him one quick, hard kiss before slipping the key into the lock and disappearing through the door.

Chapter 14

RIDING AT A sedate pace was a constant irritation. The groom riding at an appropriate distance behind her was an even greater irritation. But it was London, it was before breakfast and she couldn't go to Hyde Park alone.

Not that the park was deserted. The Season was still in full swing, and even though the midsummer weather was cold enough to be September, there were a few early morning riders in the park. Each one of them looked at her askance, as she rode her mount astride just as she had on the march. She'd learned to ignore the odd looks as people caught sight of the breeches beneath her gown.

She wanted the open space. To think and breathe and just be. Rather, she wanted to *not* think, even for a few hours.

But of course, not thinking was impossible. She rubbed the spot between her eyes where trouble concentrated. She was foolish and unwise. Being with Angelstone was ten times a mistake.

They had not made love, however. That would be tender and sweet. This had been needy. She did not want it to be anything more than a fierce, urgent coupling. God, she could not even think of love or marriage. She could not trust herself to pick a proper man.

Although, however foolish it was to take a spy as a lover, it was no worse than being married to an assassin. At least this time her eyes were wide open. What woman wouldn't enjoy sex with a skilled lover who touched her as though she was the first woman he had ever loved? Calloused thumbs brushing a nipple, long fingers stroking skin. His eyes. Oh yes. Those were just as compelling as his touch.

And thinking of it would not quiet her body.

Treacherous, treacherous body.

Lilias leaned forward and set her mare to canter across the open field. The hooves of the groom's horse thundered behind her. Perhaps she could simply keep riding. Perhaps she could outrun Jeremy and her memories of him. Angelstone had only temporarily erased six years of marriage. In the morning light she was still in Fairchild House, with a miniature of her husband tucked in a drawer. There was no outrunning betrayal.

Or murder.

She increased the horse's pace to a gallop. She needed a quick, hard ride. No light canter would do. She lifted her face to the cloud-obscured sky so the chilled morning air rushed over her skin. Wind plucked at the hat perched on her head. It felt good to simply release everything, just for a few minutes. Everything eased, muscles, temper, nerves.

She slowed the mare's pace as they neared the end of the field, settling into a light trot to let the animal work out the gallop.

With an expert twitch of the reins, she turned the horse toward the sandy track threading through the park. The groom took a position to the side and just behind her. It made her edgy to have someone follow her so closely and she fought the urge to look behind her.

"The mare is in fine form this morning, ma'am," the groom said.

As though in agreement, the horse tossed her head.

"So she is." The animal was in better form than her mistress, at any rate.

"Mrs. Fairchild!" The call was accompanied by the nearby beat of hooves. Jason Hawthorne rode toward her, looking as dashing as ever in his top hat and riding clothes.

Her smile warmed. Hawthorne had been her husband's closest friend. He'd helped her return to London after Waterloo when she'd been exhausted from the battle and grief—and he had championed her the previous evening when Angel had imperiously demanded to stroll with her.

"Good morning," she called as he drew to a stop beside her.

"I'm surprised to see you still riding astride." Hawthorne tipped the brim of his hat. "If you weren't a favorite with Wellington, society wouldn't accept it."

"I've spent too many years on the march wearing breeches beneath my skirts to change my behavior now." She looked down at her riding habit. "Riding astride is so much less precarious. And I was in need of the exercise."

"I am afraid it will be short-lived, however. I think it is going to rain." He looked up at the sky. Dull gray clouds formed a patchwork field over the city. He waited a moment, as though considering some weighty subject in the sky, before looking back at her. "Did you enjoy your social engagements yesterday evening?" he asked.

"I did." She frowned at him. He was watching her steadily, brown eyes probing. What did he want to know? "But I saw you yesterday evening, Hawthorne."

"I remember." His voice was tight. "You danced with the Marquess of Angelstone."

Ah. That was what he wanted to know about. "I did, indeed, dance with Angelstone," she said slowly.

"You have not danced since Jeremy died."

"Are you noting down my dance partners?" She raised an amused brow. With his chest lifted in indignation he looked like an offended older brother.

"Only Angelstone. I was not aware you were acquainted with him."

"I have many acquaintances you do not know about." Why was he prying into her relationship with Angelstone? It wasn't simple curiosity that lowered Hawthorne's brows so menacingly. "If you have something to say, please say it."

"Mrs. Fairchild." Hawthorne spoke through gritted teeth. "Lilias. What are you about?"

"I don't know what you mean."

"Don't think me a fool. Angelstone couldn't keep his eyes from you yesterday evening. You *danced* with him." Now he sounded like an offended father. But even with the scowl darkening his face, she knew it was concern for her that had him speaking. "He is not for you, Lilias," Hawthorne finished. A muscle twitched in his jaw as he clenched it.

"Whether he is or not, it is my decision, Hawthorne. Only mine." She lifted her chin. "Jeremy has been gone for two years. I can dance with whomever I choose."

"It's my duty to protect you. I promised Jeremy I would." Hawthorne glanced once at her groom, who was still behind them at a respectful distance. Far enough not to hear, but close enough to be proper. "Let's walk the horses."

They set the horses to a slow walk on the sandy path. Others were starting to take the morning air now, and they passed a pair of old gentlemen moving slowly.

"What is it that has you so worried about Angelstone?" She could not stand firm against his concern. They had been friends too long.

"There are rumors about Angelstone. He's a rake." Hawthorne's eyes remained forward, as though it was most proper to deliver bad news without making eye contact.

"And you aren't a rake?"

He shook his head. The dark hair peeking from beneath his hat fluttered in the breeze. "It's not the same."

"Of course it is." She tapped the butt of her whip once on his arm. "You're feeling protective, Hawthorne. I understand that. But I'm not a simpering miss or naïve widow that needs protection."

"I know. But—" Hawthorne looked over now, met her gaze with serious eyes. "There's more. He was a soldier that suddenly left his regiment. No explanation."

She sucked in a breath. *Desertion?* She didn't dare say it aloud. But no, it wouldn't be desertion. It would have been espionage. She could not imagine Angel would desert his regiment—but then, she wouldn't have expected Jeremy to be an assassin.

Perhaps she wasn't the best judge of character.

"No one knows where Angelstone went or what he did during the war," Hawthorne continued. "He disappeared one day, then would appear occasionally at various battles. Like Waterloo." He sent his gaze out across the park again. "There are rumors linking you to him."

"Rumors?"

"An affair. They are wondering how long you've been his mistress."

Of course. She should have guessed. When a widow who has not set foot onto a dance floor in two years invites a well-known rake to dance, the rumors would multiply a hundred-fold before she finished the dance.

"Already the gossips have left their mark." She tried to let the irritation roll from her shoulders. "If we are involved, it is between Angelstone and me. No one else."

"You don't have to ally yourself with Angelstone. If you are looking for companionship—" He choked on the word, swallowed, recovered. "There are any number of better choices."

She laughed at the self-conscious flush on his sharp cheekbones. Older brother, indeed. "By whose measuring stick, Hawthorne? Yours or mine?"

"Society's." He looked down at her, let out a long, low breath. His eyes warmed, reminding her of her morning chocolate. "I only want to see you safe and happy, Lilias."

The wind snatched the sigh that slipped from her lips. "I know." There was nothing he said that wasn't true. Angelstone was known as a rake. If he'd disappeared from his regiment, it was for reasons he—and she—could not reveal. It was one more secret they shared.

And suddenly, she knew that she would be with Angel again. *She* would pursue *him*. There was no one else in the world just now that knew her secrets. An exhilarating thing, that shared sense of intimacy, however strange the connection. And no other man in two years had stirred her. So she would seduce him again, and probably again, until they were tired of each other.

"I'm grateful for your concern, and for knowing that I can lean on you if I have a need. But for now, I've chosen Angelstone. When we're finished with our *companionship*, we'll go our separate ways. No harm to either of us." Her voice sounded strong.

She almost believed it.

Chapter 15

HAWTHORNE WATCHED HER steadily. "Be careful, Lilias. You're playing a deep game with Angelstone, and you are a novice."

"I will." The ribbons of her hat fluttered against her cheek. She brushed them away. He didn't know what a novice she was—at espionage, at any rate. Nor did he know the extent of Angel's experience. "Hopefully you won't need to pick up the pieces of my life again."

"I will, however, if need be." The smile he sent her held understanding.

Hawthorne had picked up the pieces for her in the Netherlands and brought her home after Waterloo. She flicked her gaze at his profile. Strong, handsome. Noble. Could he have known Jeremy was an assassin? Suspected something? Perhaps, like her, what he thought were ordinary meetings were only a cover for murder. She had to tread carefully to find out.

"Do you think often of those campaigns with Jeremy?" She twitched her skirts into place to better hide her breeches. She would have to guide the conversation. Lead him around to it. "I find I can't remember some things."

"It's been two years since he died," he said softly. "Time fades memories."

"It does." The conversation would turn maudlin in a

moment—or more maudlin than it already was. Lifting her voice over the thud and scuff of the horses' hooves, she said cheerfully, "I remember Jeremy teaching me to fence the winter after we withdrew from Madrid and went into Portugal. I borrowed your sabre. I was so clumsy, do you remember?"

"You were beyond clumsy. You were miserable at it."

"Hawthorne! It's ungentlemanly to remind me how bad I was." Relieved to be on easy footing again, she winced playfully. "Though it is true."

"By the time we left Portugal you were proficient enough."

"Quite an unladylike skill, I'm afraid." She wasn't the least bit sorry for having learned it. "Fencing passed the time that winter."

"The boredom was worse in the barracks."

"I know." She studied a pair of doves winging across the sky and contemplated her next direction. It seemed pitifully easy to guide a conversation. Is this how Angel conducted his spy business? "Do you remember when the fever spread through the barracks in Madrid? I was thinking just the other day how glad I was that even though Jeremy spent the week in the barracks with you, he never fell ill."

It was an arrow released into dense fog. She could only hope to hit a target.

"I remember that. We lost a lot of good men in Madrid." He frowned, eyes gazing into the middle distance. "But I don't remember Jeremy being in the barracks when the fever spread."

"Oh." She pursed her lips and tried to ignore the sudden thumping of her heart. She'd hit her target. Perhaps the fog was only a light mist. "I must be mistaken on the campaign. Or the city. They do blur together."

But she wasn't mistaken. She knew the date. She knew it had been Madrid when she had run into a surprised and shocked Jeremy outside the opera.

He hadn't been in the barracks.

"No," Hawthorne said slowly, eyes sharp. "No, you never forget cities or campaigns. You know them as well as I do."

Clearly, she was not being subtle enough in her questioning. She tightened her hands on the reins. The mare responded with a jerk and Lilias forced her hands to relax. Foolish to think she was as experienced at espionage as Angel.

"As you say, memories fade," she said.

"It's more than that. I can see it in your face. What has happened?" It wasn't a question, but a demand for an answer.

"Jeremy is not the man I thought he was—that any of us thought he was." The words spilled from her lips before she could stop them. "I can't tell you about Jeremy. Not yet. I will, as soon as I can." She pressed her lips together. She'd already said too much.

"Are you in debt? In legal trouble? Or—" A quick tug on the reins drew his horse to a sharp halt. The animal snorted in protest. "Are you in danger? It isn't Angelstone, is it?"

She shook her head and reined in her own mount. "No, I'm not in danger. Far from it." When a spy loomed over one's life, one was safe enough. "But the secret isn't mine to share. It will have to wait."

"Tell me if you need assistance." His gloved hand reached out as though to touch her arm, but fell away before it made contact. "You will tell me, won't you? You're not alone."

"No. I'm not alone." The smile she sent him came from her heart. "Thank you, Hawthorne. I will tell you everything as soon as I can."

"Good." His face relaxed, his shoulders eased. "I'll always be here to rescue you."

"What would I do without you?" A fat drop of rain bounced off the edge of the bonnet, another trickled cold down her cheek. Large beads of water already dotted the mare's dark coat. Glancing up, she saw dark clouds roiling above. "I think now would be a good time to return home."

"Shall I see you to Fairchild House?"

"No, you'll only get wet. The groom is sufficient." She smiled at him as she turned her horse away. He tipped his hat, then rode in the other direction with a quick wave.

She was too late. By the time they reached Fairchild House, she and the poor groom were soaked to the skin.

As was Grant, who was leaping from his own horse to stride up the front steps. He left a muddy trail behind him, which did not surprise her. He often did so, and she'd grown to learn it meant he'd been chasing after his birds.

"Did you get caught by surprise?" she asked, once inside the dry confines of Fairchild House.

"I was tracking a Cirl Bunting. I was surprised to find it in London. It's a songbird that only lives in—Well. At any rate, I wasn't watching the sky." A pair of binoculars swung like a pendulum from Grant's fingers. "But you're sopping wet and dripping everywhere. Towels, Graves!" Grant called, but the well-trained butler was already moving down the hall and calling for the housekeeper.

"I was in Hyde Park and lingered too long." She needed to strip off the wet clothing and order something hot to drink. Moving toward the stairs, she began to ascend.

"Wait, Lilias."

She paused to look down at Grant. Raindrops were liberally sprinkled through his dark brown hair, curling it at the tips and making him look a romantic figure. He came up the steps until he stood just below her.

"Your answer, Lilias?" His fingers closed around hers. He raised them to his lips. They were cool against her hand. "I'm impatient. The wait is becoming interminable."

She opened her mouth, but was not certain what to say. How does one refuse an offer of marriage from a man that one cares for, but not enough? She struggled to find the right words.

"Silence is not rejection," he said. She could see the tension in the lines around his mouth. "I care for you, Lilias. Deeply."

"I know, Grant." Oh, it was difficult to look at the face so dear to her and know she would hurt him. But temper was beginning to outweigh her pity. She had already given her answer.

"Is it me you are opposed to, or simply marriage?" His fingers tightened while he waited for an answer.

Perhaps the truth would ease the rejection. "I don't want to marry again. Ever." Now that she'd said the words aloud, she felt the weight release from her chest. And it *was* true.

"An easier barrier to overcome than opposition to me." His fingers relaxed, then released hers. "I shall try to persuade you, then, for as long as it takes for you to realize we would be the perfect match."

"Grant, that's not what I mean. Or what I want."

He only smiled at her, lightly amused, even flirtatious. "We'll talk later, after you're dry." He plucked at a long coil of hair that had fallen from beneath her hat. "Order a hot bath. You'll feel better."

Then he was striding down the steps and calling for Graves.

A hot bath wouldn't change her mind.

And damnation, she felt perfectly fine.

WHAT GOOD WAS a coat if it did not protect one's neck from rain? Cold water dribbled beneath his collar to saturate the coarse shirt beneath. Angel hunched his shoulders to fight off a shiver. He'd rather stand watch in the snow than the rain. Snow might be cold, but at least it didn't permeate everything a man wore with damp. Standing in the street attempting to look unobtrusive while being pelted by rain was his least favorite assignment.

Tugging his cap lower on his forehead, he tried to keep the wet out of his eyes as he watched Lilias arrive at Fairchild House, just behind its owner, Lord Fairchild. It hadn't been an easy matter to follow her on foot, but the rain had sent people on the street scurrying for cover. Her horse's pace had been slowed by burgeoning mud and wet Londoners.

Now she was perched atop the pretty mare, looking amusingly bedraggled. He shouldn't laugh at her, even if she didn't know he was watching. But the feather on her riding hat was drooping and one long rope of escaped hair hung down her back. He couldn't hear the sodden shush of her skirts from this distance, but judging from the way the fabric dragged over the saddle, her skirts were as soaked as his coat. She didn't seem to mind. She handed the reins to the groom, picked up the edge of those dripping skirts and calmly swept into the townhouse just behind Lord Fairchild.

The light rain became gray sheets. He flicked his gaze up, checking windows, roofs, then up and down the street. Once, twice. Rain was a blessing and a curse. It was useful to hide in, but it also hid enemies. Angel slipped around the corner of a building and into rain-soaked shadows. But he didn't leave her street. Couldn't quite bring himself to.

There was no reason he needed to stand guard over Lilias, particularly. He'd gained some information, and she was willing to provide more. She exhibited no intent to flee London.

She did not appear to be in danger. The question, then, was why was he standing in the rain, watching her townhouse? Worse, why had he lingered in the park while she rode with an old friend? Hawthorne, his name was. The soldier.

Because she'd watched him with those uncertain eyes while they'd made love. As though she couldn't quite believe what she felt and saw was real. That bit of vulnerability had lodged somewhere in the vicinity of his chest.

A carriage rumbled past, the driver huddled against the rain. He was alone on the carriage box while the family sat cozy within. Poor sod. But then Angel was standing in the street doing the same.

Except he wasn't alone any longer.

He didn't bother to turn and look at his companion. "What did you find?"

"Nothing unusual." Jones leaned against the brick wall. Now they were two idiots huddled against the rain, both of them dressed in patched coats and drab colors. "Lord Grant Fairchild has a good reputation in the House of Lords. He's a conscientious landowner. A Tory. He was a diplomat to Switzerland for a short time. Also to India."

"Hm." He knew those facts already. Jones also knew he wasn't interested in any of that. "More."

"He does not frequent gaming hells or bawdy houses. No known bastards." Jones tugged at his cap. Rain dripped from the brim, sending yet more water onto the cobblestones. "No gambling debts. No uncertain investments. He's conservative on the Exchange." He sounded as though he were reciting some passage his tutor required him to memorize.

"Nothing interesting at all?" Angel swung around the corner again to peer at Fairchild House. Apparently the man was a veritable paragon of virtue. He didn't like Fairchild, then, on principle.

"He's an ornithologist."

"A what?"

"Birds. He studies birds." Jones's face didn't change expression. It stayed blank and unemotional. "The valet was scraping dirt from his lordship's boots in the rear of the house yesterday as I was passing by on reconnaissance. I made a point of asking a question about the boots—the valet clearly took pride in their quality, so it was a simple conversation opening to make an inquiry about the boot maker."

"Birds." Angel looked up at the sky, as though a flock might be flying past. All he earned for his trouble was more rain and a glimpse of gray clouds. "Everyone has some preoccupation, I suppose. What of Hawthorne? The soldier."

"He does frequent bawdy houses occasionally. He prefers experienced courtesans, but does not have the blunt to support a mistress. No known bastards."

"Gambling?"

"No more than many other young soldiers on leave. No debts."

"Not a paragon of virtue, then, but at least he's human."

Jones's lips lifted up on one side. A quick acknowledgment of amusement before he went back to impassivity. "My source is obtaining Hawthorne's military record. But I have gathered some information already. It's not helpful."

"Let me guess," Angel sighed. "His record is as exemplary as Major Jeremy Fairchild's."

"Well, we know how *that* turned out."

"Jones, I do believe that was a jest." He raised his brows. "In all the years we've known each other, I didn't think you had a sense of humor."

"I jest, sir." He didn't smile, but Angel saw small lines form at the corners of his eyes. It was close to a smile. "Sometimes."

Angel shook his head and squinted through the rain at Fairchild House. It looked no different than it had a moment or two before, except—yes. There. Drapes that had been closed on the second floor were now open. A bedroom window. Hers, he was quite certain. And then there she was. Little more than a blurred face, though he knew it was her. The angle of her head as she watched the street, the way her arm moved to push the drapes farther to the side—both told him it was she.

What did she see? He could not tell in what direction she was looking. She couldn't possibly know it was he out here in the rain. He wanted her to, though. He wanted her to know he was in the street. In case she needed him for—something.

Chapter 16

"GRACIOUS, THE SCREECH of violin tuning is enough to put one off one's tea." Still, Catherine sipped from her painted teacup despite the quartet of stringed instruments howling on the air. "Shouldn't the gels do that before the concert begins? Perhaps upstairs? This is their home."

"I think they need to tune the violins immediately before they play." Lilias sipped her own tea and tried not to wince at the latest squeal of strings. Across the room, four young ladies were seated side by side with their violins. Plucking, turning pegs, plucking again, then a stroke of the bow. "Do you suppose the ladies are talented?"

"I hope so, for their sakes." Catherine shifted in her seat and craned to look around the turban of the lady in front of her. They were in the fifth row of Lady Milbanke's salon, in which chairs and ottomans and sofas were lined up for guests to watch her daughters slaughter Beethoven.

"Do you know why their mother is having this private concert?" Catherine asked.

"No."

"Look at the guests, dear."

She did, and saw nothing unusual at first. There were about forty guests arranged throughout the salon. Some carried glasses and little plates of refreshments from the next room, where tea was laid out. And then she saw the pattern. No young ladies. No debutantes. The women were older or married, the men, quite eligible bachelors of varying ages.

"Lady Milbanke is not particularly subtle, is she?" Lilias couldn't decide if she should be shocked or amused. "How on earth did she orchestrate this?"

"She has four daughters to marry off. One becomes quite scheming in such circumstances. It really is a desperate situation." Catherine tipped her head toward the four female musicians still tuning their instruments. "Hardly a dowry for any of them. The youngest just came out this year. They are all a year apart. Goodness, the oldest is now twenty-one and on her fourth Season and not a single marriage offer to show for it. The youngest will be offered for within a few weeks, I'm certain. Lovely chit. The others—well. Look at them."

They were not pretty. They were not ugly. They were simply plain. Hair, clothing, face, manner. Three older plain girls, and then the utterly exquisite youngest daughter. Lilias imagined the older three expected to be passed over for the youngest. No dowry, no beauty. "Poor girls," she murmured.

"Not that poor," said a low baritone voice into her ear. "Lady Milbanke has managed to invite half the eligible men of the ton by appealing to their mothers."

And there he was. Angelstone. Smelling of man and cologne and sounding like sin. Sitting beside her on the sofa, his leg brushing against her skirts. When she'd last met him, they'd made love. In a chair. And then he kissed her in the moonlight.

Ah, but flesh held memory, did it not? She breathed deep as her body remembered.

"Lord Angelstone, it is delightful to see you again." Catherine peered around Lilias from her end of the sofa, eyes bright. "Now that you are here and Lilias will not be left alone, I need to speak with an acquaintance of mine. Please excuse me." She stood and was walking away before Lilias could say anything.

"Catherine is as subtle as Lady Milbanke," she ground out. She turned to look at Angelstone and found him smiling into his glove. "*You* can laugh. Your mother-in-law is not attempting to play matchmaker."

"My mother has been attempting to do the same for the

last six months, which is doubly irritating. I am only too happy to see someone else in the same predicament." He waved his hand toward the women in the row just in front of them. "You are currently looking at the backs of all the ladies in my family, excluding my niece who is too young to attend."

Three heads. One gray haired, one brunette and a woman with hair that was not quite blond, not quite brown. It was evening, and the ladies were dressed accordingly. The dowager in light gray, the brunette in a pretty shade of pale pink with white trim. The woman with hair of an indeterminate color wore an odd combination of plum and orange. She chose that moment to turn and look curiously at Angelstone.

"Mrs. Fairchild, the lady staring at us quite rudely is Elise, the Marchioness of Angelstone, my eldest brother's widow." Angelstone said it lightly. It sounded like any polite introduction, despite the words. "She has ghastly taste in clothing."

"I can hear you, Angel."

"I know." He grinned at her.

She grinned back. Then she nodded politely at Lilias. "I do apologize for foisting our family blackguard on you, Mrs. Fairchild. But there were not enough seats in our row." Her smiled widened. "And I wish you good luck with him. Angel is quite tedious at concerts."

"Because I expect music."

"I don't think you will hear it today," his sister-in-law said.

Unperturbed, Angelstone settled more comfortably in his seat. "Then I shall take a nap."

The dowager marchioness turned her head, just slightly to the right. She did not even look at them fully, but spoke from the corner of her mouth in that way mothers had that left a child quaking. "If you nap, Angel, I shall force you to attend Lady Milbanke's amateur theatrical next week, in which her daughters feature as Greek goddesses." Threat properly delivered, she faced front again.

The third Whitmore lady, the brunette, snickered into her palm.

Lilias decided she liked all three women. They were just shy of perfectly polite.

"Perhaps I will go in search of coffee, then, instead of the tea you ladies are currently drinking." Angelstone's voice sounded properly chastened, though Lilias saw the gleam in his eyes. His mother's threat was no real threat, but he let her think it was. She liked that about him, though she didn't want to. Arm's length was where she wanted him to stay.

"Mrs. Fairchild, I intend to throw myself upon your mercy." He leaned toward her as he had when he'd first sat beside her. His thumb slid along her thigh, hidden beneath her skirt. But the contact sent hot little zings from her thigh to her center. "May I lean my cheek against your bosom if I fall asleep?" he murmured, quiet enough his family couldn't hear.

Oh, and was he ever a rake. But two could play at that game. She angled her head down, sent him a look from beneath her lashes. "Only if you pay proper attention to it."

"A bit difficult in this venue." But he smiled wickedly at her. No doubt he was trying to determine how best to accomplish the task she'd set him.

"If you become fatigued enough as to require my bosom, I imagine you'll find a way to lavish attention on it." She raised her teacup, sipped. Flirtation was an accomplishment she was skilled at.

"You credit me with creativity."

"I am certain of it. After all, I've experienced it."

A man's face could move so little, yet convey so much. Amusement, desire, laughter, need. He lifted her free hand, set it to his mouth. A brush of lips on glove. She couldn't even feel it through the fine kid leather. Her heart bumped against her ribs nonetheless. It wasn't the kiss on her hand—that was a simple matter. Easily dismissed. But those lips had tasted hers. Those hands had touched her body.

But they had not touched *her*. Some part of her had been held in check. Hidden beyond where he could reach. She slid her hand out of his grasp.

"If you do find coffee, please bring two cups." She set her teacup on its saucer and balanced the pair on her knee. The pretty white china was an oasis in a sea of cerulean blue. "I had hoped to hear music today as well and need all my wits about me." It sounded like a dismissal. Perhaps it was. Perhaps she needed to retreat and regroup.

He made a careful study of her face. Eyes, mouth. His gaze lingered on both cheeks, even her forehead, as though learning the creases that had formed there and the meaning of each dip and line and dimple.

"Coffee it is, then," he murmured. "Your cup, if you please?" He held out his hand for the china. When she placed the set in his hand, he stood and looked down at her. "I fully intend to return to this seat. Please stay, as it would be difficult to chase you down and retrieve you while holding two cups of coffee."

He was asking her to sit beside him during the concert. He was not quite sure of her answer, perhaps, and so he did not outright ask. She was not sure herself. And yet, sitting anywhere else would be impossible now.

"Yes." A simple word, but mired in meaning.

He strode away, her teacup cradled carefully in one hand. A man with purpose. One who did not flinch at duty.

A man that did not shy away from a needy woman marked by scars.

She smoothed her skirt, running gloved fingers over the blue. Wrinkles leveled out to an even field of muslin beneath her fingers. When she looked up, Elise, Marchioness of Angelstone, was watching her with curious eyes.

"I did not know you were acquainted with Angel," she said carefully.

Neither the dowager nor Mrs. Whitmore turned around. But of course, they could hear.

"We were just recently introduced." The phrase could cover a multitude of sins. But not all sins. *Deflect. Quickly.* "Have you heard the Milbanke daughters play? I'm curious how long they have been studying." A legitimate concern if she was to protect her ears.

"I have not heard them." The lady nodded toward the four young musicians. "I think they are starting."

And indeed, a hush had begun near the front of the room and was rippling its way to the rear. Lilias looked around for Catherine, expecting the lady to return to her seat. But her mother-in-law was seated near the front next to her girlhood friend Leticia, heads bent toward each other as they whispered, much as they had done at the ball.

With an amused smile, Lilias clasped her hands together and prepared for an evening of music spent in the company of Angel.

Only it wasn't really music. Perhaps each lady on her own might have sounded passable, but together, it was an off-tempo caterwauling of angry cats.

Angel returned with coffee and she accepted her cup gratefully. Perhaps it would dull the pain. He seemed unperturbed by the sounds, until she noticed the white of his knuckles on the cup. But he watched the group, vigilant gaze on their fingers, on the rush of bow over strings.

"The second oldest." He whispered the words to himself, a light frown between his brows.

"What of her?" She kept her voice low, silence being the most proper method of speech in this venue.

"She has talent. Watch her bow. It's nearly straight. Except . . . there." His breath caught. "There, she knows when to angle it. It's instinctual."

She studied Angelstone's profile. He had straightened, even leaned forward in his chair. Brows down, eyes squinting at the makeshift stage. She turned to look at the lady and saw nothing unusual. Just a girl, playing a violin.

"The bow is nearly right for staccato," he said. "Just a bit off, but she knows it. She is trying to compensate."

"You play." It was obvious.

He turned his head. There was no expression on his face now, nothing she could read. Then it softened and drew her in. "I simply understand violin playing. A friend."

"A friend." She did not believe him in the least.

"*Shhhh.*" An ancient lady two rows up turned around and held her fingers to her lips. Gray brows beetled over watery eyes. "Sh."

"For heaven's sake," Lilias began.

But Angel shook his head and set his finger to his lips. *Quiet*, he mouthed.

She frowned at him, lips pursed. He'd started the conversation, after all. And he was clearly lying to her. She had told him of her love of music, of violins specifically, on their very first meeting.

But that didn't signify, she supposed. They had been lovers only a single time. And though he knew many of her secrets, he did not know all of them.

Just lovers. But not in love.

His queue of hair gleamed bright against his dark evening clothes, catching the eye amidst all the fashionably tousled curls and cropped hair of the other men. He was watching the violinists again, without the focused concentration of before. Instead, he leaned elegantly against the sofa back and crossed his legs.

Angelstone flicked his eyes her way. Perhaps she should have flushed, as she'd been caught watching him. But she was not embarrassed. Desire did not shame her. He could keep his secrets. She would keep hers. It did not change what her body felt.

His expression changed from polite interest to something bright and hot, and her body answered that need. It grew, a sharp hunger she didn't bother to hide. Like a thin, golden rope strung between them, that desire held them together.

Lilias looked down at the painted silk of her fan. Pretty little seashells marched across the cream fabric, playing hide-and-seek between the ribs. She flicked it open, closed, open. Being with Angelstone was likely to be one of the worst decisions of her life. Aside from marrying an assassin, of course.

But making love had been glorious. Thrilling. Carnal. And she wanted to do it again. Just thinking of all that golden skin sliding against hers and the thick, soft hair she could grip in her hands sent little waves rippling over her skin.

Slowly, she raised her head, met his gaze. Her lips curved. Flicking open her fan, she sent him a look over the painted silk knowing precisely how he would read it.

She was rewarded with the flash of hunger in his eyes and a wicked, wicked grin.

———

THE ASSASSIN LAID his knife on the tabletop. Candlelight danced over the immaculate blade. One long, clean, deadly line that divided the expanse of filthy tabletop beneath.

The leader ignored the weapon. And the filth. Unfortunately, he had become accustomed to it. The back room of the Goat and Goose was as disgusting as the rest of the tavern, but at least it was private.

The assassin slid into the opposite chair. Cloth whispered against wood. His dark eyes pulled the light from the room instead of reflecting it. "The Fairchild woman went to the Marquess of Angelstone's townhouse again tonight."

"I wondered." He'd watched them together. The seduction in her smile had been unmistakable. He had not seen that particular look on her face before, not even when she was still married. "Has she returned to Fairchild House yet?" He pushed one of the two tankards of ale he'd ordered across the table.

"No." The assassin did not pick up the tankard. He never did. "The carriage that conveyed her belonged to Angelstone. It did not wait."

"Ah." She would be there for some time then. He'd always believed her to be a lusty woman. Some women were passionate deep in the bone. They usually became mistresses, in his experience, which appeared to be her relationship with Angelstone.

Lucky bastard.

"How much does she know?" The assassin fingered the edge of the blade. Not menacing. Measuring. Testing. An assassin always kept his blade sharp.

Good. He'd trained the assassin himself. It was gratifying to see one's hard work rewarded.

"It is difficult to tell how much she knows," the leader answered. "Lilias Fairchild is not like other women. She doesn't keep her thoughts in the open." But she knew something. Oh yes. He'd made a study of her inflections, her expressions. He heard more than she said. But still she surprised him, which was why she was the most fascinating woman he had ever encountered in his travels.

It was unfortunate he must order her death.

"Ten thousand pounds to the Adder that takes her." He crossed his legs and noted he still wore his evening clothes. He would have to burn them now that he'd worn them into the Goat and Goose. They would never come clean. "I want her death to look like an accident. Or, at the very least, the work of a common footpad. I want no connection to the Adders."

The assassin's brow rose. "The medallion?"

"Send it to me when the deed is done."

Chapter 17

"You don't have to seduce me, Angel. I'm in your study, it's nearly midnight and we have already been lovers once. We both know why I'm here." One corner of Lilias's lips tipped up. An enticing invitation, he decided. But then, she'd issued the invitation hours earlier at the concert. He'd accepted.

What man would refuse a woman watching him like she wanted to forget the crowded room and swallow him, bite by bite? Not him. Not the peer, not the spy, not the man.

"What if I want to seduce you?" A pleasurable pastime, seduction. From the nervous flutter of her hands, the idea discomposed her. How interesting. He reached for the crystal wine decanter on the sideboard and removed the stopper. "Would you care for a glass of wine?"

"With our limited time, it seems wasteful to drink wine. If it is daylight before you finish your seduction, every member of Fairchild House will know I've been out."

She had not said no. Ruby red wine flowed from the sparkling decanter into two curved glasses. The scent of spice and berries rose into the air. He breathed deep and brought that lovely scent into him.

"Much like seduction, wine is never a waste." He threw a glance over his shoulder before picking up the glasses. She half reclined on the chaise longue. Her gown spilled over her legs, a frilled expanse of gold embroidery and fabric the same rich shade as the wine. She was passion and practicality, all packaged in the most delectable body.

He offered her the glass. Gloved fingers closed around the stem. She set it to her lips. He watched the white column of her throat as she swallowed and imagined running his tongue over the soft skin.

Soon. He would, soon. But for all her willingness, he wanted to savor her as he had not had the opportunity before. She'd wanted fast and needy to prove that even if her marriage had been pretense, she was still alive and a woman. But this time, he wanted just a little more from her.

After all, she'd discovered a piece of him. Turnabout was fair play.

He raised his glass, sipped. The wine slid over his tongue, smooth and mellow. "Do you like it?"

"I do." She held up her wine, peering into the glowing liquid. It must have been an interesting substance, as a line appeared between her brows. She did not look at him when she spoke, but continue to peer into the wine. "What are we doing, Angel?"

"Being foolish."

A resigned half laugh dove into the glass and disappeared into the wine. "So we are. I don't seem to mind. Sit beside me."

She drew her legs in, making room on the chaise. He sat beside her. Her slippered toes were only inches from his thigh. Part of that vibrant gown tumbled over his knee. A shapely ankle peeked from beneath her skirts. He couldn't resist the subtle point of her anklebone. So delicate. His forefinger brushed the silk stocking covering the peak. Beneath his touch, her skin fairly vibrated. His body answered, though he'd been half aroused already.

"This is seduction again." Blond brows drew together. She was so unsettled by the seduction he could practically feel her muscles quivering. "We are moving backward, Angel. I don't want seduction."

"We skipped a few steps the first time."

He met her gaze and found the most intriguing vulnerability in those blue depths. She was afraid of seduction. Not of seducing someone, but of being seduced.

"I don't know." Her lips curved upward. She leaned forward,

sliding her legs over his thighs until she was nearly on his lap. "We managed all the pertinent parts."

"Except getting to know each other."

"I would say we know enough." Her eyes went dark and shuttered. A barrier rose up, something he knew instinctively he could not penetrate. "I told you, I don't want to be seduced."

"Is it only sex you're after, Lilias?" He couldn't decide if he should be delighted or offended.

The line formed between her brows, only it seemed fierce now. "It's only pleasure between us, Angel."

And death and murder and lies. It all lay between them, even if they chose to ignore it for a few hours. "We can share more than just pleasure." Though he wasn't sure why he wanted to.

"You're in a strange mood tonight." Her laugh was light and strained.

Perhaps he was. He'd let his guard down at the concert. It wasn't that the music was lovely or the violinists skilled. He'd been intrigued by the young girl struggling to work with her raw talent. She should not have caught his attention, but she had. And Lilias had seen the moment when he'd forgotten to be a spy.

It was wrong of him to want to erase that moment. It was just as wrong to want to pierce her armor. But if he gave Lilias some part of himself, he wanted some part of her in return. The brightest, most true part. Because she had found his, even if she wasn't aware of it.

"Do you know what I think of when I think of you?" he asked.

A faint line appeared between her brows. "I haven't the slightest idea." She set the glass to her lips, watching him with curious eyes. "What?"

"Waterloo. The sabre." A warrior woman. Whatever she'd been fighting for—and he thought he knew—it was that part of her that seemed most true. "Where did you learn?"

"To fence?" Her brows snapped together. "On the march. Jeremy taught me, along with Hawthorne. It helped pass the time when we were bivouacked somewhere inhospitable."

"You were more skilled in battle than I expected."

She straightened, all bright eyes and amused smile. The

darkness lurking behind those eyes had eased. "Oh, I have a range of talents. Fencing is only one of them."

"What else are you skilled at?" A question filled with possibilities. With her hand skimming along his thigh, it was full of more possibilities than his body could manage.

"Riding a horse in a raging blizzard." A dry tone, a dry look, as her hand slipped from his thigh. "I'm an accomplished rider."

He had more than enough proof of that. "Not a talent easily showcased in London." Unless she were in a chair.

Her fingers rippled across the crescent sweep of the wineglass. Coyly, "I'm better on a horse than with a sabre."

"I've seen your riding skills." His hand stroked her ankle again, then his fingers trailed beneath the edge of the skirt to the lower curve of her calf. "*Are* you skilled at fencing?"

"I've never had a chance to perfect it." Her laugh was quiet. "Not a very ladylike skill."

"But a useful one."

"Only if I need to fight off some blackguard and happen to have a convenient sword nearby. Of late I'm beginning to think I may need such skills. I may need to protect myself, now that I've taken a spy as a lover."

"The hazards of governmental service." Damnation, but she smelled like sin. He set his lips against the line of her neck, nibbled there. "But perhaps your skills have become rusty with disuse these last few years."

"Do you need a demonstration, then?" She laughed, low and throaty. "It is unfortunate I do not keep a sword in my reticule."

"It so happens I keep multiple swords in my home."

"That is the worst euphemism I have ever heard." Her smile simply bloomed. Bright and beautiful. "Most definitely a demonstration, then. Perhaps you can help me refresh my fencing skills."

Ah, he found that part of her. This was Lilias, not Mrs. Fairchild. The woman, not the wife. Major Fairchild might have taught her to fence, but it was her character that made her enjoy it.

"Well, you can't fence in that gown, my girl." A kiss, a

stroke of her cheek. The slightest dimple as she laughed at him. "Let's find you something to wear."

HE HEARD HER slip into the training room. Her tread was the lightest whisper against the floor. He didn't turn around, but continued to remove the matching foils from their case.

"This is the longest room in the house. It is the most conducive to fencing lessons." He laid the foils side by side on one of the tables at the edge of the room. The long, intricately constructed wooden floor had seen more than its share of inexperienced spies. "Are you ready?"

"Yes." She stepped up beside him to study the buttoned foils. "They're beautiful."

Candlelight shone on the thin, polished blades. Her finger slid over the length of the entwined ropes of gold forming the guard. Her touch was slow and light, the movement long.

He swallowed hard and glanced over. His breath clogged in his lungs. When he'd given her the shirt and breeches he never imagined she'd look like this in them. Aphrodite could not have looked more enticing.

"What?" Her smile told him she knew exactly what.

"I'd forgotten how thin my shirts are," he said softly.

She wore her chemise beneath his shirt. He could see the lace rising above the deep V of the neckline. Technically, she was properly covered, even swimming in clothing. But even through her chemise and the fine lawn shirt her nipples peaked against the fabric. The sight left him wanting more.

His gaze traveled over her waist, over the lush hips revealed by the breeches. She'd used a cravat to hold them up. Silk stockings with a pretty little pattern covered her calves. Those long legs beneath ended in a ridiculously sensual pair of heeled slippers.

The delicate ankles he'd admired were completely exposed. Odd that an ankle could make a man salivate.

He raised his eyes and found her watching him through her lashes. She touched the tip of her tongue to pink lips. Desire shot through him, a quick dart that took his breath. Who was seducing whom now?

"Thank you for the loan of your clothing," she said.

"It looks better on you than on me."

Her lips quirked. "You're biased."

"True."

"Unfortunately, I don't have the slightest idea how I'm going to fence in these slippers."

He grinned. "Take them off."

"A challenge, my lord?" One hand landed on her rounded hip. "Do you think I won't? Too improper, do you suppose?"

"I have no doubt you will." With a flourish, he dipped to one knee and held out a hand. Looking up into her amused face, he said, "May I?"

"Ah, the gallant knight." Her hand came to rest gently on his shoulder, bringing her scent with it. She pointed one foot, lifting it for his ministrations. Candlelight shone on the wine-colored silk of her slipper. "Very well, sir. Remove the slipper."

He slid his hand around to cup her heel. Her stockings were as thin as gossamer, and when his fingers brushed the diaphanous silk he felt the shock resonate low in his belly. The slipper all but fell from her foot. His gaze followed the line of her calf, the lovely hollow of her ankle, the high arch.

Looking at her was an exquisite torture, sharp as the point of a sword. He slid the second slipper off and turned away lest the torture become unbearable.

He pointed to the masks and jackets lying beside the foils. "For protection."

She didn't hesitate. The jacket first. Arms slid in before she ran her hands down each side of the front opening, her hands skimming her breasts. He met her gaze, saw she was watching him through her lashes. Minx.

The jacket was his, and too large for her frame. But she gamely buttoned it, still watching him as deft fingers fastened it over her breasts. A sad thing, when a pair of exquisite breasts was covered by thick fabric.

Then with a hand resting on her hair to hold it in place, she set the mesh and leather mask over her head to cover her face. Beneath the mask he could barely see the features of her face. But he recognized her grin. It was infectious, that sudden joy.

And it was a piece of her that had been missing. One of

the pieces he had been hoping to find. Perhaps his motives were not pure, but he was not pure. If he wanted to find that tiny bit of her she did not show others, he refused to consider that a fault.

She tugged at the jacket, settling it into place. "I know some of the basic positions already," she said.

"Show me, then. Slowly." Picking up a foil, he turned it to offer it hilt first.

Her brows rose in challenge. Wrapping her hands around the hilt, she took it from him. Lovely, gloveless hands. "I have only a rudimentary knowledge of the art of fencing. My knowledge is more the practical kind."

"War is nothing if not practical." He set a mask over his own head. Now her image was crisscrossed by steel squares. He could not see details, only the shape of her body, the slow and elegant movements. She seemed to be forever in a delicate dance.

"I couldn't agree more." She stepped to the center of the cleared area. Graceful as the curve of a swan's neck, she rose to the balls of her feet. "How do I stand?"

"I thought you knew already."

"Only the most basic idea." She grinned merrily. Enjoyment radiated from her.

He'd been right to think her interests were atypical—but so were his. They were two nonconforming souls. He with the ton and the life of peer, she with—well. The ton, the delicate pastimes of some women, even life in London, he supposed.

"En garde." Lifting the foil, she pointed it at him. It was a clumsy version of the position.

He clucked his tongue. "You need to be retaught the positions." The foil in his hand whispered through the air as he prowled toward her. "Fencing isn't about body positions and thrusts." He stopped to stand beside her and took up the en garde position.

"No?" She ran her eyes down his body, then mirrored his position. That quick look sent his blood humming. If a man could imagine a woman naked beneath her clothes, a woman could do the same, could she not?

He cleared his throat. "Fencing is about deceiving your opponent, and not being deceived by him."

"No wonder Jeremy excelled at it. He was an expert in deception." She paused, the foil before her motionless. "Then again, so are you. Since I apparently didn't know my husband—" She thrust the sword forward, body moving as fluidly as water. "Perhaps I don't know you as well as I think."

She could not know him. There were too many secrets in his head. There was too much blood on his hands. "Perhaps *I* don't know *you*. What secrets do you carry with you?"

That mobile, flowing body did not pause in her thrusts. "You know my secrets."

"Only some of them. Rest your weight on both legs. And don't do anything until I tell you." He moved to face her. "Equal weight on both legs."

"Jeremy said to put my weight on the left leg." But she shifted her weight as he'd asked.

"I'm not Jeremy. Bend your knees a little more." He demonstrated and she followed suit. "Some believe that the weight should be equally distributed, so that you are planted more firmly on the ground."

She danced forward. "It feels different. Stronger." Her stocking feet moved over the floor, flexing, pointing, a blur of silk and skin. "And I know you are not Jeremy."

"Good. You and me, Lilias. No one else."

Her feet paused in their movements, then started again. "No one else." She met his gaze, but he could not read the emotion in her eyes. "Am I standing correctly?"

"Ultimately, the choice of stance will be made by your body." He smiled. "You simply need to let your body tell you."

Her gaze swept over him. "My body has already told me what it wants."

Desire flickered, a low burn that spread like wildfire through his blood. To counteract it, he raised his sword. "Follow my lead, then."

He lead her through a parade of carte, step-by-step. His borrowed breeches moved against her buttocks, stretching, molding. Delight lit her eyes.

And it was he that helped put it there. Something warm bloomed in him, something that wasn't lust or admiration.

When she parried his thrust and then neatly counterattacked to put him on the defensive, he laughed aloud and let that warmth ring in the sound.

"You know more than you let on," he puffed out, pulling the mask from his head and dropping it on the floor. He wanted to see her face.

Her form was rough, but she knew the positions, the moves. And she made little breathy sounds with each thrust. Sounds he'd heard before. Her breath had hitched in, then stuttered out when he'd slid into her body.

She stepped back. Her own mask landed on the floor beside his. Her cheeks were flushed, her hair a disheveled mass of blond.

"More," she said, her eyes dangerous and bright.

It was impossible not to think of taking her, right there on the floor. He was hard, and feeling reckless enough to try the fencing bout without the masks.

"En garde."

And they began again, more delicately, but this time he could see her eyes more easily. Watch her cheeks flush with pleasure.

"You're looking at me in that way, Angel." She parried his thrust, their foils paused in midair. She stepped toward him, her blade sliding down so that the hilts locked. For a moment, they simply stood, sword to sword, toe to toe, mouth to mouth. "When you look at me that way, I can feel it in my skin. In my blood."

Lust could be brutal. A merciless need that swept a man's feet from beneath him and sent him to his knees.

He couldn't stop himself from taking her mouth. She tasted sweet, and faintly like wine. Her lips were soft and warm and opened beneath his. He wanted to be skin to skin, to feel her against him. In a bed this time. No barriers of clothing.

His arm came around her, his hand pressing into the small of her back. To draw her forward, draw her in. But their blades still crossed. Always, there was a battle between them.

He eased back and looked into that magnificent face. Her lashes swept up, a gold arc revealing bright eyes. Slowly, those kiss-reddened lips smiled.

"An interesting way to end a bout, Angel." Her tone was silky and low.

"Is the swordplay over, then?"

"A very, very bad jest." She laughed and stepped away. The foil in her hand dipped to the floor. "Can you think of nothing more original than that?"

"Come to bed, then."

Chapter 18

"Only a bed?" Laughter danced in her eyes. "How unadventurous. Surely a spy can think of somewhere better."

"Bed." He pictured her there, hair spread over the pillow, arms opening to draw him in. Unhurried, so he could feast on her. The half arousal plaguing him this last hour sprang full.

"Then we shall be traditional." She walked to the table, hips moving under the loose breeches. A silent temptation.

"Perhaps women should wear breeches regularly." He cocked his head and watched the light sway of her hips.

"I can't imagine it." The foil clinked against wood as she lay it down. "Too provocative."

"So they are," he said, unable to find a fault in that.

She looked natural wearing them. Her body moved with a confident awareness that spoke of knowledge. Of her body, her sexuality, her figure. Herself. Perhaps it was her awareness of self that caught him. It was an intoxicating combination. What man would betray his country—become an assassin—and risk losing this woman?

Christ, those breeches would make a dead man hard. What it did to a live man—well.

She held out her hand, palm up. He set his hand over hers, closed it around delicate bones and soft skin. It felt strange, as though he accepted more than her body. What he had just been gifted, he could not say.

Stepping backward, he drew her from the room, ignoring the foils. They could be dealt with later. He could not ignore Lilias when she looked up at him through her lashes in just that way.

The quiet hallways and dark stairs leading to his room seemed impossibly long. When they reached it, he closed the door behind them. There was no fire in the grate, no candle lit. Just darkness. Offering sensation, concealing secrets.

Her hand was small in his. He shifted his fingers so they entwined with hers. Brought them to his lips. A kiss, another, over a finger, then a knuckle. He found that lovely hollow between thumb and forefinger, tasted.

He set his other hand on their joined ones, then skimmed it over her arm in slow ascent. He could not feel her skin beneath the sleeve of his shirt, only the shape of her. The narrow expanse of wrist. A forearm that curved just so. A surprisingly delicate elbow. Then the lightly muscled upper arm, the arc of her shoulder. She tipped her head to the side as his fingers rasped over her collarbone. Delicate there as well.

He found the nape of her neck. Curling wisps of hair flirted with his fingers. He drew her forward, hands still entwined. Her scent met him first. Bright and clean. Then her lips touched his. Soft. Full. Opening beneath his mouth without even the slightest urging.

Now he tasted her. Wine. Woman. The essence only she could create. Her tongue played with his, as bold as the hand that snaked up his shoulder to tangle in his hair. She pressed herself against him, eliminating that small space between. Breasts were marvelous, he decided, when they were free beneath a man's shirt. Pointed nipples pressed against his chest and he could feel the fullness of her breasts.

She wanted him, and that was a satisfying thing. The knowledge of it beat a rhythm inside him. Throbbing just beneath his skin.

He could not see, was blind to all but sensation. His hands roamed. Skimmed over her cheeks. He had not realized cheekbones were composed of peaks and valleys. Beneath his thumbs was a mountain range of female bone and skin. He had to press his lips there. To touch those crests. From there it was easy to find the line of her jaw. And that led to the hollow between her collarbone. Another valley to explore.

Her fingers dove into his hair. The constraining leather cord slipped away and landed somewhere near his left foot. He did not care. The body pressed against his was lithe and pliant, the fingers tracing his jaw frantic to touch him. The moan low in her throat vibrated against his lips.

It seemed impossible that such need could resonate inside a woman and then shudder through a man. Could sexual hunger flow from one person to another?

"Lilias." He needed more of her. He could not touch enough of her. The ridges of her spine beneath the linen shirt. The smooth skin of her back. The roundness of her buttocks.

"You *are* bent on seduction, are you not?" Her words were barely more than breath.

"Only if touching you equals seduction." But he understood, with an utter clarity that comes from being in darkness, that seduction meant more than sex. It was not seduction she feared. It was the connection running beneath it. The edge of her shirt—his shirt—was an easy barrier to defeat. She raised her arms so he could remove it. A silk chemise still lay between them, so he tugged that until it pulled free of the breeches.

Hot skin. The dip of her waist. Ah, but there, that was the curve of a breast brushing against his thumb. And there, a tight nipple just begging for attention. He brushed a palm across the tip and she arched back, pressing that glorious, full breast into his hand. Her sound of pleasure was music on the air.

Her breast lifted, moved beneath his hand as her arms rose. The chemise billowed around her torso, a whisper of silk against his hands, leaving the scent of lavender in its wake. Then it was gone, over her head, and her breast settled easily in his palm again. Warm as a peach in the Grecian sun.

"Too many layers," she breathed into the dark.

He laughed lightly. "A woman after my own heart."

"No," she corrected, and he could hear the amusement in her voice. "Just your body."

Cool fingers traveled up his arms to his shoulders, then

down to flutter around the waistband of his pants. Thumbs slid between cloth and skin, around to the front to undo the top buttons of his breeches, then the exposed drawers beneath. The action was practical rather than seductive, but dear God, it aroused him. When she shimmied the breeches over his hips and down, his cock sprang free at full tilt.

And then she touched it, before his breeches even met the floor. Just the right pressure, here, there. A skim of fingers. Her fist closed around it. His hips jerked forward, bucking against that delicate, strong hand. She laughed delightedly. Utter feminine approval. A long stroke, another. He struggled to hold himself in check.

"If you continue that, my lovely Lilias, you'll be disappointed this evening." His voice was little more than a rasp.

Her hand fell away. Through the darkness he heard her tiny chuckle.

Reaching for her, he drew her in against him. His cock pressed against her bare belly, his legs against hers, still clad in borrowed breeches. Not close enough. It wasn't nearly enough.

His shirt was a rush of linen over his flesh. He barely felt it. He was listening to her movements. Her breath. The rustle of fabric. A soft vibration in the thick rug beneath his feet. Her breeches had fallen to the floor.

And there she was. One long, lean line of woman. Warm skin, smooth and soft. Against him, around him. His hands slid over her buttocks, just there, at the slight dip where they met her upper thighs. Such a feminine place. He would learn this place, and whether it pleased her. He ran a finger along that crease. Ah yes. Pleasure indeed. Her muscles quivered. Thigh, belly. Her breath quickened.

The bed. It had to be here somewhere in the dark. He'd lost all sense of space and could not tell door from bed from floor. He moved slowly, drawing her with him. Her thigh brushed against his as he sought the bed. Thick rug gave way beneath his feet. She laughed low into his ear. Could a man be harder than this?

"Wait," she whispered, stepping back.

"If you don't want—" *Dear God, would she end it now?* In a thousand years, he could not stop. But he stepped back because he must. Dropped his hands, though they throbbed from the need to touch her flesh.

"My hair. It is still pinned up." Displaced air sighed as she moved an arm, perhaps both.

He grinned, relief surging through him. He would have her, after all. "Let me."

He tangled his hands in her hair. He could not see it in the deep of the night. But he could imagine that mass of bright blond. How long was it? he wondered. How thick? One hairpin was eliminated, then another. Tiny spears of women's fashion. He let them fall where they would on the carpet.

Then her hair was free. A mass of waves he knew to be the color of wheat in the sun tumbled down. He rubbed the strands between his forefinger and thumb. His fingers traveled the length of the strands. Long, longer. To her hips. Did they tickle her skin? Did they touch that crease where buttock met thigh and arouse her? He hoped they did, so that she felt pleasure with her own body.

She shook her hair back, pulling the strands free from his hold and his mind free of his musings. Her hands were delicate against his shoulders, but there was pressure, too. Pushing him toward the bed. Or he hoped it was the bed that hit his knees, because he was powerless to do anything but tumble them both to whatever surface was behind them.

She rose over him, invisible in the darkness, but still a siren as her thighs trapped his hips. He made no effort to move from his back, but let her keep that position of power. Let her choose the position, the angle. He wondered what she preferred. Deep or shallow, fast or slow? He'd had no opportunity to learn those things the first time. He would now, by letting her guide him.

But she did not take him into her. Her hands began to roam over him. Down his chest, curling in the hair as though it were a new sensation. Her body slid over his in a symphony of curves and dips and hollows. Her sleek hair ran like a waterfall over his face, shoulders, chest. For a moment he could not draw a proper breath. Lips settled against the center of his chest. Her tongue darted out. A taste. She must have approved, as her lips moved to one side, laved his nipple. His cock twitched against her buttocks and she laughed aloud. The minx.

So he began his own exploration. He skimmed a hand up her torso, found the indentation of her navel. Then a narrow line that ran horizontally across her rib cage. No, not a line, a ridge. Thin and just slightly raised from her skin, about four inches long.

Her hands stilled. She straightened, tension reverberating through the muscles that trapped his hips. "A bayonet cut from Waterloo," she said into the revealing dark. "It was shallow, and the mark has faded now. But, still, I bear a scar."

"Ah." He set his hand against the mark. It ranged just shorter than the width of his palm. "Does it hurt?"

"No." She was shrinking from him. Pulling back. Not physically, but he felt the retreat of her emotions as though it were her body.

"I have a scar myself. Several in fact." He took her hands, entwined his fingers with hers. Bringing her back to the present. "Here," he said, guiding her hand to the back of his shoulder. A knife fight in the wilds of India. It was only one of a dozen scars he bore, but it would match hers. Her fingers skimmed the scar, curiosity evident in their smooth pads. "It does not hurt, either. But I think of it sometimes, when the weather turns."

"Yes. When the weather turns." She bent, and pressed her lips against his shoulder. So thoughtfully, so easily, that he could not find words to respond. But perhaps he did not need to speak. Perhaps all that was necessary was a touch. A gift.

Her thighs were supple, shifting beneath his hands as she rose above him once more. His fingers searched in the dark for the juncture between her thighs. Her breath was a quick intake as he found the curls hiding all of her womanly secrets. But there, ah yes. That was the most secretive place of all.

Her breath heaved in and out as he moved his hand, playing between the curls, finding that little spot that would break her apart. He grinned into the dark when he felt her hips press forward against his hand. Christ, he could slip into her if she moved just right. She was wet, hot and—he bit back a groan and gritted his teeth against the need to be inside her.

She shuddered against his hand, and her quick little moans spiked into the air. He almost expected to be able to see her, as her skin was so heated she should be glowing with it. Neatly filed nails dug into his hips, flexed, clutched even as her thigh muscles quivered. He felt her climax almost as though it were his own. Her head fell back and her hair brushed against his legs, those thighs squeezed, trembled. He could not wait any longer. He needed to have her beneath him. Willing and open, with her arms and legs wrapped around him.

He rolled, almost before she could recover, until he was ranged over her. She welcomed him with those slender arms, the leanly muscled legs. He felt the wetness of her, the scalding heat. Then, dear God, he was finally sheathed in her. Was there any place as divine as being inside a woman one respected? One admired? This woman could wield a sabre on the battlefield. This woman made him think of music. This woman made him want things he'd forgotten he wanted.

He could not smell the lavender on her skin now. Only Lilias. The scent that was uniquely her. It mingled with his own scent, until they smelled of something belonging only to them. A scent no one else in the world would share.

He buried his face in the lovely curve of her neck, pressed his lips against her pulse. *In and out, slow, deep.* Her inner muscles clenched around him. Her arms tightened across his back. She arched up, gave a triumphant cry that spurred him on. Just one more thrust, one more time to touch the center of her. And then he, too, fell over the edge and into oblivion.

Chapter 19

"I SHOULD RETURN TO Fairchild House. The servants will be waking soon." The sun had yet to cross the horizon, but she could see that pinkish band kissing the edge of the city before it faded to yellow and blue.

"Stay a little longer." Angel's whisper wrapped around her, a warm, rich cocoon of sound.

She smiled into the pale gray light as his chest brushed against her nipples. They hadn't bothered to put anything on before they fell asleep. Now she was warm and sleepy and surrounded by naked man. One of her calves was trapped between his. A hand ran up and down her thigh. Fingers swirled a random pattern on her skin, touching, caressing, moving, sliding. The calluses on those fingers excited and soothed all at once, heating her skin. Heating her blood.

Again.

"Mmm." The sigh purred out of her. She stretched against his play of his fingers. "I could be persuaded to stay."

He chuckled, the deep baritone rumbling in his chest and teasing her breasts. "I think we don't need to advertise our relationship any more than you did last night."

"I?" she asked, feigning innocence. Her hand slid down his stomach, marveling at the strength of him, until she found the rough patch of hair and the part of him that was quite ready for another round. "I have no idea what you're talking about."

"No?" he growled into her ear. The night's growth on his jaw sent little shock waves from the tender place at her neck right down to her toes. "You were disrobing me with your eyes in Lady Milbanke's salon, my dear Lilias."

She laughed and wrapped her hand more firmly about him. "Perhaps I was. But it all led here, so can you truly complain?" Tipping up her face, she nipped at his bottom lip.

"Most definitely not. But I have no idea how I'm going to face the dragons of the ton today. My reputation is all but ruined." He began to nibble at her ear. One hand flattened against the base of her spine, as though waiting for the right moment to press her close.

"Your reputation?" She snorted. "It was *I* who was warned away from *you*, Angelstone."

He stilled, the hand against her back releasing its pressure. "Who warned you?"

"It doesn't matter." She set a hand against his firm chest. Muscles moved beneath her fingertips.

"Who was it?"

"It doesn't matter," she repeated. She shook her head, hoping to erase the hardened expression in his eyes. But the heat that had been building between them had chilled.

"It might." His legs untangled themselves from hers. The circle of his arms still sheltered her, but questions had once again come between them. It was inevitable, she supposed. They were not just a man and a woman. Espionage and assassination could put a damper on sex.

"Jason Hawthorne." She sighed. This was not the conversation she'd wanted to have early in the morning. Angel was so close she could see the deep brown flecks ringing the outside of his tawny irises. "He believes you are a rake who will break my heart and warned me your reputation is not spotless."

"Jason Hawthorne seems to spend an inordinate amount of time warning you against me." He shifted and his arm slid from beneath her neck. In one smooth movement, he rolled over to sit on the edge of the bed.

Irritated, she did the same so that they were sitting back-to-back on the bed, naked. An ocean of sheet stretched between them.

"He cares for me—and it's not as though you have a stellar reputation, Angel," she tossed over her shoulder.

"It's not so bad that you need to be warned off. I'm still considered eligible."

She turned to study his back as she sat on the edge of the bed. Broad. Gold. Strong. An arrogant toss of his head sent his hair rippling over his shoulders. He stood and strode across the room to retrieve his clothing. The sight of the long, lean muscles in his legs sent her insides quivering.

All he needed were wings to be the fallen angel she once thought him.

"Perhaps your reputation isn't as bad as some," she allowed. Generously, she thought. "Still, Hawthorne is concerned for me. He was Jeremy's best friend and a godsend during those first days after Jeremy's death." Sliding from the bed, Lilias reached for her chemise and wriggled into it. When she turned, Angel was regarding her with an arrested expression.

And, sadly, he was wearing breeches.

"He was your husband's best friend."

"Yes." She slid her arms into the stays, settling it over her chemise. "Will you?" she asked, presenting her back to him.

He complied, working on the tabs and laces with quick and experienced fingers. But he was silent, and she felt the need to break it.

"You make more than a passable lady's maid. Have you had much practice?"

"A gentleman never tells." There was no teasing note in his voice, though the words themselves hinted at a jest. But they were beyond the easy companionship of the night. It was nearly daylight and the comfort of the dark was gone. Life did intrude, didn't it?

"There, you're finished," he said. "Was Hawthorne at Waterloo?"

"He marched with the regiment." Stays complete, she moved away to find her gown. She shook out the frilly silk confection with a quick snap to release the wrinkles. "They were quite close and nearly always together. Closer than brothers.

Sometimes I think Hawthorne knew Jeremy better than I did." She looked up at Angel.

He only stood there. Waiting. Watching.

Her heart thumped once. The gown slid to the floor from boneless fingers.

"Oh no. Impossible." She shook her head frantically. "Hawthorne is not one of them."

"How can you be certain?"

Her mouth went dry. She couldn't.

"You said it yourself, Lilias. They were nearly always together."

She wished he didn't sound so patient. "But, if they were both Death Adders, they wouldn't have been so open about the connection, would they?" She couldn't bear to lose Hawthorne, too. Desperately, she clutched at hope. "Being so close would draw suspicion on them."

"There's no better place to hide than in plain sight."

"I can't believe it of Hawthorne." But she had not believed it of Jeremy, either, until it was true. She picked up the gown with numb fingers.

"You don't *want* to believe it." Sympathy shone from Angel's eyes.

She would not look at him. The ribbon running across the bodice of her gown, now that was interesting. That she could look at without aching inside. She was not prepared for sympathy.

"I will investigate Jason Hawthorne," he said. "I must determine if he is involved."

"I need my slippers." She clutched her silk stockings in fisted hands. She could not think of Hawthorne. She only wanted to escape. To regroup. "They are still in your training room."

———

LILIAS WOVE THROUGH the crowd in the ballroom. In, out, around. She avoided the muslin skirts of the debutante. The cane of the octogenarian. The huge brass buttons of a dandy. She barely saw any of them.

Jason Hawthorne was the sole focus of her attention.

She circled the ballroom. Watching. She'd known him for

nearly a decade. Six years of her marriage to Jeremy, two years of widowhood. And there was that exhilarating year before her marriage when she and Jeremy had moved from infatuation to lust to love. Hawthorne had always been there.

Had she ever noticed the sharp edge to his jaw when he clenched his teeth? He was doing so now as a marriage-minded mama tried to entice him to dance with her daughter. He did dance, of course. A gentleman always did. But he was stiff as he led the girl across the floor. The poor chit ducked her head and blushed, then pulled her shawl close around her shoulders.

Lilias stopped her prowl around the room. Sliding behind a potted orange tree, she hid herself with the green leaves and watched the floor. Hawthorne and the girl separated as the country dance began. Couples moved across the floor, met, parted.

Angel could be right. If fact, he likely was right. It wasn't that hard to believe if she thought about how often Jeremy and Hawthorne were together. They fought together, certainly. On the occasions they were able to relax, they did so together. They ate together, traveled together, took their leaves together.

Worse, Hawthorne had been there when Jeremy died. Hawthorne had brought the injured Jeremy back to Lilias. Just in time for him to breathe his final breath. If Jeremy were assassinated, Hawthorne would have known. He would have told her.

Or he was the assassin.

Bile rose in her throat. She turned her head, swallowed hard. Forced herself to breathe. Was the foundation of her life nothing but sand? Jeremy, her marriage, and now Hawthorne. None of them were what they seemed. Perhaps others of the men serving with Jeremy were assassins.

If she hadn't noticed her own husband's perfidy, how would she recognize that of others?

It was as though she'd been betrayed a second time. Only this time, there was someone she could confront.

"What are you doing hiding behind this orange tree?" said a voice at her shoulder.

"Bloody—" Lilias caught herself and swallowed the curse.

Catherine stood a step behind, feathers trembling as she shook with laughter. "Lilias, dear, you came off the floor a foot at least." Her dark eyes laughed over her fan as she hid her smile. Not that it mattered. The snorted laughter gave her away.

"I just—I was just—I needed to rest."

"Mm hm. Now—" Catherine slide behind the orange tree. She peered through the branches and looked every bit the woodland sprite. "Who are we spying on?"

"Catherine." The wave overcame her, an engulfing, all-encompassing sweep of emotion. "I love you."

"I know, dear. I love you, too." Though her mouth still smiled, her eyes had turned serious. Green leaves crisscrossed over her face, hiding the roundness of her cheeks. "Don't forget that my shoulders are here to help bear your burden, whatever it is that is troubling you."

"What do you mean, whatever is troubling me?"

"You have shadows under your eyes. You've barely eaten a morsel in the last week. You'll need to take your gowns in soon as they're getting too big. Do tell me, when you're ready. Now"—she turned back to the ballroom—"who are we spying on?"

Lilias could think of nothing meaningful to say. It was not as though she could tell Catherine her son had been an assassin. The need to speak was a huge weight on her chest. But only some of it could be relieved.

"Jason Hawthorne." She swallowed hard. "What do you think of him?"

"A good man."

"You think so?"

"Dear, a woman doesn't get to be my age without understanding men. I married one and raised one. Raised two, really, if you consider Grant, as his mother died when he was so young." Leaves rustled as Catherine stepped away from the plant. "Why does Jason Hawthorne upset you?"

"Why do you think he upsets me? Perhaps I've set my cap for him."

"If you had, you would sound much happier when you spoke of him. Besides, you've set your cap for the Marquess of Angelstone." She waved her hands at Lilias when she protested. "Oh, fine. Perhaps not your cap. But your negligee at the very least."

"Really." Lilias closed her eyes and gave her head a little shake of denial. "How does one answer that?"

"I don't think one does." Catherine's tiny fingers clutched at Lilias's sleeve. "To be serious, I like Hawthorne. He's a good man, I think, but he does have secrets. Everyone has secrets, but his are darker than most. That doesn't make him better or worse than the man you see."

"No?" Some secrets were worse than others.

"Grant has arrived." Catherine flitted out from behind the orange tree. "If you intend to spy on Jason Hawthorne, I suggest you be more discreet. The rumors are bad enough at the moment. You don't need to embroil a second gentleman."

"Rumors?" Lilias swung around to face Catherine.

"Well, of course, dear." Catherine's eyebrows rose, to graying crescents of incredulity. "You're beautiful, Angelstone is handsome and your mutual interest is quite marked. Angelstone doesn't dance often so it's of note that he dances with you. He also doesn't have a mistress at the moment, so the gossips are abuzz with the idea he's pursuing a woman."

"Well, of course," she murmured, repeating Catherine's words. She wanted to press her fingers against her eyes. "I don't know how you can take it in stride."

"What else is there to do?" Catherine's eyes danced. "I confess, it's the most fun I've had in years."

"What of my reputation? What of yours?"

"What of them?" Catherine let out a tinkling laugh. "Darling, don't get upset. Your reputation will withstand it. Just be discreet. Widows are allowed to have liaisons. Heavens, I even have them now and again. My last was just a month ago with Lord Martin—"

"Stop!" she choked out. "Catherine, I don't want—" Rubbing a hand over her eyes, she tried to strike the image of Catherine and Lord Martin out of her mind.

Catherine's laugh bounced around the ballroom again. "At any rate, have a care, dear."

As Catherine swooped across the floor to meet Grant, Lilias watched her husband's cousin carefully. He was elegant and confident and full of diplomatic charm. He met her gaze over Catherine's head and smiled at her. Dimples winked.

Perhaps she could tell him the truth. Not about her relationship with Angel, or her desire never to marry, but about her husband. Grant had known Jeremy as well as she. He was a strong man, with broad shoulders that already carried the weight of his diplomatic duties. He would carry the burden with her.

And then she saw Hawthorne at the door to the ballroom.

Her heart thumped when he threw a glance over his shoulder. One hard look before he slipped between the double doors.

A secret, Catherine had said. Well, she was going to find out what it was.

Guests faded away. Her gaze arrowed to the doors closing behind Hawthorne. She hurried through the press of people, crossing the ballroom. The door handle was smooth beneath her palm, the door heavy as it swung open, then closed again.

There were others in the hall. A pair of young women coming from the ladies' retiring room. An older gentleman who nodded as he passed her. She barely noticed. Her eyes were focused on the light blue expanse of a soldier's coat.

Hawthorne stood at the top of the steps going down to the ground floor. The footman standing next to him bowed before scurrying down the stairs. Hawthorne adjusted his evening gloves and followed more slowly.

Lilias hissed at the thought of losing sight of him and picked up her skirts. Her slippers were silent on the ornate rug running the center of the hallway. Quick steps, the swish of skirts, and she was poised at the top of the stairs.

She saw his profile as the butler handed Hawthorne his hat, his greatcoat and the walking stick she knew hid a sword. From the side, his face seemed sharp and rough and much less civilized.

The front door opened. Rain pinged on the walkway outside. She darted down the remaining interior steps and leapt for the door.

"Just a moment. I need to speak with Hawthorne." She swept past the butler as though she were engaging in perfectly common behavior. "I'll be back in a moment."

The rain was light, but it would still ruin her dress and hair. Setting one hand uselessly above her head she scanned the street. Carriages lined each side, as it was the height of the ball and few guests would be leaving this early.

Hawthorne was near the end of the line. One hand rested on the carriage door handle, his head was bent as he spoke with someone. The carriage lamp above them threw shadows beneath the brim of Hawthorne's hat. More shadows ranged beneath the stranger's cap so she could not see his face. Ill-fitting clothes covered the stranger's body. Not a peer, not a servant, but a commoner. Or someone disguised as a commoner.

Metal glinted in the lamplights. A pistol. She could not tell who carried it, but—wait. Hawthorne. It was in Hawthorne's hand. Her stomach pitched, rolled. She scrubbed the back of her hand over her mouth.

She could not look away. Hawthorne and the stranger bent over the pistol, shoulders hunched. It was impossible to know what they were doing. Then the stranger slunk around the side of the carriage and disappeared into the dark.

She surged forward, not certain if she meant to stop the stranger or confront Hawthorne. *Either. Both.* But uncertainty dragged at her feet. It could be an innocent exchange. It was possible.

Hawthorne stood alone, water sluicing the brim of his hat. The pistol hung from his fingers. Not tightly, not loosely. Comfortably. Easily. Then he leapt into his carriage. The driver didn't even wait for the door to close before the carriage began moving through the rain and mud.

She'd hesitated too long. She'd faltered, and he was gone. He was disappearing into the night. He could be doing anything.

A raindrop slid between her breasts. A cold finger of suspicion. Hawthorne was the man most often in Jeremy's company. His confidant. If anyone knew what Jeremy was, it would be Hawthorne.

If he did, then she'd been betrayed again.

Anger burgeoned in her. More lies. More betrayal. It would be as easy for Hawthorne as Jeremy to hide the truth from her. After all, she never questioned Jeremy. Why would she question Hawthorne?

She looked past the rain as the hot fury growing in her fought against the frigid drops pelting her face. Hawthorne's carriage was an indistinguishable shadow in the night.

Secrets. She would discover Hawthorne's. And then Jeremy's.

Without hesitation. She would not falter when it mattered most.

Chapter 20

"CHRIST, LILIAS, IT's barely dawn." Hawthorne slammed the hackney door shut and threw himself into the seat opposite her. Shadows formed circles beneath his eyes and the stubble on his chin told her he'd yet to shave.

"I need to speak with you," she said. "It's urgent."

"So urgent you must arrive before the sun?" The words bulleted at her, rife with irritation.

"It's nearly nine. Hardly dawn." Temper shortened the words. She was still riding on a wave of fury. Had he, too, lied to her? She might not be able to confront Jeremy, but Hawthorne was here.

The carriage jerked, then began to roll. The sound of wheels on cobblestone accompanied the clop of hooves.

Hawthorne sat up straight. "Where are we going?"

His coat was buttoned crooked. He must not have been dressed yet when she sent the hired boy to the door with her note. She always thought him handsome but at the moment, she could not recall why.

"The coachman will drive up and down the nearby streets while we talk." Her fingers twitched on the object hidden in the folds of her skirt. In her mind she saw Hawthorne and the stranger, standing in the rain the night before. The glint of metal. The surreptitious glance around the street.

Perhaps he was innocent. Perhaps he was an assassin. She was determined to find out—whatever the consequences. Because death was better than betrayal and ignorance. Slowly, she raised the pistol she had been hiding beneath her soft, innocent skirts. No trembling. No hesitation. If he came at her, she would have the upper hand. She cocked the gun and looked down the barrel into Hawthorne's shocked eyes.

Not just shock, but fear. Her heart constricted, a painful reminder that this man had helped her through the darkest of days.

But she would not hesitate again.

"Tell me of Jeremy's death." Her voice held so much more command than she had expected.

"Lilias." Very carefully, Hawthorne drew himself upright. "Perhaps we should discuss whatever has overset you." The patronizing tone set her teeth on edge.

"Stop." The pistol jumped in her hand, but didn't discharge, thank goodness. The wood was cool against her skin, the pearl inlay warm. Irony, wasn't it, that she pointed Jeremy's own pistol at Hawthorne? "Don't treat me like an imbecile. We've known each other a long time—for good or ill. You owe me the truth."

His breath seemed slow and steady. Why was hers ricocheting around in her lungs?

"I'm not certain what the issue is, Lilias. Why don't you enlighten me?"

An awful shuddering pain worked its way from the pit of her stomach to her throat. She hadn't expected the betrayal to be twice as bad this time. It was worse. Instead of a ghost betraying her, it was a flesh and blood man. One that could both bleed and die.

"Jeremy was living a second life. A secret one." She did not say *assassin*. Could not. Despite the anger and fear roiling in her, she kept the word inside. If Hawthorne was one of them, he didn't need the word. He would already know. "The things he did were horrible, and he might have been murdered for them."

Hawthorne's intake of breath was as discordant as the gunshot would have been. "You cannot be serious."

"You were the man most often in his company, and you were there when he was injured. You brought him to me.

Therefore, I must ask what you know. And I must ask how Jeremy was wounded. Exactly."

"Murder." He said the word as though it were foreign, his pupils dilating. He did not answer her question. "A second life. Impossible."

"Don't play games with me." Her hand shook. She struggled to steady it and the pistol. The lump forming in her throat burned. "I have proof. It's true. And I have to believe you were working with him."

"I—" Jason lurched in the carriage seat, like a child's marionette. "No."

She set her finger to the trigger as tears gathered. She blinked, refusing to let them fall. "Tell me what happened when he died. Tell me all of it."

"I feel as though I've been dropped into a storybook." He raked a hand through his hair. "I've told you already. It was a French soldier. A sabre cut."

"It *was* a French soldier, or it *looked like* a French soldier?" Anyone could put on soldier's garb. She had done so herself.

"My God." Hawthorne stared at her, as though he had never quite seen her before. "I don't know if he truly was a French soldier. It was a bloody battlefield. I was a hundred yards away, fighting a damned soldier myself. I saw a man in a blue coat. I saw the sabre." He stopped, licked his lips. They were chapped. "It was a battlefield."

There was no answer there, and she wanted answers. Some part of her knew that there may never be an explanation. But this was the only man that could provide her one, and he was giving her nothing.

Straightening her arm, she aimed the pistol at Jason's head. Her stomach churned and her heart pumped wildly beneath her stays.

"Where did you go last night?"

His brows careened together, as though shocked by the change in subject. His eyes darted toward the pistol. "I was at the ball. You were there, too. I saw you."

"After the ball. I saw you speak with someone and then get into your carriage. It was the height of the engagement. You should have stayed for a while yet."

"I had to meet someone."

"Not good enough." She wasn't certain how she had the courage to keep the pistol so steady.

"Lilias." His eyes were dark as they flickered over her face, then to the pistol. His tone softened to a whisper. "I have a daughter. She was ill."

"A—a daughter?" Shock wasn't a gentle wave. It was a deluge. "But you had a pistol."

"I'm ashamed to say I haven't the blunt to keep my daughter and her mother properly. I've enough to keep them from being hungry, to keep a roof over their heads. But not enough to put that roof in Mayfair. I carry the pistol against footpads when I visit them." Humiliation flushed his cheeks beneath the night's growth of beard. His hand reached out, then fell back into his lap. "My daughter is ill, and I needed to be with her. I have only just returned."

The unshaven jaw, the mismatched coat buttons. His tired face. They all fell into place.

"Why did you never tell me?"

"A man doesn't tell a lady about his bastards." He scrubbed a hand over his face. "I don't know what the hell is going on, Lilias. I don't know anything about murder or double lives." What was truth? What was a lie? She could not tell. But his eyes were full of simultaneous shock and compassion. He ran his hand over the stubble on his jaw, but it did nothing to erase the haggard expression. Or the pull of his heavy, tired lids.

She couldn't believe it of him. She just couldn't.

Hawthorne was no assassin. If he was, he likely would have tried to kill her by now.

The gun fell to her lap. "I'm sorry," she whispered. The rumble of passing carriages nearly drowned out her words.

"Lilias." Hawthorne half rose in his seat, as though to approach her. But there was nowhere to go within the confines of the hackney. "Tell me what's happened. This is not like you." Then his lips quirked. "I take it back. It is like you. I just didn't expect it within the civilized confines of London."

"I don't feel civilized." She felt numb, even as her chest ached and her belly roiled. "I can't tell you the details. If you

In Bed with a Spy

133

don't already know—" She broke off and shook her head. "Tell me more of his death."

"I don't understand how that will change anything." When she only watched him steadily, he sighed in resignation. "It was after the heavy cavalry charge led by Uxbridge. Losses were significant, though the charge was successful. Some of the heavy cavalry lost its cohesion, but we kept control of ours and mounted a countercharge. We couldn't rein in the men. I saw him fall—Lilias. What do you think he has done?"

She gritted her teeth. "Tell me the rest."

"I watched Jeremy fall. It was a sabre cut across his chest, another on his thigh. You saw the wounds yourself. He fell from the horse, but his foot was tangled in the stirrup. I—" He stopped, swallowed. "I managed to catch the animal before Jeremy was dragged too far."

She hissed out a breath. She couldn't help it. There had been much worse on the battlefield—she'd inflicted worse on her enemies. But she'd seen that battlefield. Jeremy would have been dragged over uneven ground. Over the bodies of other men. She closed her eyes, but the image was stark against the darkness of her lids.

"And so I brought him away from the battlefield," Hawthorne finished.

"I remember when the note came to the farm where I was staying." Pain could have twin forces. Death and betrayal. Loss and lies. *"Major Fairchild has fallen.* That was all the note said." She saw again the grim face of the soldier that had brought the news before he returned to the front. Then there had been the hard ride to the battlefield.

And she remembered the gray face of the man she'd married and the bloody sabre cut across his chest. She choked, and the tears began to drop onto her fisted hands.

"Oh, Lilias." Hawthorne drew her in, his arms coming around her. "I wish you would explain."

Strong. Comforting. A friend's arms. Arms she could trust. Burying her face into his shoulder, she let tears of loss flow, exorcising the second round of grief that accompanied the second loss of her husband.

As her tears dried, she realized he was a little awkward

about holding her, as though he couldn't quite figure out where to put his hands and still observe propriety. She smiled. Wiping the tears from her cheeks, she pulled away. Catherine was right. He was a good man.

"Jeremy did horrible things, Hawthorne. Horrible. The life he lived—well. It wasn't what I thought."

"Whatever acts you believe he's committed, it must be a mistake." He sounded so certain.

"He lied. Everything was a lie." She hated to shatter Hawthorne's certainty. "He was never where he said he'd be. He would meet with strange people, men watched where we slept. He would jump at the slightest noise, he was often worried. He hid things from me."

"He was a soldier at war. He had to protect the woman he loved, not to mention command his men. He might have hidden the worst of war from you, but he was always honorable."

Her fingers convulsed around the pistol. Hawthorne was wrong. Jeremy was anything but honorable.

THE ADDER'S GAZE did not leave the unmarked carriage carrying Lilias. He really would have to ensure his men killed her now. She was beyond a slight danger to him and had fallen into the realm of deadly. Not because of the weapon, but because of her unpredictability.

She was ever a surprise. He had learned that long ago.

The carriage stopped at the doors of Fairchild House. He had been waiting for her to return. She must have instructed the coachman to drive around or he would not have arrived before her.

He saw her fingers first as she set them into the footman's assisting hand. Her gloves matched the dull gray of her pelisse. An odd choice for her. Gray was not her best color. Scarlet was her color. Not the bright cherry red the debutantes wore, but the deep, vivid red that pulsed with energy and passion.

He couldn't smell her from across the street, but he knew her scent. Lust. Sex. Ready as ripe fruit waiting to be plucked. He went hard just thinking of it. Of her. It had always been her. He'd tried to pretend she wasn't a weakness, but he dreamed of her.

Desperate hunger tore through him as he pictured her face

when he plunged into her. It was an old fantasy. She would wrap her legs around him, grip his shoulders with her long, elegant fingers. He knew the passion she hid beneath her curves. He wanted it. Under his hands. Under his body. His breathing grew ragged. Raw. Something dark clawed in him. His hands fisted and he imagined her hips beneath his fingers. Imagined driving himself into her, harder and harder, until she screamed with it.

He couldn't quite breathe. He was hard as stone and damn near spilling his seed in his breeches. But he could still see her across the cobblestone street, even with the haze of lust clouding his vision. He'd almost forgotten her pistol in his violent need, but the watery sunlight caught the glint of metal.

He beat back his hunger and narrowed his eyes, focusing on the metal peeking between her glove and the dull fabric of her pelisse. She was hiding the weapon from the footman as she glided up the front steps.

It was her husband's pistol. He recognized the pearl-handled weapon easily enough. It was too big to fit in her reticule, so at least she couldn't carry it everywhere without being seen. Even inside Fairchild House, she could not hide it. But it was still a dangerous weapon wielded by a woman with a volatile temper and little fear.

To be aimed at him, when she chose.

The price on her head would increase. A woman with a weapon and the willingness to kill could not be allowed to find him. Yet he could not kill her himself. Even a hint of his involvement and his career, his reputation, would be forfeit.

He'd issued his orders, but the Adders had yet to strike. They were biding their time, waiting for an opportunity to make her death appear as an accident.

But he couldn't afford to wait for a convenient opportunity.

Chapter 21

"SHALL I TAKE your pelisse, Mrs. Fairchild?" The butler closed the door of Fairchild House and reached for her outerwear in a vain attempt to do his job.

"Thank you, Graves, but I will be going back out in a few moments." Lilias moved away, keeping her hand to the side and out of view. She was lying through her teeth. She needed the pelisse to hide the pistol. "I shall keep my pelisse on."

Graves sent her the silent stare butlers excelled at. "As you wish, ma'am." He disappeared into the quiet recesses of Fairchild House, leaving Lilias alone in the hall.

She looked down at the butt of the weapon. Delicate pearl flowed from a warm cream to a pale yellow, then back again. Such a pretty color. It had felt alive in her hand when she aimed it at Hawthorne. She couldn't decide if that terrified her or not.

"Oh, good," Catherine trilled. "You're back."

Lilias jumped a foot at least. Thumping her pounding chest with her free hand, she turned around as Catherine brushed past her.

"Do come into the salon, dear," the older woman said, traipsing through the open door.

"Ah. Hm." She couldn't go into the salon to chat with Jeremy's pistol still clutched in her hand. Thank goodness she had been facing the other way. Catherine had not seen the weapon.

Catherine's turbaned head poked around the doorjamb. "Well?" She blinked. "Are you coming?"

"Yes, of course. Just for a moment." She didn't enter the room, but hovered in the doorway.

"I wanted to talk to you about attending the opera." Catherine settled into a spindly chair with curved legs.

"Yes?" She could barely concentrate with the blasted pistol behind her back. It felt as though she were waving a flag behind her—one that was embroidered with the word *Lie*.

"I do so want to see Miss Byrne in *The Beggar's Opera*." Catherine pulled a basket from beside the chair. She rummaged through it and pulled out her latest embroidery project. White curls bounced around her face. "Perhaps Grant's box is available tomorrow evening. Unless, of course, you have a previous engagement with Angelstone?"

"Angelstone?" She nearly dropped the pistol.

"You haven't come to that type of understanding then, have you?" Catherine's eyes lit from within. "Then you're still in that lovely phase where you are having fun."

Lilias sighed and closed her eyes. She needed one moment of quiet thought. One moment. She couldn't balance assassinations and pistols and operas with the logistics of an affair. When she opened her eyes, Catherine was regarding her with amusement.

"Have fun with that rake, darling." Catherine's needle poked through a swatch of thin linen. "There aren't very many of his type around."

Footsteps rang on the hall floor. Lilias whirled, still trying to keep the damn pistol hidden from the front door and Catherine.

Graves set his hand on the front door handle, waiting. He had a sixth sense for visitors. A moment later, a quick rhythm was knocked out on the front door. Graves waited just the right amount of time before pulling open the door. A draft of cool fresh air blew into the hall.

Three women stood on the steps. They were decked in jaunty hats and military-style pelisses, though one of them wore the most garish shade of pink. Curls of mahogany and gray and blond-brown waved in the wind.

"The Dowager Marchioness of Angelstone, Elise, Lady Angelstone and Mrs. Whitmore." The oldest of the three ladies held out a card for Graves, looking as harsh as any British general. She stopped, her hand in midair, when she spied Lilias.

Lovely. Just lovely. Angel's family had come for an unexplained social call when she was still idiotically holding Jeremy's pistol and trying to hide it from Catherine. As though threatening a man with a pistol wasn't enough excitement for the day. She needed to dispose of the weapon. Quickly. Before someone noticed she was acting as though she belonged in Bedlam.

Graves cleared his throat. He would have normally put the ladies in a salon while he checked to see if Lilias and Catherine were at home and receiving callers. But here she was. Clearly at home.

Devil take it. She couldn't disappear with the pistol while the Whitmores stared at her from the doorstep.

"Lady Angelstone," she called to the dowager. "Please. Come in. We are most certainly at home." Sweat slicked her palms and dampened the inside of her gloves. She didn't know the Whitmores aside from the briefest of acquaintance at the concert. There was no reason these women would come to call.

No reason but Angel.

The three women on the doorstep of Fairchild House moved into the entryway. Skirts rustled, boots clicked on the floor. The scent of rain came with them and she saw that the sky had clouded over. A storm hung in the air.

Catherine whispered from just beyond the salon door. "Do you know them? I have not been introduced."

Lilias shook her head and hoped the dowager couldn't hear her mother-in-law.

"I don't think one is supposed to call on her son's paramour." Catherine's whisper quieted as she returned to her seat. "I wonder what they could want?"

"I can only imagine," Lilias muttered. Raising her voice, she said, "Please, join us in the salon."

The dowager's sharp eyes scanned Lilias's pelisse, the entry, the paintings, the stair. One quick glance to take it all in. Behind her, the other two ladies watched Lilias with bright-eyed curiosity. The brunette was pretty in that soft, round, comforting way.

She'd been amused at the concert. The other wore the hideously pink pelisse and studied Lilias with narrowed eyes.

Lilias had, apparently, become a display. Irritation pricked. Still, she pasted a gracious smile on her face. "Please," she said again, gesturing into the salon.

She waited as the three visitors walked into the salon, her frantic gaze bouncing around the hall. She still had the pistol to hide. With the vigilant Graves remaining in the entry, there was nothing she could do.

Disaster loomed on the horizon.

Catherine, bless her, was already welcoming their guests. "We are quite pleased to have you join us. Lilias has just arrived from—" Catherine's voice faltered.

"A walk," Lilias filled in. "My apologies, I have not yet removed my pelisse." All eyes turned her way. Four gazes started at her head, moved down to her feet, then back up again. Well. Now she *had* to remove her outerwear. And she had to distract them. "We were just remarking upon Lady Milbanke's concert. Catherine, didn't you mention how much you enjoyed it?"

The eyes swung away from her and she sighed in relief as Catherine began to chatter. Lilias stepped into the room and edged along the wall. There was a potted plant only a few feet away with conveniently abundant foliage. It would do for the pistol's short-term hiding place.

". . . But I did tell Lilias she should dance more often."

The eyes came her way again. She huffed out a breath. The plant was only a few steps away. She could drop the pistol into it—if only they would look the other direction—

"I do love music." That bright tone sounded idiotic coming from her mouth. She looked at the dowager, hoping to deflect attention. "Lady Angelstone, do you like music? You seemed to enjoy the concert."

The eyes swung away again.

"Yes, I do, indeed. Particularly violin music." The dowager's severe face softened. "My son plays, you know. He's quite accomplished."

Lilias's fingers convulsed. The pistol fell into the potted soil with a dull *thwack*. The eyes turned to her again. "I didn't know." The whisper tumbled from her lips.

Angel *had* lied. She'd thought perhaps she'd been mistaken. She couldn't think why it would matter, except—no, there was no reason why he should lie. What did they share? Sex? Murder? There was very little holding them together.

Yet she felt an inexplicable something luring her in to bind her to him. She wanted to know he played the violin. She wanted to know his favorite food. Whether he preferred winter or summer.

"Yes. He plays the violin." The dowager spoke again. Her voice was sweeter, her eyes brighter.

"Has he played since he was young?" Did those words come from her lips? Lilias moved forward. Part of her thought of the pistol and hoped it wasn't visible through the leaves of the potted plant. The other part of her thought of Angel's long fingers moving over the strings of the violin. The same fingers that skimmed over her skin with such expertise would play a violin with heat and desire and pain. All the things needed to create beautiful music.

She felt the pang in the deepest part of her heart. Music was of the soul. It would be Angel's soul. Yes, he would guard that.

"He started playing when he was only six." The dowager's dark eyes were fathomless.

"He plays almost every day. The instrument comes alive under his hands." The widowed marchioness, Elise, spoke softly. "Sometimes it makes me cry."

Lilias dropped into a chair. She didn't notice the plush cushion, but she did feel the tightening of her pelisse as she tried to snatch a breath. Swift fingers unbuttoned the garment.

"I have never heard him play." But oh, she wanted to.

"He is attempting to teach my daughter, Maggie." The widow of the second son, Lady Whitmore, laughed. "She's abysmal, but he keeps trying."

"Do you play?" the dowager asked Lilias.

"Not even a little. I cannot play any instrument. Nor can I sing, I'm afraid." She intended her laugh to be merry, but it sounded strangely sad. "I do enjoy music. Very much. The violin particularly. It has the most—" She struggled to find the word. "Emotion. Depth."

"Ah." The dowager's eyes focused on her. Lilias fought the urge to squirm as silence descended.

Catherine broke it. "We were just discussing the opera. I was hoping to see Miss Byrne in *The Beggar's Opera* in the next few days. Have you seen it yet? I have heard her performance is stunning."

"We are attending the opera next week." Elise, the younger marchioness, smoothed her pink pelisse over her lap.

The dowager turned her head to look directly at Lilias. "Perhaps you and your mother-in-law would like to accompany us. There is enough room in the box, and Angel is escorting us."

Tentative approval. She recognized it in the slight curve to the dowager's lips, the tilt of her head. Unfortunately, the dowager would be thinking marriage. But there was nothing between her and Angel besides lust and espionage. Marriage was not even a glimmer, nor did she want it to be.

She almost said no, they could not attend the opera. She would not lead his family to believe there was more between them. But she wanted to see him again somewhere that was not clandestine. Somewhere not under the cover of darkness.

"We would enjoy it very much," Lilias said.

"Good." The dowager stood. "We must take our leave. But I look forward to seeing both of you later this week."

The rest of the women stood and moved toward the door. Platitudes fell from multiple lips. The dowager set a hand on Lilias's arm and held her back.

"Mrs. Fairchild, thank you for receiving us today." Dark eyes held Lilias's gaze. The hand on her arms squeezed lightly.

"Yes, of course." She looked down at the dowager marchioness's kid glove. Tiny fingers, but they held strength. She would have thought them comforting, if she weren't being eyed by her lover's mother.

The dowager leaned closer. "I don't think the dirt will be good for the pistol. You might want to retrieve it quickly."

"Ah." What could she say? "Hm."

"I won't ask why you have it—though I should—because I learned long ago with my son not to ask such questions. And if you can receive us so graciously with a pistol behind your back, you shall do nicely for my son." The dowager squeezed her arm again, and this time the squeeze radiated approval. "When you are ready."

With a final, brilliant smile, the dowager and her daughters-in-law left Fairchild House.

Lilias dropped into the salon chair and ignored the bevy of feminine footsteps in the hall.

She had once been married to an assassin. She couldn't possibly spend the remaining days of her life married to a spy.

A woman could not make that many poor choices in a single lifetime.

Chapter 22

"WHAT THE BLOODY hell do you mean, 'Mrs. Fairchild approached Hawthorne with a pistol?'"

Very slowly, very deliberately, Angel stood. He set his hands on the desktop and stared menacingly at his informant. It wasn't quite rage gripping him. Disbelief, perhaps. Shock, even. Utter incredulity, most certainly.

"She approached Hawthorne with a pistol, my lord. I caught a glimpse of it in her hand as she left Fairchild House and entered the carriage." Jones did not blink. He simply continued in his report. He might have been recounting his dinner meal. "The carriage then went to Hawthorne's lodgings. A boy was hired to take a message to the door. Hawthorne joined her in the carriage and they proceeded to drive around the block a few times. Then Hawthorne was set down in front of his lodgings again."

Lilias had approached Hawthorne. With a weapon. She must have confronted him. There was no other possibility. Damn the woman, if Hawthorne were an Adder she had tipped his hand. Four years of secrets and grief and hard work, gone in a fit of temper.

He set his hand over the round medallion on the corner of his desk. Small and silver, and washed of Gemma's blood—but never clean.

"Where is Mrs. Fairchild, at this moment?" He needed to know so he could throttle her.

"At home, my lord. It is nearly eleven in the evening, and she did not attend any social engagements this evening. I believe she has already retired." Jones stepped aside as Angel strode past.

He didn't bother calling the carriage. He went to the mews to saddle his horse himself.

He knew which bedroom belonged to Lilias. He had spent numerous nights these last weeks standing watch outside Fairchild House. He knew her nightly habits. She would read. A light novel, perhaps. Poetry. Then her light would be snuffed out and she would sleep. Sometimes the candle would be relit in the early hours of the morning. Nightmares, he suspected. He had seen the pattern a few nights himself and Jones had noted it as well.

The room was still lit when he tapped on the glass of her window. He could have entered on his own—there were ways to accomplish such things—but it would be faster and easier for her to open the window. And he was clinging to the side of Fairchild House like a damn spider to a chandelier, miles above the earth and just as precariously.

Her head jerked up, her eyes unfocused for the briefest of moments. The book she read fell from her hands to the bed. He might have noticed the long rope of braided hair over her shoulder. Or perhaps the candlelight playing on her collarbone as she pushed back the coverlet.

He was too infuriated by the case of dueling pistols set prominently on a chest of drawers.

Then she was flying across the floor in a blur of white linen and bare feet. The window popped open and her fingers scrabbled for the lapels of his coat. She drew him in, over the windowsill and onto the carpeted floor. He'd be gratified under other circumstances at her hurried movements. Just now he was itching to battle with her.

"Have you no brains in your head?" She shoved lightly at him, then turned toward the glass. "You are three stories above the ground!" The window closed with a snick.

"You confronted Hawthorne today." The idea of it, the

picture of Lilias trapped in a carriage with a potential assassin, chilled his blood.

He saw only her back as she reached for the window latch, but it went rigid. Shoulders tightened. She stilled, hand poised just above the fastener. He did not have even an ounce of sympathy for her.

"I did speak with Hawthorne." She did not turn around. Her hand landed on the fastener, twisted it to lock the window. Her skin shone translucent in the candlelight, revealing blue veins beneath. Then her fingers flexed and dropped away. She turned to face him, eyes bright, color high. "He is not an Adder."

She might have compromised everything. Everything. Years of investigations into assassinations. Monarchs, politicians, countries. Alliances with Britain. So many men and women murdered by the Death Adders. Gemma. Even her husband.

"Do you know what you've done?" He stalked across the room toward the chest of drawers. The pistol case lay atop it, as volatile as if the weapons were alive.

"I believe you are about to enlighten me." Temper sparked in her voice.

Well, he had temper of his own. "If Jason Hawthorne is a Death Adder, you've warned him. He'll go to ground before I've gathered enough evidence to—" He stopped the flow of words. *Link Hawthorne to Gemma's murder.* The words were just there, on the tip of his tongue. He swallowed them. "To link him to the Death Adders."

He flipped open the lid of the pistol case. They were exceptional pieces. All the more reason she should not touch them.

"Hawthorne isn't an Adder. I'm sure of it."

She stalked forward and flipped the lid of the case down. It snapped on his fingers and he stupidly jumped back, no better than a small boy caught doing something he shouldn't.

"Did you confront him with a pistol?" He flipped the lid open again. The pearl handles of the pistols glowed yellow-gold. He picked up one of the weapons, tested the weight, the shape. "With one of these?"

"Yes. They were Jeremy's. And don't insult me by asking if I can use them."

It didn't matter if she could use them or not. He sighted down the barrel, aiming it at the wall. "You might have died, Lilias. Even with the pistol, if he were an assassin, he could have killed you before you even fired a shot. It was an utterly foolish idea."

"He is my close friend. I have every right to—"

"No, you don't." He turned to look at her, still aiming the weapon at the wall. That she even thought she could approach an Adder was beyond bearing. Voice cold and even, he said, "This is my investigation. The *government's* investigation. You are impeding and interfering with an investigation affecting His Majesty."

She sucked in a breath. The linen of her nightgown rose with the indignant movement. "This affects my life as well. It was *my* husband that was an assassin. My friend who is under suspicion now."

She reached for the weapon in his hand. Did she think to wrest it from him? It might be loaded. This proved she was incapable of understanding the gravity of her actions. He lifted it high above his head. She would be unable to take it unless she climbed up his body.

"You're being ridiculous." Eyes narrowed to dangerous slits, she began to circle him. "Have you been reduced to childhood games? Keep the toy above your head, so other children can't steal it from you?"

Confound it, she had a point. But he didn't lower his hand. "I want your word, Lilias, that you won't interfere again."

"I won't give it." She pressed her lips together and set her hand on the lid of the case, though she did not touch the second pistol tucked into the velvet. A subtle threat. "I'm part of this."

"Only when I allow it, and I do not."

Her eyes went dark with fury, her chin rose, spine straightened. If possible, she'd grown by inches. "Only when you *allow* it?"

He lowered his hand, slowly and carefully, keeping the pistol pointed at the ground. He knew he was breaking some tie between them. Whatever relationship was building on their attraction would be broken. But he could not think of another way to keep her safe. "There is no reason for you to be involved. I have gathered all the information I need from you. I will manage Hawthorne."

She stepped forward, making no move toward the weapon. She must have learned not to approach an armed man. But her eyes were just as lethal as the pistol. "Bastard."

He did not answer. So he was—at least in character.

Color rose high on her cheeks. Not embarrassment. Anger. "Get out of my room."

"Do not approach Hawthorne or any other Adder alone. Ever. Stay out of the investigation."

She ignored him. "Give me the pistol." She held out her hand, palm up.

He was tempted to take the set with him. He should, for her own good. But leaving her unarmed didn't sit well, either. She'd only obtain another pistol, he was sure. He knew that much about her.

"Is it loaded?"

"No. Jeremy taught me how to safely unload a pistol when—" She broke off, let her hand drop. "Your mother and sisters-in-law called upon me today. Your mother saw the pistol."

"I beg your pardon?" He couldn't quite understand what she'd said. The words did not make sense.

"Your mother called upon me. Did you ask her to?"

"I did not." His mother had been in Fairchild House, on a social call. That was not good. In fact, it was very, very bad for his marital prospects. He'd have to explain the pistol away as well. "I'll set her straight. She won't inconvenience you again."

"It is not your mother that is the nuisance. It is you." She held out her hand again, her eyes daring him to keep the pistol from her.

Oh, it stung to give her the weapon. But leaving her with nothing—he narrowed his eyes and watched how she handled it. Gingerly. Respectfully. And quite comfortably. Frighteningly so.

"Stay away from Hawthorne," he ground out. "Don't embark on any more personal missions."

She paused in the act of setting the pistol in its velvet bed. "Not even when it elicits information? Such as the fact that Hawthorne has a bastard daughter? That he has no knowledge of Jeremy's actions?"

"Damnation," he whispered. He scrubbed a hand over his face. Jones hadn't discovered the bastard. Yet.

She had learned something useful. And wasn't that a thorn in a spy's side. She knew it, too. He couldn't let that matter. One incorrect step, one word in the wrong person's ear, and she would be dead.

"Do you think Hawthorne would not lie to you?"

"Yes. If he were an Adder, he would." She turned to face him, her eyes cold and distant. "I do not believe he is lying."

"You do not believe." Well, they would see about that. "No more, Lilias. Your word."

None of the sensual warmth he'd come to recognize was visible in her face. Only disinterest. She angled her head. Not a gesture of assent, not a refusal.

That, too, did not matter. For the foreseeable future she would be watched by his agents.

"Good night, my lord." Not Angel, nor even Angelstone. *My lord.*

Very well. "Good night, Mrs. Fairchild."

He strode to the window and opened the latch. It took only a moment to push it open, hoist himself onto the ledge and reach for the rope hanging from the roof.

"Do take care not to fall to your death," she said. "It would leave a nasty mess in the morning."

Chapter 23

SHE FOUGHT HER way out of slumber riddled with dreams. Jeremy's face blurring with Angel's. Hawthorne. Grant. They were all a tangle in her mind.

Fog muddled her brain. The throbbing behind her eyes told her the tears she'd wanted to shed after Angel's departure still lingered there. When she opened her eyes the nearly complete darkness smothered her. But perhaps it was only the coverlet tucked close around her face. One part of her mind thought to pull the warm, thick coverlet aside and free herself from the heavy darkness.

But she didn't move.

Awareness slid into her, a sense of unease that sent her pulse skittering. Breathing evenly and carefully, she let her eyes roam the room. Beyond the coverlet, moonlight filtered in to create silver shadows. She let the disquiet hum beneath her skin for a moment. A breeze fluttered over her face.

Her mind screamed the warning. *Move!*

She rolled fast and hard, over and over until she dropped onto the floor beside the bed. Scrambling up, she looked through moonlight to the other side of her bed. Fear shot through her as the figure dressed in black leapt nimbly onto the bed. The cloth he wore over his nose and mouth fluttered with his breath.

An arm slashed out, silent and quick as a snake. Reflex

shoved her back. Blood roared in her ears and energy pumped through her. She shrieked, one shrill note of fury, even as she grasped the bedcovers and yanked with strength born of terror. The man staggered and lost his footing. He toppled, falling with a grunt onto the soft bed.

She ran, though there were pitiful few places to go. As she rushed around the bed for the door, the man hissed out a breath and jumped from the bed. Sheer luck had her guessing his intention and darting away.

"Get out!" she shouted.

From somewhere beyond the closed hall door she heard a man's faint call. "Lilias? What's happening?"

Grant! Her mind shouted it, but her breath clogged her throat and stopped the words.

The intruder lunged. Her feet tangled in her nightgown as she scrambled away. The black knife arced through the air. *Too close.* Throwing up a hand, she blocked the strike. The blade pricked her arm, a white-hot scratch, and fueled her temper.

Instinct drove her. *Fight. Survive. Kick!* Her foot connected with his thigh. Bone and flesh was solid beneath her heel. He grunted, staggered, then glanced at the door. Footsteps pounded through the hall below where Grant and Catherine slept. More footsteps sounded above. Servants.

A minute. Two. It was all she needed to stay alive.

Catherine's voice called out, muffled through the walls and floors. "Lilias?" She must be right behind Grant, only slowed by age.

Dear Lord, don't let Catherine be hurt.

The intruder whirled away. He sprinted toward the open window and the cool breeze that had saved her life. He paused on the sill, looked back once, then disappeared into the night.

She raced over to the window and peered out. He dropped onto the small iron balcony jutting out street-side from the floor below, then scrambled nimbly over the edge of the balcony and was gone.

A Death Adder. She knew it—and had to hide it. She could not reveal the truth to Catherine and Grant.

Clarity narrowed her mind. She must move quickly. A hard jerk closed the window. Then the latch. Her robe would cover her wounded forearm. She could feel wetness on her sleeve, but it wasn't much, thank God. Nothing more than the tiniest brush with the blade.

Even as she shrugged into the robe, the door burst open.

"Lilias," Grant panted. His head turned right, left, as he scanned the room.

"I'm sorry." Her own breath was just as uneven. "I'm so sorry to wake you."

Catherine peeked into the room. Her nightcap was tipped sideways, nearly covering one eye. "What happened?"

"A nightmare, that's all." She shook her head and pressed her lips together. She dared not say more.

Grant focused his scrutiny on her face. She was grateful for the dark. He didn't speak, but only watched her with the intense care and fragile handling common after she began waking the household with screaming nightmares.

"Oh, my dear. I thought the nightmares had stopped." Catherine stepped into the room. Her hands worried the edges of the robe, as though not quite sure what to do with themselves. "A candle. You'll want light."

"No." The blood would be visible. Servants were gathering in the hall now. She could not let any of them see the blood. "I'm fine now that I'm awake. Truly."

"Are you certain?" Grant asked quietly. His robe fell open as he stepped to her. She could see the bare, muscled chest beneath for just a moment before he pulled it closed again.

"Yes." She wanted all of them out of her room, most particularly Grant. His bird-watcher's eyes were too observant.

A candle appeared behind Catherine in the hall. It flickered over the butler's face as he lifted it high. Wavering light bounced around her room. More blood was seeping onto her robe, though it was still only a little. She slid her right arm behind her back, hoping the movement looked natural.

"My lord?" The butler said from the hall.

Grant stared at Lilias, unblinking. After a long pause, he said, "All is well, Graves. Please return to your room."

"Yes, my lord." The light faded as he moved down the hall, herding lesser servants before him.

"Thank you, Grant. I'm grateful." More than she could say.

"What can I do for you, Lilias?" Catherine asked. Concerned wrinkles surrounded her eyes, showing her age.

"I really just want to be alone." Another lie. Another arrow through the heart. Turning, she moved away from them. She was careful to keep her bleeding arm out of sight. Even in the dark, she did not want to take the risk.

"Are you certain?" Catherine asked. Doubt tinged the words.

Lilias nodded. She could only hide the blood for so long. As much as she wanted the physical contact of a quick embrace, she could not.

"Very well, then. We shall leave you." Catherine was not in agreement. It was clear in the tightening of her lips, in the way she folded her hands in front of her. "But do come to my room if you need company."

"I will be fine." Guilt tugged at her. She was lying to the only family she had left.

"Good night," Catherine murmured as she quit the room. The tight angle of her shoulders told Lilias she would be angry tomorrow as well.

Grant remained a few steps into the room, utterly still and utterly focused on her. "What really happened?"

"Grant—"

"You can trust me." His voice was quiet and sure and comforting.

She wanted to give in and tell him everything. He would know what to do. He could help. She opened her mouth to tell him, but she could not. She'd already drawn Hawthorne in and shared more than she should—and placed him under suspicion. So she only shook her head and pressed her lips together.

He set a hand against her cheek. Cool and strong. She almost turned into it, but she could not quite burden him with murder.

"I'll respect your wishes, Lilias—for now. But I expect you to tell me eventually."

With a deep breath, she nodded. Perhaps she would tell him, once she decided how. "I suppose I have to say thank you again."

"I suppose you do." In what little light streamed in from the moon, she saw the corners of his lips quirk up. "Good night." He shut the door behind him.

Tensed, she stayed where she was until his footsteps faded.

Then she waited another full five minutes. The house quieted around her until she only heard the occasional creak. The faint sound of wheels and hooves filtered through the closed window, then the sound of laughter as someone passed on the street. Still she waited—ten more minutes, fifteen—until she was certain there was no one left awake.

Then she flew to the wardrobe and whipped it open.

Pushing past the stays, she pulled out a chemise and simple gown. She could only guess she had the gown she wanted. She couldn't risk lighting a candle to be sure. Peeling off her robe and nightgown, she carefully pulled the fabric away from the wound. She set her fingers to it. Barely a sting, and only a little sluggish bleeding.

Still more rummaging in her wardrobe yielded linen handkerchiefs. She took three of them, folded and tied them together before wrapping the makeshift bandage around her forearm.

She pulled on the chemise and gown. It was the one she'd sought. No buttons. It went on over her head and was cinched tight with a ribbon. Her breasts would look ridiculous without the stays, but it couldn't be helped. Drawing out her cloak, she threw it around her before sliding into a pair of half boots.

With the bloody nightclothes bundled in one arm and a reticule clutched in her hand, she snuck through the house and into the garden through the kitchen door, leaving it unlocked behind her.

In minutes she was out the back gate and sprinting through the mews to the street. Another five minutes and she was hailing a hackney a few streets away. When she gave the address to the jarvey he didn't even blink. Apparently the late night wanderings of the aristocracy were not of interest to him.

Arriving at her destination, Lilias paid the driver. With her bundle of clothes tucked in the crook of her arm, she scrambled up the front steps of the townhouse and knocked. There was no noise on the other side of the door, so she knocked again, louder.

"Please hear me," she whispered in the dark, and was shocked to find herself close to tears. But she had nowhere else to go. "*Please.*"

Relief coursed through her when she heard footsteps and

the scrape of the bolt through the wood. The door swung open.

"Bloody hell."

He was gold and tall and strong and just what she wanted at that moment. Even if he was a complete idiot.

She launched herself at him.

Chapter 24

HIS ARMS WERE full of gorgeous, warm woman. A bolt of lust shot through him, followed by irritation. Angel whipped her inside and shoved the door closed.

"Are you *cracked*?" He gripped her shoulders. "What are you doing here? It's bad enough I went in through your window. Now you're standing on my front step a few hours later?" Women could be mercurial, but not like this.

Setting her away from him, he studied her face in the bright light of the candelabra he'd brought with him. Her cheeks were flushed, her eyes bright. Light curls floated around her face. The rest of her hair was hidden by the hood of her cloak.

"I'm starting to wonder if I *have* gone daft." A strangled laugh bubbled from her throat. "It's not every day an assassin stabs a lady in her bed."

He stiffened and his fingers gripped her shoulders.

Not again. Please, not again.

"What happened? Are you hurt?" He pushed back the edges of her cloak. Ran his gaze and hands over her body. She batted his hands away, but he ignored her unspoken protest and studied her throat and chest and belly. A cursory glance showed no blood. His shoulders relaxed as that fear dwindled.

"Only a minor wound." She dismissed it with a quick

wave. "It's already stopped bleeding. But, Angel, there was a Death Adder in my room. *My room.*"

"You're a target." He sucked in a breath, held it while fury raced through him.

Her cheeks drained of color. "I suppose so."

"Come." With one hand he picked up the candelabra. With the other, he pulled her into his study. "Tell me."

She did, succinctly and without emotion, while she removed her cloak. He heard the control in her voice and saw it in the slow, deliberate movements of her hands to counteract their slight tremble. The panic he'd sensed in her when he first arrived had diminished. Fear remained, though. He saw that in her gorgeous eyes.

Good. It would keep her alive.

She pulled the cloak from her shoulders to reveal a simple, long-sleeved gown. The blond braid he pretended not to notice earlier tumbled free to brush her hips. The candlelight turned the pale blond to burnished gold.

A knock sounded on the open door. Jones stepped into the doorway, then pointed his pistol at the floor when Angel looked over. For once Jones looked disheveled. "I've inspected the premises, my lord, as you requested. All doors and windows are secure."

"Good. Lilias, is there any chance you were followed?"

"No."

"You're certain?"

"As I can be. I kept a close watch when I left."

"Then, Jones, I need you to contact Sir Charles. Tell him Mrs. Fairchild has been attacked. She's a target." And he had failed to protect her. He should have been on watch.

"Yes, my lord."

With soft footfalls, Jones moved down the hall. When Angel heard the front door latch behind the man, he turned to Lilias.

"Let me see the wound," he said.

She rubbed absently at her forearm. "It's nothing. Barely a scratch. It's already stopped bleeding."

"I'll be the judge of that."

She held out her arm. He could see a thick bulkiness beneath the fabric. She pushed up the sleeve to reveal a cloth tied around her forearm.

His fingers fluttered over the bandage. "Does it hurt?"

"Not any longer."

He hoped not. God, he hoped the wound was as minor as she'd said. He unwound the bandage and found it stuck to one small section of the wound. Her breathing caught as he peeled it away. Just one jerky intake.

"Am I hurting you?"

"No." Her breath was even and slow. Controlled.

"Tell me if I do." Small wounds could be sharply painful.

The bandage fell away. Relief tangled with guilt in his belly. The cut wasn't long, only three inches. It was narrow and thin and shallow. A scratch, she'd said. She was right. The curved, razor-sharp claws of a cat could have done worse. Still, it had bled.

"Angel, it's nothing."

Her skin was soft. Smooth. And marred by the wound. "You may have a scar," he said softly. He wished she would not. But scar or no scar, she would not forget tonight, he supposed.

"I have scars already." Her voice was just as quiet as his.

Looking up, he met her eyes. The bright blue cut hard into him. "I remember."

She breathed in. Long. Slow. Then she breathed out again. Controlled. She shifted, lashes swept down. The barely tamed braid swished in the air and brushed across his knuckles. The soft strands incited a low hum under his skin.

"I've a salve that will help it heal," he said, relinquishing her hand.

"I have something at Fairchild House as well."

"It's my duty to see to your comfort." He stood, looked down at her. She didn't need him. She could take care of herself well enough. What he couldn't decide was why he wanted so badly to do it for her. "Let me." He almost added *please*. But that would have made him sound ridiculous.

She sighed, a sound he accepted as acquiescence. Taking one of the candles, he hurried to the butler's pantry where he stored various salves and ointments. He'd used them on more than one occasion in the dead of night.

When he returned, she was pacing the room with a graceful

prowl. "If I'm a target, what do I do next?" She pinned him with bright blue eyes. "I can't go into hiding."

"Not easily, at any rate. Not until you must. Doing so would only raise eyebrows among the ton. Gossip would spread and the Death Adders would hear of it." He crossed to her and took her hand, pulling her toward the settee. She dropped onto it and let him apply the thick salve onto the cut.

"Then what do I do?"

He expected to hear some quaver or tremble in her voice. He did not. Her voice was even, her gaze steady. Both of those could be controlled. But even her hand and arm were free of tremors. She'd faced murder and escaped unfazed. Then again, she'd faced battle, bloodshed and widowhood.

"Your only choice—for now—is to allow us to keep a closer watch on you." His fingers smoothed the salve carefully over the cut. He rubbed in it with as much gentleness as he could. She didn't flinch.

"A close watch. What does that mean?"

"Sir Charles will likely assign more agents to watch Fairchild House. They will follow you to whatever social engagements you attend. Rides in the park, the lending library, Gunter's. Everywhere." It would be an imposition. The worst sort. But she had no choice. He couldn't see another way except to spirit her away, and that wouldn't flush out the assassins. "They'll follow you to ensure the Adders can't reach you."

She shook her head. "I don't want someone watching my every move." Now she looked up at him. "I had precious little privacy during my marriage. When you're on the march there is nowhere to be alone."

"The agents will be unobtrusive." Duty warred with understanding. With infinite care, he wrapped a clean bandage around her arm. In days it would heal, well before she was safe again.

"I'll know they are there."

"Yes." He smoothed out the bandage. Her skin was warm where it rested against his palm.

"How will it be, then?" Her resignation was a quiet undertone.

"Sir Charles will assign someone to lead the team and coordinate the watch. The agents on duty will rotate. If we can place someone within your household—a boot boy, a scullery maid—we will. If not, they will be stationed at both the front and rear of the house."

"I want you to lead the team." Her fingers clutched his arm, squeezed once. Her eyes were level with his. Features hard. "I shouldn't, after your manly display of protective idiocy a few hours ago. But I want no one else."

Protective idiocy. It might seem that way to her. But idiocy or not, he would protect her.

She turned her arm over so that their hands were palm to palm. Her smooth skin slid against his calloused palm. Warmth spread from his hand, to his belly, to his heart. Too much heat. Too much sensation. *Too much caring.* It was that step between being lovers, and something more.

He should have pulled away. Instead, he let her delicate fingers tangle with his. She sent him a slow, feline smile.

"Only you, Angel."

Chapter 25

"GO TO THE opera without me, Lilias. I couldn't possibly attend." Catherine flung an arm over her eyes. "It's the headache." She moaned it. Likely for dramatic effect.

Lilias wasn't fooled in the least. In the nine years she'd known Catherine, the woman had never had a headache—at least not one so debilitating she couldn't attend some ton function. She smiled down at the lady reclining pathetically in her bed. "I am worried about you, Catherine."

She rubbed a hand over Catherine's arm. The older woman wore a lovely gown of green silk with matching feathers in her hair. The feathers, poor things, were rather crushed against the pillow.

"It is just one of my headaches. I shall be fine." The arm covering Catherine's face twitched. One dark eye peeked out to dart around the room. "The dowager marchioness will be so disappointed."

Oh, the machinations. But two could play at that game.

"Perhaps, if you are feeling so poorly, I should stay home. I prefer to take care of you myself, instead of your maid doing so." She stifled a laugh when the green feathers in Catherine's hair jerked right along with their mistress's head.

"No!" Catherine's voice rose. "No, of course not," she added more quietly. "I wouldn't dream of ruining your evening. Please, go without me."

"If you are certain?"

"I couldn't concentrate, what with the pain." The sigh accompanying the words was pitiful.

Lilias rubbed Catherine's arm again before moving to the door. She opened it, stepped through. Then she tossed over her shoulder, "You know, you could have staged this an hour ago and saved yourself the trouble of changing into your evening gown."

A sharp gasp came from the bed. Lilias pulled the door shut, knowing full well Catherine would pop out of the bed the moment the door was closed. Laughing, and not bothering to quiet it, Lilias moved through Fairchild House to meet the waiting carriage.

Catherine's antics should have irritated her, but for whatever reason, Catherine thought she was furthering Lilias's cause—whether it was with Angel or his mother wasn't clear. Still, the stratagem was devised with love as its base. She couldn't be angry with love.

Graves held out a cape when she entered the front hall.

"Thank you, Graves." She smiled at the butler as he set the cape over her shoulders. "I shall be back late. I have a key, so please don't ask anyone to stay awake for me."

"No, ma'am."

Someone would, anyway. Probably Graves himself. "Have I ever said thank you for taking such good care of the family?"

"I beg your pardon, ma'am?" For once the calm butler look was gone from his face. He looked truly startled. Tugging on the hem of his jacket, he said, "We are in service. It is our duty—"

"No." She angled her head and smiled at him. "It is your duty to feed us and dress us and clean Fairchild House. It is not your duty to care for us. But you do, regardless."

Craggy features softened. Bushy brows rose. "I cleaned the soil from Major Fairchild's pistol, ma'am, and the potted plant is none the worse for wear."

The laugh burst out of her, as did the affection. "Oh, Graves, you are certainly the best butler in London." She leaned forward and kissed his cheek. "And a good friend."

"Er, thank you, ma'am." He blushed the most adorable shade of pink, spreading from protruding ear to protruding ear.

"Now, don't wait up for me."

"No, ma'am." He opened the front door. Stars, clouds and smoke from London's chimneys competed in the night sky. "Enjoy the opera."

She walked lightly down the steps, scanning the street as she went. It was night, but the street was lit from windows and carriage lamps. Vehicles moved, people walked, moonlight flickered.

Then she saw what she'd been looking for: the man at the corner. There was always a man at the corner of the street. The agents attempted to be unobtrusive. If she hadn't been watching for men walking up and down the street multiple times a day or returning to the same corner, she wouldn't have noticed them.

Their faces changed, but they were always there. It made her itchy. She felt their gazes between her shoulder blades when she walked in Hyde Park and at the nape of her neck when she shopped on Bond Street.

Tonight she would be at the opera with Angel. Well protected. Well guarded. Gathering up her skirts, she ascended into the carriage. The door slammed shut. She settled back against the seat and sighed. None of the agents watching her were Angel, though Jones had kept watch numerous times. She'd become used to seeing his face and short-cropped brown hair, he was there so often.

She hadn't seen Angel since the night the intruder had entered her room. A day had become two, then three. Then a week. Perhaps it was the separation making her itchy. She found herself wondering what he was doing at odd times of the day—and the night. She closed her eyes. Only a week, yet she wanted the brush of his hand against her cheek, his silky hair beneath her fingertips. She wanted the scent of him to surround her and the weight of him over her.

Her fingers clutched the handle of her reticule. Their behavior at the opera would be scrutinized by his mother, his sisters-in-law and all the attending gossips of the ton. She didn't care. She was determined to enjoy herself. With Angel.

He was waiting for her in the hall. She watched him as the footman led her to the curtains hiding the opera box. Leaning casually against the wall, Angel studied his pocket watch. It clicked shut. Closing his fist around it, he shook the watch lightly before tucking it into his pocket. He appeared to have no cares in the world. But his gaze was sharp when it scanned the hallway, the patrons. His back was to the wall.

She wondered if he'd learned those spylike characteristics through training, or if he'd been prone to them before.

Tawny eyes lit when they saw her. "Mrs. Fairchild." He scanned her from head to toe. Lips curved in an approving grin. "You look lovely."

She fought the urge to twirl. "Do you like the gown? I just had it made." The deep purple was entirely too bold. She loved it.

He held out his hand. She set hers in it. A simple gesture, yet it sent her heart racing. She was glad to see him, and he her. That lovely feeling warmed her right to her toes.

"Delectable." He brought her gloved fingers to his mouth. She felt his breath through the white satin. A smile still hovered on his lips. "Mrs. Fairchild, you are a treat."

Oh, his eyes were wicked. She pursed her lips, though it was hard to hide her smile. "A treat to gulp in one bite? Or a treat to savor?"

"Both. As the moment calls for." He leaned toward her. For a moment she thought he would kiss her. Her breath caught, suspended in a bubble of time. "I've missed you," he whispered.

"And I you, my lord." Angling her head, she peered between her lashes. That handsome face was a study in pleasure and longing and—she didn't know what. Need. Hunger. Something far more base than longing. She felt the answer within herself, a slow unfolding of heat. She breathed deep, and breathed spice and man. "When may I come to you?" Her voice was hardly steady.

Someone passed in the corridor. The symphony began to tune the instruments with the discordant jumble of music that meant the performance was about to begin. Angel's eyes flicked up, then side to side. Ever the spy.

When he spoke, the tone was lust over gravel. "Tonight."

It was what she hoped to hear. "Send your carriage."

"Jones will meet you at the corner at midnight."

"Poor Jones. Roused from his bed to fetch his master's light-o'-love." She tapped his arm with her fan. A coquette's gesture. It was a movement she'd used on dozens of men. But she couldn't on Angel. She dropped the fan and let her hand rest on his arm. The muscle beneath her fingers flexed. "I'll wait for the carriage. I'll come to you."

His gold gaze held hers just one more moment. Then he pulled her into the opera box. She blinked at the speed and sudden change in setting. A mild din rose from the pit, a murmur from the gallery. The lights had dimmed.

All heads in the box turned in their direction. Dowager and daughters-in-law, all in a row. Three pairs of curious eyes.

The dowager's lips were pressed into a thin line when she looked their way. "Mrs. Fairchild." Watchful eyes flicked between them. Lilias might have gained some approval at tea, but caution had overcome approval during the week's separation. "Are you alone? I thought your mother-in-law would be joining us?"

"I'm sorry. She has a headache. She sends her regrets."

The dowager narrowed her eyes. "I hope she recovers quickly."

"Have you seen this performance yet? It's truly spectacular." The younger Lady Angelstone smoothed the striped yellow and puce skirt of her gown. Lilias could not imagine a more disagreeable combination of colors.

"I have not. But I am looking forward to it." Lilias settled into the seat Angel directed her to.

"You'll enjoy the show." Lady Angelstone smiled, a small, welcoming gesture. She turned her attention toward the stage as the music began.

Angel leaned over. "I must apologize for Elise's gown. She has the most hideous taste."

"I heard that, Angel," Lady Angelstone called out, eyes never leaving the stage. The dancers had begun to take their places.

"Do you disagree?" Angel called back.

The conversation was an echo of the concert. Lilias could see the pattern now. Almost like siblings, teasing each other. A comfort to both of them, no doubt.

"No." Now Lady Angelstone slide her gaze over. "But I like it. Now, entertain Mrs. Fairchild and leave me be."

Lilias flicked open her fan to hide her smile.

"Ignore her," Angel said. Little lines fanned out from his eyes as he smiled. "She's incorrigible."

They turned to the performance as Miss Byrne took the stage. Music swelled, voices rose above it. Dimly she saw the patrons moving through the aisles, talking politics and gossiping. But she could only hear the music, the echo of it, the soul of it.

The aria stole her breath, winging it through the air toward the stage. As she tried to catch that breath back, she felt Angel lean toward her.

"Do you suppose anyone but us even hears it?"

She turned her head. His face was only inches away, his mouth just there. "Hears what?"

"The music." He nodded toward the others in the box.

His family was exclaiming over two debutantes in the next box who were making cakes of themselves ogling a pair of bucks in the pit. She glanced to the other side. A peer and his veiled mistress flirted. Below, the crowd undulated as spectators greeted one another and talked. Did no one see the stage?

"Why do they come if they don't watch the opera?"

"They see it in quick glances and small observances. But it is not the focus. They come to be seen. The opera is never about the performance. It's about society and gossip and politics." It wasn't derision in his voice, but resignation. "I was convinced I was the only person who heard the music."

"How could you not hear it?" Indeed, there was room for nothing else. The crowd was nothing more than the buzz of a bee in the midst of the symphony of notes.

She turned back to Angel. He leaned toward her in the chair. His shoulder brushed hers, the lightest of contacts. The brush of a butterfly wing. She felt it in every nerve ending of her body.

"Why do you love music?" she asked softly.

His eyes were serious. "I don't know."

"Quite unhelpful." She smiled lightly. "Your mother told me you play the violin. Why did you tell me you did not play?"

A man's eyes did not change color. Gold could not become black. But it seemed to her that Angel's eyes darkened, swirling with some unnamed emotion. He did not smile at her in return. Lips remained firm and taut.

Her own smile faded.

His shoulder shifted away. The absence of him struck as powerfully as his touch. His gaze focused on the stage as the cast flittered across it.

"I have angered you." She did not send her gaze to the performers. She could not look away as his face transformed. Cheekbones sharpened, brows lowered, eyes bored into the stage. Then he was a harsher version of himself.

"It's intermission." He stood and tugged his waistcoat into place. His voice rose to carry to his family. It was not harsh, or even irritated. "Would you care for punch?"

Two negatives, one acceptance from the Whitmores. He looked down at her. His eyes were unreadable, except that she had started to learn to read the unreadable. Or partly, at any rate. He was holding in a hurt. Some secret. He needed to step away.

"Yes, please," she said.

He would be better for that reprieve from her. Attraction was as easy as breath. Sex was easier. But emotion—that was a complicated thing. Music held emotion. He felt it deeply, that much was clear.

His long fingers pushed back the curtain to the hall. They rested a moment on the frame as he sent a last look in her direction. Then he slipped through the opening. Heavy curtains swished into place behind him. Lilias watched the sway of gold fabric.

And wondered what lay behind his music.

Chapter 26

BEHIND THE SCENES of the Theatre Royal the air was filled with noise and bustle. Lackeys darted between sets. One of the principals was half in, half out of her costume. Candles blazed everywhere, punctuated with the occasional dark corner.

Angel searched the dancers behind the stage. Skirts swirled, petticoats frothed around legs extended into high kicks and pointed toes. More than one interested look was sent his way. Though to the cast, he was just one more dandy looking for a mistress. There were more than a few men hunting their night's pleasure backstage.

A young lackey carrying a bundle of fabric smacked head-first into Angel's chest. The breath wheezed out of the lad as the fabric tumbled to the ground. With the breath punched from his lungs, Angel was hard-pressed not to wheeze himself.

"Watch where yer going you, you bleedin'—" The boy shot a glance at Angel. Ducking his head, he snatched up the fabric. "Er. Sorry, m'lord."

"No need." Angel picked up one of the costumes himself. It looked to be a very colorful woman's gown of pink silk. "Vivienne? Have you seen her?"

"Jest saw her 'ead that away, m'lord." The boy jerked his head behind him before scampering off.

Angel turned in the direction the boy had indicated. He could see an opening to the passageways leading to dressing rooms. Like the boy, actors and dancers and singers scampered up and down the hall.

Vivienne had changed her costume from the one she had been wearing onstage. Her gown was a pretty blue confection of lace and ribbon and something flattering to her curves. A crown of flowers barely held her riotous dark curls in check. She raised one arm above her head and braced the other hand against the wall. A toe pointed out, a knee bent. A leg extended, full, slow, controlled. An arm circled around, a fluid sweep of lithe limbs. Her body was like an ayre, one movement flowing into the next. Graceful and soft. Though he had reason to know there was nothing soft about Vivienne La Fleur.

Her dark eyes met his. Her lips tipped up. The slightest of acknowledgments. She gave no other sign that she'd seen him, only continuing her practiced movements.

Angel sauntered toward her and propped a shoulder against the wall. He crossed his arms over his chest. She didn't pause in her movements. Point, bend, a sweep of arm. Someone rushed past. Neither of them noticed—rather, neither showed they noticed.

"I did not mean for you to come *now.*" Her voice held a laugh. Pretty lips remained tipped up. An act for anyone that watched. "*Espèce d'idiot!*"

"Don't spout French at me, Vivienne." He grinned at her. She looked exceptionally beautiful when she was angry. Which she often was. It was difficult to see behind the light-hearted smile unless one knew where to look. "You gave no indication of timing when you gave your signal onstage."

"Intermission—with the rest of the dandies—is a bit conspicuous." She shook back her hair. A curl fell from the flowered head wreath to curve about her collarbone. "Can you not be more original?"

"No one will notice me." He reached out, flicked the fallen curl so it fluttered about her neck. "You need to see the costumer again."

"I just came from there. *Zut!*" Not by a flicker of an eyelash could one tell she was irritated. Unless one watched the sweep of her dance movements. "But, no more talk, *mon ami.*

There is an assassin in the pit. An Adder. I have seen him before."

Every muscle went rigid. His pleasure at seeing her drained. "Are you certain?"

"*Mais oui.*" Point, bend, sweep of arm. One hand let go of the wall to balance on her hip. "I saw him in Prussia. Many months ago. We had—words."

"Only words? Why do I not believe you?"

"Just so." She paused between the toe point and arm sweep to shrug. A most Gallic gesture from an English-born spy. She had perfected her Frenchness in the months since he'd last seen her. "The Adder and I, we did not speak. Not beyond the clash of knives. Quite good with a dagger, that one."

"What does he look like?" He paused as a pair of dancers rushed by. Their gazes flashed between Angel and Vivienne. Hands covered mouths and giggles arose.

"Do not mind them." She smiled at him. A flirtatious smile full of the life and gaiety she was known for. An act, he knew. One that was second nature to her. "The Adder is dark. Mediterranean coloring. Shorter than you. Thinner. Mean. Sharp eyes. I remember his eyes to be brown, but I could not verify this evening with the distance. He is wearing black and white, of course. You would not pick him out in the crowd."

"Did he recognize you?"

"I do not think so. But I cannot be certain." She stepped close. Her arm slid up to his shoulder, fluttered over the queue of hair at the back of his neck. A sign of flirtation to anyone watching. She was good at her chosen profession. Perhaps he might have felt some stirring for her if he didn't know she could kill a man in a dozen different ways. Likely more. She set her lips against his ear. "He was watching your box, *Mon Ange.* He looked once. Twice. He walked around, then returned. Looked again."

Her scent rose. Not cloying. Sharp and clean. No perfume for Vivienne.

He owed her much more than she knew. "Thank you." He kissed her cheek. He tried to make it appear loverlike. But dammit, it felt just like the kiss he gave little Maggie, his niece.

"May we not cross swords, *Mon Ange*"—she turned her face, brushed her lips against his—"but raise our glasses together at the end of days." It was the same good-bye she always gave her fellow spies. Her trademark. The spies were her only family, after all.

Her lips touched his ear. "Watch your back."

———————

AS ANGEL DISAPPEARED into the intermission activity in the halls beyond, Lilias turned back to the other occupants of the box. They all watched her. Expectantly.

"The performance is wonderful." But of course, that was not what the dowager and her daughters-in-law were interested in.

"I should not have mentioned his music," the dowager said quietly. She clutched at her fan. "It is private. Forgive me, and please do not mention it again." Her lips were pinched, drawing in her cheeks. Lilias could see that Angel had inherited his mother's sharp cheekbones.

"Do not worry." Lilias gave a tiny head shake. "It will remain private."

"Until he chooses to share." Mrs. Whitmore smiled at her. Her smile held both warmth and sadness. "Do not force him, Mrs. Fairchild. Everyone has painful secrets."

"You do not need to tell me of painful secrets. I understand them perfectly." She wondered what secrets the lady hid behind her soft brown eyes. She was a widow, which they had in common. But Mrs. Whitmore would not understand what it was to watch men die. To kill. To hold a dying love in her arms. Or to learn the depth of betrayal.

"This is the most maudlin conversation I have ever had at the opera." Elise, Lady Angelstone, stood up and crossed the box to take Angel's seat. Her eyes were bright and mischievous. "Don't let us scare you. Angel is the only male left in our family. The poor man must be continually defending himself against four women."

"Four?"

"Well, three women and a six-year-old girl," Lady Angelstone qualified. "But I daresay little Maggie counts as a woman when a man is so significantly outnumbered."

"I just barely remember the age of six." It seemed a lifetime ago. She smiled at the sudden memories of bright summers and green grass and fishing holes. And the little village boy she'd been desperately in love with. "I would have most definitely counted myself a woman."

"We're not sure if Maggie counts herself a woman or a soldier." Mrs. Whitmore laughed. "And Grandmamma does not help!"

The dowager bristled. "Nonsense. Maggie is precocious, that's all."

"Which you encourage," Lady Angelstone said, raising a brow. She leaned toward Lilias. "Maggie is also blood-thirsty."

"Which *I* encourage, much to her mother's dismay." Angel's deep baritone penetrated the box. He stood in the doorway, a glass of punch in each hand. A grin flashed. It was meant to be carefree, but it did not reach his eyes. Those eyes were hard and sharp.

Something was wrong.

"So you do." Mrs. Whitmore pursed her lips. "That better be punch for me, as recompense for your blood-thirsty teachings to my daughter."

He transferred the glass into her fingers. "Of course. The other is for Mrs. Fairchild." Gold eyes slid their way, lit on his other sister-in-law in his seat. "Have we traded places, then, Elise?"

"Forgive me, Angel. I commandeered your seat." Lady Angelstone stood and shook out her skirts before returning to her seat. "And I daresay Maggie shall overcome your lessons soon enough and become a proper little lady."

"You are likely right, Elise. But she does seem to enjoy my lessons." Angel reclaimed his seat and extended the punch glass to Lilias.

"Thank you," Lilias said, accepting the glass. She cocked her head. "Just what lessons have you been teaching your niece?"

"Napoleon's battle strategies versus Wellington's."

Lilias choked. "You haven't." She was lucky the punch hadn't sprayed across the front of the opera box. The patrons below might have disliked the slightly used beverage.

"She's partial to Wellington's strategies, but I think she may be biased." Eyes gleamed with amusement. "She might like to hear your opinion on Waterloo."

Now it was Maggie's mother's turn to choke. "Oh, heavens, no. I don't need Maggie thinking she can go to battle."

There was a collective pause in the box. Lilias's battle experiences had barred her from numerous drawing rooms. There were many that pretended they hadn't happened, simply because she was a favorite of the great Wellington. But it was never, *never* discussed.

"Is there something wrong with fighting for your country?" Angel's words were soft and dangerous.

Lilias could see the hurt roll through Mrs. Whitmore. A tremble of lips, the tightening of her jaw.

"There's nothing wrong with fighting for your country, Angelstone, as you well know." Lilias tapped her fan on Angel's arm. He did not need to defend her at the expense of his family. "But perhaps I should tell Maggie I wish I had never experienced it."

"Truly, this conversation cannot become any more awful than it is. Did we not already decide we were maudlin this evening?" Lady Angelstone smoothed out her skirts. "Do you know, Mrs. Fairchild, I love that shade of purple in your gown. But I wonder if the entire ensemble wouldn't look better with the addition of bright orange."

The entire Angelstone clan groaned. Lilias only laughed. "I hadn't thought of orange. But now that you mention it, perhaps I can find orange trim for my skirt."

Chapter 27

"THEY DIDN'T MAKE you feel uncomfortable, did they?" Angel leaned into the open door of the Fairchild carriage. The lights of the opera house blazed behind him.

"Not at all." Lilias settled back against the seat. It sighed beneath her. "But they tread lightly around you."

"What?" His brows jerked up. "Me?" The door was just barely wide enough for his shoulders. He blocked out the front of the opera house, the porter, the theater-goers as he leaned in.

"Yes. They are afraid for you." She tugged at her opera gloves. They were beginning to slide down her forearms. An inferior cut, she decided. "They are afraid something will happen to you before the title is secure. They are afraid of you being a spy—which they are quite aware of, even if they pretend they are not. And they hurt for you because of whatever pain you hold inside you."

He said nothing. Only continued to lean part in, part out of the open carriage door.

"I'm not afraid for you, Angelstone. Or of you. Whatever dark place you have, I have it, too." Why she was irritated by this subject she could not say. She thumped her fist on the front panel of the carriage to signal the coachman. The horses jerked in their harnesses, ready. "Now, get out of my carriage."

He surged forward. His hand cupped the back of her head.

Lips met hers. Hard and possessive and full of heat. Her hand fisted in his cravat. She wanted to make love to him. Here, in the carriage. Now. He could join her under the pretext of escorting her home.

But it wasn't that simple. *They* were not that simple. It had gone beyond the mindless give-and-take, the mindless need. She could feel his anger, his desperation as he captured her mouth and consumed her as though this kiss were a final good-bye and he must take the memory with him forever. Her heart trembled, her breath hitched as that desperation seeped into her.

He let her go with a final nip at her bottom lip. The door snapped shut without even a semblance of good-bye. She exhaled. One long, full breath. All that hunger and need translated to a marvelous kiss. The kind that took a lady's breath and scattered it.

The carriage began to roll. She sank into the cushions and watched London pass her window. She was becoming far too attuned to Angel. His moods, his emotions, even his slight irritations. She wondered if he was becoming accustomed to hers. And what did that mean?

His family was quite protective. But she supposed they would be. Three direct males to inherit the title but only one survives—and that one is a spy. Not particularly good odds for keeping the line intact. And they were all dependent on him to some degree.

She hadn't realized the level of his family commitment. The affection had been clear in his tone, his teasing. It was a level she hadn't thought of. He was, to her, a spy. The man with a family of females clamoring after him was someone she hadn't known existed.

The carriage rumbled to a halt with a muttered "whoa" from the driver's perch above. Lilias frowned. It was too soon to be back at Fairchild House. She hadn't been paying attention, but she was certain not enough time had passed.

She pushed the curtain aside. Beyond the window, shadowed buildings rose above the street. Curtains hid the candlelit interiors so that she could not judge the quality of the neighborhood. She didn't recognize the street. It was shabbier than the fashionable districts. Broken wrought iron fences grinned at her like mouths with missing teeth. She could wait and see, she supposed. No doubt it was a lame horse, or—no. They should not even be here. They were in the wrong part of town and stopping when they had no reason to stop.

Her brows snapped together. She half rose from the seat and pushed open the carriage door. Peering out, she searched the shadows for any threat.

Nothing. Only darkness punctuated with squares of light and the sound of faraway voices. The shadow of another carriage rolled away down the street.

Crack! A gunshot rent the air. Horses whinnied and the carriage lurched. Lilias fell back against the seat in a jumble of skirts and lace. An involuntary shriek ripped from her throat.

Shouts rang out. Running feet pounded the walkway outside. The carriage dipped and someone grunted as they jumped onto the coachman's box. The sound of flesh pounding flesh thudded above her.

They were being robbed. Footpads. Vagabonds. The driver would be injured. He was young and inexperienced. He was not trained to fight.

Hooves clattered on the cobblestones as the horses bucked in their traces. The carriage rolled back, forward. Pitched. Another shout sounded above, then a dull thump as something heavy fell.

She wasn't having it. Not her driver. He was her responsibility.

Setting her jaw, Lilias pulled up the seat opposite her. Jeremy's pistol and a short knife lay hidden beneath the expensive, plush cushion. She had never used the blade. But the knife was sharp, the pistol loaded.

Ignoring the delicacy of her new silk slippers, she kicked open the carriage door and jumped out on the cobblestones. Darting onto the sidewalk, she set her back to the buildings. Her gaze swept across the street, searching for help. No one. Her breath wheezed out. No one but her.

Instinct had her crouching, lining the sight of the pistol as she swung her gaze toward the carriage again. The sound of rending silk followed her. She ignored whatever torn gown or petticoat she'd find in the morning and focused on the moving shadows.

Two men grappled on the box. She couldn't tell which one was the driver. She couldn't even guess well enough to take aim.

Leaping forward, she scrambled toward the coach. Muddy water saturated her slippers as she splashed through a puddle. She didn't notice. Her only goal was the two men.

"Halt!" she cried out.

They didn't even acknowledge her.

"Damnation." She leapt forward, intent on climbing up the side of the coach.

Crack!

It wasn't her pistol. It was her first thought. When she watched one man atop the box slump and collapse, fear enveloped her. "No!"

It had to be the coachman. He had no training. No experience. He was just a young man, with a new wife—

The sob gathered in her throat, but she jumped back and aimed her pistol at the man still standing. He bent over, riffled through the coachman's jacket, then stood again. Light flickered over his face, but she could make out nothing aside from a strong jaw.

"Get down from the carriage." Her voice was cold. Steady, even. Pleased, she bettered her aim. Prepared to shoot. "Now."

"Ah, Lilias. You are as magnificent tonight as you were at Waterloo."

"*Damn*—" She broke off. Her knees sagged in disbelief. She'd expected the criminal to be a stranger. "Angel?"

"Of course." He bowed, sweeping his arm out as though he were a charming courtier rather than a murderer standing on a carriage seat.

"Did you kill him?" She straightened her arm, aiming the pistol carefully at his heart.

"Yes."

She swallowed the sob. *The coachman's poor young wife.* "I'll kill you for that."

"Blood-thirsty wench." He sounded approving. "But I think you'll find there's nothing to kill me for."

He flipped something through the air. Light sparkled over metal before the small object hit the cobblestones at her feet. Keeping the pistol trained on Angelstone, she reached down for the object. Her hand closed around a small metal disc.

She didn't even have to look. She could feel the engraving against the palm of her hand.

"He is not your driver, Lilias." Angel jumped down from the carriage, boots landing solidly on the street. "He was an Adder."

———————

"HE'S GETTING BLOOD on your carpet."

Lilias eyed the assassin. He was bound, arms and feet, and lying on the floor of Angel's study. The Adder wasn't dead, as Angel had thought. Yet. The bullet was lodged in his side. The wound wasn't mortal, but without care he would die. She knew it, Angel knew it and so did the assassin.

Black eyes snapped above the gag in the assassin's mouth. His gaze was as bright with fury as with pain. She turned away.

"Thank you for sending someone to take the coachman home." Lilias pushed back her cape to work at the fastening at her throat.

"It was sheer luck I saw the assassin push him off the carriage seat." Angel's fingers closed around a short crystal glass. He set it in front of him and reached for the brandy decanter. "I'm sorry I was so far away when it happened. I would have caught up with your carriage earlier." He splashed a significant amount of brandy into the glass.

Lilias raised a brow. "Thirsty?"

"As a matter of fact, yes." But he didn't drink from the glass. He turned toward the assassin.

"Here." Angel knelt beside the man and pulled the gag from his mouth. "Brandy." He held a cup to the man's mouth.

The assassin turned his head away and cursed. Savagely.

"There's a lady present, you cur." Angel cuffed him with the flat of his hand. The assassin sucked in a pained breath.

Pity stirred and Lilias drew a deep breath before burying it. She knew espionage wasn't pleasant. She'd seen death and pain and suffering herself. It was senseless. And sometimes it was necessary.

"Drink the brandy." Angel held the glass up. "It will dull your pain a little."

"And my wits," the assassin bit out.

"Likely so, with the amount of blood you've lost." Angel tipped the cup against the man's lips and plugged his nose so he had no choice but to swallow. "We'll both benefit from the brandy, then."

While the man sputtered and cursed again, Angel examined the wound with detached scrutiny. The wound was low in his side and bleeding sluggishly now.

"Damn. I aimed for your heart."

"You need more practice." The assassin bared his teeth. "You missed."

"Obviously. From the looks of it, I managed to miss every possible organ." After a disgusted shake of his head, Angel stood.

It was almost like they were discussing the poor execution of a punch thrown at Gentleman Jackson's.

"Well, infection might carry you off." Angel's conversational tone ceased and his face went hard. "If you're very lucky."

Angel moved to the doorway and gestured to her. She threw the assassin one quick look as she crossed to Angel. The Adder's dark eyes followed her every movement. He licked his bottom lip, one quick dart of the tongue. The hair rose on her neck.

"What do you intend to do to him?" she whispered.

"Ask him a few questions." Angel paused. "Alone."

He said it nonchalantly, but he didn't fool her. She slid her gaze toward the assassin. Now pity did stir in her breast. Whatever he was, he was still a man.

"Don't kill him."

"Is that your only qualification?"

"For heaven's sake—"

"I have questions. He has answers. And he's an assassin." His eyes turned to golden chips of amber. Hard. Sharp. "I need to know the name of their leader."

"I'm aware of that." Lilias set her hand on his sleeve. "I'm also not idiotic enough to believe he will come through this unscathed."

"Such calm acceptance of torture."

"Stop." It seemed he wanted to antagonize her. She slid her eyes toward the assassin, then back to Angel. "I said, I'm not an idiot. But I don't have to like it, and I don't have to condone murder."

"Then you'll obtain your wishes, my dear. He's worth more to me alive than dead." He shook her hand from his arm and stepped away from her. He was a stranger to her in that moment, as much as the assassin was—and just as dangerous. "Sir Charles will want to question him, in any case."

He turned, leaving her with nothing but a view of broad shoulders still clad in black evening wear.

She narrowed her eyes as temper spiked. "I'll wait in the hall."

Spinning on her heel, Lilias strode from the room to pace in the hall. She didn't know why he was being an ass. She'd made a simple request. She didn't whine or nag. She hadn't cried or thrown herself over the wounded assassin. She'd asked for mercy. No more, no less.

Because if Angel killed him, it would be too much like Jeremy.

A moan escaped through the crack beneath the closed study door. She flinched, then steeled herself against the sound. Truly, she didn't want to know what was going on behind that door.

But she wondered about the toll it would take on Angel. One couldn't hurt another person without carving away a piece of one's humanity. Some part of her had been lost on a field in the Netherlands.

Looking down at her feet, she saw the deep purple slippers were stained with blood. They would never be clean again.

The door opened and Angel stepped out. He looked the same. Expressionless. Merciless. Through the open door behind him, Lilias could see the assassin on the ground, panting, eyes closed. Fresh blood bloomed around his wound. But he was alive. When his eyes flicked open, she saw awareness there. And fear.

Chapter 28

"HE IS STILL alive and has all his limbs intact," Angel said. He swept his arm into the room, as though ushering her into something as innocuous as joining him in the drawing room. "Unfortunately, he knows nothing."

"I beg your pardon?" She moved into the room, her eyes on the assassin.

"He doesn't know who the leader is." Rage was a quiet note beneath the words. "He does know how to contact him."

"That's something at least." But very little comfort.

"Jones should have returned. I need to speak with him. I must contact my commander and a surgeon." His gaze flicked toward the assassin. "In that order," he added.

"What do you need me to do?" She didn't want to stand by, useless. She was a target, and she could think of no way forward but to be on the offensive.

Angel gestured to the frivolous purple reticule on the sideboard. Its delicate fringe spilled over her pistol. "I assume it's loaded?" He picked it up, inspected it.

"Yes." Her mind was reeling as he handed her the weapon. Her hand was steady as she accepted it. She'd do what needed to be done, and hoped it didn't involve cold-blooded murder.

"I'll be back in less than ten minutes. If he moves"—he jerked his head toward the assassin—"shoot him."

"Of course." She took aim at the enemy bleeding on the rug. Pity still beat in her, but she supposed that only made her human. The rest of her pulsed with hate and anger. It was not Jeremy on the floor, and yet somehow it was.

The door closed quietly behind Angel. The assassin's dark eyes darted around the room. A scared rabbit. She narrowed her gaze. But no. He was working at the bindings around his wrist. Subtly. A slight twist. A pull. Ah, not such a scared rabbit.

He did not know the information Angel wanted, however. The leader's name was still unknown, and from the fresh bloom of blood on his shirt, he would have told Angel if he did. But he must know something. The Death Adders did not work in seclusion. They did not work completely alone. If Angel knew other spies, then this Adder knew other assassins.

And if Jeremy was, indeed, an assassin, then this man might have known him.

Like a sword balancing on its edge, this moment was the tipping point. She could turn away. Leave. She knew enough about Jeremy and his duplicity. Had accepted it. Knowing more was not necessary.

But then she would guess for the rest of her life.

She smiled grimly. "Now that the spy has had his little talk with you, it's my turn to ask you a few questions."

"I do not know the man in London. We—we do not—" He broke off. Shook his head as though to clear it, coughed. Not a healthy sound, nor was his gasp of breath. She imagined the wound burned like the devil. But he bore it stoically. She could respect that.

"But I do not care about the man in London. Whether you know his name is irrelevant to me." Her palm was slick on the butt of the pistol. She couldn't betray her nerves by even the slightest degree, so she did not even attempt to change hands. "But I do intend to extract information from you."

The assassin licked his lips. "What can you do to me that he hasn't done?"

"Besides kill you?" she asked casually, setting one hip on Angel's wooden desk. She swung her leg gently and contemplated the man bleeding on the rug. "A very good question. I have no training you know, except on the battlefield."

"The battlefield?" His voice cracked.

"Waterloo. Are you thirsty? Did the brandy's effects wear off?"

He only watched her.

"Ah. You are thirsty. I can fix that." She gestured toward the brandy. "For a few answers. I'm not a hard woman."

His eyes flicked toward the decanter. "What do you want to know?"

"I'd like to know about one of your members. A soldier." She drew a breath. "Jeremy Fairchild."

"Yes. I knew him."

Hope could be a slap in the face. Sharp, sudden, it could steal one's breath away. She hadn't realized she still hoped it had all been a mistake. Had she truly believed Jeremy was innocent? She must have. Her fingers spasmed on the pistol, then relaxed again. Hope was a foolish misstep. She should have known better.

The assassin licked his lips again. "The brandy." His voice was sand over desperate stone.

"Tell me more." She moved to the sideboard and pulled the stopper from the decanter with one hand while keeping the pistol pointed at him with the other hand. She picked up the decanter by the neck and poured, splashing the liquor over the rim and onto the wooden sideboard.

"There is nothing to tell. Fairchild is dead." He squirmed, wiggling his hands and feet. Still trying to release those bonds—though she doubted he could. She heard his harsh breath, the pained moan.

She steeled her heart. "Yes. He *is* dead, isn't he?" She picked up the snifter, set it beneath her nose as if enjoying the scent of wood and caramel and spirits.

"He was my assignment. Mine. The brandy—" He swallowed audibly, strained against his bindings.

"Oh, what luck. Jeremy Fairchild was your assignment." Pity could be pitiless. *The surgeon will be here. Soon.* He would not die. And the brandy—it was only brandy.

"No one renounces the Death Adders once they are in."

She jerked, spilling brandy onto the already bloodstained rug. Angel would have to buy another carpet. "Renounce?"

His eyes had followed the drip so that he stared at the floor where it had fallen. She could see the thirst on his face, in the ravaged eyes. He must have lost a lot of blood. He needed water, not liquor. But a man in a desert would drink the sand if that was all he could see. Which meant she had something he desperately wanted.

She swirled the brandy in the glass and lifted it to her lips. Blocking out the craving in his eyes and what it did to her heart, she sipped. "Mmmm. French. And very, very good."

"What do you want to know?" The man's voice was steady, but his eyes darted between her lips and the glass.

"I want to know about Fairchild's leaving the Adders," she shot out. "Why?"

"He was done. He wanted to retire." His gaze focused on the glass.

She stepped forward. "Why?" she said again.

"His wife."

"His wife?" Woodenly, she stared at the assassin. "He wanted to leave because of his wife?"

"He wanted a normal life. The London Adder gave the order for his death after Fairchild gave his notice. He could not be allowed—" He coughed. The jerking movements sent pain shooting across his face. He panted, gasped.

She couldn't bear it. She knelt and held the glass up to his lips, still keeping the pistol trained on him. He gulped it, and she thought now of a drowning man, instead of one in the desert.

"I'll see you get water," she said softly. "You need water."

"Thank—thank you." He leaned his head against the floor and closed his eyes. He breathed in and out, slowly. "I remember you from that day at Waterloo. I did not know you were his wife when I saw you on the field. *L'Ange de Vengeance.*"

Lilias pressed her lips together and stood. She set the snifter aside and gripped the pistol tightly. He had not asked a question. So she would not answer.

"But when I saw you a few days ago, when I received the order for your death, I recognized you." His voice was rough with pain.

Orders for her death. Orders for Jeremy's death. Sorrow swelled and grew and swamped her. Once, she had believed a person could not survive grief. It had consumed every waking moment. She'd nearly died avenging her husband. Then she'd learned he was an assassin and grief had turned to hate and fury.

She did not know what the horrible pressure in her chest now was caused by. The mix of it was beyond name. Beyond knowing. It simply consumed her. Perhaps she hated Jeremy for deceiving her. Perhaps she hated herself for being blind to his true nature. Perhaps she hated him for dying.

Perhaps she hated him for seeking redemption.

He'd been trying to leave the Adders for her. *For her.* And his killer lay before her. Bound and helpless.

She felt the tears. Hot. Bitter. They swam in her eyes, blurring her vision. She blinked them back and ignored the ache in her throat. Ignored the way her chest heaved beneath the smothering storm inside her.

She turned back to the assassin and raised the pistol, aiming it at his head.

"Yes, I was at the Battle of Waterloo." Behind her, the door opened. She pretended she hadn't heard the sound. "I was avenging the death of my husband. Jeremy Fairchild."

Chapter 29

GOD'S TEETH, SHE was stunningly beautiful. And furious. Angel stayed near the door, afraid to even move into the room lest he startle her into something her soul would regret.

"Lilias." He could see her finger was taut on the trigger. "What has happened?"

Her throat worked and she audibly swallowed.

"What?" he asked again.

"Jeremy was assassinated on the battlefield—because he was trying to leave the Death Adders." She turned bright, angry eyes toward him. "He was leaving because of *his wife*."

It was like watching the slow torture of an angel in hell. Turmoil. Pain. All there in her eyes. Her husband was an assassin. How did one accept that? Worse, he'd tried to stop for her—and was killed for it.

Forgetting about the Adder bleeding on the rug, he reached for her arm. Sliding his hand over her soft forearm, her tense wrist, her rigid hand, he finally came to the weapon. Her fingers convulsed.

"Give me the pistol, Lilias." Quiet words. Soft hands. Like a startled mare, she might spook. The assassin was smart enough not to make a sound. "Give it to me now."

She continued to stare into his eyes. Lips parted, jaw firm. Eyes bright and hard and so full of vengeance. He'd seen it all there once before, after all. It was an expression he'd never forgotten. He was going to lose her. He saw it in that brilliant blue as she stared at him. She would pull the trigger.

Stay with me. He willed it. His mind screamed it. If she did this, she would never recover. He angled his body, set his back to the assassin. In effect, he put himself between Lilias and the assassin.

The hardness in her eyes eased. Her shoulders slumped. The hand holding the weapon trembled once before loosening its grip.

"It's different in cold blood, isn't it?" Her voice was raw and wounded. "Death on the battlefield is different than death in the middle of Mayfair."

He didn't answer. He only took the weapon from her shaking hand. The door opened and Jones came in. Angel heard the soft footfalls as the man crossed the room toward them.

"My lord." His voice was hushed, as a man's might be when he was trying not to startle a wild animal.

"Yes?" Angel didn't take his eyes from Lilias's, nor did he let go of her hand. Or the pistol.

"Sir Charles should be arriving soon." Not by even the slightest change of expression did Jones betray his understanding of the scene.

Lilias blinked those stunningly blue eyes and turned away, as though waking from a dream. Or a nightmare. She paced toward the opera cape draped over the arm of the settee.

"Good," Angel said, watching her jerky movements as she swung the cape around her shoulders. "Take the pistol, Jones. Cover the prisoner. I'll return in a moment."

"Yes, my lord." Jones took the weapon when Angel held it out. With competent and well-trained movements he checked the pistol and took up his position.

"Lilias." Angel kept his voice low. "We need to talk."

"I can't." Refusing to meet his eyes, she swept toward the door. "I need to think. I need to *move*."

He strode after her as she clipped into the hall. Grabbing her arm, he swung her around to face him. She snarled at him. As he'd wanted her to. If she was angry at him, the pain was buried. And he needed her angry, not full of sorrow.

"Very well, Lilias. If you need to move, you can pace the bloody hallway—"

"Don't bloody swear at me."

"—while I talk." He wanted to kiss that mouth. Why was a spitting, snarling woman who cursed when she was angry so damn attractive to him? "It's important, Lilias."

"Fine." She wrenched her arm away and did, indeed, pace the hallway in quick, strong strides. Anger flushed color into her high cheekbones. "What do you wish to speak about, Angel? I've had enough for this night. I want to go home."

"To Fairchild House? Where an assassin nearly killed you in your own bed?" he asked softly.

Her steps faltered. Stopped. She closed her eyes and drew a deep breath. "Is nowhere safe? I cannot even trust old friends."

"Hawthorne has been cleared of suspicion." Mostly cleared, at any rate. But at least he could give her this. It might be a comfort. "He does have a child."

"Thank God." Her shoulders sagged with relief.

He hated to take that away again. "But you still cannot fully trust him. There is nowhere safe."

He crossed to her, set a hand on the rigid curve of her shoulder. The light of the wall sconce played over fabric as she tensed. She shrugged off his hand and stepped deliberately away from him. Her eyes glittered like twin shards of broken glass. She did not want comfort. Nor pity.

So he would not give it. "There's a price on your head. A big one. Ten thousand pounds to the Adder that completes the job."

"Ten thousand pounds?" Her jaw dropped. "That's ridiculous. Utterly ridiculous." The notion seemed to have taken the temper out of her.

"You don't think your life is worth ten thousand pounds?"

"What an odd thought." She pursed her lips. A line appeared between her brows, as though she were truly attempting to calculate the value of her life.

"With that price, the Adders will not stop. It will be attack after attack until one of them succeeds." He fisted his hands. He could not undo the directive. He was as helpless as he'd been to stop Gemma's murder. "I want to send you into hiding."

"But—"

He held up a hand to stop her. "I said I want to. I can't." The hand he'd raised reached for her. Cupped her cheek. She did not shy away from him now. Her eyes were still bright, but it was not with that broken light of before. Her skin was soft beneath his thumb as he rubbed it over her cheekbone. "The only way to stop the attacks is to capture more Adders. When we find one that knows the leader, we'll be able to revoke his directive."

He shouldn't even touch her now. He was about to use her in the most horrific way, and she knew it.

"I'm the bait for your trap," she said.

———————

HE LOOKED EVERY inch the fallen angel just now, with his brows furrowed and those golden looks gilded by candlelight. She could not be angry with him. She could not even summon any fear at the moment. She was hollowed out by too much emotion, too much knowledge.

"It is not easy, is it?" His fingers brushed against her cheek again.

She did not pretend confusion. "Truth is never easy."

His fingers continued to glide across her skin, cheek to jaw to collarbone. A simple touch between lovers. It sent her already bruised heart reeling.

"I do not know what is worse," she said, though he had not asked a question. "Whether Jeremy was an assassin and killed men for money, or that he was killed because he wanted to *stop* being an assassin." She turned her face away. Sometimes a gentle touch could move mountains. "There is no clear right and wrong in that. Was he right to try to leave the Adders? Yes. But of course, there is nothing *more* wrong than murder. So he started in the wrong."

"The answers are complicated. As are the questions. Lilias." He waited to speak until she turned to face him again. "I know there is no time for you to recover."

"I don't need—"

"You need to regain your equilibrium." He paused, and though he was not touching her any longer, he still stepped closer. "But you do not have time. You must keep thinking.

Keep moving. Keep watching. The price on your head is beyond reason. The Adders will be following you, waiting for the right moment. There is no room for mistake. If they come for you and we don't see them in time—"

She could see the worry in the gold depths of his eyes. In the way he held his breath.

"Don't think of it." She took his hand, twined her fingers with his. The rasp of calluses against her palm was an odd sort of comfort. "I will not wallow. I promise to stay alert."

He raised their joined hands and pressed his lips to her knuckles. "I worry for you, Lilias." His words were easy, but beneath them was a heavy tone, full of meaning that could not be discerned.

Her heart thumped once, hard. *I worry for you.* She could not decide if there was more beneath those words or not.

"It could happen anywhere. A public venue. A ballroom crush." His fingers tightened around hers. "A knife through the ribs. A drop of poison in your glass. They are common methods and let the assassin disappear into a crowd with no one the wiser."

"I will be careful." But she was not stupid. She could never be careful enough.

"We'll be watching."

When his lips touched hers they were surprisingly soft. The kiss was sweet enough to have her heart flutter. He dropped her hand to grip her upper arms, transferring that delicious scrape of calluses from her palm to her arm. She opened her mouth beneath his, desperate for heat and comfort from him. For the indefinable thread that bound her to someone. She'd lost that thread when the assassin had told her of Waterloo. The losing had nearly consumed her.

And then there was Angel. A great rock in the center of a vortex of crashing waves. She gripped his biceps, anchored herself to him. And simply fell into his kiss. Into the scent of man, the heat of him, the slight rasp of his jaw that needed shaving. He was, for the moment, all that was solid and real and safe.

With a final pressing kiss, he pulled away. She nearly slid her hand against his neck to pull him back so she wasn't alone.

"You must return to Fairchild House soon, before the explanations become too complicated." He murmured the words against her cheek, then pressed a kiss there. "Agents are already stationed. I'll take the first morning watch. Jones will be taking a turn as well, and you will be able to visit me here, where we can protect you." He kissed her again. Quick and thorough. "The Adders won't know one of their number is missing until morning at the earliest. Midday by the latest. You'll be safe until then."

After that . . .

The words hung in the air. Unspoken, but there.

She was still a target.

Chapter 30

JONES DROVE THE carriage to the front door of Fairchild House as they'd prearranged. It was likely Catherine and Grant would be aware of the coachman's injuries and know the carriage was missing—with her in it. There was no use attempting to sneak into the house.

She was right in her assessment. Every window was blazing with light.

Jones called out. Quiet, sure words that scattered beneath the beat of hooves. The horses slowed with a jingle of harness. The carriage rocked to a halt.

Grant threw open the front door and jumped down the steps. He was in his shirtsleeves, his brown hair mussed.

Running to him seemed the best option. She could leap from the carriage and those arms would catch her. But she couldn't tell him the truth, and that stung.

All thought vanished as Grant swung a pistol up and aimed it at Jones.

"Damn, damn, damn," Lilias groaned, scrambling to push open the door.

"Down from the carriage! Now!" Grant shouted.

With one fast leap, she covered the distance between carriage and street usually bridged by the steps.

"Don't! Grant, don't!" Throwing herself at him, she forced

him to drop his weapon hand and take her into his arms. She buried her face in his shoulder and gripped his shirt. Female and helpless—and conniving. "He's a friend. He's not the man you're after."

His arms came around her, Jones already forgotten. The scent of cologne enveloped her. "You're well? You're fine?"

She nodded into his shoulder. It felt horribly wrong to scare him so, and be unable to tell him what had happened. She turned her face so her cheek rested on his coat. On the coach, Jones stood on the seat, his broad shoulders outlined against lighted windows. His arms were raised, palms out. The wind caught his coat and sent it flapping.

Behind her, Catherine rushed down the steps. Various servants spilled out of the door behind her. A cacophony of voices and boots and skirts filled the air.

"Darling! What happened?" Catherine's eyes were round as tea saucers beneath her nightcap and the fringe of white curls bobbing over her brow. "We received news the carriage was stolen."

"An abduction perhaps, for ransom." The predetermined story tripped from her tongue as though it were the truth. Odd, given she hadn't even practiced it. She drew back and gestured toward Jones. "This man happened to see. He followed and fought the criminal."

"How brave!" Catherine clasped her hands together and peered up at Jones. His arms were still raised, and his gaze rested on Grant's pistol. A spy always remembered the important bits of a scene.

Lilias shuddered delicately to embellish her part and bring the focus back to her. "The criminal is dead. He's been killed."

"Good," Grant said firmly, arms tightening around her. His chest was warm and strong beneath her cheek. The muscles in his chest shifted when his head turned toward Jones. When she glanced up, the look in Grant's eyes was indecipherable. "Thank you, my good man. If you'll leave your name and direction, I'll see you receive a suitable reward."

"No need, milord. 'Appy to 'elp," Jones said in a heavy cockney accent that made Lilias blink in surprise. He climbed down from the carriage and handed the reins to a waiting footman.

"Please allow me to see that you reach your destination safely." Grant's voice rumbled in his chest, vibrating against her cheek. His arms still encircled her. Comfort and torture. He still waited for her answer to his marriage proposal, and she could not say no tonight. "We can send you in the Fairchild carriage."

"No, thank 'ee, milord. I'm not far from me household." Jones tipped his head in their direction, hand on the brim of his cap. "G'nite, ma'am. Good to see yer none the worse for wear."

"Thank you again, sir." Lilias straightened, moving away from Grant, though he kept one arm around her waist.

Jones strolled off into the night, whistling aimlessly.

"I am not certain I trust that man." Grant did not turn away from the retreating shadow. She could see his slight frown in the light from the glowing house. He was questioning Jones's role in the night's events, and perhaps even the story they'd concocted. She needed to distract him.

She moaned a little and staggered. She thought it was rather well done, and when he switched his gaze from Jones to her, she knew she had him. But the deceit whittled away a part of her heart. Was it possible to live this way, always, as a spy, and still retain some decency?

"Come, Lilias, you must be overset." Grant's arm tightened around her, guiding her up the steps and into the house. "Graves, see to the carriage," he said to the butler.

"Yes, my lord," Graves intoned. His concerned eyes were flicking over Lilias just as Catherine's had done, searching for injuries.

When did one become accustomed to lying?

When they were back inside, Grant started barking out orders for food, wine, hot water for a bath. "You'll want to go to your room, I'm sure," he said to Lilias as he led her to the stairs.

His arm was still around her. Gentle and easy to lean upon. She wondered what animal was less than a garden slug. Whatever it was, she was certainly it.

They made their way to the upper floors, Catherine climbing the steps before them. "My poor dear," the lady said. Her disheveled curls twitched and bounced with each step. "You must have been so frightened. It was lucky that man was so kind and brave to come to your rescue."

"Yes, it was fortunate," Grant agreed.

"I wasn't frightened, at first," Lilias said. She had to say something. They would want to know the details. Any normal person would provide the details.

Keep to the truth wherever possible, Angel had said. *It's easier to lie that way.*

"I didn't understand what was happening. The villain kept the carriage to a normal pace, most likely to avoid arousing suspicion." They had come to the second floor now. She gently shrugged out of Grant's supporting embrace to move along the corridor. "I suppose it's why that man was able to catch up to us. We weren't moving very quickly."

"Where did the criminal take you?" Grant asked as he pushed open the door to her room. A fire snapped cheerfully in the hearth. A tray held tea and brandy—presumably to restore her nerves by whichever method seemed best.

"Near the docks." Perhaps she should shudder in disgust. Or fear. But no, if she acted too weak Grant would surely guess. He knew of Waterloo, of the marches and conditions she'd endured. She drew a deep breath as though bracing herself—though she supposed she was actually doing so. "We came to a stop and I looked out the window. I didn't recognize the street. It was poor. Shabby. Beyond shabby, actually. I knew something was wrong. Hello, Betsey," she said to her maid.

"Oh, ma'am." Betsey's worried eyes scanned Lilias, presumably looking for injuries. "Did those brigands hurt you?"

She smiled at Betsey as the girl pressed nervous fingers to her mouth. It was unsettling to realize how many people cared for her—and how many she was lying to. "I'm fine, truly. I'm glad to be home. At any rate, I heard the shouts outside the carriage." Now to blend fact with lies. "The horses spooked, taking the carriage with them. I could hear the fighting going on above, but I couldn't do anything because I was stuck inside the carriage."

Turning away, she handed her reticule to the maid. It was easy to allow her fingers to tremble. They trembled again when she fumbled with the clasp of her cape. Catherine, who had been perched on the end of a chair, popped up.

"Let me do that for you, dear."

"No, I have it. Thank you." Lilias gave Catherine a grateful smile and swallowed hard. She couldn't understand why the lady's offer of assistance made her want to cry when she had yet to shed a tear over the assassin's information on Jeremy. "To finish, by the time the horses were under control and I was able to leave the carriage, the criminal was already dead."

"What happened to him?"

"I don't know. The man who saved me found someone to dispose of the body." Lies twisted with truth. "There really isn't more to tell, I'm afraid. Once the body was removed, the man brought me home."

"You were gone for a long time." Grant watched her steadily, gray eyes probing.

"It must have taken longer than I'd thought for the entire episode to be over."

"Well, it's over now." Catherine rubbed a hand on Lilias's shoulder. "Have a cup of hot tea to settle your nerves. The maid will help you get ready for bed." Catherine took Lilias's hand and led her to a chair. "You're cold, I'm sure, so we'll have the fire built up, perhaps even a hot bath—"

"In a moment, Aunt," Grant interjected. "Can you allow us some time alone?"

"In her bedroom? Certainly not. It's improper enough as it is that you're here at all, Grant." Catherine pressed her lips into a single disapproving line.

"I promise not to ravish her, Aunt." Grant's mouth twitched. But he crossed his arms, a sign that he would not budge in his position. "I only want a word. It will take less than five minutes."

"It's quite all right, Catherine." Lilias kept her words even and measured, but it was difficult not to give way to the wild thump of her heart. Perhaps he guessed that she lied. Perhaps he saw through all of the partial truths. She didn't know what to tell him if he suspected she was lying. She couldn't tell him the truth.

"I suppose these *are* extenuating circumstances." Catherine's eyes flicked between the two of them. "Very well. Five minutes. Betsey, do come along."

"Yes, ma'am." The maid quit the room amidst a rustle of skirts.

When the door shut behind Catherine, the room echoed with silence and the crackle of flames.

"What is it, Grant?" Lilias asked, breaking the silence.

"I must ask, and there is no delicate way to do so."

"Then don't be delicate, Grant. As we both know, I haven't a delicate bone in my body. Ask me your question."

Grant walked toward her, his broad shoulders looking strong and masculine in the lawn shirt. He stopped in front of her and his gray eyes searched her face. She was breathless for a moment under that intense scrutiny. What would she be required to lie about now?

His arm came up, fingers reaching for her but not touching. "You weren't . . . *hurt*, were you?"

Ah. That was it. "No." She didn't pretend to misunderstand him. "I was not hurt. Only frightened."

She saw his muscles relax. His arms lost their rigidity. Breath whistled out. He cared so much for her. It made her heart ache, because she couldn't love him in return. Worse, she was lying to him.

"Grant." She sighed. She should love this man. She *should*. But she could not. "Thank you for your—"

The door to the room whipped open. "Your time is up," Catherine said from the hall. "I sent Graves to check on John Coachman. Lilias, Betsey is bringing up food. Something hot and strengthening."

"Thank you, Aunt." Grant let his hand fall, but his eyes stayed on hers. "Sleep well, Lilias. I am glad that you are safe."

He strode toward the door and hustled Catherine into the hall before him. With one final look in her direction, he pulled the door shut and left her alone.

Her breath *whoosh*ed out. She had been holding it and had not noticed before. She had been too busy deceiving the people she loved most.

Angel lived this life every day, she thought. He lied to his mother, his sisters-in-law. No one revealed all their secrets, of course. But Angel lived two separate lives.

Which one was the lie?

Chapter 31

"I DON'T THINK ATTENDING tea with the dowager marchioness is a good idea." Lilias tapped the prettily written invitation against the palm of one hand. She had been brooding over the invitation for days, and now the afternoon of the tea had arrived.

"Nonsense. She inquired about your health after *the incident*, and has invited you to tea. It would be unpardonably rude not to attend. And Angelstone himself may appear." Catherine's eyes twinkled as she pulled a gown out of Lilias's wardrobe. "You must wear the blue muslin, dear. It suits you."

Lilias sighed and accepted the muslin. Catherine was correct. It would be rude. But that did not make her feel any less awkward about the visit. Having tea with her lover's mother was beyond the bounds of propriety. But she dared not argue.

And so Lilias found herself greeted by the Angelstone butler, her pelisse was spirited away and she was sitting in the drawing room with a delicate teacup pressed into her hands and three Whitmore women eyeing her over the rims of their own teacups.

She smiled politely at them and calculated how long she would have to stay.

"I was so glad you could join us at the opera, but I was shocked to hear about the abduction." The dowager marchioness's thin features sharpened as she pressed her lips together. "Shocked! I couldn't believe something like this could happen right in Drury Lane."

"Was it terribly frightening?" Mrs. Whitmore asked, gentle eyes bright with concern. "I'm sure I would have been a bundle of nerves and hysteria."

"I don't think Mrs. Fairchild is afraid of very many things." Elise, Lady Angelstone, laughed. "You strike me as quite full of fortitude."

"I'm as fortitudinous as the next woman." Lilias quirked her lips. "I promise you, when one's life is in danger, it is amazing how much courage one can dredge up."

The door to the drawing room burst open on a shout. "Mama! I've learned my sums! It was ever so hard until Uncle Angel helped me." A little girl tumbled in, all knobbly elbows and flying braids. Dirt edged the hem of her pretty dress and a streak was smeared across her flushed cheek.

"Maggie," he mother said sharply. "We have a guest. You will kindly make your curtsy and then go wash."

"Yes, ma'am." The girl's face sobered into a polite little mask. But her eyes danced with mirth and mischief. "I am delighted to make your acquaintance, Mrs. . . ." Her voice trailed off. "What is your name?"

"Maggie!" Her mother hissed as she started to push up from her chair.

"I'm Mrs. Fairchild," Lilias interrupted, amused. "And you must be Margaret Whitmore. I am most pleased to make your acquaintance. Your uncle has told me about you."

"Oh." A vertical line formed between her brows. "Are you trying to warm his bed, too? Grandmamma says—"

"Oh, dear God." Mrs. Whitmore rushed toward the door, scooping up her young daughter along the way. "I'm so sorry, Mrs. Fairchild. Forgive us." She started to push the girl out the door, embarrassed color flushing her cheeks.

Lilias slid her gaze toward the dowager, who didn't appear the least bit repentant. The older woman continued to sip her tea, a brow raised as she waited for Lilias to react.

She could only laugh. Despite the fact that the dowager was sitting beside her and Lilias had, indeed, warmed Angel's bed, she could only laugh at the awkward tableau and the truth of a child's tongue.

"Mrs. Whitmore, do not think a moment about it. Your daughter is truly delightful. Maggie," Lilias said, setting her cup down on the table. "Tell me all about how your Uncle Angel taught you your sums."

The girl scooted around her mother and half ran to the settee. She leaned against the arm and grinned. The streak of dirt beside her mouth curved up.

"Uncle Angel took me to the park. He brought my soldiers with us—he knows all about formations, he used to be a soldier—and lined them up." She walked her fingers across the cushion. "Like so."

"Yes, I can see how that would be helpful." Lilias nodded, as though she, too, could see the soldiers. "What did he do then?"

"He showed me that if you have soldiers in the right flank, and you move them over to the left flank, you have added them together. Two soldiers plus two soldiers makes four soldiers. Do you see?" She lifted shining eyes. "It was ever so hard, as I said. But Uncle Angel knows everything."

"He certainly does." She wanted to ruffle the girl's hair. "So who won your war this afternoon?"

"I did. I 'most always do. Uncle Angel says I'm quite blood-thirsty." Pride beamed out of her. "And look, I have one of my soldiers right here. I carry him with me everywhere. Uncle Angel says he looks like my papa, and so if I carry him, my papa will always be with me."

Blue paint had flecked off to reveal the dull metal beneath the soldier's coat. Painted eyes stared sightlessly up. The tip of his tin nose had broken off. He was as battered and beaten as any true soldier after battle. But Maggie held the shabby toy in the palm of her hand as though it were the most wonderful of treasures.

"I think your Uncle Angel is very, very wise." The lump rising in her throat threatened to bring tears with it. "Your soldier is quite handsome."

"Thank you," the girl said solemnly.

A sniff sounded across the room. Lilias glanced up and

found the dowager marchioness's eyes wet and shining. Lilias smiled softly at her. A mother should never outlive her children, but if she did, to have such a wonderful son and granddaughter remaining could only make her proud.

"You may come play war with me, if you would like." Maggie slid the soldier back into her apron pocket.

"I would like that very much."

Someday, perhaps. Assuming she lived. There were a few pesky assassins she needed to hide from first.

And then she saw him. He filled the doorway, or at least he seemed to. His hair was disheveled from the wind in Hyde Park. His jacket was unbuttoned, revealing the white waistcoat beneath. Her breath caught, held, as she drank him in. Why did her heart stutter beneath her stays?

His gaze traveled once over her, as though ensuring all parts of her were intact. She felt it in her skin before his gaze flicked over the rest of the room.

"Maggie, my love," Angel said, finally resting his gaze on the youngest female. "You've bested me again. Not only did you humiliate me on the battlefield, you beat me into the house."

Maggie hooted with laughter and scampered over to him. He picked her up and propped her on his hip, as though it were the most natural thing in the world. He chatted with her a moment, laughed, kissed her nose. Lilias's belly clutched at the sight. This was a facet she could not quite fit into the puzzle that was Angel.

His gaze turned back to Lilias and her breath caught in her throat. There was purpose there, and a stark need that he barely hid behind the casual façade. "Mrs. Fairchild," he said, setting Maggie onto the floor. "A delight to see you again."

She ignored the self-satisfied smile of Angel's mother and curious gazes of his sisters-in-law. All that seemed to matter was the little bump of her heart. She hadn't realized how much she'd wanted to see him. Foolish, she thought. Foolish and female. Still, it was Angel she wanted to spend time with, not his family.

"And you, my lord."

He strode into the room and took a seat on the settee beside her. The two inches between their arms was as noticeable to her as if it was solid matter. How could that tiny space send her pulse scrambling?

"Mrs. Fairchild says she's fully recovered, Angel," the dowager said, pouring a cup of tea for her son. "She's a strong woman to bear such an incident with such grace."

"Indeed, she is." He accepted the cup from his mother, his longer fingers carefully cradling the delicate porcelain. "But I don't know if she's strong enough to endure the three of you poking at her."

Lilias choked on her tea and tried to hide it in her cup. It didn't work. Angel reached over and tapped her back. Just that ordinary touch sent little waves of sensation climbing up her spine. "I'm sure I can endure the three of them. It's *you* I'm not certain I can endure."

He slid her a sidelong glance, sly and amused. "No? Well, you shall have to a bit longer. I still have a full cup of tea."

Maggie leaned against Angel's knee, drawing his attention. She cocked her head and eyed Lilias with interest. "I am impressed Mrs. Fairchild didn't have the vapors." Her little nose scrunched up. "I think the vapors are silly. Do you?"

"I do, indeed," Lilias said. "Have you ever had the vapors?"

"Of course not!" Shocked, Maggie's eyes went wide.

"Well, if you do find yourself having the vapors, do you know what you should do?"

Maggie shook her head and moved closer to hear the secret.

Lilias leaned forward, all seriousness. "You should find the nearest piece of sturdy furniture and kick it. You'll feel ever so much better."

"If Maggie starts kicking furniture," Mrs. Whitmore called from the other side of the room, "I'm coming after you two!"

"I didn't do anything," Angel protested, putting his hands up in the air. "It was all Mrs. Fairchild's fault!"

"Oh, how chivalrous of you to blame me." Lilias laughed.

"Guilt by association, Angel," Mrs. Whitmore continued. "The two of you are mirror images of each other."

Chapter 32

"SHALL I TAKE your cloak, ma'am?" Jones asked blandly as he shut the front door behind Lilias. His dark eyes were as inexpressive as ever. If he thought her late night visits—or rather, early morning visits—during this past week were improper, he never showed it.

She really ought to be embarrassed. She wasn't in the least, and wondered if that spoke to some lack of moral fortitude.

"Thank you, Jones." She passed the hooded cloak to him. Tipping her head to the side, she studied him. He was handsome in that easy way some gentlemen had. Brown eyes, a nice, lean face. Lips that never smiled, though they were full and mobile. "Jones?"

"Yes, ma'am." He folded her cloak over one arm, exhibiting as much care as he would the king's garment.

"Are you a spy, or a butler with many talents?"

He didn't blink. "A spy, ma'am."

"I thought as much. Have you been with Angel for a long time?"

"A while." He regarded her steadily. Patiently. Waiting. One hand lay over the cloak. Competent fingers smoothed wrinkles from the material as though he had nothing more pressing to do.

"That's precise."

His eyes smiled at her, tiny lines fanning out at the corners. "Yes, ma'am."

What secrets did Jones have tucked away behind those expressionless eyes? "Where is Angel?"

"In the study, ma'am."

"He always is."

When she opened the door to the study, she could see his booted feet propped on a footstool and crossed at the ankles. She couldn't see the rest of him, as he was hidden by the back of the sofa. His gold head peeked over the carved mahogany ridging at the top of the sofa.

He didn't hear her enter, which was unusual. Angel always seemed to know where she was. But he didn't move when the door opened, or when she closed it again.

She pursed her lips, angled her head. Considered the unmoving Hessian boots. Very relaxed, those booted feet. A quiet snore competed with the crackle of flames in the hearth.

With soft steps, she circled the sofa. He slouched against the luxurious upholstered sofa, pillows propped beneath his back. He wore no coat, no waistcoat, no cravat—only a fine lawn shirt open in a V at his neck. One hand lay palm up on the seat beside him, fingers curled inward. The other hand held a slim volume against his chest, pages open and pressed against his shirt.

Beyond relaxed. The spy was quite, quite asleep. No surprise, as he was guarding her more than any other agent. And then she would visit his lodgings, as she had tonight, and neither of them would get any rest.

She had never seen him sleeping before, though they had dozed together after making love. The firelight flickered over him, shadowing features softened in sleep. He looked almost beautiful without the edge of danger. The glint in his eyes was hidden by lashes. She had not noticed how very long they were until now.

The fingers curled around his open palm twitched. He would be waking soon, no doubt. Her reticule scuffed against the polished top of a side table as she set it down. Angel didn't stir. Treading lightly, she moved toward the sofa. She bent over him, heard his strong inhale. This close, she could see every eyelash, the light dusting of stubble on his jawline. He breathed in again. Long. Deep. A smile curved his lips.

She set a hand on his chest for balance and kissed that mouth. He tasted of brandy. Of man. She could smell the light spice that meant Angel. She felt wakefulness slide through him. Even in half sleep, his lips firmed beneath hers. His chest muscles went from lax to hard, then relaxed again beneath her fingertips.

"Lilias." The word was barely more than a breath. A caress of sound and soul. "I dreamed of you."

His eyes fluttered open. The gold had deepened, holding her trapped. There was no barrier between them. No spy to filter out the heart of him. For an instant, she could see all of him.

Her heart stuttered in her chest. She could not breathe. Not at all.

His free hand slid around her waist, drawing her down beside him. The book fell to the floor as his other hand cupped her cheek.

"Lilias," he whispered again.

A log snapped in the fireplace, sending out sparks as bright and sharp as the thumping of her heart. His lips were soft. Gentle. They played over hers, as easily and delicately as his fingers over her cheeks.

"I was hoping you would come tonight." He drew back, tipping his head up to see her better. "I haven't seen you in a few days, aside from through a window or across the street."

"Only two days. Not so very long."

"Too long." He kissed her again. A quick, familiar kiss. It eased the wild beat of her heart.

She slid into the space between his arm and his body. Drew her feet up so they curled beneath her. A snug fit. Two bodies. Two interlocking puzzle pieces. "What did you do today? Any exciting espionage-type exploits?"

"Followed around a pretty blonde." He nuzzled her neck, pressed a kiss there. "She went shopping on Bond Street—not a safe venue, I might add—and then to a small dinner where she conveniently stayed away from windows so a shot could not be fired. Although it made it damned hard to keep track of her."

"I'm sure she tried her best to follow all the rules you have imparted to her in the past week."

His eyes smiled at her. Warm and soft, though more guarded now. He was fully awake. She missed that unfiltered bit of Angel already.

"What were you reading?" she asked.

"Poetry. John Donne."

"Ah. I thought I had read his name on the spine." His shoulder made a surprisingly comfortable pillow. She nestled in. Watched the flames dance in the fireplace. "You like poetry. Music. Quite unplumbed depths for a spy."

"Even a spy must have a respite." He tipped his head so that his cheek rested on her head. His hand skimmed down her shoulder, her side, then rested along the curve of her hip.

It was soothing to sit this way. No urgency. No demanding sexual desire, though it hummed just beneath the surface of her skin. She could turn her head, just so, and press a kiss to the underside of his jaw. Or she could nibble on his ear. Both might turn the hum to a spark.

She did neither.

"Why Donne? Why not Shakespeare? Or Byron, for that matter?" Her fingers played with the open V of his shirt. The light sprinkling of hair on his chest was stiff and rough beneath her fingers.

She felt his cheek move against her hair as he smiled. "A man that can write a sonnet entitled 'A Hymn to God the Father' and an elegy entitled 'To His Mistress Going to Bed' must have quite the dual life."

"You *would* be familiar with a poem about a mistress. Come to think of it, I should be as well." She tipped her head back to look up at him. "I am your mistress, more or less."

"Mistress." His fingers twirled one of the curls that curved around her cheeks. He frowned. "No, that doesn't seem right."

"What else would you call our relationship?" She was not certain she wanted to know. There could be no correct answer.

Chapter 33

H E WAS MADDENINGLY silent for a moment. She thought to fill the silence, but that would give him an easy retreat. So she waited, embarrassingly nervous about his answer. Which was ridiculous.

"I don't know." He sounded baffled. Endearingly so. "I don't know, Lilias. But you are not my mistress."

Odd. That made her feel ever so better. She felt quite buoyant, in fact, and decided to turn the conversation. "I barely remember the mistress poem. I do remember it was quite scandalous, though." Naughty, but she couldn't help adding, "Will you read it to me?"

His chuckle was a low rumble in his chest. "Perhaps." She shifted as he retrieved the fallen book, then nestled in against his shoulder again. He flipped through the pages. "Here it is. 'To His Mistress Going to Bed.'"

He dipped his head. Warm lips pressed against the curve of her neck. The hum beneath her skin intensified. A simple kiss could have such effect.

"*Come, Madam, come; all rest my powers defy / Until I labour, I in labour lie.*"

"That doesn't sound enjoyable."

He laughed, then set his fingertips against the page to follow the print. She didn't listen to the words, only the baritone tenor of his voice. Strange that it could vibrate inside him and still sound so smooth.

"Off with that girdle, like heaven's zone glitt'ring . . ."

"Oh. Well, that is more exciting." She set her lips to the underside of his jaw. Just where the skin arched over bone. Stubble scraped her lips in rough welcome.

"License my roaving hands, and let them go / Before, behind, between, above, below—"

"Angel!" She sat up, laughing at his outrageousness. Improperly outrageous. Scandalously so. "You concocted that bit on your own. Don't embellish!" she chided.

"I did not embellish. Look." He set his fingers on the line.

She read it carefully, then laughed herself. "Donne was a randy fellow, was he not?"

"No more than I." His eyes were bright. Gold and bright and so, so focused on her. "I want you, Lilias. Always. I think about you when I should not. When I cannot take the time to think of you."

They were not romantic words. But they struck somewhere deep within her. The stuttering of her heart began again. "When will it be too much?" she wondered aloud. "When does it become so all-encompassing that it becomes too much to bear?"

"I don't know."

It frightened her, this consuming lust. But it was more. It wasn't desire. Or not just desire, though it had begun there. She couldn't name it. Didn't want to. But she did want him. Inside her. Around her. With her.

Leaning over, she set her hands against his chest. She kissed him once, twice. The moment called for softness. For sweetness.

"Now off with those shoes, and then softly tread / In this Love's hallow'd temple, this soft bed." He whispered the words against her mouth.

Oh, his words were a stroke to the heart. And they were for her. She heard them, internalized them. Craved them. Her body went weak. Femininely so. Her breath was quick, her stomach muscles quivering as he reached for the edge of her bodice and slid it down her shoulder.

"Lilias." One hand followed the bodice, sliding over the curve, calluses satisfyingly rough against her skin. The other hand drew her toward him. "It is new. Each time, it is new and fresh. I know what lies beneath your gowns already, but each and every time I discover something different. A sigh. A whisper. A trembling." He kissed the underside of her jaw, much as she had done to him. More kisses trailed down her neck, flirted with her collarbone. Then her bare shoulder.

Her skin was alive under his touch, under his lips. She could only concentrate on breathing, on sensation. On the gentle pleasure burgeoning inside her. She wanted to reach for him, to pull the clothes from his body. From hers. But she could not. Her muscles were too yielding, her sighs too content. She was powerless against his hands as he pulled her beneath him. As his mouth touched hers, she accepted his weight. He did not crush her, but held himself just above her. The control reverberating through his muscles drew out sheer feminine delight.

She smiled up at him as she brought his thoughtfulness into her. He did not smile back. So serious, this Angel. A sober man, bent on seeking out every hidden drop of pleasure.

Hands framed her face, fingers skimming into her hair to tangle in the taut strands. But his lips did not leave hers. He tasted, possessed, then gave to her. It was not their first kiss. Yet it felt new. Captivating. But perhaps it *was* new. This grave Angel was someone she had not seen before.

It wasn't fire that streaked through her when his tongue stroked the seam of her lips. It was warmth. It wasn't urgency or hunger that sent her hands to his biceps, or her legs twining with his. Closer. She wanted to be closer.

The kiss deepened, a stroke of his tongue. The scrape of his whiskers. One clever hand skimmed along her body. The first touch. The thousandth touch. She could not decide. But it was not enough. She arched against him, telling him she wanted more. So much more. Her breasts pressed against his solid chest, one leg slid up his to press him against her.

"Not enough room on the settee for what I have planned," he growled.

And then he was standing, looking down at her. Did she appear wanton, with her hair beginning to fall from its pins and her petticoats rucked up beyond her knees? She did not move, because she saw how his body strained against his clothes, how his breath heaved in his chest. So she let him look his fill, then look again. His eyes skimmed over her body as slowly as his lover's hands could do. Now he smiled, just a little bit wicked. And oh, she saw plans in his eyes.

Excitement, just as wicked, streaked through her.

He stepped away from the settee and she turned onto her side to watch him, pillowing her cheeks on her hands. His back was to her as he stoked the fire, then added more wood. She watched his shirt stretch over his back, shifting over muscle. But it was not muscle that made her heart sigh. It was the plush pillow he brought to the floor, and the quick glance to check the height of the flames.

He was seeing to her comfort. Did he not know she required none of the trappings? Silk pillows and warm rooms were unnecessary. She had made love in uncomfortable places, because sometimes that was all she'd had to tie her to Jeremy in the last hours before battle.

Now, with Angel, she had gone far beyond the need for a soft place to lie. A chair would suffice—oh! His shirt was drifting to the floor, and then one boot was tossed into a corner. Then the other. Angel in nothing but breeches was a magnificent sight. Lean, elegant, and gold all over. Then his breeches were discarded, then the drawers beneath and then— nothing more could be thought. A naked Angel was every woman's dream.

He walked toward her. Strutting almost, she thought, and realized she was smiling at him. Well, she did want the dream. When he reached her, one arm slid beneath her knees, the other behind her back.

She laughed when he picked her up, sounding as giddy as the butterflies wreaking havoc in her belly. And when he laid her on the rug before the fire, she simply sighed. Low flames licked the logs, tongues of red heat to slowly burn away the cold wood. She felt just like that low fire. Tiny flames flickering inside, but not burning out of control. A pleasant hum in the blood, and needy heat between her legs.

"There's a romantic in that spy soul of yours, Angel."

"And a romantic in your warrior's heart." He stretched out beside her, nuzzled her neck.

And though she wanted softness, she also wanted more.

One quick move and she was above him, straddling muscled thighs amidst a froth of muslin and ruffles and lace. He used the moment to begin to unfasten the hooks at her back. One, two, three . . . the scrape of his thumb against her back sent her blood from that low hum to a bright peak. Anticipation slid along her skin.

Then the ribbon tied around her waist was loose. She set her arms into the air and let him draw the gown from her, the chemise, her stays. The petticoats were more difficult, but then those and the stockings were gone.

She was bared to him, dressed in nothing but skin and firelight. She still ranged above him, straddling him. He twitched against her, his body trying to pierce the warmth and wetness of her. She only smiled and pressed herself on him so that he groaned and tipped back his head, hands gripping her waist.

"Do not make me wait, Lilias." His voice was part groan, part whisper.

But she wanted to look, and decided he could stand the exquisite torture. Tongue caught between her teeth, she studied him. Lean muscles on his chest and stomach. Crisp hair rasping against her fingers. Eyes that were half closed and watching her.

His hand moved to her breast, thumb flicking across her nipple. The concentration on his face was complete, as though nothing in the world existed beyond her body.

And so she took him in. The hand on her hip gripped tighter and he pressed himself up, deeper. She let her body adjust to him, let her heart swell with that contact. With the sensation of being filled and being given a gift and being taken, all at once.

Breathless, she could only glory in it. A single moment where neither of them moved, and yet both *were* moved. When nothing existed but that place where they were joined, and their breath, and the beat of hearts.

She sensed the gathering in him. Saw his eyes focus on her face and the hunger come into them. She braced for the move, for the flare of his desire and the snap of his control. When he pulled her beneath him she simply rolled with him and vised her legs around his hips. When he buried his face into the curve of her neck, she wrapped her arms around him.

He thrust into her, slow and even, drawing out the pleasure. Some part of her heart ached. Not a hard pain, but the type that moved its way to the throat, then built behind her eyes. Her head tipped back as he found the rhythm, as his body melded with hers.

Torture built in her, pleasure and pain and need and passion. It all tangled together, just as her hands sought one of his and their fingers tangled. Then his other hand found hers, so they were joined by both hand and heart.

His body claimed hers again and again, his fingers tightening in hers. That grip was the last bastion against drowning in sensation and emotion. Until it was no longer enough. The last bastion failed, and there was nothing but the exquisite pressure building inside her like so many starbursts.

And then there was nothing but gold behind her eyes and his lips against hers as she cried out. When he joined her beyond that moment of reason, his body was slick with sweat, his muscles rigid with the release. He withdrew, thinking again of her comfort and safety, no doubt.

The thought had her pulling him onto her, so that now he did crush her with his weight. But it did not hurt. Her arms cradled him, her legs held him. They stayed there, wrapped in the firelight and each other, until the flames died low and nothing but burning coals remained.

Chapter 34

"WHEN I FIRST saw you, I never would have thought that I would be lying here with you. Like this." He lay beside her, propped on his elbow and looking down at her. One of his hands lazily cupped her breast.

"*En déshabillé?*" she suggested.

"This is a little more than *en déshabillé*." A corner of his mouth ticked up.

She laughed. It *was* more—so much more. She was loose and satiated, and had no driving need to leave the rug in front of the fire.

"You were so fierce that day on the field," he said. "And so beautiful." His thumb brushed across her nipple, sending tiny aftershocks to her belly.

"And you were covered in sweat and blood, and looking fierce yourself."

"It's battle. There's no choice." His hand fell away from her breast, only to skim the length of her belly.

She slid her foot along his calf, part caress, part comfort. The sleek muscle of his leg beneath her toes felt hard and strong. But she sensed an odd pensiveness about him. Something had disturbed him. She had no guesses as to what it was, so she seized his topic of conversation. "What do you remember most about Waterloo?" she asked.

"Aside from you?" His hand moved along her hip and thigh in an absent caress.

She laughed softly. "Yes, aside from me."

He was quiet for a long moment. Perhaps he wouldn't speak. Even in the light of the single candle across the room, she could see his gaze turn inward.

"The smell. More than the blood and incessant pounding of the guns, I remember the smell."

"Gunpowder." She could smell it even now. Sharp, acrid, burning her eyes and nose.

"And the scent of death. So many dead." His fingers jerked once, digging into her hip, then releasing. He looked down at her. His mouth was so serious. "Do you ever dream of it?"

"Do you?" She laid a hand on his chest, curling her fingers in the rough hair sprinkled there.

He raised a brow. "That's not an answer."

She hadn't wanted to answer. But she could see in the deep gold that the answer mattered.

"Sometimes." She ran her fingers over his serious, sculpted lips, pressed the pad of her thumb there as though it were a kiss itself. "I stopped dreaming of it for a while, but since I learned the truth about Jeremy the dreams have started again. They're all mixed up with the medallion now, and I can't tell what is memory and what is only dreams. All I feel is sadness."

"I'm sorry." He kissed her palm. Softly. Tenderly. "I wish I didn't have to tell you the truth."

"But you *did* have to."

His eyes never left hers as his mouth lingered on the sensitive skin of her palm. Those gold eyes stripped something raw in her. She felt the kiss all the way to her soul—where it shook her very foundation. She couldn't catch her breath as his fingers twined with hers.

"I could have been gentler." He bent his head and brushed his lips against hers. "In the beginning, I didn't know you. Now I do, and I care."

Pleasure and pain welled up in her. *I care.* Simple words. How could they bring such joy and such fear at one time? Her heart clutched, split, then hardened. She could not fall in love again, and she was perilously close to it.

So she did not return the words. Could not. "I do not

require gentle handling, as I think I've sufficiently proven." She pulled her hand away from his, though the movement arrowed into her heart.

He continued to lean above her, but his face had lost all softness. "I suppose not," he said slowly. He watched her one more moment, as though trying to read beyond the skin and bone and into her eyes.

"I did stand my ground against French soldiers and two assassins, after all." Words that tasted foul. She should have answered him with something better. It was too late now, so she plowed forward. "In fact, what happened to our opera-loving assassin?"

A shutter came down over Angel's expression, turning his face cool and serious. "It does not signify." Lean muscles bunched in his arms and shoulders as he pushed up to a sitting position.

"Of course it does." She sat up as well. Feeling awkward now, she set her arm across her breasts—something she had never done in all her life.

"I meant it is not significant to you."

Her mouth opened in surprise. "He attempted to abduct me. He's a Death Adder."

"But you are not a spy. Not one of us." His tone was harsh. "You do not need to be involved any more than you currently are."

Not one of us. No, she was not. She stood, naked, to search for her clothing. "I am a target. I'd think the outcome of my intended murderer would be my concern." Chemise first.

"No." He stood as well and reached for his breeches. "It is our duty to protect you. It is also our duty to protect the government and His Majesty. That means keeping some information unknown to civilians." Breeches buttoned, he stood in front of the fireplace, arms crossed. "I want you kept out of this, to whatever extent you can be."

Oh, she could see that. In the hard line of his jaw, in the temper in his eyes. Some part of her knew he was striking out at her because of the words she had *not* said to him. But another part saw the seriousness in his eyes. He did not want her involved. He did not quite trust her.

"So be it," she said softly. Turning away, she shimmied

into her petticoats and ignored the stays. She would carry them beneath her cloak.

A muscle in his jaw clenched. "It's not a personal affront. It is policy. We only share with those who need to be informed."

"And I do not. No matter that I'm a target." She did not want to face him just now, so she kept her back turned as she pulled her gown over her head. She wanted to be angry, to let temper bubble and brew and spill over on him. But it was layered over by hurt, a thin sheen that covered the temper so she couldn't use it.

"Let me work the hooks," he said.

"Just leave them," she snapped. She didn't want him touching her just then. "The cloak will cover them."

"Don't be ridiculous."

She knew she was being ridiculous. She couldn't go around London with no stays and partially dressed. And his fingers were already on the hooks, so she let him continue. But the little brushes of his fingers that had excited her earlier were now like small scrapes on her heart.

"You don't need to be involved, Lilias. I don't *want* you involved. I shouldn't even be having this affair with you." Frustration rippled through his voice.

She didn't want to hear it. "I must return to Fairchild House. I know there is yet time before the morning, but Grant is becoming suspicious. He has been asking about my early retiring."

Angel swore, and she felt him tug hard at her dress. "These bloody hooks." Another curse. Another tug, then he stepped away. "It's done up well enough. You won't have a gaping gown in the front. And you must keep Fairchild uninformed."

She knew that. Of course she knew that. "It isn't that simple. He's asked me to marry him." She tried to feel the back of her dress, stretching her arm around. Crooked. He'd done the damn hooks up crooked. "Grant cares enough that he—" She broke off at Angel's muttered curse.

"What was your answer?" he asked, voice low and controlled. "Have I been making love with another man's fiancée?"

"I said no, but he refused to accept it." She narrowed her eyes. "Do you believe I would agree to marry one man and make love with another?"

He rolled his shoulders before picking up his shirt, but

didn't answer her. He looked irritated and masculine and gorgeous. Which was quite irritating in itself.

"Apparently, you do not trust me at all." She stalked to the door, temper boiling.

"I'm a spy, Lilias." His shirt billowed out as he slipped it over his head. "Someone is always lying to me."

He was right, damn him. And for her, it was time for the truth.

Chapter 35

"HAS HIS LORDSHIP returned?"

"Yes, Mrs. Fairchild." Graves took her pelisse and the umbrella she'd carried against the threat of heavy gray skies and drizzle during her walk. "Lord Fairchild was in his personal study after a turn in Hyde Park, but then retreated to his room to change his attire. I believe he will be back in his study shortly."

"Thank you, Graves." Lilias smiled at the butler before striding toward the study.

It was time to tell Grant the truth. Past time. She'd been a coward, she could admit now. It was so much easier to find excuses than to tell him the truth. Any little distraction would do. But it was not fair to Grant to let his marriage offer go unresolved.

The study was empty and quiet, though a low fire burned in the hearth to ward away the rain. It was considered Grant's domain. She did not often come here. Few did, aside from the servants. Every shelf space was full. So full, in fact, that books were stacked in front of the typical vertical spines. They littered the desk, the side tables.

She stepped to the desk and flipped open a treatise on ornithology. Riffling the pages, she barely registered the sketches of crossbills and thrushes and woodpeckers.

She suspected Grant knew her answer, though he wasn't

ready to accept it. His marriage offer was not out of passion, but convenience. Yes, she would be able to withstand diplomatic travel, the rigors of foreign courts, hostess duties here at home. Perhaps she could fulfill wifely duties and provide an heir as well. But none of those qualities moved her soul. They did not give her joy.

Marriage to Jeremy had taught her two things. First, one could not trust even those one loved most. Second, if she was to marry again, it would be for love. Anything else would pale in comparison. Because for all Jeremy's faults, despite the assassinations, the betrayal, he had made her happy when he had been alive. Before she knew the truth, she had known happiness and love and desire.

It was as much of a juxtaposition as Donne's poems about his mistress and his hymns to God. Jeremy had shown her true happiness. And true betrayal.

She shut the book on birds and opened another volume stacked on the desk. Drat. More birds. Beside the book were feathers and sketches and binoculars. All of them irritated her. Unreasonable response, but she couldn't care. She shut the second book as well, snapping it closed in a fit of temper.

The book slid from the desk. The spine landed on the carpet with a dull *thwack*. The cover fell open. Pages fluttered like a whisper on the air.

And she saw it, inked onto the page. A circle with a black "A." Her pulse beat an irregular tattoo as she stared at it. Weak light from the window filmed the pages in pale yellow. She blinked, certain the symbol would disappear in the light. But it did not.

The symbol of the Death Adders.

Movement was impossible. She couldn't quite grasp what she was seeing. A mirage. A hallucination. Certainly people hallucinated in a London study at midday. A log snapped in the fireplace. The sound fueled her. She swiped the book from the floor and frantically thumbed through it.

Birds. Just birds. Sketches, descriptions. All by Grant himself. She recognized the slanting scrawl of his handwriting. An ornithology diary. Some pages held blots of ink, others scratched-out sentences or paragraphs. They were all dated, with details of where he was and what birds he had seen. Behaviors. Colors.

Every few pages she saw the sign of the Adders. It was small, not even as large as her smallest fingernail. Always in the upper right corner. But the design was recognizable. If she didn't know it belonged to the Adders, she would not have thought twice about it.

But she did know.

Swallowing, she scanned the pages related to the last few weeks. A crossbill. There was a little sketch of a bird's wing. *Loxia curvirostra. Drank from puddle. Hopped four times, flew twenty meters to a spruce* . . . Then, in the middle of the page, *Lord P_____. #9.* A series of numbers followed it.

Ice pooled in her veins. She flipped through the pages, going back in time. Only a few days from today. In the middle of a description of a kingfisher observed near the beach, *Mrs. L_____ F_____. #6.* More numbers followed the reference.

But it was the *L _____ F_____* that caught her eye. Those initials, on that date, with the Adder symbol.

Oh, God. The ice that had stopped her veins turned to shards of glass. Her very bones felt brittle.

"It is me." Terror and betrayal scored her throat. Numb fingers turned more pages. Backward. 1817, 1816. What about other years? Horror etched itself on her heart. What about 1815? What about Waterloo? Her hand shook as she flipped to June.

Major J _____ F _____ . #4. The numbers following it were insignificant. Meaningless. The initials and the date were all that was necessary.

She staggered, knees giving way. Gripping the edge of the desk, she stared at the page. Denial rose to her lips, but no sound came out. She read the very first page. 1814.

Were there additional volumes? Grant had maintained bird diaries for as long as she'd known him. She went to the shelves on shaking legs.

It was an easy matter to find the other volume. An easy matter to skim the words and sketches. The mark was there every so often. Initials and indecipherable numbers followed. 1813. 1812. Pages rustled. 1811, 1810, 1809. Eight years. The same year she had married Jeremy. 1808. 1807. Ten years.

Nausea reached cold, dark fingers into her chest. It seemed impossible. He was keeping track of the deaths.

Ten years.

But perhaps there was an innocent explanation. He was a diplomat, a member of the House of Lords. Perhaps he, too, was a spy and Angel was unaware. A dozen scenarios flitted through her mind.

She was grasping at loose threads, and she knew it. Grant was an Adder.

The diary in her hand seemed to burn her fingers. She must tell Angel. Quickly.

Bitter anger surged through her. Choked her. For Jeremy. For herself. For all those who died by the hand of an Adder. Fists clenched. Unclenched.

"*Bastard*." The word slipped unbidden from her lips and tasted like vengeance. Then she heard the footsteps. She recognized the uneven beat of his boots.

Grant.

She whirled to face the door, all hate, all fury, swelling viciously inside her. Curses tumbled in her brain, formed on her tongue, ready to be heaped upon Grant. But logic was a hard jolt of fear. He would be skilled in death. An assassin. She had no weapon.

She glanced at the second diary before shoving it back on the shelf. She needed to live long enough to tell Angel the truth. She buried the pain, the rage, beneath a cold, hard barrier where it could fuel the part she was about to play.

The door handle turned. Slowly. Inexorably. It might have been five minutes before the oak panels opened. It might have been seconds. It might have been a single heartbeat. And then he was there. A smile on his lips, warmth in his deceptive eyes.

She returned Grant's smile, and could not understand how her face did not crack in two. She suppressed a shudder and felt it ripple beneath her skin. Beneath her bone.

"Lilias." A pair of binoculars dangled from his fingers. "Did you enjoy your walk this morning?"

She gulped air as her lungs constricted. She couldn't play this role. She couldn't. She wasn't prepared for it, wasn't trained for it. She couldn't—

"I did enjoy it, though the skies were quite threatening." Shocking that the voice coming from her mouth sounded so normal. "I think it's about to rain."

"It's always about to rain." He crossed the room to the

fireplace. Binoculars marched across the mantel, a little line of spying soldiers. He set the binoculars he carried in their reserved place. "There is a concert at Lady Burlingford's this evening. Will you be attending?"

She frantically searched her memory for evening plans. "I haven't decided." Her brain was moving at the speed of a snail. She could not think of something as simple as a concert. "I think so."

Grant's large hand rested on the edge of the mantel. His blunt fingertips pressed against the white marble as though trying to dig into the stone. "Who will you be attending with?"

It seemed his words held some hidden meaning. Or perhaps she was reading meaning where there was none. "What is it you are asking me?"

"There are rumors linking you and the Marquess of Angelstone." He turned toward her. The warmth in his face had seeped away. She searched his eyes for some sign he knew she was a target. There was nothing there. She couldn't read anything.

But then, she did not know him at all.

She drew a deep breath as fear fled. There could be no fear when hate and betrayal consumed every inch of her heart and mind.

"You are wondering what is between Angelstone and me."

"Can you blame me?" He stepped forward, reaching out a hand. "I offered you marriage."

She thanked God she had not accepted. "And I have kept you waiting. I'm sorry for it." Lies. But she must sound natural. She must be able to leave this room.

He took both her gloved hands in his and stepped close. Closer. He raised them to his lips. She could read his expression now. It was not quite pain in his gray eyes. Not quite excitement. But they were bright with something. Her eyes flicked over his face and she caught her breath.

Lust. Basic, animal lust.

His voice was rough with it. "Give me your answer, Lilias. I deserve to know."

She could smell his cologne. The scent was as familiar as the scent of tea. It would have been as comforting—if she hadn't known he was a liar and a murderer.

But it also brought clarity to her thoughts. Her mind

sharpened, like a thin, slender blade. On one side she analyzed how best to avoid detection. On the other side of that keen edge, her heart held the knowledge of his betrayal.

It only sharpened the blade.

So the deception would start now. Before she was ready. She would have to play the coquette. Feign attraction. There was no other choice. She met his gaze and again saw nothing that indicated he wanted her dead. She wondered what he read in her eyes. It couldn't matter. If it did, she *would* be dead.

"Grant. It hasn't been fair to you, but—"

"You are saying no." He let go of one of her hands and raised his to her cheek. He wore no glove. His hand was surprisingly cool against her skin. "I promise you, I will be a good husband. I know how badly you hurt when Jeremy died. But I shall live a long life. I shall make you happy and see to your every comfort. I don't want you to be hurt again."

Did death not hurt?

His thumb brushed her cheekbone, ever so softly. It felt like playing with the devil. She took a long, slow breath that turned ragged at the edges. When his eyes went dark with desire, she knew he'd mistaken her steadying breath as her reaction to his touch.

"Grant." She turned her cheek into his palm and tried not to be repulsed by the smoothness of his skin. "I'm sorry I made you wait for my answer. But I had to be sure."

"I've tried to be patient." His other hand came up so that he cupped both of her cheeks in his palms. "The rumors about Angelstone have proved to me how much I care for you."

Oh, how cleverly his tongue lied.

"I appreciate your patience. I—" She swallowed hard as his head dipped toward hers. As his lips came close to hers. Her fingers convulsed around his upper arms. She could not help it. "I know my answer."

"What say you?" he asked. How had she never noticed the underlying sourness beneath the scent of his cologne?

"Yes," she breathed, trying desperately to feign desire rather than showing the absolute disgust roiling in her stomach.

He stilled, his eyes dark and focused on her, before a tremor ran through his body. Then his lips swooped down to crush against hers. His mouth was hot and tasted bitter. His lips were hard, even harsh. When his arms pulled her to him, she gripped his shoulders—not in heat, but to repel him. Only she couldn't. As her body told her to push him away, a cold part of her mind told her to play the game.

She had to stay alive. To escape. But she wished desperately for a knife she could slide between his ribs. Even if she wasn't sure she could kill him, she wished for the knife so she could have the choice.

"Thank God." Grant buried his face in her hair. "I've been waiting. Lilias, I care for you so much." The liar. Then he kissed her again, roughly, as though trying to take possession of her. "I don't know how long I can wait for you."

"You'll have to." Breathing through her nose in an effort to control herself, she stepped away and smoothed her skirts. "I need to wait a few more months before announcing the engagement."

"Why?" He said it in a flat tone that warned her his passion had turned to irritation.

"For Catherine. The second anniversary of Waterloo has barely passed, and she may not be able to contend with our marriage yet. That day was very difficult for her." She willed herself to put a hand on his arm. "Please wait two months at the very least."

"Very well. For Catherine." After a quick, hard kiss, he stepped away and opened the door for her.

She swept past him and into the hall, then hurried up the stairs to her room. When she reached the bedchamber she'd called sanctuary for two years, she set her fingers on the smooth panels of the door. It shut with a quiet, final *snick*.

She waited a heartbeat. Two. Then she whirled and raced to the basin stand in the corner. Bile rose in her throat and she fought the urge to wretch. Pouring water into the basin, she scooped a handful and drank from her cupped palm. Inelegant, but she desperately needed to wash Grant's taste from her mouth.

When she'd rinsed, and rinsed again, she lifted her head and stared at her own white face in the glass mounted on the wall.

So this was the game. She was, effectively, a spy.

She hadn't known it would be so difficult.

Chapter 36

HER CLOAK SWIRLED around her body as Lilias and a sharp breeze rolled through the door. The air smelled of women and thunderstorm. Angel shut the door and blocked out the night air, but the mix of scents remained, along with the faint scent of wet leather. Narrowing his eyes, he studied the arms crossed over her chest. Beneath her cloak, he saw the butt of her pistol side by side with a dark swathe of leather.

"I must speak with you." The urgency in Lilias's voice sent his heartbeat spiking upward. Something was wrong. Something had changed.

"The study, then. Jones is there." He didn't bother to ask for her cloak. She was already halfway down the hall and scattering raindrops behind her. Her cloak disappeared through the study door. He was a step behind.

"I know the identity of a Death Adder."

Her statement fell heavy into the room, as solid as the pearl-handled weapon she set on his desktop. A weight pressed against his chest, his lungs. He was conscious of the crackle of flames in the hearth, the tick of the clock on the mantel, Jones's utter stillness in the corner, hands hovering over the dismantled pistol he was cleaning.

"Who?" His voice scraped against his throat, rough as tree bark over skin. "How?"

"It's Grant." She was nearly breathless. "Look." She thrust something at him.

Two slim volumes. Leather bound. Worn. Ordinary. He took them and ran a hand over the smooth cover of the top one. Ordinary often concealed the most extraordinary secrets.

"Open it. Find the entry for the day we went to the opera." She was reaching for the first journal, ready to do it for him. Not eagerness, but urgency.

He flipped it open just before her fingers snagged the cover. Her haste echoed inside him. Blood pumped and rushed and roared through him in a deluge of anticipation.

Sketches of birds flew across the pages. Scrawled notes of feathers and flights followed. He saw them. Dismissed them. He found the date, stopped. He didn't even need to read it. The sign of the Death Adders was there. Just there. Small, but clear.

Terror howled in his heart. Rage thundered though his mind. *She had been living with him.* Fairchild could have murdered her while she slept. While she ate breakfast. During tea. A primitive bloodlust hazed his vision, blurring the words on the page. But he could still see enough to know he'd found an Adder.

Mrs. L _____ F _____ . #6. Then an indecipherable code of numbers.

He struggled to bring himself under control. "It's a record," he said softly. "Son of a bitch."

"I called him a bastard when I found the books," Lilias said drily. "But I think the sentiment is about the same."

Jones snorted, then coughed politely into his fist.

Lilias moved beside Angel and peered down at the page. "Grant killed Jeremy. He tried to kill *me*."

"We don't know he killed." He ruffled the pages, searching for the sign. Each time he found the inscription, numbers were listed beside a name. "This is proof he is involved, but not an explanation of how."

"I agree. But he kept track of the deaths." She looked up, eyes bright and hard. "At the very least Grant is involved with the Death Adders. If he's keeping track in this way, it seems likely he's organizing the assassins."

"Agreed. Jones? Take a look." He passed the books to

Jones when the man approached. He turned back to Lilias. "How did you find the books?"

"They were right in the open." She fiddled with the clasp of her cloak. Her fingers trembled on the silver hooks. "I found the recent one on his desk. I knocked it onto the floor, and there it was. The sign of the Death Adders. I found the second one on his shelf, but I knew where to look. Angel, he has been carrying those diaries with him for years."

"What do you mean?" He reached for her cloak as she swung it from her shoulders. He could still smell the rain mixed with the scent of her soap.

"He carries the diaries when he goes bird hunting. That's what he calls it. 'Bird hunting.' He walks around in the country, hunting birds, but also here in London. Or he always said he was hunting birds."

"That's one way to put it."

"He found me in his study, right after I discovered the books."

"What?" He jerked his head up to stare at her. Beside him, Jones did the same. "What did you tell Fairchild?" Though his actual question was *what did you reveal?*

"Nothing. I promise." She slid a glance at Jones, then back to him. Her shoulders hunched a little—a most un-Lilias gesture.

"Jones, can you give us a moment, please." He kept his gaze steady on hers. When the door closed quietly behind Jones, he asked, "What did Fairchild do to you?"

"He wanted an answer to his marriage proposal. I told him yes. I did not know what else to say," she added quickly. "I could not tell him I knew about the diaries. Or the Adders. I had to do something to distract him."

"That is not all." He saw it in her face. He cupped her chin in one hand and raised it to look more clearly at her.

"Stop." She jerked her chin away. "I do not want to be manhandled again today."

"Tell me." Something possessive and manic and primitive rose in him. "He did not hurt you, did he?" Fairchild would pay if he had. In blood.

"No." She shook her head, took a step forward. "He kissed me. I couldn't stop him. Or rather, if I had stopped him, he might have questioned what I was doing in his study, or what I had found."

She turned into him. A sob rose in her throat, then was suppressed again. He drew her in, as natural as breath. There was nowhere she belonged just now but holding on to him. He ran a hand down the ridge of her spine, the curve of her back just above her hips.

"He had no idea what I knew or what I had found. But he will know the diaries are gone soon."

He feathered his hands over her cheeks. The oddest sensation settled in his chest. "Do you know, Lilias, that you've all the makings of a proper spy?"

Her laugh was low and relieved, and her shoulders relaxed. One corner of her lips tipped up. "I've learned from the best."

Safe. She was safe and here with him. He caught her mouth with his own. Tasted her. Breathed her in. She was never the same. Always new. Hunger and need swirled around her. A low hum sounded in her throat. Approval, he thought, as her hands slid up his shoulders. Her mouth was hot and willing. He felt the need in her, as strong as in him.

But he drew back. There was a time for need. For now, there could only be action.

Chapter 37

A BRIEF KNOCK PRECEDED Jones's entrance into the room. "Sir Charles has arrived, Angel. I heard his carriage out front." Even as he spoke, the front knocker fell hard, once.

"I'll speak with him." Angel stood, long body unfolding itself. "Stay here, Lilias."

There was little chance to argue, given that Angel was through the door. She started to follow, but Jones stepped in front of her. In his quiet, dispassionate way, he blocked her from exiting the room. She narrowed her eyes at him.

"I will give them two minutes, Jones. That is all."

"Yes, ma'am." That was all he said. As though he were not protecting his compatriots, and she were not threatening him.

But she had no intention of being left behind. Angel might believe she did not need to be informed of the circumstances, but this was her battle. Her life. If she needed to fight to be included, she would. She wasn't waiting even two minutes. She sized up her opponent, his broad shoulders, the narrow hips. He was bulkier than Angel. More solid. She looked him over, trying to decide on his most vulnerable area.

Jones squared his shoulders, as impenetrable as a stone wall, just as Angel and Sir Charles brushed past him.

"Where are the books?" Sir Charles moved into the room as he had before, with purpose and strong strides.

"Here, sir." Angel picked them up in one hand and passed them to Sir Charles. "I think they're coded—or partially coded."

"Will you arrest him?" Lilias said, stepping up beside Angel. "If he is an Adder, he must not be allowed to go free."

"Lilias." Angel set a staying hand on her arm. "There isn't enough evidence to arrest him."

"Not enough—what about the books?" Shocked, she swiveled her head between the two of them.

"They're likely coded." Sir Charles riffled through the pages, as though that was all she needed to know to understand their logic.

Well, she didn't. "Explain."

"He's a peer," Angel said, his hand firm on her arm. "Fairchild is a member of the House of Lords and is well respected. The books aren't enough information to arrest him on. We don't know what they say. Once they are decoded, or if we find more information, we can act. Until then, there is nothing that can be done but search for more evidence."

"Catherine may be in danger every moment she stays in Fairchild House. The household servants as well," Lilias bit out. She could not let them stay there. She did not know what Grant was capable of, but if he was involved with the Death Adders, he could kill them all.

"There is no reason to believe he will kill any of them now," Sir Charles said calmly, picking up the second bird volume to thumb through that. "Presumably, unless he becomes aware he is under suspicion, he would not want to be linked to any deaths—yours included. It's likely the reason you are still alive."

Angel let out a breath that sounded suspiciously like a growl. "We need the volumes decoded. Quickly."

"Agreed. Use Maximilian Westwood. He's fast and he's the best." Sir Charles tossed the second book on the desktop. The slap of it made Lilias jump and stare at it.

More evidence.

"How much evidence do you need to arrest him?" She set her hands on the edge of the desk and leaned over so her face was inches from Sir Charles. "I will obtain it."

"Lilias, no." Angel stepped beside her, tried to push her back from the desk.

She angled her body away from him, ignored the heavy hand on her shoulder and kept her eyes on Sir Charles. However much it hurt her heart, Angel would have to wait. "I will obtain whatever evidence you need," she repeated.

"But, sir—" Angel was cut off before his protest could even begin.

"She must return, regardless." Sir Charles's fingers tapped the journal as he frowned. "If she does not—if even a whiff of suspicion reaches Fairchild—he may bolt. We can't risk that."

"I can search the house," she said. Ideas began to grow in Lilias's mind. Where would Grant hide weapons? Documents? Medallions? She could think of a dozen hiding places in the townhouse. "There are unused attics upstairs for storage. There might be something there. I could search Grant's room. Linen closets. Wardrobes."

"She's not trained. She'll make a mistake, perhaps forewarn him without meaning to." Angel's hands fisted, unfisted. "Send an agent during the night. Myself. Jones."

"If Fairchild is trained, he'll be ready for a night intruder." Sir Charles stood, stacking the journals one on top of the other. "Mrs. Fairchild has the opportunity to search during the day while he is away, and has an excuse to be in almost any room of the house. You do not," he said to Angel. "Send her back to search."

She let out the breath she'd been holding. She could not decide if she was satisfied or terrified. It was her duty to find the evidence now. Her duty to save herself, Catherine, the servants—and to avenge Jeremy. Or at least, to avenge the life and love she'd thought she had.

"Good," she said. "Good." She would not let fear overwhelm her, whatever it took.

She stepped to the ubiquitous brandy decanter in Angel's study, poured herself two fingers and tossed it back. It scorched her throat, her heart, her stomach. Drawing in a breath, she welcomed the heat. Snapping the glass onto the tabletop, she turned and faced them.

She sent them a savage grin. "May the best woman win."

––––––––––

LILIAS'S WORDS COMPETED with a furious buzz in Angel's ears. She could not go back into the lion's den. Fairchild could kill her at any minute. His blood chilled. He was putting a woman between himself and the Adders—putting her at risk.

"A word, Angel," Sir Charles said before disappearing into the hall, calling for Jones and his greatcoat.

Angel spun on his heel to follow, filled with a vicious fury that had no proper direction.

"Sir," he said, once they were near the front doors. "She cannot go."

"It's the plan with the least amount of risk and the most chance of success. Decode the books, let Mrs. Fairchild search—"

"I'm not letting her go back." The words were a shock to him. He hadn't planned to say them, but once they were out, he could not deny them. He was not putting Lilias in harm's way. He could not let another woman die by the hand of the Adders.

Sir Charles paused in the act of putting on his greatcoat. A brow rose, slowly, coolly.

Perhaps Angel should have taken it for the warning it was, but he did not. "She's not trained. She has no experience. She should not go back to Fairchild House."

"Angel," Sir Charles said softly. "You are bordering on insubordination." He shrugged into his greatcoat with deliberate movements.

"She may be killed." Even the thought sent his gut churning.

"Indeed. A risk she is aware of and willing to accept. I believe it does not need to be stated." Sir Charles picked up his cane without looking at Angel, as though his concerns did not matter. "It is a risk I, too, am willing to accept."

"But, sir—"

"She will go back." Sir Charles opened the door, letting in rain and a cold wind. "It is nearly midnight. You will spend the next few hours giving her instructions. You will ensure she gets a few hours of sleep. Then you will return her to Fairchild House and take the journals to Westwood. *That is a direct order.*"

Angel nodded once, hard, in acceptance. But he could not speak. There was nothing to say. It was no longer a warning, but a command.

Sir Charles did not even wait for an answer, but stepped into the night and closed the door quietly behind him.

Panic gained a slippery foothold in his chest. He could not let her go back, and he could not disobey his commanding officer.

Chapter 38

YOU WILL SPEND *the next few hours giving her instructions.*
He had done so. Instructions on weapons to search for.
Tricks to avoid detection such as searching for hairs in cabi-
net doors, the placement of books, the folds of a coverlet.

You will ensure she gets a few hours of sleep.

Now they were in his bedchamber, as per Sir Charles's
second command, though he doubted Sir Charles had planned
for her to sleep in Angel's bed.

"You need to sleep, Lilias. A few hours is all you have
before—" He choked on the words, but she did not seem to
notice. He pulled off one boot, then the other and set them
next to the bed, side by side, as was his habit. If a man had to
move quickly in the middle of the night, he wanted his boots
close by.

"Yes, but I'm concerned about coded documents." She
toed off her half boots and set them neatly on her side of the
bed. It would have been a mirror image if not for the fact that
his Hessians were tall and black and polished, while her half
boots were shorter and tan and soft kid leather. "What if I
don't recognize what I'm looking at?"

"Then you bring it to me." Could she hear the displeasure
in his voice? She had not noticed it yet, despite the hours of
questions and answers.

You will return her to Fairchild House and take the journals to Westwood.

Sir Charles's third command.

Some howling monster in his chest was fighting with itself. Tearing itself apart the same way a trapped animal might chew off its own leg to escape.

He glanced at Lilias, at the curve of her jaw as she angled her head to study her bundled cloak. She rummaged through folds of fabric and drew out one pistol, then the second. She'd left the fancy wood and velvet box behind when she came to him with the journals. It would have made them even more unwieldy to carry with her than the pistols alone.

For some reason, that single fact arrowed through the fog of exhaustion and worry. She'd left the box and brought the pistols. Even now, she was carefully setting the weapons on the bedside table.

Christ, he could love a woman who knew how to use a pistol and thought to set it out before bed. He *had* loved a woman like that.

And damnation, he did again.

He'd fallen in love with the widow. With Lilias.

It was good the bed was there to sit on. He needed the support just then.

He pulled his shirt over his head, let it fall beside his boots. Behind him, Lilias began to pull pins from her hair. He could sense she was coiled tight as a spring, her movements erratic and irregular.

Did she think of the fact that this might be the last night they were together? That tomorrow she could die?

"The attics seem like the most likely place to start. No one ever goes into those rooms." She presented her back to him, turned her head to the side to look at him over her shoulder. She didn't even ask him, as though it were a nightly routine for him to undo her buttons and the gesture needed no explanation.

He reached for the tiny pearl buttons that marched down her back. They were slippery under his fingers, and he felt clumsy. But he worked his way down the row of lustrous sentinels guarding the curve of her spine.

Damn if his male parts didn't want her. Always, he wanted

her. It was that deep part of the night, past midnight and hours before dawn. They would only get a few hours of sleep at best. Protecting her was his job for the night—it was why she was in his room. In his bed. It was no time for his body to stand at attention. But he wanted to press her to the mattress. To sink into her and pull her close and around him. Into him. To hide her from prying eyes and assassin's knives.

He wanted to run a finger down the line of her spine, covered by the soft fabric of her chemise. Press a kiss against each one of her vertebrae. And then just stay there, holding her.

When he reached the last button she shrugged out of the gown and let it fall to the floor. She bent to pick it up, an efficient movement that spoke of routine. She snapped the fabric and moved away to lay it over the arm of a chair. Perhaps she hadn't noticed his violent need. Perhaps she did not see the vicious fist of lust and fear that tightened in his chest.

She wore only a chemise beneath the gown. No stays, because she'd dressed herself at Fairchild House before bringing him the journals. The hem of the linen chemise brushed the top of her white stockings and the ribboned garter holding them up.

"Where would be the mostly likely place to hide more evidence, do you suppose?" She set a foot on the chair and untied the garter. She dropped the garter over her gown, then rolled the stocking down. The simple cotton skimmed over a slim thigh, the curve of calf.

"His study, where the first journals were." But then, if it were he, additional documents would be in a separate location. Divide for maximum concealment.

The second garter followed the first. Feminine fingers with short, rounded nails rolled the second stocking down, over another shapely thigh, over skin he knew to be soft and silky. She kept the chemise on, as she had no nightgown. Practical, his Lilias. She turned down the covers of the bed with an efficient flick. Looking up at him, she raised a brow. *Are you coming?*

It was all very domestic, wasn't it?

He could see it all happening again. The domesticity. The complacency. On another day, someday in the future, perhaps they would make love in that bed, perhaps they would laugh. The highs and lows of the day would be discussed.

Then an assassin would slip into the room and the world would end. His lover's life would end.

"Get some rest." He could not escape. The door led to the hall, to the other levels. But leaving meant leaving her vulnerable. "I'll be staying up to keep watch." The chair before the fire beckoned.

Cynical blue eyes watched him stride to the chair. He pushed the pillow behind his back into shape, tested the fluff of it. Still, her eyes watched him. She got into bed, the chemise still skimming her thighs. He could just see the shadow of her sex beneath.

Damn her. He had no right to a woman. Not when he knew what could happen to her. Not when he was about to drive her to death's doorstep and leave her there.

"Who was she?" Her words were low and quiet, but not sympathetic.

How the hell had she known? "I don't know what you're talking about."

"I know there was someone." She drew her knees up, creating a mountain of fabric with the coverlet. "Whoever she was, she was someone important."

Her eyes were curious and sharp and kind. All of the things he admired her for. No artifice there. Just Lilias.

"I loved her." The words popped from his mouth before he realized he'd thought of them.

The chair before the fire was bloody uncomfortable. The fabric prickled against his bare back. He wanted to be in the bed. But there she was, watching him with those bright eyes, her head angled in that half-coy, half-challenge way. She wasn't smiling, but her eyes were knowing.

"What happened?"

"She died."

———————

LILIAS SUCKED IN a breath. "How?" But she did not need to ask. The answer was as plain as day.

"Assassinated." His tone was flat, his face expressionless.

He was silent and still in the chair. Neither of them could be sure if he would continue. She wondered if anyone knew the details besides himself. Pushing back the covers, she slipped from the bed and went to him. He watched her with slitted eyes as she approached. His body was flesh stretched taut over muscle and sinew, a hunter ready to pounce.

She set a hip onto the arm of the chair, bent one thigh to drape along the arm, toes of the other foot pressed against the piled rug below to balance her. She looked down and met his amber eyes.

"She was a target because I was hunting one of them in Pamplona." Quiet words. Churning gaze. "Gemma was on assignment with me. I was posing as a wealthy merchant and she was my mistress. We tossed money around Pamplona, buying a ridiculous number of gowns and trinkets and boots. Whatever we wanted. In short, we made ourselves conspicuous."

"On purpose, wasn't it?"

"Yes." A muscle in his jaw jumped as he clenched his teeth. "Yes, it was on purpose. It was part of the mission. Be conspicuous so no one would guess our mission. It should have succeeded. *Would* have succeeded. But I heard rumors of an Adder killing. Sir Charles sent word we were to come in, but I disobeyed his order. I thought we could delay our departure by a day, perhaps two, so that I could gather information on the Death Adder assassination."

She wanted to tell him to stop talking. What came next was as clear to her as if she'd already heard the story. Setting her hand on his bare shoulder, she opened her mouth to tell him just that. But the words began to tumble from his lips in a mad rush.

"I went out to follow a lead. I was gone only an hour. That was all. But when I returned, the door to the rooms we had rented was open a crack. I knew what I would find." His voice trembled, then firmed. "They had slit her throat. One clean cut. There were no other wounds, which I was grateful for."

There was little comfort she could offer.

"She would have been aware," he said fiercely. He turned bleak eyes toward her. His cheekbones stood out in stark relief, the skin stretched tight over bloodless cheeks.

He could have spared her the details. Perhaps he should have. But it was a heavy burden to carry alone. So she would carry it with him. "Tell me."

"She would have seen the assassin standing over her as she

died. She would have tried to call out. To call for me—" The words became a croak, then trailed into nothingness.

The gold of his eyes had turned dark as his pupils dilated. Misery etched lines into his face. With aching eyes as she fought tears, Lilias slipped right over the arm of the chair and onto his lap. She wrapped her arms around him and felt his hands grip her waist and cling there.

Then his arms went around her, drew her in until she could not tell where he began and ended. Skin pressed to skin, heart to heart. She gave him what comfort she could, knowing that it would never be enough.

"It wasn't just any assassination, Lilias." He whispered into the crook of her neck. "They left a note, telling me my pursuit of the Death Adders placed her on the top of the target list. They didn't know my real name, but we were too casual with our disguise. They followed me to our rooms. She was killed because of me."

His face was hollowed by grief and guilt. There was nothing she could say to ease either one of those. Only time would do that. But she could help in other ways. "Then let's hunt the bastards down."

With a raw laugh, Angel set his forehead against hers. "Christ, Lilias. You should be terrified."

"Perhaps I should be." She flashed him a ferocious grin. "But so should they."

Chapter 39

FIRELIGHT FLICKERED OVER the battered violin case. The warm glow fragmented over the nicks and scrapes in the leather. Angel ran a hand over the thin tear from a knife. The edges of the cut were smooth. He remembered the occasion vividly. He remembered a hundred other occasions just like it.

It would never change. Even now that he had the title, his life would not be different. Though his mother wanted him to marry, he would not. His life wasn't one that could be shared. He had tried that once, and his lover had ended up dead. It was an immutable, absolute fact.

But that still left Lilias. The lovely Lilias, with her bright eyes and her tough nature. He turned his head to look at her, sleeping fitfully in his bed. She had not settled into restful sleep, but rolled over and murmured in her sleep. One hand fisted into the bedclothes and brows moved into the shadow of a frown.

It was like loving a Valkyrie. Her sabre was as bright as her eyes, her smile as fierce. She carried such passion inside her. It could not be hidden. That passion had led her onto the field of battle. If they lived, and they stayed together, where else would that passion lead? Marriage? It would be too conventional. They would be stifled. Could he bring her into the Service? That would only lead to her death. If she survived the Adders' knives, that was.

He looked away again, as desperate fear pounded in his chest. If he sent her to Fairchild House and the lord *was* an assassin, then it was Angel himself who killed her. Her blood would be on his hands.

With a heavy heart he lifted the lid of the violin case. It would travel with him next month or next year, wherever his assignment took him. It always did. But he would give it up, let the music go unplayed forever, if he could take Lilias with him instead.

The wood was smooth beneath his cheek when he tucked it there. Fingers brushed over rough strings. He closed his eyes and let her melody play through his head. When he set the bow against the strings, it was only Lilias that he thought of.

It was Lilias he played for.

MUSIC FILLED HER, drawing her out of sleep. The melody haunted the air, coloring it with vivid violin strains. But it wasn't just a violin. It was a heart weeping. She could feel the sorrow echoing in her own heart. The music swelled and her throat ached from the sheer beauty of it.

She almost didn't want to look. Music that deep, that visceral, was private. It was a piece of someone's soul. But she had to look. She *had* to.

Powerless to resist, she opened her eyes and saw Angel, standing in the center of his bedchamber, his eyes on her. Somehow, seeing him with the violin tucked under his chin was the most natural thing in the world. He wore only a shirt and trousers. Beneath the straight gray trousers, bare feet shifted in time with the music. Beside him, a small table held a battered violin case and a single candle.

The candlelight flickered over his face, lighting the planes and hollows of it. They were smoothed out, more relaxed than usual—but not peaceful. Even now, lost in music, there was no peace about him.

The sorrow of the music gripped her as the lonely violin notes rose and fell. The bow glided over the strings in long, sinuous movements. His fingers played over the instrument. Long fingers. Strong fingers. What a joy to discover they were a musician's fingers.

Those fingers were calloused. She'd felt the calluses on her skin and had wondered at them. She knew how they felt skimming along her thigh. Cupping her breasts. His body carried other scars, other calluses. She had touched all of them when he lay above her, when his body slid against hers. Low in her belly something began to pulse, beating with the rhythm of her blood. With the rhythm of the music.

Pushing back the coverlet, she slid from the bed and walked toward him. His gaze fastened on hers and his arms fell slowly so the violin and bow dangled from his fingertips, as though he felt awkward now that she had seen him play.

"Don't stop," she murmured. Her feet swished against the carpet as she came forward. "Play for me."

"I don't usually play for anyone." His face held little emotion. Perhaps, after baring so much in his music, he was hollowed out. For a moment, he did not look at her. Then slowly, he brought his head up, set those eyes on her face.

"Lilias."

A single word could impart all the emotion of the soul.

"Just one time, let me play for you." He took her hand. "Come," he said, leading her to a cushioned chaise.

She settled onto it, anticipation thrumming in her veins. She could smell spices in the air and wondered where else the violin had traveled. Beneath the spice was wood, polish, resin. He set the instrument beneath his chin.

His eyes held hers as the bow hung suspended above the strings. "This is 'Lilias's Song,'" he said, and set the bow to the strings.

Understanding rushed over her even as the first note sang on the air. It was his song, for her. His eyes drifted half closed though he watched his fingers move over the strings. A stroke, a slide. The sorrowful music of before had vanished and in its place was something ripe and sensuous. A little lively, a little brazen. The notes were full and rich, with a lick of heat that sounded like a battle of notes.

He played with a half smile on his lips, but it was not mocking amusement or charm that she saw on those lips. It was sensual and erotic, as though he caressed a woman instead of the instrument.

She felt as taut as one of those strings, just waiting to be plucked.

His eyes moved from the violin to her, and though the music still played she heard none of it. What more did a woman need than a lover's steady gaze and a song just for her? The bright gold of his eyes focused on her, the music stole into her breath, her heart. As though he knew the core of her and had drawn it out for the music.

Her fingers dug into the cushion beneath her. She barely felt the give of the fabric. Her body had grown tight, aching. The melody mesmerized her, the brush of his fingers against the strings made her yearn. It wasn't a sob that caught in her throat, but the sound was close.

He had turned her soul into a song. And she had done something stupid and fallen in love with him. It was impossible not to love a man that saw you with such clarity he could translate it to notes.

Her heart simply fell at his feet. Not because he was beautiful, or because he could play for her, but because he saw her. Truly saw her. No one else ever had. And worse, she had never known it.

She could not sit. Her legs carried her to him, into the circle cast by the single candle. When she stood before him, he only watched her, his body swaying with the music he created, those eyes at half-mast so that he looked at her with two brilliant slices of gold.

The notes became elongated, the smile on his face faded. His lips turned serious, his eyes full of heat and hopelessness and, God help her, love. When the last note lost itself to silence he stood there, waiting. The violin still pressed against his cheek.

"Did you like it?"

He should not have to ask. Tears welled, pressing against her eyes as love pressed against her heart. She swallowed, then curved her lips in a slow smile. Instead of speaking, she laid her fingers against his free cheek. He was a feast of textures, rough stubble, smooth skin, firm jaw. As complex as the musician beneath the spy.

"Make love to me." Her heart swelled with a fierce and joyful pain. She didn't think. Her body was too wound, her heart already pounding. Heat had already gathered between her legs. "Now." She tipped up her chin. "Here."

His eyes went hot and dark. Silence pulsed between them,

full and ripe with need. A heartbeat passed, two. Perhaps he would turn away. But no, the arm holding the bow came around her waist to draw her in. She met him eagerly, sliding her hands up his shoulders to wrap her arms about his neck.

His mouth took hers, hot and urgent. For an instant it was like being consumed by fire. She couldn't think beyond the heat. His lips were firm and hard, a brand on her own mouth. She met him. Matched him. Need for need. Her mouth moved beneath his, their breaths mingled.

His lips trailed down from her mouth to her jaw, to the sensitive place where her pulse pounded. Then he simply pressed his face against the curve between her neck and shoulder.

Chapter 40

HE WOULD ALWAYS remember the look of her, just that way. The sly smile, the curve of her cheek, the play of the single candle over flushed cheeks. A luminous light in her eyes that brimmed with emotion he could not name. Would not name.

Music swelled inside him. Her song. The never-ending melody in his mind. For the first time in his life, he did not want an instrument in his hands. He only wanted Lilias.

The smooth surface of the violin dropped away. He replaced the instrument in its case. He barely had to watch his hands. It was an efficient habit. Pack the instrument quickly so he could leave quickly. Time was precious, even when he thought it wasn't, and he could never be certain when he would play again. So he did not neglect to lay the fabric over the violin, or set the bow in its little velvet bed, or even flick the clasps. When he turned back to her, he saw she watched him with sultry eyes and a half smile.

"Angel, do you know that you touch a woman with the same care with which you touch a violin?"

"I would hope I give the woman more attention." Her collarbone was a peak of soft flesh and strong bone. It sloped into a valley of candlelit shadows. His fingers followed the peak, the slope. The calluses of his fingers rubbed against her skin. "You are not delicate. I always expect you to be fragile, but there is steel beneath your skin."

"Steel is not very attractive. But then, an angel is not particularly entertaining." She held his gaze. "Neither of us are what we appear to be."

The wide scoop neckline of her chemise beckoned. Frilled ribbons cinched it tight. They slipped in his fingers as he loosed them. "Are you cold?"

"No." She set her fingers on the edge of the fabric where it kissed her shoulders. A touch of her fingers and the garment slipped from her body, brushing her breasts, skimming her hips. It pooled at her feet, a white froth of linen that hid slender ankles and pretty feet.

She could not be more beautiful. Or more untouchable. He would be damned for this single act alone, if he was not damned already. He would make love to her one last time. Then he would save her.

"'Lilias's Song' came to me that first time on the battlefield. I heard it in my head." Her breast fit perfectly within his palm. Ripe, round fruit, full and ready. He brushed a thumb over the peak and reveled in her sigh.

"A man doesn't compose a song on the battlefield." Her eyes drifted closed as he tested the weight of the other breast. His thumbs met in that lovely space between them. The candle glowed on her skin, burnishing the white skin gold, the pink nipples a warm rose.

"I didn't compose it, Lilias." He could not explain it properly. Not with her body standing slim and straight and tempting before him. "It was just there. Inside me."

She shuddered beneath his hands. He could not hold back. He wanted to touch every inch of her skin, to breathe her scent. His hands roamed over her. Hip, stomach, the long muscles of her thighs.

She pressed her naked body against him. But he could not feel her through his clothes. Hungry to feel her skin against his, he removed his trousers. They landed on the floor in a heap. Drawers followed. Then finally they were skin to skin.

The construction of a man's body was an odd thing. Bone, sinew, skin. Knitted together into a moving whole. But parts of it were made simply to fit together with a woman's. He could feel the cadence of her heart against his chest. The cleft between her legs. That soft space between her shoulder blades. He could not touch her enough. He could not kiss her enough.

He set his arm beneath her thighs and lifted her. She sighed and wrapped her arms around his neck.

"You make me feel utterly female when you do that—and a little foolish for it." She nestled her face against his shoulder and laughed at herself. He smiled, content to hear that soft amusement.

He carried her back to the chaise and laid her there. Willing woman poured over brocade. Limp and pliable and ready. When she reached trusting arms for him, the fist of betrayal punched his belly. But his need was greater.

The last time. He would make it perfect. He started at her toes. Nibbled and kissed and sucked his way to her calves. Strong calves. Beautiful calves. He lingered at the soft spot behind her knees. The little moan deep in her throat told him it was sensitive.

He moved up to the long arch of her thighs. She had walked for miles, ridden for days. Traveled for months. Endurance. It was etched into the very flesh of her thighs. Every military march could be found here, in the memory of her muscle and bone. In the lean shape of the thighs that had gripped the side of a horse. Thighs that wrapped around him and brought him home.

His gaze moved to the curve of her hips, the indentation of her waist, the roundness of her breasts. The shapes didn't matter. Only that they were her shapes. Her hips, her waist. And when he spread her thighs apart to touch the core of her, it only mattered that it was her.

Her scent was intoxicating. Her heat, alluring. He captured her mouth with his and moved his fingers within her. Strong thighs quivered, her hips bucked. Lovely hands clutched the edge of the chaise. He felt her come undone in that slow, bone-melting way. His gift to her. Satisfaction burgeoned within him. A gift, but it would not be the only one.

Some sound of pleasure purred in her throat. She drew him to her, wrapping long legs around his hips. Her heels pressed against his buttocks. The slick heat of her core pressed against him. Her touch was the flutter of butterfly wings against his shoulders. He propped himself above her and looked down.

The candle was too far away. He had wanted to see her eyes when he entered her. But her eyes were only shadows among lashes. So he watched the rest of her face. Her lips curved when he pressed himself at her opening. He held himself still, just there, at the edge of heaven. His muscles trembled with the need to plunge into her. Yet to go quickly would never be enough.

A small movement. The fire of her lured him in. Deeper. The smile faded as her mouth opened on a sigh. Deeper again. She opened to welcome him. Now the sigh was his.

Her head tipped back, the sweep of her jaw outlined in the candle's glow. He pressed his lips there. Not a kiss, just a touch. A taste. And he slid deeper until he could go no farther. Until there was nothing in the world but her heat, her scent. The press of her thighs, the embrace of her body. He was steeped in her. In Lilias. In love.

"Say my name." His request was a whisper. She had never said his first name. He needed to hear it.

A sigh on the air. "Alastair."

He was lost in her now. Taste and texture, shadow and light. Strands of hair swirled between them. She was all that was need. All that was comfort. She was sensation and sound. He could not touch enough of her, or kiss enough of her.

Her fingers dove into his hair, tugging at the thin leather binding it. He felt the urgency in her movements. Her mouth was sweet and desperate. Her muscles clenched around him, driving him farther and harder.

Sorrow met joy as he dragged his mouth back to hers. He wanted to taste her pleasure when she took it. And she did, shuddering around him, her whispers both meaningless and full of knowledge.

He could not prolong release. Desire to stay here forever with her, on the edge of the precipice, did not overcome physical need. So he wrapped his arms around her, drawing her as close as he could until they did not have an ending and a beginning. And when he withdrew, their hearts bumped along in unison.

THE BROCADE WAS itchy against her back. Angel was heavy on her body. She did not want to move, however. Perhaps she would be able to move next week.

It was the brush of his breath against her neck that held her pinned beneath him. The rough stubble of his cheek and jaw rubbed against her and sent little vibrations through her body. She set her lips to the stubble, kissed him.

"I love you." She wasn't quite certain how it had happened. She ran a finger through his hair. "I had not expected to fall in love again. But there it is."

He did not answer. Instead, he pulled away and sat up. It was as much a withdrawal from her declaration as her body. She scooted herself up and leaned back against the upright portion of the chaise. Perhaps she had miscalculated by telling him.

"Angel?" He did not look at her. "Alastair." A quick shudder ran through him.

Alarm ran through her.

"You are not returning to Fairchild House." He stood and strode toward his clothes. Snagging his trousers from the floor, he pulled them on.

She narrowed her eyes. Had he somehow misunderstood Sir Charles's plans? Had he forgotten the hour he'd spent instructing her on how to conduct a search? He sent her a quick glance, but she could not read his face. His spy look had dropped into place.

"I am not leaving this mission incomplete, Angel. Sir Charles has agreed I must return—I thought you had as well." She was *not* going to have this conversation while in the nude. She shimmied her chemise over her head and body.

"You aren't going. I'm taking you out of London. Perhaps even out of England."

She froze in the act of tying her bodice ribbons. Angling her head, she watched him continue dressing as if the earth hadn't crumbled beneath her feet.

"Bastard." She said it softly. His head jerked up. "You think I will fail."

"I think you will die." His face was set. Grim and hard, nearly emotionless. But she could read his eyes now.

"You bloody idiot." Temper and fear and hurt streaked through her. She thumped a fist on his chest.

"Lilias." He rubbed a hand on his chest. But the grim face and sad eyes didn't change. "It's for your own protection."

"My *protection*? It is up to me to see enough evidence is found to charge Grant. This is not about protection." She jerked at the ribbons of her bodice, trying to close it so her breasts didn't leap out. She pulled her hair away from her face. Tears threatened to overwhelm the temper. She would not allow it. She knew where this sudden course stemmed from. "I'm not Gemma. And even if I were, I don't think she would walk away from this."

"I'm not confusing you with Gemma."

"No? You're afraid to love again, Angel. You're afraid I'm going to die like she did. Well, that's a risk I have to take."

"I'm not afraid to love." He stepped forward, anger sparking from him.

"Do you think I'm not afraid you will die?" Her voice broke. She felt the tears on her face. Salt stung her tongue. Stupid to cry. She never cried. But for who? Jeremy or Angel? Once again, they were all wrapped up together. Just like she and Gemma."

"Lilias."

"We both loved." Weariness pervaded the very marrow of her bones. She could not fight such emotion. "We both lost. There can be no undoing that. You have to live with it, or not at all."

His face hardened. "This is not about Gemma, or Jeremy."

It was. How could he not see that?

He didn't speak again, but simply stood with his shirt balled in his fists. Immovable as a mountain, eyes dark as a fallen angel.

"I'm returning to Fairchild House," she said. "Now. It's close to dawn." She picked up her dress from the arm of the chaise.

"Lilias," he said softly, stepping forward. He set a hand on her cheek, sent a thumb across her cheekbone. "I'm not commanding you. I'm committing insubordination and risking my position. I'm *asking* you. Do not go back. I could not bear your death."

She wished she could comply. Her heart ached with the desire to ease his pain. But there was more than love at stake.

"I will not leave Catherine and the servants under Grant's power. If he's an Adder, I'm the best chance we have of protecting them and bringing down the entire ring of assassins."

His face hardened, his eyes becoming two blank, golden stones. "So be it."

He strode from the room. His bare back faded beyond the candlelight and into quiet shadows of the house. Unseen footsteps faded away.

Alone. It could be as easy as an hour to oneself. Or as enormous as forever. It could bring peace, or stifle the breath. She stared at the single candle and its circle of light. It held no warmth. But perhaps that was just her body. It had become nothing but an icy wasteland where she could not breathe.

Except for the tears. They branded her cheeks and blazed a trail of anger through her heart. She swiped them away again and wished desperately for a handkerchief—or a large, blunt weapon to beat Angel with.

Chapter 41

"MY APOLOGIES. MR. Westwood is unavailable at the moment. Good day." Daggett, the code breaker's assistant, started to close the door to the residence that housed one of Britain's secret weapons: Maximilian Westwood.

"It's urgent." Angel slapped a hand on the door, then shoved a foot against the jamb to keep the door from closing.

If there was damning evidence in the journals to prove Fairchild was an Adder, he could take Lilias out of the Fairchild townhouse. All he needed was enough information that Sir Charles would be willing to arrest the man.

Daggett sighed. "It's always urgent when it's a spy. Come in, then, Angel. Mr. Westwood is just finishing up a translation for the Greek ambassador."

The assistant led the way down the hall and into Westwood's study. It was a large, well-lit space. Books were piled onto every surface, as were papers and quills. Angel counted six ink bottles on various tables throughout the room. The code breaker himself was hunched over a large wooden desk strewn with papers, spectacles perched on his nose.

"I'm not done," he barked. "I told you not to interrupt until I was done."

"My apologies, sir. Another spy has arrived for you."

Westwood's head jerked up and around to stare at Angel through tiny, round lenses. "What do you want?"

"Another spy?" Angel asked, striding into the room.

"The Flower was here earlier."

Ah yes. Vivienne La Fleur. Westwood didn't care for Vivienne's method of entering houses. She had a talent for sneaking in and sneaking out again.

Westwood shrugged and pushed his spectacles up his nose. "Left her damn scent in the air," he muttered.

"Women do that sort of thing." He ought to know. His bedchamber had held Lilias's scent long after she left that morning. "I have two journals I need decoded. Urgently."

"I'm busy." Westwood leaned over his work again, shoulders rounding up to block out Angel.

"They pertain to the Death Adders." He held the journals out, knowing Westwood would take them.

Westwood removed his spectacles and slowly turned to face Angel. He blinked once, twice. "Those bastards came close to designing a code I couldn't break."

"We think we found an Adder in London."

"Well, well." Westwood took the journals. He thumbed through the pages, studying the numbers added on the pages with the signs. "I don't think this will be difficult. It might even be a straight substitution."

"Good. Then I'll wait."

THE ATTIC WAS the most logical place to start.

Lilias pushed open the door to the attic that stored Jeremy's trunk. It was in the same place, the lid latched, just as she'd left it. But there were dozens of other items in the room. More trunks, hatboxes, an old settee. In the corner, paintings leaned against the wall, backs facing her, just waiting to be flipped around and viewed again. Tables of various heights and shapes were lined along one wall. Desks that had once taught Fairchild children sat side by side, books stacked on them.

It might take days to search each nook and cranny.

The idea sent a ball of dread into her belly. Did she have days? Gritting her teeth, she set down the candle she'd brought, in case the windows didn't let in enough gray, rain-soaked light.

If she didn't have days, she had better get started.

She systematically moved through the room, starting in one corner and working her way to another. She found nothing but old clothing, family portraits and knickknacks that no longer matched the house's décor.

She ignored Jeremy's trunk in the corner. She already knew what that held—memories she didn't want.

Eventually, she exhausted every drawer and shelf and corner. It was frustrating to spend so much time and find nothing. With a last look, she shut the attic door behind her.

Where should she search next? The answer seemed logical. She made her way down a staircase, then another, until she came to Grant's bedchamber.

Lilias stared at the partially open door. She had never been inside. She wasn't the least bit curious as to the colors, the furniture, how he lived. It was a room no one entered besides the maids and his valet. If he wanted to hide something, he could do it well enough here. Angel had taught her how to find a false floor or panel in the wall. If Grant had such a hiding place, it would surely be here.

With quick footsteps she entered the room and shut the door softly behind her. She leaned on it and studied the space. The shades of blue were pleasant enough. The bed was large and appeared comfortable. A writing desk pressed against one wall, a wardrobe against the other. Rugs and tables and chairs blurred in her vision. Where to start?

The desk. It was of dark wood, with spindly curved legs. Papers were strewn across the glossy surface and drawers ran down one side. She would have to search carefully, as a document could be coded, perhaps in some way that was not readily ascertainable.

But she had time. Grant had said he wouldn't be back until after luncheon. There was an hour or two, at the least, before he returned.

———

"It's a little more complex than I expected." Westwood's fingers flew across the journal page, number by number, mark by mark. "But I've got this bastard's code now." His other hand moved nearly as quickly, writing down the translation. The quill was a feathered blur as it traveled over the paper.

"What does it say?" Angel leaned over Westwood's shoulder. It wouldn't be coded if it wasn't incriminating. Anticipation darted through him.

"Wait. I'm not done." Westwood's elbow jerked back, just shy of Angel's stomach. The warning was clear.

Struggling against impatience, Angel straightened and stepped away. Every moment was precious. Every moment Lilias was in Fairchild House, she bore the risk of discovery. He wondered what she might be doing now. He'd given her the tools to conduct a proper search, but that did not account for unexpected servants' tasks or other interruptions.

But perhaps Fairchild had another explanation for his records. Perhaps she was safe with him, and this investigation was nothing more than a fool's errand.

"The bastard is ordering their deaths," Westwood said softly, his fingers pressed against the page so that his knuckles turned white.

"What?" Panic arrowed through him, sharp and hot.

"Look at this." Westwood leaned back, letting Angel get a good look at the translation.

Lord P_____ . #9 assigned. Met with client on 4 April. Order for poison. Mission completed with knife. Money received, though client unhappy with method. There were more. Dozens. Line and after line. Then he saw an entry that chilled his blood. *Mrs. L _____ F_____ . #6 assigned. Order for knife at opera. Mission failed. #6 to be punished. Order reinstated.*

Raw fury scraped a hollow through his body. He'd known Lilias was a target, but seeing it on paper was a kick in the gut that stole his breath.

"Son of a bitch."

"Agreed." Westwood pushed the papers toward Angel. "Both books are finished."

He couldn't know if Sir Charles would count it as enough evidence. It should be, and Angel could argue that it was. But he could not be certain.

Footsteps clattered in the hall, a harbinger of news.

"Sir!" The assistant's voice echoed through the hall. "Sir, he barged in!"

Jones skidded through the doorway. "The assassin from the opera. He's escaped," Jones huffed. He bent over, hands propped on knees. Rain curled the ends of his dark brown hair. He gasped for air as a drowning man would. How far had he run?

Daggett clattered in after him, chest heaving with indignation. "I tried to stop him, sir. He didn't listen—"

"What happened?" Angel strode forward and clasped a hand on Jones's shoulder.

"Agents were transferring him from headquarters to one of the prisons. I don't know which one." Jones straightened, chest heaving. "They were ambushed. Someone was waiting for the carriage. We lost one man, they lost two. But the assassin escaped."

Angel was already leaping for the door. "Fairchild?"

"We don't know. He lost the agent assigned to him on the streets shortly before the ambush."

"Bloody hell." He sprinted down the front hallway of Westwood's townhouse. The assassin would have told Fairchild that Lilias knew of the Adders. "Send a message to Sir Charles. We have to get her out of there."

Chapter 42

THERE SHE WAS. In his bedchamber. The place he had wanted her to be for eight years. But she was not in his bed, as he dreamed of. She was not naked and welcoming him into her body. Lilias was bent over his desk, riffling through papers, methodically searching his belongings.

The traitorous bitch.

Grant Fairchild watched her gown shift over her body as she pulled open another drawer. He could take her here, in his room. She was so conveniently available. And there were ways to make a woman silent.

But he did not want Lilias that way. He'd had others that way, but it could not be the same for her. Did she not realize what he had offered her? Not just marriage, but life. If she'd married him, he would have rescinded the order for her death. But instead, she chose the spy. A milksop who took orders instead of giving them.

Still, she looked exquisite, even in profile as she was now. Bent over the desk, opening drawers, finger skimming over documents. She had no doubt looked exquisite with her legs wrapped around the spy, too. And that could not be forgiven.

Compound her whoring with the fact that she knew he was an Adder, and, well, she would have to die. In due time, of course. He would use her to draw out the spy first. He could thank assassin number six for the most recent news. Or he would have, if the assassin weren't dead.

Such was the price for failing to kill a target and worse, being captured by the enemy. But number six wouldn't be making that mistake again.

"I DID NOT expect to see you here."

Lilias fought the urge to bolt upright. The smooth tenor of the voice was quite familiar. She knew it as well as her own voice. Fear became a wave of gooseflesh rippling along her skin. But she could not show panic or she would lose any possible advantage.

"Grant? Is that you?" The conversational tone of her voice pleased her. She turned to face him and forced a smile onto her face. "I am glad you're here. I was looking for sealing wax. I've used all of mine." It was difficult to appear calm when terror rolled through her.

Grant was only a few feet away, leaning comfortably against the doorjamb. Rays of slanted light shone over him as the morning sun streamed through the bedchamber window. He looked handsome, his grin broad, his jaw square and strong. For the first time, she noticed his smile did not reach his eyes.

"My apologies, Lilias. I shall see to it that Graves brings wax to your room." His voice was not normal. Something was off in the tone, the words.

The hair rose at the nape of her neck, but she widened her smile. "Thank you so much, Grant. It would certainly save me the trouble of finding it."

"I'm happy to be of service." He twitched his cuffs into place, appearing to be nothing more than a leisurely gentleman speaking with an acquaintance. Not an assassin. Not a criminal.

Her palms were damp when she clasped them together. He suspected. She was certain of it. She kept her face bland. "Well, I'm going to finish my letter, then." She started out of the room, her heart pounding in her chest as she tried to brush past him.

His hand shot out, gripping her upper arm. Fingers dug into her muscle, squeezing painfully. She gasped, then sucked in a breath when she saw his eyes. Hot lust swirled there, but it was not that emotion she focused on. She saw death there.

Unadulterated, quiet, reasonable death. Fear flooded her, an icy deluge that shivered down her spine.

"Not a bad performance, Lilias, but you are inexperienced." His voice was soft, but she heard rage lurking beneath the surface.

"I don't know what you're talking about." It was a pathetic response. She tried to wrench her arm away, but he only gripped it tighter.

"No?" His smile was terrifyingly pleasant. "Where are my journals? They are missing, which I would not have looked to you for. But now I find you searching my room. Did you go running off to your lover with my journals?"

"I don't have them." This time when she wrenched her arm away he let it go. She took a fast, panicked step to the door, but it was too late.

She didn't see it happen, but suddenly there was a pistol in his hand. Odd that such a small opening in the barrel could seem so huge.

Horror was a living thing inside her, crawling and scratching to get out. Beating it back, she struggled to think clearly. She could start screaming and bring the servants running, but Grant might kill her before she finished the first scream. She could run, but if he didn't catch her he could certainly shoot her. She had no weapon beside what was in arm's reach—which was pitifully nothing, as the only item was the elegant desk chair.

"I can see you are trying to decide what to do next. The wisest option, Lilias, would be to stay just where you are so I don't have to shoot you. Yet." Broad shoulders, elegant movements. The tailoring of his clothing only accentuated an already appealing physique. But the threat of the pistol loomed. His gray eyes held hers steadily, full of confident power. "Though I will if I must."

"Very well." He would see through any pretense that she had no idea who and what he was. "I won't feign innocence."

"Good. Lies never serve anyone."

There was a hysterical edge to the laugh that tumbled from her lips. "You have been lying for the last ten years. You're an assassin."

"Yes, one of my men told me you had learned the truth." He set the fingers of his free hand on the desktop and pushed around papers, as though mentally counting them. The pistol never wavered.

She gripped the edge of the chair. "I know you killed Jeremy."

"I gave the order for his death. That is entirely different than wielding the weapon." It sounded reasonable when he said it. He could have been discussing the anatomical differences between the wood warbler and the willow warbler. "Where are my journals?" he asked again.

"I don't know."

"Of course you do." He sent her an amused, superior look. "I've known you too long, Lilias. I know when you're lying."

So much for her performance. Still, she could appear fearless. "Apparently I don't have the same skill for detecting lies." She set her hands on the chair back, leaned into it and tried to imagine they were just two people, calmly engaging in an enjoyable tête-à-tête. "I never suspected either you or Jeremy were assassins."

"I found your lack of knowledge fascinating." He continued to casually point the pistol at her, all relaxed elegance. A strange light came into his eyes, full of some disturbing emotion she could not name. Chilled fingers of dread slid down her spine as he continued, "You are a beautiful, clever woman who could not see the truth in front of her. I often wondered what you would do if you discovered the Adders. Join us, I had hoped. You have all the qualities I want in an Adder. Courage, passion, intelligence, ingenuity."

She recognized the light in his eyes when it blazed again. Avarice and lust. *He wants me.* Her blood chilled, but she forced herself to stay calm. Anything could be a weapon. She would use Grant's own lust for her against him.

"All those qualities?" She angled her head, pursed her lips. "You think highly of me."

"I know you well, Lilias." His gaze lingered at her breasts, her waist as she drew herself up. How long had he kept that greedy want in check? He licked his lips and drew his gaze back up to her face. "You should have married me. I would have let you live," he said softly. "Instead, you whored yourself for Angelstone and sealed your fate."

In a move as swift as a lightning strike, Grant seized the

hair at the back of her neck and yanked. She had time for only a short cry before he'd spun her around and shoved the pistol in her ribs.

Her elbow rammed into his stomach before the idea coalesced in her brain. Satisfaction bloomed when she heard his pained grunt and his breath wheeze out.

Then the pistol smashed into the side of her head and she saw nothing more.

Chapter 43

SHE WOKE IN darkness. And silence.

Through the pounding in her head, Lilias struggled to discern where she was. She lay on the floor, though there was a rug beneath her cheek. A bed was beside her, but—yes. It was her bed. Her coverlet. Her bedside table.

She sat up, biting back a moan as blinding pain darted through her head. She didn't need even a moment to remember what had happened. Crawling to the door, she set a hand on knob. She had to hurry. To warn Angel. She jiggled the knob, tried to turn it.

Locked. She was locked into her bedroom.

She swallowed a panicked sob and sat back on her heels. What of Catherine? The servants? Grant could not keep her locked in here for long without some explanation.

She stood, staggered as her head pounded anew. She had to leave, by any means possible. She had no skill picking locks, and she couldn't break down the thick, solid wood door. It would alert Grant.

She spun around, stared at the window. If the Death Adder could get in, then she could get out.

A scratch came from the other side of the door, a sort of scrabbling. Then, "Ma'am?" The whisper was hardly perceptible. "Are you awake yet?"

"Graves?" Hope sprang inside her chest. "Is that you?"

"He's dismissed the servants for the evening. All of us." She could almost picture Graves's mouth at the keyhole. "He won't let me stay much longer, but he's hidden the keys to your room. I can't get them."

"Catherine?"

"She's at a soiree and plans to attend a ball after that. She won't return for hours yet." Graves's breath was harsh and shallow. "What's happening?"

She shook her head. It was too much to explain. Too strange. "Get out of here, Graves. Find the Marquess of Angelstone and tell him I'm locked in. Then don't come back. Keep as many of the servants away as you can. Catherine, too, if you can find her." Was that enough? Would that save them?

"What of you, ma'am? He's in a cold rage. I don't know what he's capable of."

She turned to look at the window again. "I'm getting out."

FAIRCHILD HOUSE WAS dark aside from a single window on the first floor. Angel reined in his horse a few houses down the street and jumped from the saddle. With a quick loop he tied the reins around the iron area fence to secure the horse.

Drawing his pistol, he moved down the street. The weapon was solid and heavy in his hand, and as familiar as his own breath. His gaze scanned the street, the windows, waiting for an ambush. Few houses had lighted windows just then, and an attack could come from anywhere. Fairchild had to know Angel was coming for Lilias.

Pistol at the ready, Angel strode to the door and pressed the latch. Unlocked. The door was open.

Fairchild was waiting.

Angel slipped in through the door and let his eyes adjust to the interior darkness. The house was silent and seemed unoccupied. The usual signs of life—servants' bustle, voices, candles—all were missing.

Sliding through the hall, he did a quick visual search, letting his pistol lead the way. Entry, clear. Hall, clear. He toed open a door to the drawing room. Empty and quiet. The adjacent dining room was the same. He finished searching the ground floor and began a slow ascent to the first floor.

He saw the open door to the study and the light spilling out of it. It was the only room that seemed inhabited on this floor. Angel checked the ballroom, the card room, even the small salon before moving to the study. If there was anyone else on this floor, he wanted to know.

He went into the study pistol first, and found exactly what he expected. Lord Fairchild sitting casually in an armchair facing the door, holding a pistol at the ready. Angel's gut twisted as he saw it was Lilias's pistol, one of the matched set that had belonged to her husband. *Where was the second pistol?* A flick of his gaze around the room revealed the second pistol nestled in its box.

"Ah, Angelstone. How good of you to finally arrive. I've been waiting for nearly an hour." Fairchild gestured to a brandy decanter and snifter on a table beside him. Firelight glinted on the empty crystal of a second glass. "Would you care for a drink?" He gestured with the pistol at the empty glass.

"No."

"Pity. I poisoned it, in the event you were stupid enough to drink it." He lifted his own snifter, pretending to be unconcerned. He swirled, sniffed, then sipped the amber liquid, his eyes never leaving Angel. The pistol stayed steady, its dark opening ready to take Angel's life.

"Where is Lilias?"

"Ah yes, my delectable little cousin-in-law." He set the snifter down and easily crossed his legs, as though their conversation was nothing more than two gentlemen meeting in the card room at a ball. "She has been quite busy, searching my house. In fact, I believe she has given you something of mine that I need back. I require my journals for my work."

"I don't have them," Angel answered conversationally. "Unfortunately, I already surrendered them to my superiors."

Angel tensed as Fairchild half rose from the chair, rage distorting his face. But the man sank back down into the seat. He sucked in a slow, calming breath.

"Unfortunate." Fairchild's voice was no longer steady. "I had hoped to trade Lilias for the journals."

"It's too late for that. The journals have already been decoded. We know everything."

Fairchild's eyes went from cold to hot. "Then I believe we are at an impasse."

———

WEAPONS FIRST. SHE flew to the chest of drawers where she'd hidden the pistol case. They would be unwieldy, but effective. She rummaged through stockings and fichus. *Where were her damn pistols?*

The case was gone. Grant had taken her pistols.

"Bloody, buggering hell." She slammed the drawers shut and gritted her teeth. "Fine. Just fine. You might have taken the pistols, but I have the sabre."

She whirled around and threw open the wardrobe doors. In moments she'd grabbed the sabre, its gleaming scabbard a long, thin line lying against the back of the wardrobe. If that was all she had, so be it.

In minutes, she'd stripped off her gown and pulled on the breeches she wore for riding. She tucked her chemise into the waistband, then shrugged into a short spencer to block out as much of the cold and rain as she could. Not pretty, but it would do.

A quick change from slippers to half boots and she stood at the window, heart thumping in her chest. A flick of the latch and the window popped open. Rain pattered on the side of the building. The wind blew in damp air and sent her mussed hair flying around her face. The street was mostly dark, the inhabitants away from home at dinners and balls and the opera. A single carriage disappeared into the dark at the end of the street.

Leaning over the windowsill, she studied the ground two floors below. She couldn't accurately toss the sabre that far, so she dropped it onto the balcony below. Swallowing hard, she clambered onto the windowsill. Balancing there, she gathered her strength.

Her lungs screamed with a hideous pressure. How many minutes did she have before Grant decided to check on her?

"Damnation." She refused to look down again. The ground was too far below, and much too hard. "Grant is going to pay for this."

She didn't hesitate again. Bellying over the edge of the windowsill, she fumbled for a toehold. A jagged brick, ropes of ivy. Anything. When she found something, she moved her hands down. Skin tore on the brick as she fought for a finger-hold. Rain pelted her back, soaked her clothes. Sodden breeches clung to her legs. She ignored it all, focusing only on her toes. Her fingers.

Hand by foot, she scaled the building and dropped onto the narrow decorative balcony below. She quickly tossed the weapon to the ground below before readying herself for the final descent.

Then, through the window, she saw Angel crouched in the drawing room door, weapon drawn and aimed at Grant, who sat easily in a chair, brandy by his elbow, pistol in his hand.

Her heart slammed into her throat. She nearly went through the glass, panic beating a wild tattoo beneath her breasts. Caution stayed her. She had no weapon, having thrown it to the ground below. Angel might be facing an assassin, but he was strong. He was quick. He had battled the Adders before.

Except this was Grant, and she no longer knew what he was capable of—certainly more than she had ever thought. Candlelight flickered over Grant's handsome, cool features, turning them into a grotesque mask of casual elegance. Angel looked just as casual. Just as worldly.

She scrambled over the edge of the small iron balcony and braced herself to drop to the ground.

Then she heard the shot.

Chapter 44

THE BULLET TORE into Angel's shoulder. The force of it swung him around. He staggered, gritting his teeth against the agony blazing through muscle and sinew. He tried to swing his arm up, to aim the pistol at Fairchild and get in a shot, but his right arm was useless.

The pistol fell from numb fingers.

He dove for it, reaching with his good arm. But it was too late. Fairchild was already kicking it out of the way.

He landed hard on the floor. Pain shuddered through him as his shoulder rammed into the leg of a settee. He groaned and rolled onto his back as white-hot pain raged in him. He saw Fairchild's boot just before it slammed into his stomach. He coughed, wheezed, curling around himself.

"Unfortunately, Angelstone, I can't wait here for my bullet to do its work. If my journals are decoded, there's little reason for me to stay in England."

Fairchild set a boot on Angel's shoulder, pressed, so that wave after wave of pain rolled through him. Gritting his teeth, Angel groped for the boot to try to knock Fairchild off balance. It was no use. The edges of his vision were going black as excruciating pain radiated from his shoulder.

"Seems your aim needs some work," he gasped. Even that

took effort. "You missed all the vital parts. But then, you usually order others to do the work for you."

The boot ground into his shoulder and he cried out. Intense, hot pain shuddered through him.

"Do you think I would ever use a regular bullet, Angelstone? That one was dipped in poison. Laurel water, to be precise." Fairchild removed his foot and crouched down. "I was easy on you, Angelstone. A sedative poison, rather than one of those nasty ones that sends a man into convulsions."

Angel put his good hand to his shoulder, trying to stanch the blood. It slicked his hand and told him he was losing blood fast. *The bullet had gone through.* It was pitifully little hope to cling to. He could feel the heaviness in his limbs and the fog in his brain. It wouldn't be long before he succumbed to the dark.

"If the bullet doesn't kill you, which it likely won't as it's only in your shoulder, the poison will." Fairchild's eyes gleamed as a smug smile spread across his face.

Angel heaved himself forward, intent on setting his hands around Fairchild's throat. But he knew it was too late. His limbs were already too heavy. His skin already burning as his insides went cold.

Fairchild took the second pistol from Lilias's case before stepping through the open door to the hallway without a backward glance.

The Death Adder would go free.

"BLOODY HELL." SHE couldn't manage more than a whisper beyond the terror clogging her throat.

Lilias dropped to the ground, her half boots landing solidly on stones. The jolt sent pain shooting through her legs and her knees gave way. Pushing herself up, she cast around for the sabre.

She had to get into the house. There was no one to ask for help. No one to stop the horror about to happen. Panicked mewling erupted from her throat. She gulped it back, steadied herself even as her fingers continued to search for the sabre.

Please. Don't be too late. Don't let him die.

She could picture Grant bent over Angel as he lay dying.

She closed her eyes, pressed her fingers against them. Not again. She would not lose another man she loved, whether he was an assassin, a spy or a king.

Fierce determination swept through her. She let it fill her. Breathed deep. Her fingers gripped the sabre and she pulled the blade from the scabbard.

Angel might die. She might as well.

But so would Grant.

The front door was open and she leapt through it, conscious only of reaching the next floor. Running up the steps, she didn't bother to move stealthily. She heard a sharp cry rend the air and increased her pace.

When she reached the next floor she charged down the hall to the open door. She heard other running footsteps at the end of the dark hall, then the door to the servants' stair creak open and slam against the wall. She almost followed those unknown footsteps, but she stopped in the doorway to the study.

Her breath ripped at her throat. Blood roared in her ears to match the panicked beat of her heart and the pounding of her footsteps as she ran across the room.

Candlelight washed over him, shadowing lean features and highlighting his golden hair. He lay on his back, his features slack, his arms limp. Blood soaked his shirt. She smoothed the hair back from his face—that gorgeous fallen angel's face.

"Angel." The word croaked out, impeded by the aching lump in her throat. She swallowed and leaned over him. She set a hand against his shoulder, trying to stanch the blood flow. She had no petticoats to rip up to do the job.

His eyes fluttered open, his mouth set grimly. "Don't bother," he panted. "The bullet was poisoned."

"Poisoned?" Shock spun through her. Words screamed through her mind. Through her heart. She couldn't voice any of them. Was there an antidote? She didn't know, and there wasn't time. A sob clogged her throat, caught there as despair washed over her.

She never thought she could have felt such anguish again after Jeremy's death. This time, with this man, the anguish was greater.

"Get out of here, Lilias." He started to roll over, then sucked in a breath and fell onto his back again. "Fairchild is on the run, but he might return. Or the Adders might swarm the townhouse. Go to my townhouse and find Jones. Leave London." His words were slurred.

"You expect me to flee? To run away and let Grant escape?" The pressure in her chest was unbearable, a tight, aching ball that drowned even her rage. She tasted salt, felt the hot tears on her cheeks. "You expect me to leave you here, like this, alone—" She couldn't say the word *dying*. She swiped at her tears. "Well, bollocks to that."

"Christ, Lilias. Bollocks?" A short laugh wheezed out of him. "Is it any wonder I'm in love with you?" His eyes started to fall closed, then rose open again. "My vision is going black, Lilias. Get the hell out of here. Go find Jones."

"Damn you, Angel." She pressed a frantic kiss to his lips. Even now, bleeding on the floor with an assassin on the loose, he could infuriate her. And even as he lay dying, he could flood her heart with love.

But he did not kiss her back.

"Angel?"

There was almost nothing from him. Just the tiniest sigh. Then nothing at all.

A violet frenzy beat inside her chest, threatening to overwhelm her. Shoving it aside, she softened her touch and kissed Angel once more. Gently. A last kiss. She wanted desperately to linger. But she knew what she had to do.

With a final caress of his stubbled cheek, she stood. Grabbing Angel's pistol from the floor, she shoved it into the waistband of her breeches.

"I'm going after that bastard."

Chapter 45

SHE WAS ALMOST flattened by Grant's horse as she ran through the alley leading to the mews. The animal reared up, hooves pawing at the air. She jumped back, skidding over uneven cobblestones.

Grant met her gaze as the animal's hooves clattered back to the stones. She saw the desperation in his eyes. He was running. Trying to save his hide before the British government arrested him.

She wasn't going to let him.

He wheeled his horse around and Lilias ran toward the open stable door. The place was empty, the grooms no doubt being dismissed with the rest of the staff. Still running full tilt, she grabbed her horse's bridle from its peg on the stable wall. There was no time to waste on a saddle. It would take too long to put it on properly. She could thank the long army marches for the ability to ride bareback and astride. It was ironic she could thank her assassin husband for that skill as well.

In seconds she'd looped the bridle over her mare's head and was leading the animal into the alleyway. Using a mounting block, she threw her leg over the horse and sent the animal down the alley. When they reached the street, she looked around. Which way did he go? She saw Angel's horse tied to a nearby iron fence, but no other movement on the street.

Then Grant and his horse flashed through the light of a

window at the end of the street and disappeared again in the shadows on the other side. Well ahead of her, but at least she knew which way he'd gone.

BY ALL THAT was holy, Lilias was a stubborn woman.

Angel struggled to keep his eyes open. He rolled to the side, the pain excruciating in his shoulder. But he could flex his fingers. The rest of the arm was still useless, but by God, his fingers could move.

He didn't know how long he had before the poison took its toll. How long had he been unconscious? Not long judging by the melted candle wax. Minutes, perhaps. He pushed himself up to sitting with his good arm. Dizzy, he gulped in air, waited for the spinning room to slow.

God, he wanted nothing more than to lay down and sleep. But that damn fool woman of his had gone after an assassin.

He made it to his knees, breathing hard through his teeth, and looked around for his pistol.

Damn if she didn't steal it from him.

MIDNIGHT WAS NO time for a horse chase. Especially in the driving rain. It was like riding through soup.

Lilias gripped the mare's broad back with her thighs. Wind rushed in her ears. In the dim light, she could see Grant ahead of her, bent low over his horse's neck. Gritting her teeth, Lilias did the same and was shocked by the metallic taste in her mouth.

It seemed determination tasted of blood and hate.

The mare's hooves thundered on the street beneath her, a rhythmic beat that echoed the wild beat of her heart. Beyond that she could hear the hooves of Grant's horse. They were louder now and he was closer.

She was gaining on him.

He was on Park Lane now. He wove through the few carriages bearing the ton to their social engagements. Lilias cut off a hackney and had the driver swearing at her. She ignored it, looking only at Grant's back.

Where was he going? Was he taking a packet to the Continent? Had he booked passage on a ship? Worse, what if she lost sight of him? He could disappear into the bowels of London or the green expanse of England's countryside. Urging the mare to move, she flattened herself against the horse's neck.

"Come on. Faster." The mare heeded her, and Lilias was grateful. But she couldn't keep the horse running at this pace for much longer.

Then again, neither could Grant's horse continue. It was already tiring, its pace beginning to slow.

Surprise swamped her as Grant made a sharp turn into Hyde Park. She followed, guiding the mare with her knees as much as the reins, and set her path at an angle to Grant's to head him off. She cut through a stand of trees, jumped the horse over a line of low bushes. She slid on the horse's back and struggled to keep her seat. Cold rain showered her body with icy, stinging darts.

Grant was just in front of her, his mount's hooves flying over the grass. He turned his horse so it followed the bank of the Serpentine. Ahead of them was a short bridge spanning the length of the river. Her mare moved up beside him, inch by inch. Grant glanced over his shoulder, and she saw eyes full of wrath and snarling lips.

She was nearly level with him now. Shoulder to shoulder, thigh to thigh. She didn't think. Couldn't. There was nothing but anger in her, a cold fury that had buried itself deep.

The leap was desperate, an action that had no basis in thought. Her body slammed into his, stealing her breath and sending them tumbling to the ground. The hard earth jarred her bones and her head snapped back. Pain blossomed in her ribs, tearing a short scream from her throat.

Dimly she heard the horses' hooves still pounding, the sound of Grant's sharp, ragged breaths.

Circling an arm around her rib cage, she rolled and sent fresh pain singing through her chest. Pushing up on one arm she surveyed the ground for Grant. He was scrabbling forward on his hands and knees, trying to reach something on the bank of the river. Gritting her teeth against the pain, she squinted into the dark. Moonlight glinted on metal and she recognized the object.

The pistol.

Fresh terror rolled through her, but she forced it down and rose to one knee, then the other. She pressed a hand against her ribs. *Not broken.* The pain was already fading. She took a deep breath. The pain sharpened again, but the sight of Grant's hand closing over the pistol had her staggering to her feet.

Again, she didn't think, but dove through the air and used her body momentum to shove him back. They both toppled into the river. Water closed over her head, filled her mouth, before she landed hard on the shallow bottom. Scrambling to her feet, she coughed it out as the current sucked at her knees. Yanking the pistol from her waistband, she tossed it onto the shore. It was useless wet—but so was Grant's.

She fumbled for the hilt of her sabre, felt the familiar grip. The steel sang as she pulled it from the scabbard and raised it. Ignoring the dull ache of her ribs, Lilias bared her teeth in a vicious grin and eyed Grant's single knife. "It looks like my blade is bigger than yours, Grant."

"Magnificent." Grant smiled as he faced her. He crouched slightly in the water, the knife clutched in one hand. "All that hair. All the feminine glory. I imagine this is what you looked like at Waterloo, my dear Lilias. *L'Ange de Vengeance.*"

"It's too bad you weren't there. I could have cut you down in the heat of battle with no one the wiser."

"And now you've been forced to resort to cold-blooded murder." He clucked his tongue. "Do you see what depths espionage has brought you to?"

The knife arced fast, a sharp and wicked crescent. She could barely see it in the near darkness, but she felt the wind rush past her, heard the *whoosh* of Grant's breath as he lunged and the splash of water. She leapt backward, instinct propelling her.

Block! Her mind screamed it. She should have blocked the knife with her own sabre. Instead, her weapon was clutched uselessly in her hand. Water slicked the hilt and her palm slid. Gripping it tight, she lunged forward, thrusting the sabre.

He moved back easily and she fought the need to simply strike out at him.

"This is Jeremy's cavalry sabre." She spoke calmly even as she raised the weapon. "Fitting that I use it to kill you, yes?"

Grant's movements faltered, just a touch. She saw it, and satisfaction curled in her belly.

"He was a coward, Lilias. He never quite understood the beauty of what we were doing."

"The beauty?" She sent her feet splashing right, left, lashed out with the sabre. Grant dodged the blade and Lilias gritted her teeth. She should have had an advantage. Even if his reach was longer than hers, her sabre was longer than his knife. And she knew how to use the blade.

A few steps forward, a flash of the metal. She felt the tip of the sabre brush something and knew she at least caught his clothes, if not flesh. He made no sound, only circled to her left. She turned instinctively, following the sound of his feet in the shallow water.

But he fooled her, moving back just enough that she had turned too far. She felt the knife graze her ribs, sucked in her breath at the burning line that spread across her ribs.

Jeremy's training came back to her, a quiet voice in her ear. She'd been his sparring partner on those long marches when he needed something to do—when they both needed something to do. Then Angel's voice echoed in her heart. *Deceive your opponent, and do not be deceived.*

"First blood, my darling." The taunt hung on the rain-soaked air.

"Luck, Grant," she hissed at him, retreating slightly. "Remember, I have experience on the battlefield. You are only a puppet master that sits in the shadows and lets others do the work."

"Perhaps." But he lunged again, quick as lightening.

She spun away, skidded on rocks on the edge of the bank. She fell on one knee, rocks tearing through fabric and stinging flesh. But she brought her blade up in time to block Grant's knife from cutting across her breasts. Springing up, she used the momentum to push him away.

Not enough strength. She only saved herself because he was toying with her. She recognized he hadn't used his full force.

He stepped back and onto the grassy bank, then tossed the knife to his other hand. "Another wound, and I didn't have to do any work. The river did it for me." His grin was feral.

"Typical," she snorted, trying to catch her breath. *She would not show weakness.* She clambered up the bank and out of the water, her eyes never leaving him.

"You're a poorly trained spy, my dear. Did the estimable Marquess of Angelstone leave his untrained pupil alone to battle the enemy?" He clucked his tongue. "A shame."

Her heart was thudding hard and she could feel the warm blood soaking her clothing and trickling down her stomach. A small flesh wound, she knew. The pain had lessened to little more than a light burning, though she knew she'd feel it later.

If she lived.

The edge of despair crept in, a little black cloud to cover her heart. She could not beat Grant. She would not win. Her ribs, her knee, the thin knife wound. Her breath was coming in ragged gasps. Pain was beginning to fog her brain.

It was Angel she thought of now. *Alastair.*

Raw fury swelled, burning bright and harsh and hot. Then it was gone, and all that was left was cold hate and the need to finish what she had started.

"I swear to you, Grant, that I will kill you. If I die as well, so be it." She spoke in a low voice, devoid of any emotion. Then she smiled. One slow, cunning smile. "Good-bye, Grant." And she let the rage fill her.

The sabre swung up, was blocked. She rose on the balls of her feet, pushed forward. He was bigger, stronger, but she was faster. She ducked beneath his arm, spun away. As she turned she struck out with the sabre, felt it slice something unyielding.

Grant grunted, his hand pressing against his side.

"Is there such a thing as third blood?" She laughed and shook back her hair, though it cost her some energy.

Jumping forward she thrust again, was blocked. Again she thrust, and again. He lost ground dancing away from her and she could hear his breath wheezing out. The sound was music to her aching soul. The wound must have been deep. It was tiring him.

But then it happened. He struck out, fast as a snake, slicing the knife across her arm. The white-hot burn spread, thin and sharp. She stumbled back, shock running through her.

He pounced.

The weight of him knocked the breath from her. The ground was as hard as a stone wall when she slammed into it. Then his hands were around her throat. Tightening, squeezing. She clawed at him, kicked her feet. But he was pressing in on her, straddling her as she flailed. All she could see was his grin; all she could hear was the blood roaring in her ears.

As the world went black, she swore she heard the voice of an angel.

Chapter 46

SHE WAS SO pale, her face a white beacon in the dark, her hair spilling over the wet earth. Her face was all Angel could see as he flung himself off his horse, the poison and the wound still slowing him. Lilias's legs were kicking, her torso bucking against Fairchild. Her hands were scrabbling in the dirt, trying to find her sabre.

Except she stood no chance against Fairchild's wide, tough hands. No chance against the man ranged above her, squeezing the life from her.

But by God, he wasn't too late. *Not this time.*

He saw Gemma's plain, well-loved face in his memory. He heard Lilias's gasping breath.

End it.

The dagger had been hidden beneath his coat in a plain leather scabbard. Now it was in his hand. He tested the weight a moment, gripped it. The poison still coursed through him. His body wasn't obeying the orders from his brain. His hands were stiff, his fingers clumsy.

But he had no choice.

The dagger flew through the air, not as straight and true as he hoped. It rotated, over and over, and in another second, it was buried in Fairchild's side.

Angel dropped to his knees, all the strength in his legs gone.

———————

GRANT'S HOWL RANG in Lilias's ears, competing with the ringing already there and harsh breath in her throat. The thumbs around her throat fell away and the pressure eased. She bucked, hard. Grant reared up, and she used all of her remaining strength to dig her fingers into the dirt and fumble for her weapon.

She coughed, winced at the blinding, burning pain in her throat.

Above her, Grant snarled, a wild, bestial sound. He yanked a dagger from his side and raised it up into the air. Fear coursed through her as she saw that blade arc down. Her chest felt tight, her skin crawled with the need to run. She nearly screamed—but her fingers closed over the hilt of the sabre.

She didn't hesitate. She swung the sabre up and slashed it across his chest. Then again. When he toppled, she rolled over, turning away from the man, from the sound and look of death. She could not bear to watch it.

Crawling through the dirt, Lilias inched her way up the bank, little mewling sounds erupting from her throat. The tip of her sabre scratched a rivulet in the earth behind her. Her hair hung down in wet, dirty ropes.

But she raised her face up to the rain and saw him. He was struggling to stand. His gold hair blew around his face as the wind plucked at it. He'd never looked so dear to her.

"Angel." The word was nearly a whimper. "Alastair."

The sabre fell completely into the dirt now. She rose to her knees, then her feet, and limped forward, her arms reaching for him. He folded her in, burying his face against her neck. He smelled of rain and himself. She lifted her lips to his. He didn't ravage them, but kissed her as a man in the darkness might worship the sun. His lips were warm, and oh, it was like finding home.

"If you're going to be poisoned," she said against his lips, "then have the decency to do it right, so I don't have to sit in suspense of the final moment."

THE PHYSICIAN CLOSED his bag and set the latches. Two brisk, irritated snaps.

"Accosted by thieves," he muttered beneath his breath. Bushy white eyebrows came together over kindly eyes. "Then I'm the king of England."

"Yes, your majesty," Lilias murmured. The chair back was a solid resting place for her head, so she left it there.

"Impertinent chit." But she heard the laughter in the physician's voice.

"I would disagree with you, but since you gave me an excellent prognosis, I'm willing to overlook that comment. Bruised ribs are much better than broken ribs." She sighed and winced at the aching pain in her chest. She would have to remember not to breathe too deeply. The medicinal scent of liniment rose from beneath the tight linen bandage. "Thank you."

"Knife wounds. Poison. Bruised ribs and throat. A dead man I ought to report somewhere—"

"But you won't." She angled her head. "Will you?"

"No." He yanked his old-fashioned breeches up over a substantial stomach. She liked the laugh lines that fanned out from his eyes. "But mind that cut of yours doesn't become infected, miss."

"She'll mind." Angel's lazy voice drifted up from the nearby settee. "I'll see to it."

"You'll be lucky if you see to yourself for the next month. How you managed to run around with a shoulder wound contaminated with laurel water, I'm not sure. If the bullet hadn't gone straight through, you'd be dead from the poison instead of just groggy."

"Luck, doctor." Angel's eyes cracked open the slightest bit. A gold gleam shown from beneath his lashes and warmed her heart. "Sheer luck."

"Well, the two of you are full of luck. The other man wasn't so lucky." A frown settled on his pursed lips. "I really should report—"

"We'll notify his family. We've already taken steps." An outright lie. It was Sir Charles they had sent a message to. The commander would have to find an appropriate lie for the death of a peer of the realm.

Lilias pushed up from the chair she was sitting in and gasped as her ribs protested.

"Don't bother seeing me out. Just rest, for heaven's sake!" The physician waved her away and left the room a moment later. She could hear Jones in the hallway, giving the doctor his hat and greatcoat.

Lilias looked at Angel's lean body, sprawled on the settee. His eyes were closed again, his breath even. He appeared to be healthy, if weary and pale from loss of blood. The clod.

"I thought you were dead." She limped over to him, ignoring the pain in her side, and smacked her hand against the side of his head.

"Ouch!" He rubbed his abused head with his good arm. His fingers were still awkward, as though he couldn't quite bring them under his control. The sight made her swallow hard. He opened his eyes to look at her. His hand came up to briefly run fingers over her bruised throat. "We're a mess, we two."

"But alive." Her legs simply wouldn't hold her up any longer. She slid to the floor beside the settee and laid her forehead against the rough brocade. His hand tangled in her hair.

"Marry me, Lilias."

Her head jerked up, stared at him. "What?"

"Marry me. Be with me. I'll be a horrible husband. Running off whenever I receive orders—"

"Oh, be quiet." She couldn't think beyond the pounding of her heart. It would be a uncertain life. There would be nothing simple or normal about it. She would never know if she could travel with him, or if he would come home. A life of instability.

"Yes." She must be crazy, but she wanted nothing more than to live that uncertain life with him. "Yes, I'll marry you. To my everlasting regret, I'm sure." She launched herself at him as well as her ribs would allow. "But I forbid you to go up against an assassin with a poisoned bullet."

Gold eyes gleamed as a self-satisfied smile curved his lips. "Is that all I had to do to get you to love me? Be shot by a poisoned bullet?"

She lay atop him, pressed against his body. Long and lean and male. And he belonged to her. She framed his face with her hands and touched her lips against his. "You only had to be yourself."

KEEP READING FOR A PREVIEW OF
ALYSSA ALEXANDER'S
A SPY IN THE TON NOVEL

*The Smuggler
Wore Silk*

Now available from Berkley Sensation!

Chapter 1

August 1813

H E COULDN'T SPEAK, couldn't think. Couldn't *breathe*.
In front of him, the spymaster's lips moved, but the sound issuing from them was tinny and thin. He struggled to focus on the words.

The man couldn't have said *retire*. Impossible. Spies did not die as old men in soft beds. Death took them in the field. A knife to the throat. A bullet. Even poison was preferable to this.

"With respect, sir, I cannot retire."

Julian Travers, Earl of Langford, uncurled clenched fists. Blood roared in his ears. He was being *asked* to retire. As though the request did not decimate the life he had carefully rebuilt. As though ten years of atonement meant nothing.

"There are no other options." Sir Charles Flint's voice was brisk. If the spymaster was disappointed to be losing an agent, he didn't show it by a flicker of an eyelash. "The French know you are the Shadow."

Julian's hands jerked reflexively. "Sir—"

"The traitor gave your identity to the French. You and two other agents have been compromised." The lines around Sir Charles's mouth deepened. He pushed aside a stack of documents and leaned over his worn oak desktop. "If we send you to the Continent and the French capture you, they'll use every method of torture in their arsenal to extract information from you. You *must* retire."

The words punched into Julian's belly. He pushed to his feet to pace the cramped government office. "Austria has officially declared war on France. I could travel to—"

"No. You're the best agent I have, but I can't send you on a mission abroad." Finality rang in Sir Charles's tone. "It's time for the Wandering Earl to return home."

Julian ignored the moniker. He much preferred the Shadow, his alias among the other spies, to the ton's pet name for him. Still, the Wandering Earl's bored and spoiled persona served as a useful cover for his frequent trips to the Continent.

"The other compromised agents are also being forced into retirement," Sir Charles continued. "The threat to our network of spies in France and on the Continent is simply too great to allow any of you to continue."

"I still have a job to do, sir." Julian stopped pacing to stand in front of the room's only window. He gripped the smooth wooden windowsill and stared down at the cobblestones of Crown Street.

"Langford, you're an unofficial agent. Assignment to an official position is not possible. Unless you want to work within this building, behind a desk—"

"That would be worse than rusticating in the country or haunting the drawing rooms of the ton, which are my other choices." Julian suppressed a disgusted snort. His gaze fell to his knuckles, the flesh white where his fingers gripped the windowsill.

"The Shadow served king and country for ten years." Cloth rustled against leather. The chair beneath Sir Charles creaked. "During those ten years, the Earl of Langford turned his back on his title and his heritage."

"I never wanted the title," Julian said flatly. Beyond the window, gray fog drifted around carriages and buildings. Diplomats and clerks and secretaries scurried to and from their offices. They went about their business, blithely unaware that only a few feet away, the earth was shifting beneath Julian.

"Nevertheless, you are an earl. You belong in the London

drawing rooms. Your duty is to marry and create heirs. It's the way of things."

Julian's gut turned to ice. The world did not need another Travers. Therefore, Julian needed no heir. The logic was inescapable. He couldn't change the past, but he could ensure the Travers legacy did not continue.

He forced his fingers to release the windowsill. The war continued. Napoleon was a threat. He could prove to Sir Charles he was still useful and return to active duty. All he needed was the right leverage. The right mission. He thanked whatever fate had sent him to the filthy pubs lining the docks of France on his return home.

"I have information that may lead us to the traitor, sir." Julian faced his commander. He knew how to give a report. Straight shoulders. Steady gaze. No emotion. Only the facts mattered. "I may have found one of his contacts."

Sir Charles let out a resigned sigh. "How did you receive this information, Langford?" Impatient fingers tapped the scarred surface of the desk.

"From another British agent. Our paths crossed in Cherbourg." He stared steadily down at the spymaster. The desk seemed like an ocean of oak between them.

"Sit down, Langford." Sir Charles rubbed the back of his neck and sent Julian a baleful look. "My neck is beginning to ache from looking up at you."

"Yes, sir." Julian settled himself into the armchair facing the desk and resisted the urge to stretch out his long legs.

"Now give me your report."

"The agent overheard a conversation in a tavern while waiting for his vessel to sail. Two men were arguing about secret documents and whether they should be delivered to Cherbourg."

Sir Charles's brows rose. "What type of documents?"

"I don't have specific information. The agent was unable to pursue the men without compromising his own mission. However, he did overhear that the documents contained military information and the two men would talk to a Miss Gracie about the documents."

"Miss Gracie? Is that an alias?"

"With a few inquiries, the agent discovered Miss Gracie is

Miss Grace Hannah. She lives in Devon with her uncle, Lord Thaddeus Cannon. They live near Beer." Julian paused. "She is definitely not an innocent. Miss Hannah has strong ties to Jack Blackbourn."

"Blackbourn? I thought he had retired from smuggling."

"He has, sir. For now, at any rate. He's running a public house."

"I can't believe Blackbourn would abandon smuggling to be a publican." Sir Charles frowned, brows drawing together over cool brown eyes.

"I was surprised myself."

"Still, it would be easy enough to transfer military information to France through the smuggling channels," Sir Charles mused, absently reaching for his quill and tapping it against the desktop.

"If the documents were smuggled out of Devon by Grace Hannah, then someone in the War Office or Foreign Office gave her that information. There must be a channel of communication between them." Julian leaned forward, resting his elbows on his knees. "I believe we can flush out the traitor in London by pressuring the smugglers in Devon."

"A reasonable strategy." Sir Charles pursed his lips as he considered the feathers of the quill. Then, with a frustrated grunt, he tossed the quill down. "My best agents are all on the Continent. With so many agents compromised to the French, I don't have anyone I can send." He broke off, eyes narrowed as they focused on Julian. "Which you are perfectly aware of."

"Sir." He didn't shy away from the commander's gaze. Lying would be useless.

"Your family seat is in Devon."

"Yes." Childhood memories crowded Julian's mind. He gritted his teeth and willed the images away.

"Damn if I don't have a final assignment for you, Langford." Sir Charles steepled his fingers and regarded Julian over their tips. "I can't send you to France, but I can send you to Devon."

"Sir." His muscles tightened. Anticipation snaked through him. He had the opportunity he needed to prove himself. To avoid a slow and meaningless death by boredom. To prove he wasn't like his father. The mission hung before him, plump and ripe and as easy to pluck as any red apple.

Coiled muscles twitched at the perfunctory knock on the office door. Julian's head jerked toward the sound. He stared at the young man peering around the doorframe. Fashionably tousled brown curls topped a handsome face dominated by long-lashed brown eyes. The face, however, held a decidedly apprehensive expression.

"Sir?" Miles Butler's voice cracked on the word. "A dispatch has arrived for you from the foreign secretary."

"Thank you." Sir Charles held out his hand without looking at Mr. Butler. When the clerk did nothing, he glanced up. "The dispatch?"

"Oh, of course." The young man hastily crossed the room and laid the folded letter in Sir Charles's hand.

"Excuse me, Langford. I must read this before we continue," Sir Charles said distractedly as he broke the wax seal and perused the communication. Then he reached for his quill, dipped it in ink and began to scratch out a reply. He glanced at Julian as the quill bobbed across the page. "The circumstances in Devon require further inquiry. I expect you to conduct an expeditious investigation of Miss Hannah." Sir Charles ended the note with a flourish and blotted the ink.

"Yes, sir." Julian struggled to keep his voice calm. Success. He could taste it. If he found the traitor, Sir Charles would reinstate him. He knew it.

"Mr. Butler," Sir Charles said as he folded the note and sealed it. "See that my answer is delivered to the foreign secretary. Also, I'm sending the Shadow on a mission in Devon. I need you to inform him of the channels of communication for that area before he departs."

"I will, sir," Mr. Butler said, beaming. "Is there anything else I can assist you with? Any correspondence I can answer, sir?"

Sir Charles waved him away. "I'll notify you when I have another task for you."

Miles Butler backed out of the room. His shoulders had wilted, poor sod. Julian sent him an encouraging smile. He'd been just as young and earnest once. A lifetime ago.

"I expect to be informed of your progress in Devon at regular intervals," Sir Charles said after the door closed. "Use your discretion regarding what information should be relayed in person and what can be sent in writing. If we discover any new information in London, I will send word. In fact"—Sir Charles glanced at the door to the hall—"if anything new arises I'll send Mr. Butler to Devon as my emissary. You'll keep an eye on him and see he doesn't get into trouble, won't you?"

"Yes, sir." And he would send Mr. Butler back to London as quickly as he could.

"This is your final mission, Langford." Holding Julian's gaze steadily, Sir Charles leaned back in his chair. "When the investigation is complete, you may consider your service to His Majesty concluded and attend to your estates."

An angry protest rose in his throat, but he swallowed it. He'd bought a reprieve. "Understood, sir." He pushed himself out of the armchair to stand in front of Sir Charles's desk, waiting for dismissal.

Within minutes, Julian was flicking the reins to spur the matched bays harnessed to his high-perch phaeton. Instinct navigated him through the busy streets of London, but his mind was on treason.

Innocent soldiers fighting for England had died because of this traitor. The country was at risk, and the bastard had betrayed Julian. Fury lanced through him, hot and sharp. Retirement was simply not tolerable. *Retribution*, he thought. *Redemption*. He would pursue Miss Hannah, find the traitor and turn him over to Sir Charles. Or kill the bastard.

Sir Charles would reinstate him if he found the traitor. He had to.

There was no alternative to spying.

Chapter 2

"MOST UNFORTUNATE, MY lord." The valet's nasal tones cut through summer birdsong. He poked his head out of the open carriage door as the vehicle rolled to a stop in front of the Traverses' ancestral home.

"What is unfortunate, Roberts?" Julian shifted in the saddle as he reined in his mount. Beneath him, the horse's hooves danced over gravel, then stilled. Dust puffed up to hang in the humid air. "The heat or the dust?"

"Neither, my lord." Roberts squinted up at Julian's mount. "If I may say, the dust would not be such a difficulty if you traveled *inside* the carriage instead of on that ill-tempered beast."

"I'd rather be covered in dust than baking in that stifling carriage." Julian studied his valet and fought back a grin. The man's heat-flushed face resembled a bright red posy on the skinny stalk of his neck. Roberts stubbornly insisted on traveling inside the carriage, but that same stubbornness made him the perfect loyal assistant for a spy. "Besides, this ill-tempered beast carried me through enemy lines and back again. Come to think of it, Roberts, this beast saved your hide a time or two."

"True enough, my lord." Roberts sniffed and stepped gingerly onto the carriage step.

"In fact, I recall an escape from a jealous husband in Italy."

"My lord, I—she—" Roberts sputtered. "She had information necessary to the mission—"

"Oh, cheese it." Julian laughed. "You're an easy mark."

"Well." Roberts's lips twitched into a smile before he could hide it. He brushed a speck of nonexistent dust from his sleeve. "To return to our initial subject of unfortunate happenings, I was referring to our location. It's quite unfortunate your mission brought us to the wilds of Devon."

"Devon isn't wild, Roberts. A Parisian salon is considerably wilder these days." Julian dismounted to stand beside the valet. A groom jumped down from the carriage to take the reins.

"Perhaps," Roberts conceded. "Still, Devon isn't London or Brussels or Lisbon."

"Indeed not, but my informant tells me the traitor isn't in London or Brussels or Lisbon. The traitor is in Devon." He narrowed his eyes at the Jacobean architecture of his ancestral estate. He had intended to go the whole of his life without ever seeing it again. "She has much to answer for," he added softly.

"Quite." Roberts straightened his waistcoat, sent his thin nose into the air and turned to the carriage. "I shall see to the trunks, my lord."

"Good. I was beginning to wonder if the coachman would be required to hold the horses here indefinitely." He set his hand on Roberts's shoulder to take the sting from the words.

While Roberts grunted and muttered behind him, Julian stepped back to study the façade of the home he hadn't seen in twenty-three years.

Thistledown spread its wings across acres of green lawns and gardens brimming with bright summer blooms. Towers speared toward the vivid blue sky, long fingers reaching for the clouds. Mullioned windows caught the August sunlight and reflected it in a thousand tiny rays.

He hated the very sight of it.

It was unfortunate that Thistledown was only a few miles away from Grace Hannah. The traitor had sent him to the one place he'd vowed never to return to.

Wheels crunched over gravel as the carriage trundled toward the stables. Julian glanced at the wide front steps of Thistledown and sucked in a breath as memory flashed, as clear and focused as though it had happened yesterday. His father dragging him by the collar down those steps, kicking and screaming. Being tossed into the carriage and held down.

It was the last day either one of them had been there.

The day of his mother's funeral.

Anger stabbed through him. He did not have the choice to turn away. He could not climb onto his horse and ignore the memories.

He forced himself to take the front steps two at a time. Pushing open the heavy paneled front door, he stepped into the dark, cool interior and breathed deep. It smelled of home. Grief rose in him, bittersweet and raw. The clean scents of linseed oil and beeswax mingled with aged wood and dust. But the sweet scent of fresh flowers he remembered from his childhood was missing.

Julian let the door fall closed. Brooding silence surrounded him. He wasn't surprised at the lack of life. There were no residents at Thistledown aside from the butler and housekeeper, Mr. and Mrs. Starkweather. The other servants came only to do the necessary tasks to keep the house from falling into neglect and left again.

He poked his head into nearby rooms in search of the caretakers. Silence rang in the empty chambers. Fireplaces were bare and curtains were drawn. Furniture and paintings were draped in wraithlike dust covers, as though life had stopped and only ghosts remained.

As he turned away from the great hall, he heard laughter echoing. *Finally*, Julian thought. *Signs of life.* He followed the sound through the halls toward the upper kitchens. The air here carried the delicious scent of roasting meat. Savory herbs mingled with it and set his mouth watering.

Cautiously, Julian pushed open the door to the kitchen and paused on the threshold to scan the room. Mr. Starkweather, older and plumper around the midsection than Julian remembered, sat in his shirtsleeves at the kitchen table, a cup of tea and an empty plate before him. His feet were propped on an adjacent chair and he was gazing fixedly at the roasting oven.

Rather, he was gazing at what was in *front* of the roasting oven.

Two derrieres bobbed side by side. One was wide with

ample hips that shook as its owner made a movement inside the oven. The second, however, had slimmer hips with a bottom that was lush and rounded, and clad in a light wool riding habit that pulled tantalizingly against the curves it covered. A pair of serviceable leather ankle boots extended from the long skirts.

Yes, a fascinating view, thought Julian, eyeing the shapely bottom. And not bad as far as homecomings went.

"I think it could use a touch more rosemary. What do you think?"

Julian assumed the voice belonged to Mrs. Starkweather, the caretaker's wife.

"I agree. Perhaps basil might be added as well?" The second voice was younger, smoother, with the clear, modulated tones of an aristocrat. He could just make out a shining coronet of white-blond hair floating above the lady's shoulders.

"You know, basil might be just the trick," the older woman agreed. "Mr. Starkweather? Your preference?"

"I think your roast is superb, dear. But you should add whatever you think best."

"A diplomatic answer." The young woman's laugh bounced through the kitchen like a beam of silvered light on the air. "Clearly, you are the wisest of husbands, Mr. Starkweather."

Julian glimpsed a full, smiling mouth and delicate features as the young woman swung to face the butler. Her smile died when her gaze lit on Julian. To his regret, the pretty features blanked.

Vaguely discomfited, as though he'd been revealed as a voyeur, he infused his smile with charm. "What incredible feast do I smell?"

The comment resulted in a flurry of movement. Mrs. Starkweather backed up and whirled around, narrowing her eyes for one long, appraising look. Mr. Starkweather jumped to his feet, frantically snatched his coat from the back of his chair and shrugged into it.

The young woman, however, exhibited no such distress. She didn't smile in greeting, but rather regarded him with the polite indifference of an ancient statue, pale as marble and carved of stone.

Unlike Mrs. Starkweather, who planted her hands on her

hips and beamed at him. "Well, young master! I barely recognized you—it's been three years since you last had us brought up to London for an accounting. You are a sight for these old eyes!"

Julian plucked up the woman's hand and brought it to his lips. "Never old, my darling Mrs. Starkweather. Why, you're as lovely as ever." He bowed, adding a flourish to amuse her.

"Go on with you, Master Julian." Her round cheeks pinked. "Though I suppose you're 'his lordship' now. You should have told us you were coming. We would have readied everything for you. Instead, you give us not a word of warning."

"I do beg your pardon." Julian laughed. "I didn't know I would be taking up residence until the day I left London."

"Welcome home, my lord," Starkweather added to his wife's greeting, tugging his coat into place.

"Thank you." Julian sent an appreciative smile toward the caretaker.

Turning to the pretty blonde, he warmed his smile. She remained in precisely the same position, fingers linked together in front of her, quietly watching. Her eyes were silver gray, a perfect complement to the fair hair.

"I quite forgot myself!" Mrs. Starkweather gestured to the young woman. "My lord, may I present Miss Grace Hannah? She lives a few miles away."

Surprise had him quirking a brow before he slipped his mask into place.

How convenient to find Miss Hannah's head in his oven.

"WELCOME HOME, MY LORD." Grace hoped her voice didn't crack. She hated to be caught unprepared. Forcing her fingers to loosen, she extended her hand to the earl in greeting.

"Miss Hannah, a delight to meet you." His lips curved, at once beguiling and sensual.

On purpose, she was certain.

She sent him a polite half smile as their gazes met over their linked hands. His eyes were the bright blue of a cloudless sky in midsummer, a color that would have been attractive if not for the calculating light behind them. Her pulse skittered as those shrewd eyes scanned her face.

"Had I known such a fair lady would greet my homecoming I would have returned fifteen years ago," he said.

"I would not have been here fifteen years ago." The words sounded stilted. She struggled to add something witty and engaging. "Your homecoming would have been bereft of my presence."

"Ah, then I shall be content with today, and count myself fortunate to be honored with your charming company."

He looked truly disappointed. But she knew the reputation of the Wandering Earl, as well as the reputation of his father, grandfather and great-grandfather. Wastrels, gamesters and womanizers, every one. A lady couldn't trust a rake and wastrel.

Then again, she wasn't a lady.

She schooled her features into the polite, expressionless face she had mastered for dealing with aristocrats and their ilk. "Regrettably, my company is about to end, as I must be on my way."

"Alas, must I be deprived of such beauty so soon?"

Her instincts leapt again as his watchful and cunning eyes continued to hold her gaze. The hair on her nape rose, sending a shiver down the line of her back. She suddenly felt like prey.

Uneasy, Grace collected her riding hat, more than ready to depart. She secured the plain hat by its long ribbons beneath her chin and wished it had been fashionable even three years ago, instead of five.

"Mrs. Starkweather, Mr. Starkweather, thank you for your hospitality. If you will excuse me, my lord? I must return home." Acknowledging the earl with a nod she hoped appeared regal, she turned toward the door to depart.

"I shall return as soon as I have escorted our guest to her carriage, Starkweather," the earl said.

"My lord, there's no need—" Grace began.

"There is every need. My afternoon would be incomplete without a few additional minutes of your delightful company." He offered his arm, extending it with a short half bow.

Nearly ten years of being the poor relation had taught her when to hide behind the pretense of submission. Resigned, she nodded in acquiescence and took his arm. It was strong and hard beneath her fingers. Their shoulders brushed, just the lightest touch as he steered her through the house. She felt the heat of him, and rising with it was the scent of man and leather and outdoors. Fresh, earthy and oddly appealing.

They left the silent interior of Thistledown and emerged into the bright August sun beyond. Grace glanced over at the earl, studying him quickly. His gaze absorbed the lawns, the drive, even the horizon in one quick glance. A breeze teased his light brown hair. The tips faded to gold at the ends, as though they had been dipped in sunlight. Lean and handsome features held a subtle tan that set off those blue eyes.

She turned away, refocused her attention on the grounds of Thistledown. It wouldn't do to be caught staring.

"Thank you for escorting me to the stables, my lord," she said.

"I take my duties as host quite seriously. Courtyards are dangerous places, you know." He smiled at her in that way people did when they shared a private jest. Flirtation came easily to him. "And I'm ever a gentleman, Miss Hannah."

Absurd. And amusing. She should remain quiet. She should refrain from responding to his banter. And yet—"It's quite difficult to traverse a courtyard, is it not?"

"Extremely. One must be forever on guard against wayward guests interrupting your walk."

"Or wayward residents." Gravel crunched beneath her feet.

"Residents as well," he agreed. "In fact, residents may be worse than guests, since they never leave." He paused, glanced around. "But where is your carriage?"

"I rode from my uncle's."

"What did you ride?" he asked, turning smiling eyes toward her. "A dainty palfrey so delicate her feet barely touch the ground? A proud, high-stepping mare? But no." He laughed. "Something more fantastic—a dragon covered in jewel-toned scales, perhaps? Or did you use your own exquisite wings? For surely only an angel could be so beautiful."

Hard-pressed not to laugh at the sheer nonsense of his words, she tried to keep her features bland. "None of those, my lord. I arrived on an ordinary horse."

"Alas. My enchanted visions dashed. Well, an ordinary horse can be raised to extraordinary by its rider, as must be the situation here. I trust you do not have a difficult journey home?"

"I have lived at my uncle's estate for the last ten years. I probably will not lose my way," she said drily.

"I hope not." He slid a glance in her direction. "I may be a gentleman, Miss Hannah, but a few miles across the Devon countryside may be beyond my escort skills."

"Gentlemen are just not what they used to be." She sighed. Despite his amused smile, her mind chastised her tongue. What devil was pricking her sense of humor?

"Having lived here for so many years you are probably familiar with the people in the community and countryside," he said. "No doubt there would be any number of friends to help you find your way."

Grace cast a glance at the earl. The calculating, watchful look returned to his eyes, turning a rogue into a predator. "Indeed, my lord," she answered warily. "One can meet any number of people in ten years."

"I've met a fair number myself."

"In London?"

"And on the Continent."

"The Wandering Earl. I have heard the sobriquet."

"My reputation precedes me."

"You are an earl, my lord. The only one in these parts, in fact, which makes your various activities interesting."

"I haven't been to this part of Devon in years."

"That doesn't negate the fact that you are the only earl. The others are merely barons, knights, honorables or, as in my case, mere misters and misses."

His eyes gleamed. "Somehow, I don't think you are a mere miss."

"I'd like to think you're correct."

The earl pulled open the stable doors and stood aside for her to enter. The faint scents of horse and hay drifted on the air. Grace let her eyes adjust to the dim light as he closed the door behind them. In the first stalls she saw what must be the earl's horses busily munching their feed. They passed the animals and Grace pointed to a large stall near the end of the row. "My mount is there."

As they approached the stall, a massive black horse thrust

its head over the door. The stallion's head was huge, his eyes a little wild. Grace watched man and beast eye each other with distrust. The horse snorted, nostrils flaring, and a hoof pawed the ground. His ears pricked forward and a decidedly irritated glint appeared in his eyes.

"An ordinary horse, Miss Hannah? That horse is definitely not ordinary. In fact, he looks to be a Thoroughbred."

"Demon is descended from the Darley Arabian." She crossed the few feet to the stall that housed her stallion. The animal whinnied softly at her.

"I assume he earned the name *Demon*."

"Would you expect otherwise?" Grace stroked the stallion's muzzle. "Demon has the speed and stamina for racing, but not the temperament, poor fellow. He has trouble following directions. Which is why my uncle dislikes him and handed him off to me." She was lucky, really. If he didn't bring in a fee for acting as stud, her uncle would have sold him years ago.

The earl eyed the horse again. "I would be remiss, Miss Hannah, if I did not ask whether you could handle this animal. I don't believe I've met a lady that would ride a stallion."

"Such ladies are rare, I'm sure." She tilted her head, met his gaze. "But she only needs to know how best to handle the stallion."

He paused. The blue of his eyes was intense. "An interesting theory."

Grace glanced at the watch pinned to her riding habit. It was nearly five, and she was allowing herself to be caught up in a conversation she shouldn't have. She schooled her features. "It is past time for me to depart, my lord. I must return home to—" To what, she thought frantically. What could she tell him? To oversee dinner preparations? To ensure the linens were properly washed and aired?

"Beggin' yer pardon, Miss Gracie," a voice called out. A young groom hurried between the stalls, carrying Demon's saddle and other tack. "I would've 'ad Demon ready for you, but 'is lordship came home and is—"

"Right beside me," she said quickly.

"Milord." He acknowledged the earl with a nod before hurrying to saddle Demon. The horse shied away from the groom, as usual.

"I'll hold him steady." She slipped into the stall to murmur to Demon, stroking his forehead. When the groom stepped back she took the reins and led the horse through the stable and into the sunlit courtyard beyond.

She approached the mounting block, but the earl stayed her course.

"Allow me to assist." He linked his fingers together and offered her a leg up.

She couldn't politely refuse and leave him standing there. With an inward sigh, she placed her foot in his linked fingers and boosted herself onto the sidesaddle. Her breath caught, then rushed out again when he gripped her waist to steady her. His fingers, hot and strong, lingered for a moment, imprinting their heat onto her waist. He squeezed gently, then let his hands glide down her hips and drop away.

Breathing seemed impossible. The caress was intimate. Too intimate. Worse, her reaction—the sudden awareness of her body, the drumming of her pulse—was discomforting. She struggled to keep her expression serene.

"Welcome home, my lord. And good-bye."